Holding Their Own XI: Hearts and Minds

By

Joe Nobody

Edited by:
E. T. Ivester
D. Allen

PrepperPress

Post-apocalyptic Fiction & Survival Nonfiction

Holding Their Own XI: Hearts and Minds
ISBN 978-1-939473-78-3

Other Books by Joe Nobody:

Find more titles at
www.JoeNobodyBooks.com

and

www.PrepperPress.com

Chapter 1

For the last three weeks, José had been watching the trucks. He spotted them in the mornings, standing on the deck as the shrimper headed out to Corpus Christi Bay. Most days, they were still there on the return trip to port, the deckhand often sitting exhausted on the main hatch after 12 back-breaking hours of working the nets and clearing the catch.

The small fleet of pickups, panel vans, and two semis was never parked in the same place. Every day, scores of workers carted in gallons of paint in an attempt to return the resort to its original luster. More than a few times, he'd noticed crews in hard hats lugging rolls of electrical wire, bundles of lumber, and other construction materials inside the mid-rise condo building. Someone was trying to reopen Ocean Towers... someone with access to labor, equipment, and money.

A lifetime ago, before the collapse, he'd been one of the hundreds of construction workers contracted to create Texas's newest, most luxurious seaside address. And what a structure it had been.

José could recall with exacting detail the soaring foyer, opulent décor, and spacious flats. The pools, both indoor and out, reminded him of brochures he'd seen of waterparks. The golf course was said to be the highest rated in the state. The list of amenities and facilities was second to none.

Billed as a retreat for the Lone Star State's newest generation of millionaires, Ocean Towers offered everything the ultra-wealthy could ask for. The full-service marina sported 75 slips for the most discerning captains of yachts as well as sailboats. No expense was spared in outfitting the onsite health club, spa and salon either. Award-winning restaurants offered a variety of selections for social climbers, while others elected private meals prepared by on-staff personal chefs. For those who preferred to soar above gridlock traffic, a private airfield was available. Residents could sip champagne and nibble on caviar while getting an anti-aging seaweed wrap, set sail on a gulf excursion or buzz the tower at the landing field.

José had never been the envious type, content with his well-paying construction job and his ability to feed, clothe, and shelter his growing family. He'd even made enough money to have his parents, two brothers, and sister smuggled across the border from Mexico to the United States. He'd become a hero in his clan – an important, respected man.

Then came the collapse.

It had never crossed the immigrant's mind to ponder how Ocean Towers had fared after society vanished. He'd moved on since its completion, landing countless other projects. His resume had expanded as well, and demand for his time was high. He mastered skills quickly... everything from bricklaying to building custom cabinetry. Even when the economy had fallen into recession, he'd still been able to find employment. Sometimes the hourly rate wasn't so rewarding, but even the worst wages here were far better than anything available in his childhood village.

Then practically overnight, there was no work. Nothing. Nada.

His father had saved the family from starvation. Fishing from shore with a second-hand rod and reel, the seafood and other saltwater fare had kept them alive. Barely. The women worked a humble, backyard garden. José and his brothers foraged anything they could find.

Night terrors plagued his sleep – memories of his family huddling in fear as the food riots raged across Corpus. Like it was yesterday, he recalled wrapping an arm around his shivering wife as they watched a downtown skyscraper burn in the distance, columns of black smoke and eerie, red flames visible for miles.

Only a few days later, José and his brothers battled roving packs of desperate, starving men who pillaged the neighborhoods, scavenging for canned goods and ammunition... hell-bent on capturing and enslaving local women. The family relied on the strength of its numbers, working together to overcome threat after threat. But sometimes, that just was not enough.

For one of José's brothers, the end came via a street gang's ambush and the blast of a shotgun. Even more sickening was the demise of his beloved, younger sister who had fallen victim to a gang rape. While José survived the skirmish that followed, his heart was irreparably broken. Both body and soul seemed to be in constant peril from the barrage of attacks, and often José marveled that he still walked this earth.

The months had turned into years, every day a struggle for food and survival. Then the fire had nearly accomplished what malnutrition, sickness, and armed raiders had failed to do – slaughter them all.

José had no idea how it had started. Candles and oil pots were common in his modest home, the only source of light now that electricity was a bitter memory. Perhaps a child had knocked something over, or maybe a curtain had stirred too close to an open flame.

2

Whatever the source, he remembered dreaming of a hell-hound sitting on his chest, the demon's weight and hot breath making it nearly impossible for his lungs to draw air.

The nightmare had saved them. Rising sharply to find his residence consumed with thick, choking smoke, José had managed to wake his family to the inferno's horror. They had escaped with their lives, but that was it. The children were still wearing their nightclothes as they stood in the front yard, mesmerized by the sight of the hungry flames consuming the place they called "home."

Utterly dejected and hopeless, the family had begun their trek at dawn with only the clothes on their backs and a few items salvaged from the yard. It had been the bottom of a pitiful existence. José remembered a strong desire to slash his wrists, but he didn't have a knife.

Nearing the end of her term, his expectant wife fairly wobbled away from their little piece of the American dream. José assisted his childhood sweetheart as much as he could, his attention further divided among their three little ones and his fragile mother who hadn't stopped coughing since her son had pulled her from the flames. They walked. No destination, no path, no plan. They merely placed one foot in front of the other and kept the sun at their backs.

By chance, the ragtag parade of refugees wandered into a neighborhood that hadn't been ravaged by fire or completely plundered by looters. Out of desperation, he approached a small bungalow, hoping the occupants would show mercy to his children and provide a drink of water or morsel of bread.

There was no answer when he knocked on the door, so he decided to check the backyard. Perhaps there was a rain barrel or pump that could provide the desperately needed hydration. He found nothing there but a vigorous crop of weeds.

Anger swelled inside him, an internal rage and desperation that spawned recklessness. In a fit of temper, he returned to the front door and kicked with all his might. He would demand water and food, take it if necessary.

The home, however, was unoccupied.

He found a few canned goods in the cupboard, along with closets full of clothing. The interior was appointed with dusty furniture, threadbare curtains, a healthy maze of cobwebs, and what appeared to be a lifetime of memories. From the scattered pictures dotting the walls, he deduced that the occupants had been an elderly couple, not unlike his own parents.

The interlopers moved inside the abandoned building, the extra space and security a blessing for the imminently expanding family. A few days later, his wife gave birth to their fourth child. José's mother died shortly after her newest grandbaby entered the post-apocalyptic world... her lungs damaged from the poisonous smoke and eventually, after weeks of coughing and struggling, unable to draw oxygen into her body.

Life was hard after the crash. Absence of medical care left the surviving population vulnerable to rampant disease and epidemics that only a few years before would have been controlled via a round of antibiotics. Survivors' numbers continued to dwindle. Eventually, there weren't enough people left alive to form gangs. Those still above ground didn't seem to have enough energy or the ammunition to fight. José and his family fell into work patterns defined by one overriding goal; putting food on the table.

The occupied home became their own after a time. Routine, the never-ending struggle to find calories, and the constant need to watch out for each other led to a sense of belonging. Still, the residence was cramped, the two bedrooms and single bath a tight fit for his family. Regardless, it was shelter.

Ultimately, word of the Alliance and her recovery started spreading by word of mouth. A man from Galveston had been the first to speak of the movement, his claims dismissed as wishful thinking and exaggeration by anyone who took the time to listen. Maybe they were true, but from where José stood, his family had lost everything.... What good would a recovery do them anyway? They had nothing to go back to. Nothing to call their own.

Food and fuel began arriving, as well as the military. Suddenly, there were men in uniforms passing out rations and organizing labor. José had signed up to work on a shrimp boat because it was the only option that wouldn't require relocating his family to some distant farm or ranch. He could walk to the piers, so he became a fisherman.

It was brutal work, much of the equipment aboard the aging fleet in disrepair. The hydraulic winches used to haul in the catch had broken long ago, spare parts nearly impossible to find. The nets were now brought in the old-fashioned way – via manual, spine-crushing labor.

It seemed like everything on the old dinghy was broken. Today, he'd spent four hours in the sweltering hull, working a manual bilge pump in the 120-degree air. The original electric units had failed months ago.

For his toil, José received 2-3 pounds of shrimp per day and ten dollars. It was better than starvation... but just barely. Still, things could be worse. They had been not so long before.

His wife would take half of today's wages to the market and

barter for vegetables, rice, oranges, and occasionally a beer or two. There was a military medical clinic just under a mile from his home. Gossip was going around that a school would open soon for his children. Things were definitely looking up.

His first reaction at seeing the trucks and construction crews was another fleeting flash of hope. Was returning to the building trades in his future? Would life eventually revert to the way it was before everything had gone to hell?

That feeling dwindled as the grueling weeks aboard the shrimper began to wear him down. José would stare at the trucks, a deep-seated injustice simmering, eventually generating a core of hot anger that commandeered his soul.

It wasn't so much the hard work – he was used to that. Labor and toil were a man's role in life.

Nor was it the horrible wages or conditions. He knew he was one of the lucky ones. Two or three pounds of shrimp could feed his family for a day.

No, what really began to eat at José's previously empathetic and lighthearted nature was the squalor of his surroundings. Every day, his path home took him through blocks lined with the burned-out shells of homes and businesses, rusting hulks of abandoned cars, weeds, trash, and decay.

His children played in filth, his oldest son already terrorized from straying too close to a building that crumbled and nearly buried the boy alive. There was never enough water to bathe or do laundry. Air conditioning and heat were luxuries from a time he could barely recall. Rodents and insects were unwelcome tenants in their personal space.

His family of 11 lived in three rooms, dug holes in a weedy lot for a makeshift bathroom, and washed up for meals using rain catch from an old tub in the backyard. Despite the passing of so many months, the city still reeked of melted plastic, human sewage, and rotting flesh. His wife's hair, once filling his senses with its sweet perfume, carried the odor of cinder and cooking fires. The rare bar of soap was a gift from God above.

Before the reconstruction drew his attention, none of it seemed to matter. Sure, his environment wasn't improving, but everyone else was suffering the same dilemmas. The sense of hopelessness was easy to digest because the entire world was cast into a similar struggle. Life was difficult for everyone, no matter how rich or poor before the apocalypse.

The appearance of the trucks had altered José's line of thinking.

Evidently, the recovery had progressed far enough that extravagance and comfort were available for some, and that ate at what little sense of humanity he managed to preserve.

Why did his family have to suffer and toil just to obtain the basics of survival when others were spoiled and overindulged? Why weren't resources allocated to clean up the rot and debris? Or at least thin out the burgeoning rat population? Why wasn't help arriving on his street?

Sitting on the hatch as the captain plied the channel, José realized that since the collapse, the only improvement in his life had been the occupation of a home that didn't belong to him. Everything else, from the substandard food to the deplorable surroundings was the same, miserable existence.

His eyes drifted back to the gleaming glass and steel tower, memories of the sparkling pools and trash-free, manicured grounds filling his mind. *Now that would be a better life*, he thought. *Everyone's attitude would improve. We would feel like we were making progress in this world instead of spinning our wheels in the same muck and mire.*

Mr. Cunningham surveyed the glistening marble floors and the spotless, towering wall of glass that defined the lobby. The dark blue waters of the bay were just beyond, framed perfectly by the deep belt of green foliage that bordered the property.

Turning to the contract manager with a nod, he said, "Excellent job, sir. She looks as good as the day we had the grand opening. Your men and you are to be commended."

"Thank you," the smiling supervisor responded.

Cunningham reached for the briefcase at his feet, handing the locked container over to the man who would pay the construction crews. "The final installment."

"Of course, sir," the man nodded. "I look forward to working with you again."

After watching the contractor walk away, Cunningham turned to one of his staff and quipped, "Ocean Towers is once again the prime address in all of Texas. Our first clients should be arriving in the morning. Please make sure everything is in order."

"Yes, sir," sounded the curt response as the two staffers hustled away, each apparently with several items on their lists of assigned duties.

After inspecting the placement of the expensive couches and chairs that composed the lobby's common seating area,

Cunningham turned and headed for his office. He, like the staff, had a series of items to be cleared from his itinerary before the residents were received.

A fleeting glimpse of two children prompted the facility manager's head to snap toward the pool area, a look of disdain crossing his face. Hurrying to a nearby house phone, he called security with a quick punch of three buttons.

"This is Cunningham," he barked once the call was answered. "We have trespassers by the outdoor pool. Please see to it that they are immediately removed from the premises."

Not waiting for a response, he replaced the phone in its cradle and then strode with purpose to the location where he'd spied the tiny gatecrashers.

Two uniformed security men appeared a moment later, hustling around the clear, blue pool while heading toward one of the emergency stairwells.

Cunningham followed their gaze and spotted the heavy steel exit door closing behind two wet, scurrying youth.

"Why are they going inside?" he whispered, now both intrigued and annoyed.

With surprising speed, the Ocean Towers honcho jogged after his security detail, reaching the steps just as his employees sprinted onto the first landing. A moment later, he was taking the stairs two at a time, hot on the guards' heels.

The children's wet feet provided an excellent trail, finally exiting the concrete steps on the third floor. It was a little more difficult to follow their path along the plush carpeting. For the next clue, Cunningham and his two men only had to use their ears.

Unit 3C was clearly occupied, that fact confirmed by a woman's voice shouting for the children to pick up their wet towels off the floor. "What the hell?" mumbled one of the security men.

Cunningham clenched his fist and rapped loudly on the door. "Facilities management," he announced with authority.

The door cracked slightly, a Hispanic man peeking out through the opening. "May I help you?" José responded.

"Sir, this is a private facility," Cunningham said politely. "You must leave immediately."

"Why?" José responded. "We live here now."

"Oh, no, no, no," the building manager replied. "These units are privately owned. This specific apartment is the property of Mr. Harrington. Please, leave the unit straightaway before I am forced to call the authorities."

"Mr. Harrington gave me this apartment," José countered with a straight face. "I saved his life during the riots, and he said I could have this place as a reward."

Cunningham was stunned, now wondering if the man on the other side of the threshold might actually be telling the truth. "Did he provide you with any sort of documentation? A deed? Bill of Sale? Even a letter?"

"No," José responded with a shrug, continuing the deceit with an innocent face. "There really wasn't time. He thanked me and said if I ever needed a place to live, I could go to Ocean Towers, Unit 3C. So now I'm here."

After exchanging a frustrated look with the two security men, the building's manager tried again. "But, sir, surely you must understand this is most unusual and very difficult for me to accept. This condominium cost Mr. Harrington over two million dollars.... That's not something most men give away to complete strangers... heroics or not."

"He said I could have it," José answered, now growing angry. "We live here now. Please leave us alone, and stop scaring my children."

With that, José closed and locked the door.

Cunningham stood aghast, staring at the entrance while his mouth moved without sound.

"Do you want us to throw them out?" one of the guards questioned.

"No... no, that won't be necessary. I don't want our organization to have a heavy-handed reputation in the community. Please drive to the police station and ask the authorities to remove them."

Shrugging, the security man responded, "If you say so," and then pivoted to execute his new assignment.

"I have a very bad feeling about this," Cunningham mumbled, moving quickly to follow the guards.

Deputy Morgan had never been thrilled with his career in law enforcement before the world had gone to hell. Now, with no other option to feed his family, he thoroughly despised the occupation.

Not only had the rules changed, but the population as a whole was far more dangerous. Seldom, if ever, did the deputy have backup, handling the worst situations as a solo responder. His vocation now reminded the 34-year-old man of the old Westerns he watched as a kid.

Those flicks often featured a plot starring a lone marshal, perpetually outgunned, and receiving little support from the local citizens. Those old timers never knew who was going to ride into town and cause trouble. They didn't have computerized background checks, instant access to criminal history, or a SWAT team to handle gangs of bank robbers, rustlers, and other vermin. They lived by instinct, common sense, and the speed of their gun hands. Somehow, however, the white hats always carried the day, at least by the time the credits rolled.

As he matured, Morgan developed an understanding of the difference between Hollywood productions and reality. While still entertaining, those old horse operas weren't historically accurate or a fair representation of Western law enforcement. Little did he know that one day his beloved childhood fiction would so closely parallel his adult reality.

"At least those cowboys had rules to live by," he mumbled. "Most of the time, I only have my own sense of right and wrong. The problem is, things are rarely black and white."

Deputy Morgan had to admit that the situation described to him by the Ocean Towers security man was unusual, if not unique. Most of his days were spent keeping the local populace from killing, raping, and stealing from each other. This would be different.

The lawman had heard the gossip about Ocean Towers, rumors circulating that the former showpiece was being repaired and refurbished. It had been just one of a dozen signs of hope that had occurred in the area since the Alliance had taken control. Now, the harbinger of recovery was turning into a bad state of affairs.

From a trusted source, the deputy had learned that 50% of the state's population had perished during the downfall. Several months ago, a man in uniform appeared at his door, asking Morgan to rejoin the newly formed law enforcement department being organized around Corpus. No one had mentioned that the force would be less than a tenth of its original size. Half of the people being policed by 10% of the officers was a formula that equaled a lot of dead badges.

Unlike before, there was little organization, few rules, and no hierarchy of command to fall back on. District attorneys no longer existed. Instead of a sergeant, captain, and county sheriff for support and guidance, Morgan often found himself making complex decisions without any sounding board of advice or a superior's experience.

In his decade of law enforcement before the apocalypse, Morgan had only ever drawn his weapon once in anger. Now, his holster's leather was well-worn.

Yet there were few other career opportunities available, and a man had to eat.

His occupation, however, did offer some rewards.

The deputy fully understood that they were all going to have to do their part if society was ever to recover. Those who carried a badge and gun were no exception, and in Morgan's opinion, were actually playing a more critical role than most. His job was to keep the public from tearing itself apart until the Alliance programs bore fruit and improved the average Joe Nobody's life.

The fact that someone was allocating money into private property like Ocean Towers was nothing short of uplifting. While Morgan didn't know who the investors were, their optimism was refreshing. On the other hand, the deputy's days were filled with visions of suffering, desperation, and encounters with a citizenry facing a substandard lifestyle. If resources were available, couldn't they be better utilized for the greater good of the whole community?

Pulling into the parking lot of the luxury address, Morgan was impressed. While he hadn't visited the mid-rise since the collapse, it was obvious that someone had poured a great amount of effort in cleaning the place up. It was the first pavement he'd seen in years that was free of litter, rubble, and overgrowth.

After exiting his cruiser, Morgan was met at the main entrance by a man who furthered the impression that today was going to be a unique experience. Resplendent in a freshly-pressed suit, white shirt, and flawless silk necktie, the fellow carried an air of sophistication and class.

After introducing himself, Mr. Cunningham jumped immediately into an explanation of the problem at hand. "I know Mr. Harrington, the unit's rightful owner," he began. "He is not a benevolent soul. My employers will not tolerate indigents or other riffraff taking advantage of this facility. Unless those people in Unit 3C can provide suitable documentation, I want them out of here immediately."

"I understand, sir," responded the deputy. "Let me go up and talk with them."

The officer was shown to 3C by Cunningham and one of the security staffers. After motioning for the two civilians to stay back, the deputy rapped loudly on the door.

A female voice answered from the other side, "Who's there?"

"This is Deputy Morgan of the Sheriff's Department," the officer responded. "Please open the door. I need to speak with you."

Morgan heard the lock click, and then the face of a young, female Hispanic appeared in the opening. The deputy noted that the woman had left the chain attached.

The lawman could see the fear in her eyes, and quite frankly, given the times, he didn't blame her. "Ma'am, the building manager claims that you and your family are not the rightful owners of this property. I am here to investigate their complaint."

"This is our home," she began excitedly, the words erupting in a heavy accent. "We live here now." Her declaration was then followed by an unintelligible eruption of Spanish words that the deputy couldn't follow.

Morgan, recognizing that his own inferior Spanish skills could start an international incident, decided that he'd try to speak with the man of the house. "Is your husband home?"

"Working on the boat! Working today. He will be home soon. You talk to him!"

Sensing that things weren't going as planned, Cunningham was not about to let the situation go at that. "Officer, these people do not belong here. Please order them to leave."

Evictions had never been one of Deputy Morgan's favorite tasks. Throwing folks out of their home was difficult enough with a court order and the comfort of knowing a detailed legal process had been executed. Now, he was faced with the dilemma that all police officers dreaded. It was the building manager's word against the frightened mother peeking through the crack in the door.

"Sir, I completely understand," the lawman responded as he turned to the now red-faced manager. "However, I am hesitant to toss someone out on the street without more facts."

Cunningham appeared shocked, his eyes opening wide while his brow knotted in displeasure, "This is ridiculous! These people clearly do not belong here. They are squatters! I have documentation in the office indicating that Unit 3C was purchased by Mr. Harrington. These people are now living, illegally, on his property and must be removed at once. I insist that you do so."

Morgan was suddenly more annoyed at the man facing him in the hall than the lady behind the door. "With all due respect, sir, I am under no obligation to respond to your demands. Is it really going to make any difference if we wait for the husband to return?"

"The tenants will begin arriving tomorrow morning," protested Cunningham. "What am I supposed to say if Mr. Harrington arrives only to find an uninvited family of... of... vagabonds living in his home?"

With a smirk, Morgan spread his hands wide in exasperation, "If Mr. Harrington were to arrive, then we could clear this whole mess up very quickly. Couldn't we?"

"I have no way of knowing when Mr. Harrington or any other resident is going to move back. In the meantime, those people could be pilfering his personal property. Our clients have valuable art, jewelry, and furnishings within their units. That's not even addressing the private possessions every person keeps inside a home. Would you want absolute strangers rummaging through your belongings?"

The lawman ignored the question, "Well then I suggest you post one of your security men out here in the hallway to make sure they don't abscond with anything that doesn't rightfully belong to them. Now if you'll excuse me, gentlemen, I have other citizens to serve. I will return this evening around dusk and interview the husband. We will see if all of this can be cleared up at that time."

Cunningham didn't like it, but the deputy gave him little choice. Shouldering his way past the building manager, Morgan again repeated, "I'll be back in a few hours. Until then, I highly recommend everyone stay calm."

For once, José was looking forward to coming home. He had left his wife and brother very specific instructions not to let anyone inside of their new residence. As he approached the lobby, the deckhand half expected the building manager or some of his men to try to block the way. It was for that reason that he had invited a handful of his coworkers to come over for the evening and admire the new hacienda.

His crewmates from the shrimper were impressed by their surroundings, oohing and aahing as they entered the lobby. The elevators were not functional, but none of the grimy, sweaty men seemed to mind climbing a few flights of stairs. After their day on the boat, the physical effort was hardly noticed.

When they encountered the building security man in the hallway outside of his door, José tensed, ready to confront the burly fellow. Either because he was completely outnumbered or was strictly following orders, not a single word was exchanged.

José's wife was also surprised by the number of men who piled through the front door. After a quick explanation from her husband, she was all smiles, the perfect hostess as she offered the guests cold drinks.

"The building has generators," José explained. "We not only have a working refrigerator, but also clean, running water. Ice, too!"

The production of clear, gleaming glasses of ice water was received as if the missus had produced an expensive, rare, chardonnay. All of the guests stared at the sparkling tumblers, sighing with pleasure as if it had been years since any of them had tasted something so wonderfully refreshing.

"Next, you're going to tell us that the toilets flush," joked one of the crewmen.

"Yes, they do. No more digging holes for us."

The haul from the boat that day had been light, each man receiving just over two pounds of shellfish for his wages. Despite the weak performance, each of the guests volunteered to contribute to the evening meal. Everyone was pleased to see the potatoes José's brother had secured at the market. It was going to be a grand feast, a fitting celebration to match the good cheer that filled the air.

With a pot boiling on the electric stove, José offered each of his band the opportunity to shower and clean up for dinner. The host was rewarded with another round of congratulatory backpats and genuine amazement as he showed each guest to his own private bathroom.

"There are really four bathrooms?" questioned one of the astounded men.

"No," José grinned, "there are five!"

Like peasants invited to spend the night at the king's castle, the deckhands couldn't help but admire the fluffy towels, pristine running water, and abundance of elbowroom. When José offered the first man shampoo, the reaction was one of pure joy.

"No wonder we didn't have a catch today," another co-worker teased. "You smell too good to snag shrimp."

Twenty minutes later, the group was standing at José's floor-to-ceiling windows and admiring the spectacular view. A loud knock at the entryway immediately put a damper on the celebratory atmosphere.

Shrugging his shoulders, José made for the threshold and then opened the door.

"Sir, my name is Deputy Morgan, and I'm here investigating a complaint from the building's management regarding your occupation of this suite. May I come in?"

José had been prepared for another encounter with the complex's security staff, not a law enforcement officer in uniform.

After taking a moment to flush the surprise from his face, José replied, "I'm sorry officer, but my children are asleep. My wife had a lot of trouble getting the little one to settle down. I'll be happy to come out in the hall."

At this point, Morgan was willing to take whatever he could get. After casting a nasty look at Cunningham and his henchmen, the deputy stepped back and allowed José to enter the corridor.

"Sir, if you have any documentation substantiating your claim to this address, we can resolve this entire matter quickly and let you get back to your family."

"As I told these men before," José began. "Mr. Harrington wasn't exactly able to provide me with any sort of written proof. He was right in the middle of being ambushed while riding in his car. My brother and I saved his life, and then later, while we were checking him over to make sure he was okay, he asked us what he could do to reward us for saving his life. I was almost joking when I said, 'I sure could use someplace better to live.' I was stunned when he asked me if I ever heard of Ocean Towers. He told me I could have his apartment here. Unit 3C."

Rubbing his chin, Morgan suddenly brightened. "So can you tell me what Mr. Harrington looks like?"

"Of course I can," José replied. "He was a man in his middle 60's, shorter than I am, sporting very little hair, almost completely bald on top."

Unable to restrain himself any longer, Cunningham surged forward, his tone accusing. "Deputy, this is ridiculous. This man has been living inside of Mr. Harrington's home for two days. Any fool could look at the photographs hanging inside and then be able to describe the owner's appearance."

The lawman had to admit Cunningham had a point. Still, there was very little he could do. "How exactly did you save Mr. Harrington's life?" He asked José.

"My brother and I had shotguns, and we fired into the looters' gathering. The thieves scattered."

The story he was hearing gave the deputy an idea for a different line of questioning. "Is your brother here?"

José shook his head, a look of sadness clouding his face. "No, sir, my brother was killed just a few months later in a similar ambush." It was the first truthful statement José had made during the entire interview.

Cunningham was again tugging at his leash. "Isn't that convenient? There is nothing in this man's story that adds up."

The deputy stood... pondering his options. His sixth sense nagged that he wasn't getting the entire story from José. Yet, there was no way he could disprove what the man was saying.

Evicting a citizen and his family, especially given the state of society, was a serious action. Before the apocalypse, it had been a necessary evil. Now it was most likely a death warrant.

Still, allowing squatters to move in any residence was a slippery slope. There were few people still walking the earth that had the resources to accomplish a renovation project like Ocean Towers. That elite group of individuals would become hesitant to invest those resources in the future if any ne'er-do-well or drifter was allowed to set up camp on their properties or utilize their assets.

Cunningham seemed to sense he was losing the debate in Morgan's mind. "Deputy, if you don't remove these people, I will be forced to do so myself. Again, I ask you to enforce the law of the land, to use your common sense."

With his fists balling in frustration, the cop's tone was harsh as he responded. "Do not take the law into your own hands, sir. You're just going to make things worse. I suggest the resolution of this issue is to wait and see if Mr. Harrington shows up. This man could very easily be telling the truth, and it would be a travesty to throw his family out onto the streets. Unless further evidence is uncovered, I am not going to evict them. There is still some question as to who owns this unit, sir."

From the color of his face, the deputy could tell the building manager's head was about to explode. Morgan repeated the warning. "Seriously, Mr. Cunningham, do not take action on your own. I promise to return in a few days and continue to monitor the situation. Until further facts are presented, I strongly advise you to leave this man and his family alone."

Morgan then pushed past Cunningham and his two security men, making it clear that the conversation was over.

"So much for the rule of law and order in our new society," Cunningham hissed as he watched the cop enter the stairwell. "We'll see about this."

From his elevated view, José watched the police car leave the otherwise-empty parking lot. Turning to his brother, he said, "I have a feeling our friend Cunningham is not going to take no for an answer."

"Is there anything we can do?" offered one of the deck hands.

"No, thank you. You have done enough already, my

friends."

After seeing his coworkers to the door and then watching them leave via the stairwell, José turned to his brother and announced, "We had better make sure the guns are clean and ready."

"Do you really think it will go that far?" the sibling questioned.

Nodding his head, the older brother answered, "Perhaps, perhaps not, but we need to be ready regardless."

Accepting José's logic, the younger brother strolled to the closet and quickly removed the two Remington shotguns. The hunting pieces had been discovered at the bungalow. After quickly unpacking the weapons, the two men began counting the remaining ammunition. It didn't take them long.

"Go with my wife to the market tomorrow," José said. "Take what little cash we have and anything of value from this apartment that will fit in your pocket. We need bullets."

Mr. Cunningham's temper and disgust simmered throughout the night and into the next day. When he saw José's wife and children utilizing the sauna, along with the courtesy towels, he finally lost control.

Finding the head of security in his small office, the facilities manager asked the question that had percolated in his brain since law enforcement had failed to evict the squatters. "Is your staff capable of removing those hobos?"

"We will have to be armed," replied the confident ex-cop. "Like everybody else, I'm sure our uninvited guests have weapons. I won't ask my men to carry a club into a gunfight."

Cunningham had expected as much. While he was a nonviolent individual, the need for firearms and security was not beyond his sphere of knowledge. "Do your men have the personal weapons necessary to do the job?"

"Of course," the security chief responded. "My guys are all survivors of the downfall and are not strangers to violence."

In a way, Cunningham regretted hearing the anticipated response to the question. Weighing the ramifications of forcing the squatters out via the barrel of the gun, he eventually sighed and said, "See to it then. I want those people out of here... today."

After watching his employee rise and move off to organize his subordinates, Cunningham stood and contemplated the potential results of his decision. Ocean Towers had originally been constructed as a retreat for the ultra-wealthy to escape a variety of personal demons and public pressures. The tenants spent millions of dollars of their hard-earned money to purchase privacy, discretion, and a refuge away from prying eyes of the press, competitors, shareholders, and other monkeys that often rode on the backs of the super-affluent.

Now, Cunningham felt that the role of the luxury building had changed.

Ocean Towers and its restoration were an experiment. Rather than a haven of privacy, the building was now a port where those of substance could safely dock their investments, family, and pride. It was a protected harbor from the storm of anarchy that still raged across much of the planet.

If the reestablishment of Ocean Towers failed, it would be a setback for society as a whole. While a significant undertaking, the cost of restoring the building to its original glory was a mere drop in the bucket compared to the resources that would be required to bring a manufacturing plant or oil rig back into production.

Everyone involved understood that the complex was much like the cavalry forts in the old West. Constructed in the heart of wild, untamed territory, those military installations had become far more than a bastion of safety. Commerce, trade, and settlements had thrived in the proximity of those early, wooden castles. If Ocean Towers were overrun, the ramifications would run deeper and wider than just a few wealthy men having wasted their money.

If the fort held, however, prosperity was sure to follow.

Never a man to beat a dead horse, Cunningham left the security office comfortable with his decision and confident in the path of future events. As he made his way through the halls adorned with quality art, tasteful decorations, and general atmosphere of wealth, the man in charge of Ocean Towers felt satisfaction for the first time since the interlopers had been discovered.

The afternoon passed quickly. Despite its lack of occupants, the luxury complex required a significant portion of Cunningham's day be devoted to forms, paperwork, and a host of small, nagging details. By the time the chief of security was knocking on his door, the sun was low in the western sky.

"I have gathered six of my best men," the security honcho began. "We are ready if you are."

For some reason, the size of the team surprised Cunningham. "Why do you anticipate needing such a large group?"

"The smart way to do this is to use overwhelming force. That and speed of action will be the key to ending this quickly and hopefully without bloodshed. If he's facing six men, our squatter may think twice about starting any trouble. In the end, isn't that what we want?"

Cunningham pondered his employee's logic for a moment before commenting. "You are the expert. We'll go with your recommendation."

The party of armed men, along with Cunningham in tow, made their way to the third floor. None of them spoke a word as they proceeded down the hall, all of the volunteers carrying long guns as well as having secondary sidearms strapped to their belts or legs. Cunningham knew nothing about firearms or fighting... but had to admit that their display of weaponry was impressive.

After motioning his boss to stay back and out of the line of potential gunfire, the security chief stayed to the side of the 3C's entrance and began slamming his fist against the door.

"Building security! Please open up!"

No one breathed while they waited for the answer. After what seemed an eternity, the chief glanced back at Cunningham and said, "You don't suppose they wised up and left already?"

Shaking his head, Cunningham whispered, "We wouldn't be so lucky."

Again, the door was rattled, the pounding sending an echo down the hall. "Building security! Please open the door, or we will force our way in!"

There was no answer.

Shaking his head, the team leader motioned for his men to prepare for a breach. Long ago, before reaching mandatory retirement age, he'd been a cop and knew the techniques by heart.

Bracing himself against the opposing wall, the heaviest fellow gathered his wits and took a deep breath. He then launched a vicious kick, his boot impacting just above the doorknob.

Ocean Towers had been constructed of quality materials. That fact became evident to the men gathered in the hall as their teammate bounced off the door as if he had just tried to topple a concrete wall with a pillow.

With another lung full of air, the heavy security man again

launched himself at the barrier. The result was as disappointing as the first attempt.

Slightly embarrassed and rubbing a now-throbbing knee, he began looking around for anything he could use as a battering ram. Exchanging a look of frustration with one of his team members, he pointed to a nearby firebox, indicating the ax hanging inside.

Before he could speak, a rustle came from behind the door, immediately followed by an angry voice. "Go away! I have a gun! I will shoot!"

"Don't make this hard on yourself," countered the head of security. "Think about your family. There's no sense in anyone getting hurt today."

There was a pause on the other side before José's voice rang strong. "This is my home! I will die to protect it. Wouldn't all of you fight to keep your family safe?"

For a moment, Cunningham thought that the squatter's argument might actually have an effect on his security team.

His concerns, however, were unfounded. Whether it was professionalism, competition, or a case of ego-driven bravado, the private police force seemed unaffected by the pleading from within.

The team leader motioned for another large gent to join him. Whispering a quick count to three, both of the hefty fellows threw their weight against the opening. The frame began to give, small cracks of splintered wood appearing around the knob.

As the duo of human battering rams gathered themselves for another strike, the door exploded outwards, showering the security team with wooden shrapnel. The man assisting the security chief grasped his chest and howled in pain as the 12-gauge deer slug tore through his lung.

That first shot was followed almost immediately by a second, and then a third, the lead slugs ripping and tearing through wood, plaster, and flesh.

Bedlam erupted in the hall.

Whether it was the sight of two coworkers withering in pain or the splatters of bloody tissue running down the wall, the remaining breachers fell back.

Only a few seconds passed before they regrouped, some motivated by pride, others wanting revenge. With faces flushed with rage, the remaining men moved forward with weapons ready at the shoulder. One brave soul kicked hard at the now-weakened door, sending it flying inward while at the same time firing several blinds shot through the opening.

Evidently, Mr. Harrington was a man who appreciated greenery. When José and his family had moved in, they had discovered over a dozen large potted plants throughout the expansive flat, the shriveled, brown foliage succumbing from a lack of water. But the remaining potting soil had another use.

José was barricaded in the corner of the living room, secure behind a heavy chest, each drawer filled with dirt. It was an extremely effective bullet stop.

Surviving the apocalypse had not only provided José with a basic knowledge of ballistics, but the normally-peaceful father had also developed a certain sense of rhythm as applied to gunfights. He instinctively knew when to stay low and when it was time to rise and use his weapon.

He was also well aware that the men in the hallway could only enter his residence in a single file. Breaching experts often referred to this as a "fatal funnel," such narrow obstacles neutralizing the deployment of their superior numbers. It was one-on-one, defender versus attacker, whenever such physical barriers came into play.

José rose from behind his wooden mini-fortress just as the first invader appeared in the now-shattered doorway. His shotgun sang its song, a deadly spread of 00 buckshot stopping the assaulter's forward momentum before the poor fellow could acquire a target.

Three times the corridor shooters attempted to enter his home. The end result was two more bodies partially blocking the threshold while the thick carpeting ran with a crimson hue.

Not only did José understand the concept of a fatal funnel, but years of surviving on the mean streets had also provided him with a basic grasp of small unit tactics.

After hearing the first exchange of shots, the defender's brother gathered himself and then sprang from a fire exit door. Blindsiding the Tower's team, his presence added the critical element of surprise.

Neither as coolheaded nor as experienced as his older brother, the sibling's first shot veered high.

Frantically working the duck gun's pump, his second blast caught one of the attackers full in the upper thigh, sending the man groaning to the carpet in a corkscrew motion.

Now the remaining team members forgot about José and his barricaded position, their weapons snapping around to address the new threat to their rear.

With no cover, and slow to work his weak, nervous limbs on the shotgun's pump, the sibling went down in a hailstorm of gunfire from the assaulters.

The small victory gave momentum to the survivors in the hall and they began firing wildly into unit 3C. The impacting rounds shattered glass, punched through walls, and peppered José's cover with such a ferocity that he was forced to keep low.

During the barrage of incoming rounds, it dawned on 3C's lone defender that his brother's weapon was no longer firing from the hall. He could only assume the worst.

The thought of losing another brother, combined with the hailstorm of lead, choking smoke, and unbearable noise caused something to snap in José's mind.

His presence at Ocean Towers was hurting no one. The odds were that the original owner had died during the collapse. Yet, the men out in the hall were bound and determined to keep him down, to put their boots on his neck and make him stay in his wretched place.

Fueled by the injustice of their actions, rage overwhelmed the normally composed defender. Screaming at the top of lungs, José came out from behind his shield and began firing at the entrance as quickly as his adrenaline-fueled arm could work the 12-gauge's action.

The bold, unexpected charge was almost successful. Stunned by a seemingly insane man rushing at them with a blazing scattergun, one of the security men actually stopped firing and took a step backward, blocking his comrade's line of fire.

Straddling the body of his own coworkers with blood-covered boots, another of Cunningham's employees had the wherewithal to round the corner and blindly pour rounds into the opening.

Two high-velocity hollowpoints struck José in the chest, the impact knocking him sideways as he fired the final round from his weapon.

The rifled deer slug tore through the kitchen wall and pierced one of the Towers' 3-inch water mains.

While José's failing lungs gulped their last gasp of air, his younger sibling pushed aside the pain and managed to lift his weapon with weak, shaking arms. As his vision began to darken around the edges, he squeezed the trigger, releasing a swarm of buckshot into the cowering Cunningham and a survivor of the security team.

Three of the pellets caught the building manager in the back of the head while the remainder of the deadly load tore through the neck of the nearby guard. Both men died instantly.

A full 20 minutes after the sickening thud of a body slumping against the bedroom wall, the surviving trespassers ventured out. Nothing but the sound of gushing water greeted José's family members when they finally emerged from the unit's rearmost room.

Deputy Morgan almost didn't return to Ocean Towers after his shift.

In addition to the dilemma of trying to resolve that ambiguous situation, the lawman had experienced an especially trying day.

Still, he'd made a commitment as a servant of the community. Perhaps more importantly, Cunningham and whoever was funding the refurbishment of the complex were going to be prominent members of the region he served. *No sense pissing off the folks in charge*, he mused.

After parking in the empty lot, the first hint something was wrong came as the deputy approached the front door. There, he noticed a small stream of water escaping down the stained concrete steps.

"Now Cunningham is really going to be testy," he whispered. "I'm sure he will blame the leaky roof on the squatters."

When Morgan opened one of the heavy glass doors leading to the lobby, a small tidal wave of water sloshed down the steps. "Oh shit, this looks like more than just a leaking pipe."

Splashing across the floor, the deputy couldn't help but feel that something was seriously wrong. Several ceiling tiles were already sagging under the weight of the flood.

He found the first two flights of stairs had now been transformed into a waterfall. Careful not to fall on the slick surface, he negotiated the steps as quickly as possible.

The carpeting on the third floor was also saturated, the thick material squishing under his shoes as he exited the stairwell. All that was soon lost on the deputy as the carnage in the hall came into view. He was taken aback when the loud torrent of gushing water was overwhelmed by lamented moans and languishing cries. Not knowing what to expect, he drew his weapon and approached the horrific scene.

In all of his days as a law enforcement officer, Morgan had never seen anything to prepare him for the blood and slaughter that filled the corridor.

Gingerly stepping over the bodies with his weapon drawn and ready, the deputy soon discovered the source of the sobbing. José's wife and elderly father were huddled over the body of their beloved one. Three small children and a baby, all apparently in shock, were clustered nearby.

After verifying there were no longer any active shooters,

Morgan holstered his firearm and began checking for pulses, feeling the bloodied, shredded bodies that seem to be scattered throughout the area. Other than the noncombatants, he found no survivors.

At that moment, the flood reached one of the building's main generators. Gallons of water began pouring into the large, diesel-powered turbine. The entire building shook violently as the incompatible mixture of water and electricity reacted, the explosion sending heavy metal fragments into the support columns and nearby foundation.

Dust falling from the ceiling and flickering lights warned the deputy that Ocean Towers might no longer be a safe place. He was just about to hustle the mourning family out when the second explosion rocked the entire floor.

The detonations served to bring the survivors out of the sorrow-induced trance. Making eye contact with the deputy, José's wife acted instantly to the threat and began gathering her children close.

Morgan followed the grieving relatives to the stairway. A few minutes later, he watched the old man, widow, and small children begin wandering toward the waterfront.

Even with the recovery, the lawman knew their chances of survival were slim. Taking a final glance at the once-glimmering structure, he returned to his car and exited the parking lot.

There was nothing else he could do.

Chapter 2

The two black SUVs rolled out of Alpha, speeding west toward Fort Bliss. The lead unit's front and rear seats were filled with the Alliance's best security team, each having been handpicked to protect the fledgling republic's highest elected official.

All four were uneasy, their eyes scanning the road ahead for anything unusual that might threaten Diana.

They were men paid to be nervous, to question everything, and take nothing for granted. They all understood their charge's importance to the Alliance and her citizens. Any of them would die to protect her.

Since Nick's hospitalization, Diana had been making frequent trips to the distant base, journeys that caused her protectors to clench their teeth from stress. Redundancy led to predictability, and in their business, that often meant death.

Like most governments, the Alliance's capital was a relatively docile environment, heavily patrolled and well policed. Not all of the territories could make such claims. El Paso fell into a category the security forces called a "frontier town." Unofficially, the border city was often referred to as the "wild, wild West."

Except Fort Bliss, much of the city was still on the fringe of law and order. Houston, Dallas, Austin, and San Antonio were all at various stages of reintegration and recovery.

Today, their heightened senses were taxed far beyond the usual trip to El Paso. Instead of one of their own behind the wheel of the leader's personal vehicle, Bishop was doing the driving per Diana's strongly worded request. That was a change from the security team's well-established protocol, and they were men who didn't appreciate even the slightest deviation.

They all knew the man, trusted his loyalty, and respected his willingness to fight. His reputation was well known throughout post-collapse Texas... and even beyond. But he was a lone wolf, and they were a team. Their methods and tactics were unique and well drilled. If trouble did rear its ugly head on the way to Fort Bliss, Diana's protection would be handicapped by having him onboard.

Even more troubling was the fact that Nick was being released from the hospital today. None of the protectors knew what to expect when their boss returned to duty. Throughout their careers, all of them had seen the impact of such serious wounds and how their comrades had been affected. Sometimes the experience could make a man timid, other times the result was dangerous aggression. Now and then, a hollow, empty shell was released from the doctor's care.

Nick was exceptionally well liked and respected. No one wanted to see the big man damaged in any way.

Which led to the primary reason why Diana's bodyguards were on edge.

Since Nick's hospitalization, the Alliance's leader, their boss's fiancé, had been spending a tremendous amount of time with Bishop. So much so that rumors were beginning to circulate among the security forces.

Being professionals, they had all initially taken a position that the relationship was none of their business.

But as time passed, a state of melancholy began to descend over the innermost ring of Diana's team. Trouble between their commander and someone like Bishop could easily escalate to violence. Domestic disturbances were still a leading cause of homicide within the territories. No one wanted to see the Alliance's first and second couples soiled by scandal or split in half. Some of the men had even speculated that an internal feud could lead to civil war.

At first, Bishop's constant presence had made sense in a way. Nick was at Bliss, Bishop's wife in New Mexico. Everyone knew the two couples had fought side-by-side numerous times to create the Alliance. If the stories were only half-exaggerated, Bishop and Nick had saved each other's lives a dozen times.

Late night laughter drifting from Diana's private quarters had begun to erode some opinions. Bishop's delivery of a few gifts had furthered the slide. After a few weeks of watching the pair, even the most optimistic witnesses began to have doubts.

To many of the professionals guarding Diana, Bishop's actions, even if completely innocent, were treacherous behavior. Nick was supposed to be his friend and had stood by the Texan during the worst of times. Wearing a path to Diana's back door while the boss was incapacitated was dastardly.

The fact that Nick was being released today could spell trouble, and guarding someone like Diana was difficult enough without internal strife and turmoil. A thick fog of apprehension filled the lead SUV.

The eastern sun was barely peeking over the horizon as Alpha faded in Bishop's rearview mirror. Sitting beside him in the passenger seat, Diana was giddy. "I've been looking forward to this day for weeks. I finally get to bring Nick home from the hospital. It's been wearing me a little thin, driving back and forth, worrying about the big lug, and trying to manage government business all at the same time."

Bishop understood. "I hear ya. I know how much I miss Terri and Hunter, and they're in good health. They're supposed to be back from New Mexico in a few days. We should all get together and have a celebration."

Beaming, Diana gushed, "Now that's one heck of an idea. But you have to promise me that you'll keep Nick from coming back to work too soon. The docs wanted to keep him another week, but I guess he's being a difficult patient."

"Imagine that," Bishop said, his tone dripping with sarcasm. "Hard to picture Nick being anything but a low-key, meek, cooperative soul."

Both of them had a good laugh over the vision conjured by the Texan's words. Both felt a little sorry for the staff at the hospital.

"As far as making you that promise," Bishop continued, "No deal. I'm not the smartest guy in the country, but I'm not the dumbest either. Other than you, no one makes Nick do a damn thing he doesn't want to."

"He'll listen to you, and you know it's true. Please, Bishop, I don't want him trying to do too much too soon and having a relapse."

Nodding, Bishop responded, "I remember when Terri and I were bugging out from Houston and I took a bullet... lost a lot of blood. Getting shot by those kidnappers was even worse. I was on the same floor of that hospital for weeks," he paused as his brain surged with memories. "It's tough. Your mind is just fine. It wants to get up and move, do things, and start living again. But your body won't cooperate. It's a difficult, frustrating situation to manage. No worries, Diana. You have my word that I'll do my best to help my hardheaded friend deal with it."

"Thanks. By the way, speaking of hardheaded, I've got a scheduled call with an old associate of yours today, the President of those United States."

Bishop laughed, "Why do you surround yourself with these types of men? Give the Colonel... err... I mean the president, my regards."

Diana hesitated for just a moment, and then said, "I'd like for you to be there, Bishop. It's going to be an important call, and normally I'd have Nick at my side. I could use a sounding board."

"Of course," Bishop replied. "I'll do my best. Besides, it will be good to say hello to the Colonel again."

A smile lit Diana's face, "Thank you. I swear I won't be burdening you with this crap much longer. You've been a wonderful friend these last few weeks. I don't know if I could have made it through without you."

Bishop waved her off, "You would... and have done the same for Terri and me. None of us would have survived the apocalypse without each other. Together, we're all stronger."

The Alliance's leader nodded and then turned her attention to the passing West Texas countryside. Bishop had been there for her, filling a void created by Nick's absence. Like no one else in the bubble that surrounded her office, she could share her fears, anger, and doubts with him. He would never betray her... or Nick. He would never run off at the mouth or wield her humanness as a political weapon.

She wondered how many of history's great leaders had benefited from such a trustworthy circles of advisors. *Probably all of them*, she decided.

Bishop had been there when the monthly report estimating the death toll in Alliance territory had arrived. While outright famine no longer racked the population, disease and illness associated with years of malnutrition were still reaping thousands of souls every month. There simply weren't enough doctors or medicine to go around. Diana had been devastated by the document's projection that another 40,000 had perished, a large majority of which were children under the age of ten years.

She had wept on Bishop's shoulder for over half an hour, confident he wouldn't judge her too weak or inadequate to lead the Alliance.

And then there was the anniversary of her adopted son's death. A horrible day that she dreaded every time it rolled around on the calendar. Atlas had died with honor, saving her church and its flock from being overrun, but that made little difference to the grieving mother who could still feel the warmth of his blood on her hands.

It wasn't always sorrow or grief. Anger was a constant companion to those who lead the recovery. On the day after reading about sick, dying children, Diana was informed of a man-made tragedy that had occurred just outside of Huntsville.

When the lights had gone out for the last time, it was estimated Texas had over 120,000 inmates in her jails and prisons. Many had starved, locked in the cells without food or water. Tens of thousands more had escaped, turned loose on a society that couldn't dial 9-1-1.

Atlas had died fighting just such a gang of thugs.

Many of the criminals were violent, sick individuals who had been locked away to protect the innocent. Now, many of them were still on the loose. The downfall of society had set law enforcement's efforts back decades. Seasoned felons left to their own devices, coupled with seriously limited resources to corral them often led to more lawbreaking than the general population liked.

On the day in question, Sheriff Watts brought the heartbreaking news of a large family having been found dead in their home. They had suffered badly before being murdered. Deputies had eventually tracked down the culprit, a serial killer who'd escaped during the collapse. He'd been marauding through the central Texas countryside ever since.

Then there was the political strife. While the council's directives had been successful, all five of the mandated priorities were being challenged by one unavoidable circumstance – how to manage the ownership of physical property.

The incident at Ocean Towers in Corpus had made the headlines for days, sending a wave of apprehension throughout the territories. If wealthy men with resources couldn't safely invest in Texas, how could the recovery possibly continue?

Texas had suffered over 15 million dead, or roughly half of the population. Those causalities had left behind unclaimed businesses, farms, homes, and other assets. Who owned them? How were they to be disbursed? Should the government keep them? What about the banks that held the mortgages... what if those institutions reopened? The Alliance would need banking if the economy were to grow and prosper. Free enterprise was already demanding to take its rightful place as a leading role in society. Everyone on the council knew that centralized planning would only jumpstart a stalled system. It was time to get out of the way and let the engine of capitalism run free.

Bishop, however, had strongly disagreed when the time came for the council to vote. "We're not far enough along, in my humble opinion," he stated after reviewing the latest proposal addressing property ownership. "The Alliance hasn't established itself well enough just yet. There's no shortage of problems to address across the land. Give it some more time before you take this one on."

Unlike so many surrounding Diana's office, Bishop didn't pout or become angry when she disagreed. After informing him that he was dead wrong and the issue was now the most critical on their agenda, he had simply shrugged and smiled. "That's why you make the big bucks, and I carry a rifle," he'd grinned. A minute later is was if the debate had never taken place.

Normally, she could face the never-ending string of challenges and deal with the death and violence. Political unrest, outside threats, and the usual internal turmoil were all in a day's work for Diana.

But not with Nick's life on the line, her future husband's mental well-being still in question after such serious injuries. Not without Terri being there. Not with Kevin still mending from what had been a terrible ordeal of torture and abuse in New Mexico.

On top of it all, the ramifications of the council's latest decisions and policies were far reaching. If they got it wrong, the outcome could lead to another collapse and chaos. The future quality of life for the survivors was at stake. The stress was nearly incapacitating, stretching her, and all of the leadership, to the limit.

Bishop had come to the rescue, offering a level head, kind smile, and unwavering support. Beyond all that... more important than anything else... was the trust shared between them. She would never forget his support during the last few weeks.

Glancing over at her driver, Diana wondered why she was so amazed by such a simple thing as his friendship. Hadn't Bishop always delivered? How many times had he saved the upstart movement? She'd lost count.

It finally dawned on her. Bishop had always used his rifle, or combat skills, or bravery to save the day. She wondered if he knew how important this latest bout of heroism had been.

Probably not, she decided. *No one was shooting at him. It must have seemed like a vacation.*

Cameron James Lewis pushed away from his desk and turned to the window.

As usual, the unremarkable Oklahoma countryside served as a reminder, the image having fueled his efforts and focused his energies on what had become life's only meaningful objective – returning to Texas.

They called themselves the Alliance now. He called them murdering, thieving bandits. Barbarians from the West.

Months had passed since that fateful day when his security forces had been attacked. He'd watched as his men fell by the dozens, hundreds of Philistines storming the gates and destroying everything he'd done to help the people of Midland Station survive the downfall. The jealous traitors of his hometown had turned on him... every man, woman, and child. *Revenge is sweet, my friends,* Lewis mused. *When I return triumphant, I will line the streets with your lifeless, disloyal bodies hanging by the noose.*

A homegrown army of irregulars had encircled his corporate headquarters, and only a mad, scrambling evacuation via rooftop helicopter had saved his life. It was all as fresh in his mind as if it had occurred just a few hours ago.

As the emergency flight had lifted off, Cameron could still see the hundreds of dead and dying employees lying in a street that was named in honor of his father. Horror filled his soul as the hordes from the west poured into the office building that bore his family's crest.

The copter pilot had deposited him here, a remote exploration facility deep in the middle of nowhere. And here he'd stayed, revenge simmering in his core as he began working to rebuild the empire of his father's dreams.

It had been difficult, the vast majority of the corporation's assets falling into the Alliance's hands. He'd been forced to do little more than watch and stew as the only working refinery in Texas had enabled the thieves' expansion all across the Lone Star State. *His* refinery. *His* engineers. *His* town. *His* family's oil fueling the recovery.

At first, Cameron had considered a counter-attack using force. He still had dozens of steadfast, armed men at his disposal. That option, however, was quickly ruled out. There were too many of the thugs, and their dominance was spreading like wildfire all across Texas.

He'd ventured to Oklahoma City, hoping to solicit help from the federal authorities. He'd found the state capital in absolute anarchy. There was no government there, state or national. Only roving gangs fighting each other for territory and what few assets they could scavenge.

So he, along with the staff at the facility, had waited, plotted, and improved their situation as circumstances allowed.

Their big opportunity had arrived via Washington. The U.S. desperately needed petroleum, or more specifically gasoline, diesel, and natural gas. An emissary from the president's office had driven up one day, sent on a fact-finding mission from the nation's struggling capital. The federal representative had spent the entire morning talking with the former executive. Cameron knew the petrol business, was well aware of certain regional facilities and capabilities, and seemed eager to help kickstart the nation's recovery.

Natural gas had been the first priority. With Cameron's skills and confidence, the Department of Energy had given him more and more authority and responsibility as the months passed. Progress was slow, but over time he'd begun to deliver badly needed energy to the military and key civilian users. It was a drop in the bucket compared to what the deprived nation needed, but every little bit counted.

With prominence came power and control. Slowly, he gathered a war chest of men, equipment, and most importantly, knowledge.

There had been setbacks. When news came that Washington was pulling the U.S. Army out of Texas, Cameron had been discouraged. Rumors of the Alliance slowly restoring electrical power to the state's larger metropolitan areas had further darkened his mood for weeks. There had been periods where it seemed that returning home was nothing more than a distant, fading dream.

Now, that had all changed.

Turning back to the two men seated in front of his desk, Cameron found himself needing confirmation of what he'd just heard. "Are you sure of this? Absolutely certain?"

"Yes, sir," answered the older of the two. "The Alliance's council made the decision just a short time ago. Our sources are confident this new program will be initiated in the next 10 days."

"It's also part of the public record," the other visitor stated. "The meeting minutes of the last four council sessions all contain numerous discussions about the ownership of private property and how the situation is growing critical. Diana Brown even stated that it was the Alliance's single largest issue, now more important than the five directives."

Cameron's eyes darted between the two men, waiting for more. His visitors were happy to expand.

"They've hit a wall," continued the first, "They're trying to restart the banking system, industrial production, and service based industries. But no one has paid on a mortgage since the collapse. Over half of the debtors are dead or missing, another significant portion of the population is sick or not working. Most of their economy is barter, and they just started collecting minimal taxes."

"They have hundreds of thousands that are homeless, many living in tent cities and working the fields by hand. Houston alone has armies of transient workers, bussed in to clean up the half of the city that burned. Yet, one estimate presented to the council claimed that 40% of the homes left standing were empty. The problem is, what do you do with them? Who owns them?

Where are the owners? Which bank holds the note? It's a huge mess."

One of the visitors chuckled, "I heard a story about a farm equipment dealership outside Brownsville. There were hundreds of new tractors, just sitting on the lot gathering dust. The owner and his family were all dead. The entire inventory had been there for months and months, half of the tires were flat, or so the story goes. Anyway, along came the Alliance... and they needed transportation. They were trying to organize work crews to plant fields, and they had a limited supply of gasoline. So they started taking the implements and using them. Two months ago, a woman showed up and claimed she's the owner's daughter... says she deserves to be compensated for all the missing vehicles. She told a great story about being trapped in New Orleans ever since the collapse. Had an ID with the same last name as the owner of record. Presented a yearbook from the local high school with her picture. The Alliance paid her off, only to find out a short time later that there never were any daughters – only three sons. They still haven't found her or their money."

"That's not even taking into account the fiasco at Ocean Towers," added the other.

Cameron grunted and then rubbed his chin, imagining the dilemma facing the Alliance leadership. "So they're going to set a time limit? They're going to give people a window to make claims. Anything that's left over will be divided between the government and the banks. That's not a bad idea."

"No," responded one of the visitors. "There's really no other way to go about it. Records, computer servers, files, and even entire courthouses have burned, been ransacked, or are just missing. If you're a survivor, you'll be able to file claims for all of the assets, property, resources, and facilities owned before it all went to hell. Of course, stocks, bonds, and other investments will be dealt with later."

Nodding, Cameron said, "That's welcome news. Thank you, gentlemen, for the update. I hope your travels back to Texas are safe, and I look forward to seeing you both again soon."

Once alone, the shunned executive returned to the view outside his window.

For the first time since his exile, he noted the clear horizon and expansive, flat landscape from a positive perspective. *There is beauty in it*, he surmised. His hard work was about to pay dividends.

When it became apparent that para-military force wasn't going to dislodge the Alliance, he'd settled on a different strategy. In a way, the fledgling government now in control of his homeland was a competitor, just like the dozens of corporations he'd bested before the apocalypse. Why should he treat a bunch of amateurs from West Texas any differently? It was all business.

Inheriting control of the U.S. Army's assets within the state made his nemesis nearly impossible to dislodge with force, but there were other ways.

More than once Cameron and his father had beaten back a larger, more powerful enemy. Stock options, futures manipulation, greasing the pockets of regulators, and an army of the best lawyers in the oil patch had resulted in some impressive victories. As the old adage went, often it wasn't what you knew, but whom you knew that could win the day. Cam knew a lot of people.

Now that rule of law, banking, high finance, and a system of justice were being reestablished in Texas, why shouldn't he use the same methods to defeat this newest foe?

He had people on the inside providing an excellent pipeline of intelligence and perspective. He had the financial assets, legitimate claims, and a growing political clout. The Alliance was struggling, her people growing impatient for progress that always seemed to be slow in coming... and disappointing in the application.

Just a few weeks ago, pounds of nuclear waste were floating through the air toward the Texas heartland, nearly setting off a panic. War with the United States, for the third time since the downfall, had been a realistic threat.

There had been so many dangers, potential disasters, and setbacks for the Alliance, it was no wonder her citizens were a potential tinderbox. It would only take the right match to set it all ablaze.

Cameron stood and exhaled a deep sigh. It was time to make his move. Confidence was high.

Unlike all of the external threats that had served to pull the people of Texas together, his would be an internal assault, exposing the rot and decay that was the Alliance's government. He would use their own weaknesses against them, wield their own systems and rules as a weapon.

He would split their leadership, instill waves of doubt through the population, and prove to the people that it was all a big lie.

"A house divided cannot stand," he whispered, paraphrasing President Lincoln's famous line.

Diana entered the secure communications room, thanking the specialist for rolling over a chair. Bishop elected to stand.

"The president is on the frequency, ma'am."

Pressing the microphone's button, the Alliance leader said, "Good morning, Mr. President."

"Top of the day to you, Miss Brown, and thank you for coming. As usual, my day is overbooked, so I'll get right down to brass tacks. Given the calamity that nearly occurred in New Mexico, I would like to offer an exchange of ambassadors between Alpha and Washington. It's the tried and true method to avoid such misunderstandings, and I think both of our governments will benefit from such an arrangement. It's not foolproof, but it's the best idea I've heard so far."

Glancing at Bishop and receiving a reassuring nod, the Alliance's top elected official popped the question that troubled the fledgling Texas government the most. "While I agree with the concept, Mr. President, I have to ask; does this mean that the United States is officially recognizing Texas as an independent republic?"

There was a pause, Diana always uncertain if the gap was due to the other party considering her words, or if the computers that scrambled their conversation were having a slow day.

Finally, a chuckle sounded, followed by an audible inhalation. "No. I'm neither prepared, nor authorized to offer such a permanent status. Like you, I've got my hands full just keeping this runaway train on the track. Be that as it may, I still believe we would both benefit from having a trusted advisor in both capitals. They could assist in economic discussions, trade, joint development, resource allocation, and a host of other topics. Most importantly, they might keep innocent misunderstandings from getting out of control."

Diana threw another quick glance toward Bishop. She wasn't seeking permission, more akin to asking a reliable consultant, "Do you see anything wrong with this?"

The Texan shrugged a response. The idea had face value.

Turning back to the microphone the Alliance leader responded, "I can't see any issue with better communications and representation, sir. Like you, I'm not a dictator. I'll have to clear this with the council, but I don't foresee anyone having an issue with it."

"Good," the president's voice assertively boomed through the speaker. "I have the perfect man already in mind to represent our side of the equation. He's a native Texan from Houston, former military, and someone who has proven valuable in our own recovery. Let me know of your council's final decision, and good day, Miss Brown."

"Before you go, sir.... There's someone here that would like to say hello."

Bishop stepped forward, bending to the microphone. "Good day, Colonel. I hope your current duties go well, sir."

"Bishop? Well, hell's fire and brimstone, son. It's good to hear your voice. That was some excellent work over in New Mexico. Saved a lot of lives and trouble for all concerned. Give my regards to that exceptional woman that lets you hang around. Terri's giving my people fits out there, but they'll be stronger for the experience. And that fine looking boy. I hear he's charmed everyone from my representatives to the local tribes. Good thing he takes after his mother, eh?" A genuine chuckle drifted across the airwaves, Bishop smiling at the insult. It wouldn't be a conversation with the Colonel without such banter.

"Thank you, sir. I'll pass along your best wishes."

As they left the HQ building, Diana meandered along the sidewalk, her mind a whir of electrical impulses and a tumble of thoughts. "We need to come up with two different people if the president's idea is to be effective," she mused. "We need somebody we can trust to move to Washington, and we must identify a liaison for their ambassador here."

"I'm not moving to Washington if that's what you're thinking. Nope, not going to do it."

Grinning, Diana replied, "You are a lot of things, Bishop, but an ambassador isn't one of them. No, that's not what I was thinking. I do, however, believe your lovely bride would be a perfect fit to work with whomever Washington assigns to us. She could stay right here and help me plan my wedding. Might be my best chance and getting a ring on that man of mine," Diana chuckled.

The Texan rubbed his chin, considering the concept. "You'll have to talk to Terri about that. I learned a long time ago not to stand between her and a career move."

"My gosh, Bishop. What good are you?" Diana teased. "You won't commit to keeping my future husband out of trouble, and now you're shying away from talking to Terri about re-entering government service. You need to pick it up a step, trooper."

Bishop laughed and then dropped his head in pretend shame.

Grim's voice rang out just then, the grizzled contractor waiting at the hospital's entrance. "Give him hell, Miss Brown. He deserves it."

Butter was there as well, waiting alongside. As usual, the big kid was all tow-headed smiles.

"We're off to help Sheriff Watts deal with a couple of hard cases," Bishop announced. "With Kevin being out of action for a while, we can't operate as a SAINT team, so we're going to earn our paychecks by helping our friends in law enforcement."

"I'd heard as much," Diana responded, stopping short and turning to face Bishop with a serious expression. "Thank you," she said, wrapping her arms around him in a tight embrace. "I wouldn't have made it through these last few weeks without you."

Bishop returned the hug, patting the most powerful figure in the Alliance gently on the back. "You're doing grand work, Diana. Never forget that. And tell Nick I'll see his sorry ass in a few days."

Despite being anxious to get Nick out of what he called, the "medical dungeon," Diana paused to watch the trio of men walk toward the front gate. "Terri is one lucky-ass girl," she whispered, "and I think she knows it."

Chapter 3

Two squad cars and a SWAT van idled at the base's front gate, Sheriff Watts and a pair of his men standing in a group while they waited for Bishop's team to arrive.

After a friendly greeting and round of handshakes and introductions, the Alliance's top lawman got down to business.

Ramrod straight, with every detail of his uniform polished, ironed, tucked, and proper, the lanky sheriff was the picture of authority and confidence. "We're having some issues in the panhandle that are pressing my people to the limit. It seems that a group of aggressive individuals has taken to growing marijuana in and around Palo Dura Canyon, and we are overtaxed in that region as it is. Last week they wounded two of my deputies in a gunfight."

Bishop was a little surprised by the first assignment and said so. "I thought we were going to help you with some truly bad men, Sheriff. Doesn't the Alliance have bigger issues than a bunch of kids growing some weed?"

The officer grimaced at the comment, "Normally, I'd agree wholeheartedly. But these 'kids,' as you refer to them... well, I believe they're actually a bunch of escaped federal inmates. They were using their cash crop to barter with the survivors in Amarillo, which again is way down the list of sins worth pursuing. The problem is, when they can't trade for what they want, they take it. Mostly at the end of a barrel. They've taken to terrorizing the region, and their numbers are growing stronger with each passing day."

Bishop nodded, "I see. My apologies, Sheriff. I've had a little trouble adjusting to the Alliance's new posture and authority."

Watts didn't smile back. "I heard about your run-in with my men in Meraton not long ago. We're just trying to do our job, Bishop. I'd appreciate it if you'd avoid fighting with my deputies. We're losing enough men as it is."

"I'll be fine, Sheriff. Now, about these pot growers in Palo Dura... how many of them are there?"

"We estimate at least 30, perhaps as many as 50. They're pretty well armed and have gotten quite familiar with the terrain. With over 70 miles of canyons, caves, gullies, and offshoots, we don't have the manpower to search the entire area. Fort Bliss loaned us a helicopter, but the aerial search didn't turn up any results. They're very well hidden."

Grim whistled, "That's a pretty good sized operation. And when we find them?"

"Call us in once you know the location of their hideout. I'll be there within ten hours with the cavalry."

Butter spoke up, "Ten hours? That's an awfully long time, sir."

Watts didn't look down, "It will take me that long to gather enough men and reach the area. That's very rugged, remote terrain up there, son. But we'll be there. You can count on it."

Grim still didn't like it. "This sounds like more of a job for the military, Sheriff. Can't you get some help out of Fort Hood or Bliss?"

It was obvious from Watt's expression that Grim's question had struck a nerve. "I'm told by General Owens that every available man under his command is busy in Houston, Dallas, and some of the other big cities back east. He made it clear that a violent gang of 30 to 50 individuals didn't rank high on his list of priorities."

Bishop shrugged, looking at his team. "We don't have to engage, just track them down. We've faced worse problems. Let's get moving."

Palo Dura Canyon was often called the "Grand Canyon of Texas." Stretching over 70 miles end-to-end, the formation was the second largest canyon system in North America. Being number two meant that the area wasn't nearly as well known or oft visited. Many of the tourists who did settle for second best left believing they had uncovered a little-known gem.

With sheer walls that rose nearly 1,000 feet, Palo Dura wasn't as deep nor as wide as its larger sibling to the west. But it's multi-hued red rock and jagged formations were a sight to behold.

It was also far more accessible with public roads, hiking trails, campgrounds, and climbing facilities sprinkled throughout the canyon floor and rims.

Bishop had only visited the place once before the collapse. A college buddy had been raised in the area and boasted of the great climbing and awe-inspiring scenery. A weekend road trip had been planned for the fellows to get back to nature by sleeping under the stars, burning a little food over a campfire and honing their rock climbing techniques.

Like that first visit so many years before, the unveiling of Palo Dura was a bit of a shock to the three trackers.

For miles and miles across the panhandle of Texas, the travelers had seen nothing but mind-numbing, board-flat fields and prairies. No trees, no hills, no features to distract the eye.

Then suddenly, without warning, the canyon just appeared, carved into the earth by the Red River. Splendid. Massive. Stark in contrast to its tabletop smooth surroundings and bursting with so much color and shape.

Bishop had once read a quote by a famous painter who had lived in the area describing it as, "… a burning, seething caldron, filled with dramatic light and color." The Texan couldn't conjure up a better depiction.

The small convoy of police units wound their way to the north rim, finally rolling to a stop just above a seldom-used trailhead leading down into the red rock walls below.

Grim and Butter immediately moved to the edge, their eyes scanning what would be the two operators' home for the next few days. The older man wasn't inspired. "Damn… that's some rough looking countryside."

Bishop didn't have to gawk, "This op is going to be longer and harder than a bad girl's dream," he said. "But look at the bright side; you'll be able to tell your grandkids about all of the famous tourist attractions you've visited in our great republic."

The only reply was a grumbled, "I'm getting to old for this shit."

The trio began unloading packs, weapons, and gear from the back of the old SWAT van. All were sweating profusely before they'd finished snapping buckles and checking weapons. Bishop was the second best long-range shooter, and given Kevin's absence, was tasked as the team's designated marksman. He was not happy about having to tote the heavy .308 adorned with a big optic. Butter and Grim rolled with their favorite carbines.

The only positive aspect of the location was the abundance of water. Despite the surrounding terrain being nearly as dry as the Texan's native desert, the Red River would provide an adequate supply of the life-giving substance. Each man carried a pump water filter as well as backup iodine purification tablets. It would be an extra task each day, but that was the far better option than carrying several pounds of liquid on their backs.

While Butter and Grim finished checking each other's loadout, Bishop and Watts studied a map spread across a squad car's hood. With a long finger tapping several marked spots on the chart, the sheriff announced, "These marks indicate where we've had contact with the gang. Looks like they are based at the eastern end, around the old state park. That makes sense, as the locals tell me that area is thick with caves and slot canyons."

Next came the most important part of the operation – communications.

Bishop pulled a military-issued satellite phone from his kit while Sheriff Watts produced an identical model. After a quick sequence of numbers had been punched, the lawman's unit began ringing loudly. A successful test.

"This will be monitored 24 hours a day," Watts promised. "As soon as you find their hideout, call and we'll be coming in force."

As Bishop checked his team, Sheriff Watts approached with a small can of bright orange spray paint in his hand. "I'll have a deputy drive along this rim road every morning before lunch. If the satellite phones fail for any reason, spray the symbol of a cross where it can be seen from the road. We'll get here as quickly as we can. Good luck."

Bishop nodded and smiled, "Backup plans are always wise. Thanks, Sheriff. We'll see you in a few days."

The team leader then turned to his men and said, "Let's go fellas. My wife is supposed to return from New Mexico soon. I want to be there to greet her. She's not had the pleasure of my company for several weeks."

"Lucky girl," grumbled Grim. "I wonder how much she'd pay me to slow this operation down?"

The descent was steep, treacherous, and exhausting. Halfway to the canyon floor, Bishop's muscles were screaming for mercy, his entire body drenched in salty perspiration. "Let's take 10 on that next ridge," he instructed between breaths. "I don't want you guys getting hurt."

Grim threw a "You're full of shit," look at his commander, but didn't say a word. Butter, in pure innocence, said, "I'm fine, boss. We don't have to stop."

The two older members of the squad outvoted the younger legs and lungs in a silent election. Grim was suffering as well, just too damn proud to admit it.

"I don't think that sheriff likes you much, Bishop," Grim finally mumbled, dropping his pack to the dust. "That son of a bitch picked the most difficult trail in the entire canyon on purpose. I bet he's up on the rim over there, sitting in his air-conditioned car and watching us through binoculars. Probably having a grand old belly laugh at our misery."

"You're probably right," replied the Texan. "I should have given your charm and diplomacy more of a chance to win the man over."

Butter, slowly getting used to his teammates' constant banter, ignored the back-and-forth prattle. "Sir, how are we going to find these bad guys? This place is huge… with a million places to hide."

Bishop grunted, "That's simple. We follow the river and look for tracks. Anybody living in this canyon and growing crops has to carry a lot of water back to their camp. We'll just find their trail and follow it."

The younger man was confused. "But if it's that easy, how come the deputies didn't do the same thing?"

Grim smiled, shaking his head, "Bishop said it was simple, not easy. They'll have lookouts, maybe snipers posted. They're probably smart enough to try and cover their tracks. We have to search 28 miles of river without exposing ourselves, and that is going to suck."

Bishop nodded his agreement. "We'll go with Grim and me in front, you bringing up the rear, Butter. We'll move like a triangle, always keeping good separation. There's no way one man can watch for signs and keep an eye out for sentries and ambushes at the same time. Two of us in front will give us a better chance of coming out of this without a backside full of buckshot."

The two team members nodded their understanding.

"Let's mount up. We're burning daylight."

Terri was touched by the number of tribal elders and local officials that gathered to see her off. While her work in New Mexico had been rewarding, she was anxious to get home. Hunter didn't seem to mind their extended stay, having made several new friends.

"We'll come back and visit, I promise," she shouted and waved from the back of the Alliance SUV.

The two security men Diana had tasked to escort her home were the typical stoic professionals. As they sped across the New Mexico desert on the way to Texas, she couldn't help but wonder how Bishop had ever tolerated such low-key, anti-social coworkers.

The thought prompted another round of worrying about her

husband. Without thinking, she asked the two men in the front seat, "Has there been any word on Bishop's mission? Do you know if he's still up in the panhandle?"

Before the words had left her throat, she regretted the questions. Even if they knew, or had heard a rumor, they wouldn't tell her. It just wasn't done.

What happened next struck Terri as strange. Instead of the anticipated, immediate response of "No, ma'am," the two bodyguards exchanged an odd gaze. She had just spent several weeks intensely studying expressions during heated negotiations. It was easy to read this one as, "If she only knew."

Terri realized that if she didn't handle the next few exchanges of conversation carefully, both men would retreat into the sanctuary of feigned ignorance. She decided that making them spill the beans would be her final challenge of the trip. A car game that would help pass the time.

"Been causing trouble again, has he? What's he been up to now? Chasing the pretty girls around Alpha, I'd wager?"

The accusation was so ridiculous, she expected the tactic to yield a quick denial and then open a different door. Instead, the driver looked into the rearview mirror and flashed a clear nonverbal response with his raised eyebrows. Terri interpreted the look to mean, "You know about this?"

Now Terri's interest in the little game became serious. No way would Bishop ever cheat on her. What the hell was going on back in Alpha?

She played along, "Yeah, I've been aware of his wandering eye for quite a while. Relax guys; we're trying to work through it. It's no state secret."

"How long have you been married, ma'am?" came the question from the passenger seat.

That did it! These two muscle-bound goons knew something... or thought they did.

"A long time. But it's not all Bishop's fault, I suppose. He's not a bad looking sort, and I know lots of women are attracted by his reputation. No matter, though - If I ever catch him with his pants down, both the bitch and he will receive a dose of my 9 millimeter's lead."

For the second time, Terri's fishing expedition yielded unexpected results. Her threat actually caused both of the men in the front uneasiness. The driver shifted nervously in his seat. The passenger shot the driver a look that indicated he clearly took Terri's threat seriously.

If Bishop and I ever get short of money again, I need to get these two in a poker game, she thought.

A foul fog of silence clouded the interior as the miles rolled past – so much so that Terri became uncomfortable herself. To break the ice, she upped the ante, "You guys just wait until Nick hears about this. If Bishop's playing around, Nick will take care of his sorry ass for sure."

The two security men exchanged a look of pure terror, the passenger and senior man turning abruptly to meet Terri's gaze. "Ma'am, we never said a word. I want that on the record. We both like our jobs."

Terri was stunned. What on earth could cause such a reaction? She was sure both of the guys in the front seat would walk into a hailstorm of bullets or charge an active shooter without a second thought. Why had her empty threat to talk to Nick caused such fear?

Less than a mile had passed before she put the pieces of the puzzle together. Diana.

Both of the men in the front seat were probably on Diana's security detail. The last time she'd talked to her dear friend, the troubled Alliance leader had praised Bishop for being there while Nick was in the hospital.

"You've got the best man in the whole wide world, girl-friend," Diana had claimed. "He's been propping me up while you've been gone, day and night, and I owe both of you a huge debt."

Terri started laughing, the ridiculousness of the entire affair striking her as humorous. Bishop and Diana? Seriously? She'd speak to Nick all right. He needed to give his security men some awareness training.

"Guys, do you really think my husband is having an affair with Diana? Really? Come clean with Aunt Terri. I promise I won't tell Nick if you give up the truth."

Again, neither man in the front answered, but the small beads of perspiration on their foreheads were telling. The driver reached to turn up the air conditioner.

Terri finally stopped giggling, "Look, guys, you can specu-late all you want. I'm well aware my hubby's been keeping close company with our fearless leader. Diana told me so personally. I even know he's been there a few times into the wee hours. They're extremely close and have fought side by side. She's going through a rough period right now, and Bishop is helping her like any good friend would. You need to tell your security buddies that they're completely off base and misreading the entire thing. If Nick finds out about this, he'll have all your asses running across the desert until your feet fall off."

She could tell her words were making them both think, instilling doubt into their perspective. When neither man offered any proof, or countered her statement, she knew they were only speculating.

Is the Alliance really so stable and boring that security men have to resort to high school rumors and gossip? Is that good or bad, she pondered.

Bishop wanted to swat the sand dragon, or mega-deer fly, or flying tarantula, or whatever the damn pesky insect was that kept buzzing his face. It was a big bastard and notably aggressive. Despite the harassment, the tracker didn't dare move quickly. Motion drew the human eye, and right at that moment, he was slightly exposed on a ridge. Attracting the attention of a competent shooter with a large-caliber rifle could ruin one's day.

Again, the winged pest buzzed his nose, but the Texan didn't move. At least not quickly.

"You're letting that little bug distract you," Grim whispered from nearby.

"Little?" Bishop hissed back. "That son of a bitch is wearing biker boots and sporting prison tattoos."

Grim grunted, "Maybe he thinks you're cute?"

Gradually working the cross hairs along the canyon wall, Bishop studied a dark indentation, keen to detect any sort of movement or shape that didn't belong there. Nothing.

Another slow sweep through the 24x magnification brought a large pile of boulders into view. There were 100 hides in that formation alone. He began studying each. He was scanning the elevated ground ahead and growing bored with the entire affair. Scouting in an environment with multiple elevations and a billion perfect concealments was proving to be monotonous work.

Bishop was surrounded by walls of the brightest crimson rock he'd ever seen. Over the last few days, the Texan had noted that the sunlight changed the stones' hues like a prism. The scenery was breathtaking, ranging from formations that looked like they belonged in a classic Western movie, to oddly rounded hoodoos sprouting from the canyon's floor.

He estimated the walls were about six miles apart at their current location. The river seemed to prefer the southern rim through this stretch, often hugging the steep cliffs so tightly that his team had to backtrack in order to find a good crossing and continue upstream. No one was in the mood for a swim.

So far, they hadn't found a single clue or indication that humans occupied the massive stone and sand formations. Not a footprint, whiff of campfire smoke, or telltale dark green of growing cannabis. For the hundredth time, Bishop wondered if the good sheriff had his facts straight.

Watts was a competent man tasked with an impossible job. Being a lawman before the collapse was tough enough. Trying to establish law and order after an apocalypse could make even the strongest character shiver. *No*, Bishop thought, *those guys are in this canyon somewhere. How on earth we find them is another matter. But they're here.*

About the only advantages Bishop had were knowledge and experience. He knew most sentries and lookouts would be posted on the high ground. It only made sense to allow the guards the longest possible viewing angles and thus give the maximum amount of warning.

It would have been impossible to visually search every nook and cranny of the canyon's walls and formations. There were so many places where a man could hide and shoot... and kill the unsuspecting intruder. So he narrowed each sweep to the higher elevations. Places where he'd post an accurate shooter with a big optic.

There was nothing.

For four days, they'd been repeating the same process, working their way along the river at an extremely slow pace, stalking, and keeping to cover. All of Grim's bravado aside, Bishop understood why law enforcement had given up searching for the banditos. It was like trying to prospect for gold in Indian country; you could never stop watching for hostiles long enough to properly hunt for the treasure.

In a way, the people they sought were a more difficult problem than any war parties faced by a 49'ner. The dope growers didn't want to be found, and that added a level of complexity.

People involved in illegal acts, like harvesting an outlaw cash crop, probably developed certain skills. They'd been hiding from the authorities for years. Just because society had gone to hell around them didn't mean they'd get careless or abandon what worked.

Palo Dura was gorgeous, a wonderful place to camp with the family, hike, maybe even do a little climbing. It was hell on earth to search for a relatively small group of men. The perfect place to grow weed if you didn't want to be found.

The insect chose that moment to bite Bishop behind the ear, the sharp pain drawing an unthinking slap from the frustrated Texan.

The swift movement and noise drew a harsh look from

Grim, but even the grizzled old contractor was too tired to comment. For a moment, neither of them moved, both waiting for the sniper's bullet to slam into their flesh.

No lead arrived.

Bishop waved his man back, the two retreating down into a shallow ravine that afforded some cover.

"That's it," Bishop spat. "I'm so tired, I'm making stupid mistakes. I'm going to get us all killed. We're done with this."

"What about the sheriff and his crooks?"

"There's got to be a better way," Bishop declared. "We could have a thousand men on horseback and still never find these guys. We're out here risking our asses for a hopeless cause. I've got better things to do with my life."

Grim shook his head, "Now what can possibly be better than humping a 60-pound pack up and down these rocks in 90-degree heat, brother? This is the high life. That last rabbit we snared was excellent fare, and the filtered river water is like wine."

Bishop grunted but didn't reply. He just didn't have the juice.

Grim noted his boss's lack of comeback and got serious, "I can't say I disagree with throwing in the towel. We're covering less than five miles a day, but it seems like 50 on my knees and back. We could sure use some aircraft to help narrow down the search."

Bishop scanned the cliffs surrounding them, something tickling his mind. A large hawk was soaring above them, the Texan jealous of the bird's effortless hunting technique. It reminded him of something....

"I've got it! That guy in New Mexico... the toymaker dude. We need some of his drones."

Grim liked the idea. "Think they might loan us a couple of those flying observation posts? They sure gave us hell, and that U.S. Special Forces Team didn't fare so well either."

Bishop's mind returned to the current mission. Their lack of success didn't sit well, the Texan finding it difficult to accept failure. Yet, they were out of food, low on morale, and completely lacking confidence. Watts would be disappointed, no doubt about it.

Sometimes you get the bear, sometimes the bear gets you, Bishop thought.

"Let's get out of here. If I never see a red rock again in my life, that'll be fine with me. I'll ask Terri to contact our new friends in the Land of Enchantment and see if they can loan us one of those drones," Bishop announced.

It was still early, and the team could make good speed over

the ground they'd already cleared. Two hours later, a sole SUV rolled down the rim road, a sheriff's emblem on the door.

The deputy spied the orange cross and reached for the radio as Watts had ordered. Before he could push the mic's button, three dirty, exhausted-looking men appeared beside the lane. "Don't bother," Bishop shouted. "We don't need the cavalry; we just need a ride out of this shithole."

Terri was glad she'd decided to stay in Alpha. Nick was being uncooperative, wanting desperately to be back at work... or out of bed... or to fix his own grub. In a way, she'd didn't blame the big guy. He wasn't the sort to quietly suffer weeks in the hospital and the restricted movements that accompanied recuperation. Diana needed all the help she could get.

Then there was Bishop out gallivanting around some remote canyon up in the panhandle. No one knew for sure when his team would be returning. Nick thought it would be any day now. While the recovery and associated law and order made her feel safer at the ranch, it still wasn't the place for a lone mother and small child. She missed home, but could wait a few more days until her husband returned.

Finally, there was the new ambassador from Washington. Diana had asked Terri to attend the emissary's welcoming reception, a casual affair to be held at the courthouse.

Diana had been upfront with her best friend, "I want your opinion on this guy. You read people better than anyone else I know."

The Alliance's leader had also dropped numerous hints that she would like for Terri to be the diplomat's liaison. "I need someone like you who can keep him out of our hair and cool his jets if a problem does come up. Besides, it will give us a chance to work together again."

To be honest, the job didn't sound all that intriguing. Hunter was going to be walking any time now, her son crawling like a little beach crab and constantly getting into anything he could reach. He was also talking up a storm when it suited a need.

Hunter needed his mother and father, and Terri knew that Bishop's return to government service was going to result in travel and danger. He might be away for days, even weeks at a time.

The thought of having to spend her time with some stuffy, old blowhard wasn't very appealing.

Terri buttoned a conservative, dark blue skirt that broadcasted, "No nonsense, professional woman," checked her hair, and then strapped Hunter into a borrowed stroller. The kid looked good in his best outfit.

It was only a few blocks to the courthouse, mother and son enjoying the cool breeze that signaled that autumn might finally break what had been a punishing blister of a summer.

She could see several vehicles parked in the council members' reserved spots, the need for such marked spaces another sign of the ongoing recovery. As she pushed the baby buggy to the front steps, she spied Pete sauntering down the sidewalk.

"Terri!" the councilman shouted. "Good to see you're back from New Mexico!"

After a quick round of hugs, checking on Hunter's progress, and a few pleasantries, Pete helped her maneuver the wheeled carrier up the steps.

Terri nodded to a security man outside, recognizing him as one of her escorts from the Land of Enchantment. With a motion of her hand and a wink, she zipped her lips and threw away the key.

Pete saw it. "What was that?" the councilman asked after they had passed through the main entrance.

"Nothing," she grinned. "I don't know why, but sometimes people just feel the need to share secrets with me."

Knowing he wasn't going to get a real answer... and not really caring, Pete let it go. The trio continued toward the main council chambers where a background of voices signaled the reception was well underway.

Terri decided to keep Hunter with her rather than utilize the daycare room. The child would provide an excellent excuse for her to skip out on the festivities early. Maybe Bishop would be home tonight.

Everyone was there, the elected council members, General Owens, and a lot of folks Terri had never met. Someone had provided a case of wine, Pete's brewery no doubt the source of more potent libations. A bartender in the corner, complete with Western string tie, was busy filling glasses and mugs.

With Hunter on her hip, Terri made for the center of the room. Diana was there, alongside a stronger-looking Nick. They were holding court with a stranger who had his back to the door.

Terri began sizing up the delegate from the United States immediately. Almost as tall as Nick, no one could miss him, especially since he was the only man wearing a suit jacket. Even so, he seemed to exude a sense of confidence and familiarity. She was struck by the relaxed laughter drifting from the trio, as if the visitor had been well received by her comrades.

As Terri approached, Diana said, "Oh, there she is now," to the stranger, who turned to face Terri. The young mother almost dropped Hunter.

"Chase? Chase McGuire?"

"Terri? I'm.... oh, my God... I had no idea Miss Brown was talking about *that* Terri," he stammered.

Diana exchanged puzzled glances with Nick and then responded. "You two know each other?"

"Oh... ummm, as a matter of fact, yes," Terri answered, now embarrassed by her reaction. "We were students at A&M at the same time."

Chase appeared to have heard none of her words, his eyes glued onto Terri as if he was hypnotized. "You haven't changed a single bit," he finally mumbled. "Still as stunning as ever. What a small world."

"Yes," Nick repeated, clearly intrigued. "What a small world."

The man appeared completely enthralled with Terri's presence, his eyes refusing to look elsewhere. The attention was obviously making her uncomfortable. Diana tried to come to the rescue, "I didn't know you graduated from A&M," she said.

"I didn't," Terri responded with a smile, thankful someone had finally said *something*. "My mom got sick, and I had to move back to Houston. I finished my last year at the University of Houston."

The question also seemed to snap Chase out of his spell. "Terri was the one who got away," he explained to Nick. "We were so young then. I didn't know what was important in life."

Then to recover, the U.S. Ambassador redirected the party's attention to Hunter. "And this strong-looking young man... this is your son?"

As he was prone to do, the child decided to be shy at that moment, squirming away and hiding his face in his mother's hair. "Yes, this is Hunter," Terri said, kissing the babe's head. "He's going to be walking soon."

Pete and another councilmember wandered up just then, relieving Terri of her position as the center of attention. The change in dynamic also allowed her time to study a man she hadn't seen for over 15 years.

Chase had always caught the female eye. Just shy of 6'5", and ruggedly handsome, he was well known around the university as the captain of the swim team and one of the most desirable bachelors on campus.

Terri had accepted his offer of accompanying him to an Aggies football game just to make her friends jealous. She had been sure he was a jerk at best, most likely a complete ass. Anyone that good looking had to be self-centered, right?

That initial perception had been incorrect. In fact, she soon discovered he was quite insecure, a young man certain that his life's ambitions far exceeded his grasp. Over the next semester, she'd found him a serious student who desperately wanted a career in politics.

He'd not been accepted into West Point, the first step of what she later learned was a detailed plan of ascent through the ranks of elected office. Texas A&M had been a second choice, a setback that had shaken the ambitious young man to the core.

The detour had only been temporary however. After graduating with a law degree, he began a short, but honorable stint in the military before entering public life. That impeccable resume, combined with his good looks, warming smile, and endless aspirations would one day lead to the oval office, or so he dreamed.

Terri couldn't relate at the time. She wanted to work in the corporate environment – travel, and experience the world. Politics was boring. Having to keep your nose squeaky clean for fear of future background checks seemed a misplaced priority and a symptom of borderline paranoia. She wanted to meet a nice, young man who worshipped the ground she walked upon, get married, buy a little pink house, and raise 2.3 children and a dog.

Yet, the two had connected at some level.

She had surprised herself by agreeing to a second date. The next year had been a whirlwind of classes, dances, parties, and intimate evenings at Chase's apartment.

When Rita had become ill, Terri had handled the situation poorly. Chase's reaction had been even less diplomatic, seemingly unable to relate her mother's sickness to the need to finish school closer to home. He never came to Houston to visit, never called. She, being just as stubborn, refused to be the first to pick up the phone. The passage of time, life events, and the world in general had dulled both of their memories.

Now, he was here, in Alpha, still as tall and athletic as ever, still possessing that same killer smile. While she had a million questions soaring through her mind, one thing was certain. Chase had made it to the Oval Office, at least close enough to sit in the chair when the president wasn't looking.

Diana pulled her aside under the pretense of getting a drink. "What a charmer, right? I had no idea you knew him. What an amazing coincidence. Tell me. Tell me everything. Were you lovers? What happened?"

Terri picked up her glass of wine and took a sip before answering. "Really, Diana, it was sooo long ago, and it was not a big deal at all. The highlight of the whole relationship was tailgating at the Aggies' football games. I remember him as a nice guy who had some pretty lofty political ambitions, and that's about it."

The Alliance's leader was savvy and wise. She didn't fall for her friend's smokescreen, not for a single heartbeat. "No way. I saw the way the two of you looked at each other. Come on, woman; spill the beans. And that's an order."

Nick appeared just then, rescuing Terri from what was sure to be a relentless interrogation.

"I think you have an admirer," the big man whispered as if he was clueing both of the girls in on a secret. "As a matter of fact, since you've arrived, he's acted more like a love-struck puppy than a representative of the White House."

"You can say that again," Diana chimed in with an evil smile. "He was drooling so much, I was going to offer him one of Hunter's bibs."

"Come on guys, knock it off. We're old friends, that's all."

"Uh huh," Nick teased. "Whatever you say, little 'Miss One-who-got-away.'"

Before she could set the big man straight, Chase separated himself from the gaggle of locals and strolled to Terri's side. This time, he managed to maintain a more professional demeanor, but just barely.

"I've heard so much from the president regarding your husband," he opened. "It seems they have quite the history together. I was hoping to meet him. Is Bishop here this evening?"

"No, but I expect him home any time now," Terri said just a little too fast. "He's off on a mission for the Alliance with his team." She was glad Bishop had finally entered the conversation, even if only in abstention.

"A lot of the people in this room fought beside Bishop after the collapse, Miss Brown and me included," Nick chimed in. "If the Alliance ever builds any statues to celebrate its heroes, Bishop's will probably be the first."

"He saved my church and congregation from some very vicious men," Diana added. "I wouldn't claim he was our version of Ben Franklin, but he would definitely be on the short list invited to sign the Declaration of Independence."

While Nick didn't possess Terri's uncanny skills to negotiate, nor Diana's laser-like focus, that didn't mean the warrior was completely unperceptive. He sensed that Chase didn't really want to talk about Bishop, at least not in the current context.

"The president was telling me several stories about both their pre and post-collapse relationship," Chase replied, his voice carrying a tone that implied, "Don't coat this guy in sugar. I've heard a lot of bad things, too."

"Bishop's not perfect, that's for sure," Nick replied. "Like any of us, he's made his share of mistakes."

Not Chase, Terri thought. *Chase probably hadn't made any mistakes. And that had always been the problem, hadn't it?*

The gathering continued, small numbers of guests clustering here and there, most of the politically active individuals trying to make the rounds and leave no social stone unturned.

Hunter was obviously a hit, but before long, the youngest attendee was showing signs of fatigue. Mom decided it was a good time to skedaddle.

Making one last round to voice her good nights and best wishes, Hunter was easy to strap into the stroller. "You and I will take a little walk, big boy. I'm sure you'll be out like a light in less than three blocks," she said, tucking the lad's favorite blanket around his chest. "You're just like your dad, not a party animal by any means. And that's why I love you."

Wheeling Hunter toward the courthouse's main entrance, Terri hoped someone would be around to help her carry the contraption down the steps. She was sure one of the security men would lend a hand.

The sound of footsteps from behind altered her plan. "Let me help you with that," sounded Chase's voice. "I've been dying to speak with you privately all evening. I thought you'd never leave," he added with a wink.

While Terri was tired, she had her own curiosities and questions. She could count on one finger the times she had run into an old lover, especially since society took a nosedive. She decided not to shoo him away.

"You look like you've weathered the apocalypse well," she said with a friendly smile. "How have you been?"

He didn't answer immediately, focused on gently carrying Hunter's carrier down the steps before peering into Terri's eyes. "I managed to pull through. You, however, are more stunning than I remember. Who knew the evaporation of society could be good for some people?"

Terri laughed at the compliment as she began pushing Hunter down the sidewalk. "I'm going to enjoy the cool air this evening with a short stroll," she said. "You're welcome to join me. I think the walk will put Hunter out for the evening."

Shrugging, Chase stepped quickly to join her stride. "So what happened to your mother? Tell me about Houston, please. I've thought to look you up... or try to call... or search on Facebook a thousand times."

"But you never did," she said with a little more edge than intended. And then, softer, "It's okay. I married a wonderful, kind man who I love with all of my heart and soul. We wouldn't have made it without each other."

"I'm so happy to hear that. I married as well, but my better half was in Washington when the riots broke out. She was a senator's daughter, and neither she nor her father survived the violence. "

Sadness momentarily veiled Terri's eyes, "I'm sorry, Chase. So many have lost loved ones. We're both lucky to still be here and in one piece."

He shook his head, "Survival is one thing, but from what I can see, you've thrived. I kept hearing about Terri and Diana, the Alliance's iron maidens. If you listen to the guys in Washington talk, Miss Brown and you are demons disguised as supermodels. You've obviously made quite an impact on the recovery. I have to say that I am impressed, since you were the girl who wanted nothing to do with the political process, as I recall," he chuckled.

Terri flushed a little red, but not much. "We've had our days for sure. It's rarely dull around here, and that's the way I like it."

"So what happened after you left A&M? And how did you meet Bishop?"

The questions prompted more blood to rush to her cheeks. "After graduation, I wanted to get into finance, but the economy was so bad the only thing I could find was an entry-level position in the banking business as a teller. You'd think I would meet a lot of people in a job like that, but I really didn't happen upon anyone I was interested in," she paused to adjust the stroller on the sidewalk, taking the moment to compose her thoughts before continuing. "I guess I'm embarrassed to admit it, but I met Bishop through an online dating service. I knew after our first date he was the love of my life."

When Chase didn't respond, Terri decided to do a little catching up herself. "Enough about me, though. I see you finally made it to Washington. 'Fess up, young man... how did it all happen?"

He shrugged, "I graduated and joined the Army. They wanted to assign me to the Judge Advocate General's office, but I wanted the infantry. I won and served two tours before resigning my commission. I met my soon-to-be wife at one of her father's political rallies. The rest, as they say, was history. She was a good woman, and I miss her very much."

They continued walking in silence, both second-guessing the wisdom of sharing so much so quickly. The thin, crisp air of the high altitude town was a joy, however, and soon both of their moods improved.

"I always heard the stars out here were spectacular," Chase noted, his head tilted toward the sky. "It's hard to believe I spent all those years in College Station and never made it this far west. I guess I missed out."

"The skies here are remarkable," Terri responded, pausing to study the Milky Way's nearly solid carpet of twinkling white.

Chase turned to her and said, "The stars aren't the only thing I missed out on. Look at you. I still can't believe this."

Bishop paused, unsure of what to do next.

An unhappy Sheriff Watts had deposited the team less than ten minutes ago, just down Main Street from the courthouse.

Being a curious sort, he thought to gather a little personal Intel regarding all the lights on in the courthouse at such a late hour. It was clear from the number of cars and trucks parked nearby that some sort of shindig was in process. There might even be trays of those little sandwiches... or toothpicks with little pieces of meat... or a cold beer. *Now, that would certainly be a fitting welcome for a man back from a mission to defend his country,* he mused.

A quick sniff of his armpits discouraged crashing the festivities. He'd been in the field for four days, and it had been dusty, hot, sweaty work at that. A shower was priority one. He'd rinse off his gear with a garden hose if one were around. No doubt his wife would appreciate the gesture.

Besides, the well-heeled political class of the Alliance probably wouldn't welcome some guy in a full combat load barging into their gathering. He'd ask one of Nick's guys guarding the front door if Terri was back. They'd know which guesthouse she had been assigned.

The Texan's next problem had been remembering where he'd parked his truck. He was dying to strip off some of the weight he'd been carrying around during his tour of Palo Dura. It would probably improve his aroma as well.

At that moment, the love of his life rounded a corner... with some big guy... talking and laughing while meandering down the street and pushing a baby buggy. He started to call out, to greet the woman he'd missed so very badly. But something was off. Terri was nervous, uptight, stressed. He could tell by his wife's stride and the way she held her shoulders.

It's probably some government thing, he considered. *Maybe I shouldn't interrupt. Could be an important negotiation or some shit.*

Without thinking, his legs began to follow his wife and the stranger. He was a big dude, obviously well dressed. Bishop judged the man towered just over 6'4", probably topping the scale somewhere between 240 and 250. Not in Nick or Butter's weight class, but not a little feller by any means.

Then they stopped, both of them gazing up at the stars like a couple of high school kids on a Saturday night. *What the fuck?* Bishop thought, his legs now moving faster.

Chase had been drinking.

Terri was stunning, as was the night.

Memories came flooding back, images of a time when two young lovers explored each other's emotions and bodies.

Chase reached for Terri's face, gently putting a hand on each cheek and looking deeply into her soul.

"No," Terri said, trying to be soft, but firm.

He didn't seem to hear, his head leaning closer, his eyes full of fire.

"No," she repeated, trying to pull back. But he was strong.

Bishop was twenty feet away when he saw Terri try to break the asshole's grip. Fury roared through the Texan's veins, fueled by four days of frustration and fruitless toil. *I'll kill the son of a bitch*, flashed red through his mind as his muscles primed for an assault.

Chase felt Terri pull back and released her instantly. "I'm sorry… I shouldn't have…" he started to say, just as the sound of Bishop's footfalls caused the new ambassador to pivot.

Out of the shadows a figure charged, the image barely registering in the low light. The attacker looked like some sort of homeless bum or vagabond. Then, the ambassador realized the aggressor had a gun. Chase reached for the firearm under his jacket, thinking to protect Terri.

Bishop spotted the movement, knew the man was drawing a weapon in less than a hundredth of a second. He's seen men reaching for a pistol far too many times. The Texan launched, uncoiling legs that were driven by rage.

The weapon cleared Chase's coat just as Bishop's shoulder slammed into his arm. It fired, the bullet missing Hunter's stroller by inches.

It was all so clear in Bishop's mind. Like so many times during a fight, he could see the angle of the shot, knew his son had almost been killed. Blind, sulfuric, ferocity powered the Texan now. This was something beyond a threat against his own life. He was fighting for Terri and his son.

The two men landed hard, rolling on the ground in a flaying ball of arms and legs. The pistol, bouncing harmlessly across the pavement, was no longer in play. Terri shouted something that neither of them heard.

Chase wasn't without skills. He was heavier but was suffering from the element of surprise.

Bishop was hindered by his gear, including the unloaded rifle strapped across his back and 55 pounds of pack. Still, the Texan landed the first clean blow, snapping Chase's head backward as the bigger man tried to make it to his feet. It slowed him down but didn't halt the effort.

With surprising speed, the ambassador's right leg shot out, landing a punishing kick to Bishop's head. The impact rolled the Texan across the grass.

Pressing his advantage, Chase dove after the still prone attacker. When he was a step away, Bishop's own leg moved in a flash, sweeping the bigger man's feet out from underneath him.

Both scrambled to stand, Terri still screaming for both of them to stop. She'd seen the bullet just miss Hunter and wasn't sure who should receive her wrath.

Why isn't Terri helping me? Bishop thought, trying to shake the cobwebs out of his now pounding head. *Why doesn't she draw and fire?*

Bishop, his vision still fuzzy, decided he'd had enough fun for one evening. In a flash, the silver steel of his fighting knife appearing in the Texan's fist. *I'll gut the colon piper. Right here. Right now.*

Somebody yelled "Freeze!" and then there were people all around. "Put down the knife," shouted another fellow, his sidearm pointed at Bishop's head. The security men, upon hearing the shot and fearing Terri was in trouble, had responded.

Bishop was scanning the new arrivals, his mind trying to reconcile the odds. Surrender wasn't an option. *Who were they? Why are they pointing their guns at me and not the rapist?* The Texan slowly backed away but didn't drop the knife.

Nick and Diana arrived next, their presence and bodyguards adding to the confusion. Flashlight beams pierced the night, probing the darkness and blinding anyone in their path. A dozen people were talking and shouting at once. One of the officers had a laser on his weapon, the eerie red hue of its aiming dot raising the stress level.

"Bishop, at ease, trooper," Nick said calmly, putting himself between the two combatants. He'd seen that look in his friend's eyes before. It was like some predatory animal had possessed the man, and he knew it was dangerous as hell. "Back it down. We're all friends here. Easy partner. It's cool," came the soft words as the big man slowly stepped closer, palms in the air.

"That piece of shit was assaulting my wife," Bishop snapped, his eyes never leaving Chase. "Why is everybody pointing their guns at me? Shoot *his* ass, damn it."

Terri then came into focus, now satisfied that Hunter was unharmed, stepping toward her husband. "Bishop, chill, please. It wasn't what you think. It's okay. I'm fine. Please, just settle down and put away the knife."

Terri's words seemed to be registering, Bishop's wild eyes focusing on his bride's face.

The security guys picked that moment of distraction to close in, their weapons up and ready. They didn't like Nick being in the line of fire. Bishop was looking like he'd gone completely insane. They didn't want such a person close to Diana.

Nick saw his men out of the corner of his eye and knew things were about to get completely out of control. He waved them back, ignoring the questioning look on their faces. "Stand down," he hissed. It was too late, Bishop already back in an aggressive stance.

Terri thought the big man's attempt to de-escalate the scene was wise. Turning to the gathering crowd, she pointed to one of the security men and said, "You! Get Chase out of here. Right now. Take him back and get a doc to check him out."

As confused as everyone else, the bodyguard hesitated, but not for long. Diana began repeating Terri's orders, desperately wanting to defuse the situation.

Bishop heard his wife and was now completely lost. *Why was Terri trying to rescue her attacker? Wait... was it really an assault? She had been walking with the shit-roach.*

Chase, however, didn't want to go. Shaking off his escort, he made it clear leaving wasn't an option. Wiping the blood from his nose, he said, "I'm fine. Just a scratch. That man assaulted me, and I want him arrested immediately."

Bishop took a step forward, weight shifting to the balls of his feet, knife lowered for a thrust. "I got your arrest right here, Assjacker. Come and get it."

Then things got worse, two shadowy figures appearing from the darkness, each taking a stance behind Bishop.

Grim and Butter, having heard the ruckus, came rushing up to find out what all the shouting and shooting was about. In the darkness, they could only see a bunch of people pointing guns at their friend and leader.

"Got your six, boss," Grim's voice sounded from the darkness. "Butter's here, too. What's happening?"

Both of the new arrivals had their rifles up and primed, the barrels pointed directly at the security men who seemed all too anxious to shoot their supervisor.

"Grim, Butter, it's Nick. Stand down. That's an order."

"Nick? What the fuck's going on here?" Grim replied, his voice unsteady. His weapon remained high and ready.

"There's been a huge misunderstanding," Terri pleaded, still trying to make sense of it all herself. "Everybody, please, just put down the weapons, and let's talk this over."

Something in his wife's voice now resonated with Bishop. His body visibly relaxed, and then he said, "Grim, Butter, it's cool."

Everyone exhaled when Bishop's knife returned to its scabbard. Without another word, he began backing away. "On me," he whispered to Grim and Butter.

As the two SAINT members closed ranks with their leader, Bishop flashed Terri a look that she could only describe as the reaction of a crushed, betrayed little boy. Nothing in her life had ever hurt her so badly.

A second later, they were gone, disappearing into the darkness.

Terri stood looking at the empty space where Bishop had been just a few moments before. She shook her head and whispered, 'Bishop, meet Chase. Chase, this is my husband, Bishop. I hope you two can be friends."

"He did what?" Nick exclaimed after Terri had recounted the evening's events, including the prelude to what was sure to be an attempt at a kiss. Then the big man whistled, followed by, "Does our new ambassador have a death wish or something? Does he have any idea what Bishop would do to him?"

"He was just a guy with a few drinks in his system," Terri replied, not sure why she was trying to defend Chase's actions. "He didn't mean anything by it. If I had a dime for every time some drunk guy tried to plant a kiss on me, I'd...."

"Bullshit he didn't mean anything by it," Diana interrupted, moving to comfort her friend. "But still, it sounds like Bishop over-reacted... at least a little."

Tears started rolling down Terri's cheek, the emotions finally catching up with her. "Where is he, anyway?" she sobbed.

"He's with Grim and Butter over at a guesthouse. Last I heard, he was taking a shower and winding down. Word is their mission didn't go so well, and no doubt that's playing some part in all this. Chase's nose isn't broken, so we may have avoided an international incident. At least for the time being."

"I need to talk to Bishop," Terri announced, rising from her perch with purpose.

"Are you sure, girlfriend? Might be best to let things cool off a little. If you're set on it, I'll watch Hunter if you want some private time."

"No, I know Bishop will at least want to see his son."

"He did what?" Grim snapped, watching Bishop towel off his still-wet hair. "Who on God's green earth would be stupid enough to try and put a move on Terri? That woman would cut 'em off."

Pulling on a fresh shirt, Bishop nodded, "If it was uninvited."

"No, not Miss Terri," Butter interjected. "She's not that sort of lady, sir. I see how she looks at you."

Bishop and Grim exchanged glances, both questioning Butter's knowledge of female ways and means.

"I bet this is an ice cream truck," Bishop mumbled, lacing up his boots.

"A what?" Grim asked, now completely confused.

Bishop sighed, "An inside joke. Before we were married, I was away on a job and the phone connection wasn't very clear. I told her that when I got back, I was going after her like a fat boy chasing an ice cream truck. Somehow, Terri heard that little analogy wrong and thought I had insinuated she was like a fat boy chasing an ice cream truck. Ever since then, whenever we have a miscommunication or misunderstanding, we both call it by that name."

Butter found the nuisances of his supervisor's relationship fascinating; Grim was still trying to work it out. Bishop ignored both of them. "Do either of you know where Terri is?"

"One of the security team told me she's still at the court-house. Turns out that the guy you punched is the new ambassador from the good ol' U.S. of A. I gotta hand it to you, Bishop, you sure know how to find the deepest shit around."

"I have to talk to Terri," the Texan said. "I'll be back in a bit."

"Let me go with you," Butter said, rising from his perch. "We don't need another fat... ice cream truck."

Bishop smiled at his teammate and friend. "Thanks, big guy, but no. I need to do this alone. I promise not to start another international incident. I'm cool."

Both members of the SAINT team relaxed a little when Bishop didn't take his rifle or knife.

He saw her coming two blocks away, her outline against the backlight of Alpha unmistakable. She was pushing Hunter, on a direct path for the guesthouse. Bishop instinctively increased his stride.

Terri spotted her husband a second later, her legs involuntarily lengthening their step.

Both of their stomachs were churning, both had weak knees. Both kept coming, each keenly aware of the collision course that lay between them.

They met in the middle of an intersection, studying each other in the pool created by the streetlight above. "I'm sorry," both said at the same instant.

And then she was in his arms, the embrace sending waves of relief surging through their cores. Bishop held her so tight, Terri melting into his chest. They felt warm, safe, and finally secure.

After a very long time, he held her at arm's length, having a million things to say all stuck in his chest. Nothing would come out.

"I need to explain," Terri finally blurted.

"No, you don't. I love you, and I trust you. It's all good."

She shook her head, "No, I need to explain for me. I have to make you understand."

"We had an ice cream truck," Bishop said with confidence. "That's all there is to it."

Terri laughed, the analogy making her adore him even more. "Yes, we did, and I'm glad it's over. I love you more than anything, Bishop. You have to know that."

"I do."

"Come on, let's take a walk. I don't want to let one little old fistfight ruin such a perfect evening."

After Bishop had checked on his son, they began walking. It took Terri almost 20 minutes to explain the earlier events. For the most part, her husband pushed Hunter's buggy and listened, only occasionally asking for clarification.

"Well that explains why you didn't shoot him on the spot," Bishop teased after she'd finished.

"He had a little too much wine and was always a bit aggressive. Right before you slammed him to the ground he was apologizing."

Bishop digested her remark but wasn't quite finished. "After you've spelled it all out, I have no issue with you, darling. I did, however, clearly see Mr. Chase McGuire's eyes and body language. He still has the hots for you, and I think you need to be careful. If there is ever a next time, I promise he won't see me coming."

"There won't be a next time, darlin'," she replied honestly. "I'm not going to be so stupid as to put myself in that situation again. Besides, from what I hear, he's just as embarrassed as I am. I imagine he's still stinging with regret."

"And my right hook," Bishop teased, flexing his sore hand. "Damn that guy has a hard head."

Terri stretched long and kissed his cheek, "I seem to attract men with that quality."

Chapter 4

A light tapping at the door pulled Bishop out of a deep, satiated slumber.

Terri was asleep on his arm, her position requiring a careful maneuver to extract his limb without disturbing her rest.

Pulling on his pants, the Texan padded quietly to the door. He could see Grim standing on the front porch, the contractor's face about as close to embarrassment as it got.

"Morning," Bishop croaked, opening the door.

"Sorry, boss, but Nick asked me to come by. He's already ripped Butter and me a new one for not following his orders last night, so I didn't want to press my luck."

"It's okay, Grim. I needed to get up anyway. What's going on?"

"You and the missus are hereby summoned to present yourselves at the courthouse at ten zero hours. That dude you whupped last night is raising a bit of a fuss, and Diana wants to have an air-clearing powwow. Nick hinted that your arriving un-armed would be beneficial to the international diplomatic relations."

"I see."

"I hated coming by so early on your day off, but I'm already on the big man's shit list for not backing down last night. If you want, Butter and I will sneak you out of town. I know this bar over in El Paso that...."

Bishop cut him off, "It's okay, buddy. Everything's cool. Terri and I will straighten it all out."

"If you say so. You want Butter and me to be hanging around? Just in case?"

The man's loyalty was warming. "Thanks, pal. I appreciate the offer, I truly do. But I don't think this is going to be that big of a deal. You two both recharge your batteries and take care of personal business. We'll be going back to that damn canyon soon, and I want both of you fresh and frisky as new kittens."

"If you say so, Chief. Good luck."

Grim turned to leave, but Bishop stopped him. "Hey, seri-ously, thanks for having my back. You don't know what that means to me."

The contractor waved him off, "Save that mushy, politically correct crap for your meeting. It all rolls off me like water off a duck's ass. I'll see you in a few days, and my regards to the missus and the boy."

Returning to the master, he found Terri awake and stretching. "I get the bathroom first," she stated.

Bishop faked a hurt expression, "No 'Good morning, love?' No, 'Oh baby, you were ab-so-lute-ly amazing last night?' Not even 'I love you?' How long have we been married?"

Hunter announced his need for a diaper change and breakfast right then, Terri pointing toward the spare bedroom with her head. "Good morning; you were amazing last night, as usual; and yes, I love you. I still get the bathroom first because I know our son is going to require my attentions. You, my love, are to make coffee, toast, and four eggs with cheese."

She rose from the crumpled sheets, stretching again with a hearty yawn. Bishop received a kiss on the cheek, and then she was closing the door behind her. "Change your son's diaper while the eggs are cooking, and wash your hands somewhere in the middle."

"Yes, ma'am. Oh, by the way, that was Grim at the door. Nick and Diana want to see us at 10. It seems your old boyfriend is raising a bit of a fuss."

"Great. Terri go here; Terri do this; Terri do that. I need a vacation," came her voice, muffled by the bathroom door.

Bishop chuckled, "I know that. But remember our last holiday didn't turn out so well. We ended up right in the middle of a salt war as I recall."

"I didn't say I was taking Hunter and you with me," the young mother responded.

"My, my, somebody got up on the wrong side of the bed this morning," he mumbled, heading off to retrieve the ever more persistent Hunter.

An hour later, the family was on the way to the courthouse, nodding and greeting the good citizens of Alpha, Texas as they wandered along the sidewalk.

Terri checked Hunter into the daycare and then hooked arms with Bishop. "Why do I feel like I'm being called into the principal's office?"

"Fuck them," Bishop said, a serious thread in his voice. "The Alliance needs us more than we need them. I'm going to keep quiet and let you handle this... up to a certain point. After that, we probably won't be welcome in this building anymore."

Terri raised a finger to his lips, "You just keep that famous temper of yours under control, young man. I've got this."

They arrived at the conference room right on time. Nick was there, as well as Diana and Chase. Bishop noted four security men who all were giving him the eye. In a lackluster attempt to break the ice, the Texan spread his arms wide and announced, "I come in peace." When the no-neck security detail seemed unimpressed, he elaborated, "Gentlemen, I am unarmed."

The snarky remark fell flat.

Little eye contact was made while everyone took a seat. Diana started off, "I want to thank everyone for coming. It should be known that having this little informal get together was my idea. Ambassador McGuire's first evening in Alpha ended up being a bit more eventful than planned, and I don't want any ill will or hard feelings gumming things up. The Alliance is implementing a new set of guidelines regarding private ownership of property in the next few days. This is a huge endeavor... and critical to the future of our citizens and way of life. We can't afford any more distractions."

Chase spoke next, "First of all, I want to apologize to Terri and the Alliance Council for my behavior last night. I should have known better than to drink wine while suffering from jetlag. However, my actions were inexcusable, and I assure everyone that it won't happen again."

Terri, after clearing her throat, said, "Apology accepted, Chase. I think we all regret the events of last night. As far as I'm concerned, it's all forgotten."

All eyes then moved to Bishop, but the Texan didn't say anything. Terri bumped his leg under the table.

"What I have to say is simple, straightforward, and the honest truth," Bishop explained in a low tone, his eyes fixed on Chase. "You respect me, I'll respect you. That's all I have to say."

The ambassador didn't quite know what to make of Bishop's words but quickly decided it was about the best he was going to get. "Well then, now that this has all been settled, I guess we should get down to business."

Bishop abruptly stood, nodding to everyone but Chase. "Today's my day off," he said evenly. "If you good folks are going to conduct business, then I should excuse myself."

The Texan headed for the door, wanting nothing more than to put space between himself and the jerk from Washington before he worked himself into a mood and ruined the day. He'd just arrived at the daycare room when Terri caught up with him.

"Are you mad at me?" Bishop asked, trying to read his wife's expression.

"No, I'm not. I suppose, given the circumstances, that was about the best I should have expected. I think Diana is a little pissed though."

Bishop shrugged, "I'm not going to apologize to that assclown. I'm not sorry for what I did or how I acted toward him."

64

Terri thought for a moment before speaking, "Let's say we were in Pete's, and some old drunk came up and tried to plant a big smooch on my kisser. Would you kill him?"

"Depends," Bishop responded. "Did he know you were married? Did he try to pull a gun on me? Did he fire off a shot that almost killed our son? And after I put him on his ass, did he try and have me arrested? If the answer to any three of those questions is yes, then he's a dead man if I'm capable."

Now Terri was getting upset. "You are incorrigible, stubborn, pigheaded, and living by some testosterone-fueled system of honor that is completely unreasonable. You would really take another life just because a buzzed man would try and kiss your wife?"

Bishop shook his head, calmly putting a soft hand on each of his wife's shoulders. "No. Of course not, and it's a little insulting that everyone thinks that's where I'm coming from. This isn't some high school feud over the prom queen. It's far more important than that. First of all, Chase What's-his-name isn't just a random drunk in a bar. He's an ambassador representing a man who I respect and call my friend, the President of the United States. Now I know everybody thinks I don't have a diplomatic bone in my body, but to me, getting liquored up your first night at a new posting shows a tremendous amount of arrogance. If I were Diana, I'd already have his ass on a plane back to Washington. If that's not enough, following you out of a formal reception thrown in his honor tells me he isn't taking this assignment seriously. Think about that – who would do such a thing? I don't care if he had a hard-on for the pretty married woman or not. And finally, to hit on one of your host nation's most regarded citizens is just plain disrespectful. Does the Alliance want someone like that playing such an important role in our future? That guy has the president's ear. Can we really trust what he whispers?"

Terri was stunned, her eyes remaining locked on her husband's face. She knew everything he was saying was true; she just hadn't put it all together in such matter-of-fact terms.

"I'm sorry," she said, looking down. And then, "Seems like I've been saying that to you a lot lately."

Bishop gently lifted her chin, his face showing nothing but admiration. "If I had gotten pissed and put some Joe Nobody on his ass, and later found out it was just some dude who thought you were the princess of the ball, I'd be the first one in line trying to make amends and apologizing with all sincerity. While I think you're hotter than Pete's chili, trying to kiss you isn't a capital offense. But that's not what all this is about. Chase now occupies an extremely powerful, a critically important position. He proved to me last night that he isn't the right man for the job, and that's why I'm not playing nice."

"Bishop, I love you. You're right. I completely missed where you were coming from. Do you really think Diana should send him packing?"

Bishop shrugged, "How Diana and the council deal with Mr. Chase is their business. It's above my paygrade, and I have no part in the decision. Hell, for all I know, he learned his lesson last night and will toe the line from here on out. But I doubt it."

"You should talk to her, Bishop. She trusts your judgment."

"No, she trusts my friendship, my rifle, and my loyalty. Anything I said from here on out would sound like I was a jealous, unforgiving husband. The same goes for you, by the way. If you went to Diana right now and spelled it all out, she'd think you were just trying to get rid of his royal highness to placate me."

Terri's expression made it clear she was thinking about her husband's words. She needed time to analyze his point of view.

"Look, I've not seen my son or wife for weeks," he said kindly. "I'm going to take Hunter to the park, try and find some ice cream, and forget about the world for a while. I've missed you both terribly. If you need to stay here and work, then I understand. If not, please join us. We both love you, and it will be more fun if Mom is along."

"Ice cream?" she brightened. "I'm in. To hell with the government."

"The Toymaker is sending over two of his best drones," Terri announced, setting down the single sheet of paper that had just been delivered via Alliance courier. "This note also says one of his best Apache operators will come along to help find the pot growers."

"Excellent," Bishop nodded, pausing the tickle fight that Hunter seemed to be winning.

Terri stood watching her two boys return to their roughhousing. Hunter's cackling laugh filled the room with a unique joy that could only come from the throat of a happy child. The world seemed perfect.

"Ball," the kid announced, suddenly bored with the current contest. Dad agreed.

Bishop retrieved a large plastic sphere from a nearby box of toys, and a few moments later, they were rolling it back and forth across the old rug.

"Isn't ball a new word for him?" the smiling father asked.

"I think so, but he's talking so much I'm having trouble keeping track."

"He got that from your side of the gene pool," Bishop teased.

Terri was conjuring up a rebuttal when a knock sounded at the door. "That's the third interruption this morning," she complained, "and it's not even lunch yet."

Sheriff Watts was on the front porch. Removing his hat, he greeted Terri with a stoic face, "Morning, ma'am. Would your husband be about?"

With Hunter on his hip, Bishop appeared over his wife's shoulder. "Morning, Sheriff. What's up?"

The lawman glanced from wife to child, and then back to Bishop. "A word in private, Bishop? We've got a bit of a situation on our hands, and I was hoping you and your boys might be able to help."

If it weren't for the serious look on the man's face, Bishop would have chuckled. The good sheriff was old school and didn't want to discuss criminal activity or nefarious acts in front of women and children. Terri took Hunter as Bishop stepped out on the porch.

The lawman got right to the point, as usual. "We've had trouble brewing up at Fort Davidson for the past few weeks, and it came to a head this morning. I've got a deputy with a slug in his leg and a barn that somebody set on fire. We've got two big ranching outfits up that way, both with extended families and lots of hired hands. There's a tract of land between their spreads that's been a point of contention since the collapse. Things got a little out of hand last night, and the shooting has started."

Bishop rubbed his chin, trying to visualize the situation. "Who has rightful claim to the land?"

"Well, that's the problem. Both sides have a legitimate claim. Decades ago, there was a convenient marriage that seemed to resolve the dispute. Both outfits had been quarreling over the parcel since the late 1800s. In fact, if it weren't for having to join forces and fight off the Indian raids, there would have been a full-out range war a long time before. Cooler heads prevailed when a Baxter boy married a Pomelos girl. According to local lore, that settled things down."

"So?"

"That bloodline didn't survive the collapse. The heirs thinned out, and the last Baxter occupying the homestead was a bad diabetic. He passed away about nine months after the insulin ran out. Both sides were probably too busy just trying to put food on the table for a while afterward. Now that things have recovered a bit, the age old dispute has again reared its ugly head."

"Why don't they just split the land and be done with it?"

"The only year-round water in that area flows through the property in question and forks to feed both spreads. The creek shifts its course from time to time, and there's no good place to draw a line in the sand. The original solution treated the place kind of like the Vatican in Rome. It was neutral ground with an understanding that the water would always flow freely to both sides."

Bishop shrugged, "So why not just keep it that way? Why escalate now?"

"Because the Alliance is making it known that new rules concerning property ownership are coming down the pike. There have been all sorts of rumors and gossip, and somebody got the idea that possession was going to be a big part of the new law."

"Unintended consequences," Bishop mumbled sarcastically. "Who would have thought?"

"Normally, I'd bring in some extra deputies, plop them down right in the middle, and pretend we were a United Nations peacekeeping force. Problem is, about half of my men in that area are decedents of one clan or the other. Trust in authority has eroded, and things have degraded to the point where a badge doesn't mean much. That's why I'm on your front porch interrupting your family time."

Bishop nodded, now understanding the sheriff's predicament. "So you need to keep them from becoming the Hatfields and McCoys until the new rules are officially announced. I get it, but we're only three men. I'm not sure how effective we would be."

Watts shook his head, "I didn't come here with a plan, only with a need. I was hoping you and your boys could come up with something… and do so quickly. If somebody gets killed up there, all hell will break loose. The whole county could be pulled in, folks aligning with one side or the other. We need to keep them separated until the government can set up the new law and a system to handle disputes. If I knew how to do it, I wouldn't be troubling you."

"My wife is a wizard at this sort of thing," Bishop stated. "Come on in. Let me get you a cup of coffee, and let's have a quick skull session. Maybe she can hatch a plot."

"I was hoping you'd say that, sir. I saw what she did to end that dispute over the salt down south. I'm trying to nip this one in the bud before it turns into a running fight like what you encountered by the border. By the way, that's some lady you've got there."

"She has her days," Bishop smiled.

Bishop opened the door for the sheriff, calling out, "Honey, I'm home. I found a stray emergency on the way from the office, and I couldn't help but bring it back to the house. Come see."

The expression on Watt's face indicated he didn't get the cornball humor. Terri did.

From the kitchen, "Oh honey, not another one. We can't rescue every lost dog, cat, and emergency in the neighborhood," she sighed. "But I do have a few minutes now that Hunter is busy. Bring it on in here. Let me see it."

The two men stepped toward the back of the home, finding Hunter in a highchair, practically all of his face covered by some green substance. Seeing his dad, the boy's smile lit up the room.

Terri put down the canning jar of whatever emerald-colored, mystery vegetable she was serving and then set a couple of crackers on the chair's tray. She had to use a towel before offering the sheriff her hand.

"Honey, this looks like a law enforcement officer, not a stray emergency," she grinned. Then to Watts, using her more serious tone, she offered, "Coffee, Sheriff?"

"That would be wonderful, ma'am. Black, please."

It took another 15 minutes for the lawman to rehash the situation. Terri had a lot more questions than Bishop, and Hunter wanted to participate in the conversation.

At one point, the lad offered his father a bite of green-goo-coated cracker. Watts winched when Bishop bent and accepted the nibble. The tough old lawman actually choked on a swallow of coffee when Bishop smacked his lips and said, "More!"

"Moh-ah!" the kid commanded his mother, and then let loose with a huge, wet burp. Everyone but the sheriff thought it was hilarious.

Right when it seemed Watts was beginning to regret his visit, Terri's demeanor became somber. "This is easy," she stated matter-of-factly. "We need some squatters."

"Ma'am?" Watts replied, his brow wrinkling in puzzlement.

"Both sides of the feud need someone or something that is a bigger, common threat. We have to give them something to fear and hate more than the opposing ranch. A group of squatters moving onto the property would do just that. Basic stuff, guys. Do you both need more coffee to get those brains working at full speed?"

"The enemy of my enemy is my friend," Bishop mumbled, his gaze clouding over while his mind sped to an empty point of

69

time and space.

"But wouldn't that lead to more violence?" Watts asked, always the skeptic.

"Perhaps," Terri replied. "From what you're saying, in the long term there's little doubt of things escalating to a full-out brawl. That being said, you only need to keep them apart until the Alliance implements the new rules. That should be in the next few days."

"And where would I find these squatters?"

Bishop shook his head and sighed in with reluctant acceptance. "*They*, sir, would be my team and me. Here we go again."

Terri watched as the short parade of one Army truck and two squad cars pulled into the empty lot. Butter and Grim were already there, the younger contractor balancing Hunter on his shoulders, pretending to be a cowboy in search of the Grim-Indian.

Her son's constant cackling, intermixed with short bursts of howling laughter, was a therapy Terri badly needed about then.

There had been such a rush getting Bishop and his men ready. Team members had to be located and called in. General Owens had to be tracked down, briefed on the situation and convinced to sign orders. Everything including clothing, food, and transportation had to be secured, requisitioned and packed.

Before she knew it, Bishop was jumping in a police car with Sheriff Watts and heading to Fort Hood. It all happened so fast.

Now she waited, dreading the conversation she needed to have with her husband. She hated doing this right before he was leaving on a dangerous mission. She'd started to cover the topic a dozen times in the last few days, but had been stopped by a precious moment that she didn't want to spoil.

And then he was gone.

The three vehicles rolled to a stop, Butter and Grim returning her child with disappointed expressions. "Sorry, Miss Terri," Butter said. "We have to unload."

She strolled over to the sheriff's car, watching as Bishop climbed out of the passenger door. "I always knew seeing you in a police car was in my future. Mom tried to warn me," she teased.

"Your mom liked me," Bishop countered, walking up to hug his wife and son. After the greeting, he continued with a wink and said, "Come here often, gorgeous?"

"Seriously, Bishop, I need to talk to you. It's important, and, well, we need to discuss it before you leave."

Realizing the timing of his humor was off yet again, he became subdued. "Sure, what's wrong?"

"Come on," Terri motioned with her head, "Let's take a walk."

She deposited Hunter in the stroller and kissed the now-sleepy child's forehead. Bishop did the same, taking a moment to enjoy his son's round face peeking out from under his blankets. "I love you, little guy. Daddy will see you in a few days."

After they were well away from the hustle and commotion by the trucks, she stopped and faced him. "I know Diana is going to ask me about being Chase's liaison. Nick hinted about it yesterday like he was trying to feel me out. I wanted to talk to you about it, but thought I had more time before you'd be leaving."

Bishop stayed neutral, "I know. I've been bouncing it around the last few days. I think my answer might surprise you."

"Oh?"

"I think you should accept the position. Now, don't misunderstand. I would be completely wary of that ass-hat. I'd watch his every move and always have my pistol ready to shoot off his over-achieving balls. But... there's an old proverb that sums this situation up about as well as any words that come to mind; keep your friends close, your enemies closer."

For the first time in hours, Terri smiled, "I had the exact same phrase rolling around in my brain. Amazing."

Bishop kissed the top of her head, taking a moment to enjoy the aroma of her hair. It was his favorite scent. "Brilliant minds on the same track," he said, holding her tight and inhaling again. "Which means you know what I'm thinking right about now."

Smacking him on the chest and playfully pushing away, she started giggling. "Stop that. And yes, I know what you're thinking right about now because that's what you're *always* thinking. No brilliance required."

The couple stood for a moment, enjoying a special embrace.

Grim's voice interrupted their hug, the contractor's tone indicating he wasn't pleased with the Army driver's bill of lading. "I ain't signing for no three cases of grenades, Specialist. There were only two on this truck. What the fuck has happened to this man's Army since I got out? Somebody had better come up with a third case of party favors, or I'm going to start kicking some mother-green ass right here in front of God and the civilians."

Bishop shook his head, giving Terri one last kiss. "Gotta

go," he whispered. "The kids are fighting. I love you. I'll be home soon."

Chapter 5

The doctor watched Nick button his shirt, noting the slight grimace as the big man moved in a certain way. "You're showing no signs of infection, Nick, but that doesn't mean you're 100%. Take it easy. Give your body a chance to recover."

"I feel fine," replied the big man. "Good to go, Doc."

"No, you aren't, and I wish you'd park the bravado at my door. The surgeons at Fort Bliss did an excellent job, but they aren't miracle workers. Your body took a lot of punishment, and it is going to take months before you're back to normal. The more you aggravate and strain yourself now, the longer it will take."

Nick nodded, a bit sheepish after the scolding. "Yes, sir. What about my... my drive... my libido? It's not like me to have no interest or desire."

The physician had been dreading the question. It was always the alpha-types that worried more about their reproductive equipment than hearts, lungs, or limbs. "Most likely, things will get back to normal soon. That's what I keep trying to tell you; take it easy. Half days at most. No physical activity. No stress."

"Would you mind telling Diana that we're going to have to delay the wedding? Can you come up with some medical excuse or something? I keep pretending... putting off the conversation."

The sawbones rubbed his chin, "She is a wonderful, understanding woman. Just tell her. She'll be fine, I'm sure. Besides, there's no medical reason not to go through with the ceremonies. If you two love each other, sex is only part of the equation."

Nick shook his head, "I can't ask her to marry half a man, Doc. She is a young, vibrant lady who deserves intimacy and everything special that goes along with it. I can't be that selfish."

"Nick, you're making a mountain out of a molehill. Just talk it through with her. Hell, there's a good chance having that conversation might speed along your recovery. Trust me on this."

"I suppose you're right. I just keep hoping my God-issued equipment will start functioning again."

Returning to his charting, the physician scribbled notes and then made for the door. Nick was right behind.

As the two men left the examination room, one of Nick's lieutenants rose from a hall chair. "Sir, I hate to interrupt, but we've got a bit of a situation down at the courthouse. I tried to handle it given your schedule today, but I'm afraid this is going to require your attention."

"What?" grumbled the big man.

"It seems our new ambassador has taken it upon himself to bring in his own security. A small team showed up this morning, and they are already butting heads with Diana's watchers."

"Shit," Nick growled. "Come on, let's go de-wad everybody's panties."

With his subordinate struggling to keep up, Nick stamped out of the doctor's office, his long stride eating up the distance. A few blocks later, they approached an impromptu meeting on the courthouse steps. Three of the Alliance's senior security men were involved in a heated discussion with a pair of strangers and the new ambassador.

"Nick! There you are," Chase called out as he spotted the ex-operator approach. "I'm glad you're here."

The head of Alliance Security Services offered his hand to the two newcomers, both of whom looked like serious professionals. After introductions had been exchanged all around, Nick turned to Chase and suggested, "I wish you had talked with me about this situation before bringing in people we are unprepared to accommodate."

"My apologies, sir, but I really didn't think it would be an issue," Chase replied. "After the incident that occurred my first evening in Alpha, I decided to put in a request for a standard emissary protection package. While technically there isn't an embassy here, I am on extended assignment and qualify for some level of protection."

"If you feel threatened in any way, we would have been happy to provide coverage," Nick replied, eyeing the younger man suspiciously.

Chase had on his best diplomatic face, dismissing Nick's offer with a casual wave and a broad smile. "There's no reason why the Alliance should be burdened with my security, sir. You good folks have enough on your plate already. No, the U.S. government can provide for my needs, and in reality it's their responsibility."

Nick mulled over the ambassador's words for a moment, finally nodding. "So here's the deal. Just like the White House or Capitol Hill, your people are allowed anywhere but inside Ring-1. If you, ambassador, enter that inner sanctum, I expect your team to stop at the line and coordinate with my staff. It's just like visiting the president, the Secret Service holds domain wherever the chief executive is located at the moment or will be traveling."

After exchanging glances with his two men, Chase nodded his acceptance. "Sounds fair and practical."

Again, a quick round of handshakes passed among the

gathered men. At Nick's suggestion, the new arrivals from the United States were offered a tour and the chance to meet some of the Alliance team they'd be working with. "Show them around and introduce them to our people," Nick had ordered. "It may avert an accident later."

After watching the bodyguards walk away, Chase turned to Nick and said, "How did things go at the doctor's office?"

For a second, Nick thought the ambassador was implying something. "Fine. Why do you ask?" he questioned with a little more venom than intended.

Chase knew instantly he'd struck a nerve, but had no clue why. He decided to pry a bit deeper. Again, with the best possible smile, he explained, "Just concerned about a new acquaintance's health and well-being is all. Besides, Diana and you are both critical to the Alliance, and *that is* my job."

"While that may be true, Mr. Ambassador, my personal relationship with Diana is none of your concern," the big man spat. Then without another word, Nick pivoted and clomped away.

"My, my," Chase whispered, watching Nick enter the courthouse. "Someone is very sensitive this morning. Maybe it's that time of the month."

The old Baxter place wasn't anything to write home about... although the layout of the land was a welcoming change. A lane that wound through well-established vegetation led to a modest bungalow that had seen better times. Weeds sprouted knee high around the foundation, cobwebs and mud dobber nests' thick on the front porch. Two windows were boarded up and a patch of shingles was missing.

The nearby barn didn't add to the curb appeal, the once workable structure now reduced to a pile of smoldering ashes and blackened studs projecting at odd angles.

Bishop could see beyond the dilapidated structures, noting the formation of the sheer black rock that defined the valley and the rich green of the plant life thriving in the rich bottomland. Less than a half mile away, he knew a wide creek meandered along, life-giving water for those downstream.

According to the maps Nick provided, two small springs fed that creek. Between them, enough water was produced to keep the brook bubbling, flowing fresh and clear even in the driest of times.

The three pickups pulling up the driveway were all chock-full of supplies. Bishop, driving the lead unit, was carrying an ATV and a motorcycle in the bed.

The contents of the second truck were covered by a tarp, Butter behind the wheel.

Grim brought up the rear, his bed stuffed with cardboard boxes, old duffle bags, and a random assortment of ratty-looking suitcases.

The squatters had arrived.

Once the team had parked and exited the cabs, Grim began making his initial assessment while the other team members unloaded the vehicles. "This ain't a bad place at all," he called out. "Easy to defend. The house needs a little sweat equity, but Butter needs something to occupy his mind anyway," he chuckled as he tried out the rocker on the porch of the Victorian farmhouse. A wide grin spread across his face. "And I get to sleep in a bed for a change," the contractor beamed as he checked the stability of the railing. "You know," he continued as he bounded down the steps and headed for the truck, "I can't help but notice that you're doing a better job when it comes to getting us work, boss. Much improved."

Bishop had to agree with Grim on one point. Whoever had picked the original spot to build the homestead a century ago must have had an eye for tactical defense.

Over the years, Bishop had found himself always visualizing how to defend a home, business, or section of land. It was a habit garnered from working security in some of the world's most hostile environments. He'd discovered the older structures around his home state were often situated in prime defensive locations, taking calculated advantage of the natural elements of their surroundings. This, he concluded long ago, must have been due to the prevalence of outlaws, Indians, or hostile neighbors.

In the case of the Baxter hacienda, it was the sheer walls of the surrounding hills that had been utilized as a three-sided bastion of protection. Adding to the strategic, fort-like surroundings, the highest ground suitable for building had been selected, allowing clear fields of observation... and fire... to the valley beyond.

This was both good and bad news in Bishop's way of looking at things. The home could only be approached from the front, which made setting up defensive positions much simpler. Yet, having only one way in also meant there was only one way out.

"I don't think we'll be getting much sleep," Bishop replied, scanning the surrounding hills. "And remember, we're here to keep them from killing each other, not to fill a graveyard. This is going to be difficult at best."

"Are you saying we can't shoot back, Mr. Bishop?" Butter asked, a rare frown painting his face.

"We can, but just don't hit anybody unless it's down to you or them. The rules of engagement on this op are going to be frustrating as hell. That's why we got all that stuff from the Army."

Hunter and Grim began unloading while Bishop moved to the home and officially became a felon. Putting a boot to the front door, the Texan was surprised to find the interior in relatively good condition. Dusty for sure, with timeworn chairs and lamps scattered around the living room.

There were still dirty dishes in the sink. The Texan didn't have the guts to open the fridge. Rodents had clearly had their run of the place.

Grim was right, he concluded. *Despite its lack of upkeep, the old house beat the hell out of sleeping on the ground.*

Finding a solar-powered well pump out back, Bishop decided running water would be their first priority. "Think like a squatter," he mumbled. "Play your role and act the part. You plan on staying here for a while."

Grim and Butter were piling boxes in the living room, unloading the trucks and bickering back and forth about who was carrying the majority of the weight. Bishop joined in, claiming both of them were slackers and panty wastes.

The team was rolling the ATV off the back of the truck when Grim nodded toward the east. "Riders coming in, Boss."

"Already? That was quick," Bishop responded, moving for a nearby rifle. "You guys know the drill. Scare the hell out of them."

Butter and Grim split, both moving to cover positions without any instruction. The Texan was pleased with their reactions.

Four riders rumbled toward the homestead, a middle-aged woman in the lead. "This is private property," she barked without any greeting. "Get off this land right now."

"And who might you be," Bishop retorted, making a show of chambering a round in his rifle.

"My name is Katherine Baxter, and this is private property. Now get out, before we run you out."

Bishop scanned the three men accompanying the rather bossy woman. *Standard issue ranch hands*, he surmised. *Tough men, willing to fight, but not pros. They're bunched up and nervous.*

"Now that's not what the men in town were saying," Bishop said, surprising the riders by stepping closer. "From what I heard, the owner of this place died some time ago, and obviously no one is living here. I overheard folks talking, and they were saying there wasn't any clear claim on this place."

"Those blowhards are full of shit," she barked. "This place has been in our family for a hundred years before you were born. Now get out, mister, before there's trouble you can't handle."

On cue, one of the ranch hands made a show of moving a hand toward his holstered sidearm. Grim countered, stepping from around a truck and holding out a hand grenade for all to see. The contractor made a show of tossing the safety pin over his shoulder.

"Go ahead, fill your hand with that blaster, sonny," Grim challenged. "Then we'll all play a little game of hot potato with this fragmentation device."

Kathy Baxter wasn't as impressed as her riders. "Who the hell are you people?" she snapped, trying to keep her now-jittery mount under control.

They're scared, Bishop thought. *The animals can sense their masters' fear. Good.*

Back to her question, Bishop found himself lacking an answer. He hadn't thought of that.

"My name is Clint," he finally replied with a shit-eating grin. "Clint Wayne. My friend over there is John Eastwood."

She didn't get it for a second, finding no humor in Bishop's response once the names did register. One of the cowhands did, however, grunting and pointing toward Butter. "And I suppose he's Chuck Norris?"

"Nope," Bishop smirked. "His name is Yul Fonda. Now, why don't you nice folks act a bit more neighborly and ride on out of here? My friends and I just left the service of the U.S. Army and have been driving all over hell's half acre looking for a place to hang our hats. We don't want any trouble, but if it comes to a fight, we'll hold our ground."

"This isn't over," Mrs. Baxter spat, turning her horse and spurring the beast. Her men followed.

Butter and Grim soon joined their boss, the trio watching the riders fade into the distance. "That went pretty well," Grim offered.

"Mister Bishop, sir, I've got a question," Butter said, his voice colored by bewilderment. "Who is Yul Fonda?"

Despite the late hour, the courthouse in Alpha was buzzing with activity. The Alliance was preparing the public launch of its property ownership solution, and that was taxing everyone.

Posters, public notices, manuals, printed rules, and guidelines were all part of the campaign. The same activities were underway in Austin, Houston, and Dallas.

From there, hundreds of government representatives and volunteers would spread out across Texas, traveling to small towns, ranches, farms, and all points in between. Most smaller communities had established some sort of building or central location for a bulletin board. Often this was in the old post office. The new laws were typically posted there.

As she worked on sorting several large stacks of copies, Terri couldn't help but wonder about the wisdom of such an ambitious effort being undertaken before communications had been established throughout the territories. The north side of Dallas now had cell service, at least part time. All of the major population centers had at least eight hours of daily AM radio broadcasts.

Television was still out of the question, the huge transmitters and home receivers requiring too much of the limited electrical energy that was badly needed elsewhere.

The internet was months, if not years, away. Despite the commonly made claim that the worldwide web had been built to withstand nuclear war, the absence of spare computer parts, knowledgeable personnel, and neighborhood-level communications equipment was a challenge that even the most optimistic engineer thought would take a significant period of time.

So that left the printed word as the primary method of communications throughout the land.

Paper was already in short supply, ink nearly as expensive as gold. In the early days, the Alliance had burned through ink cartridges at an amazing rate, trying to get information out to the people.

Now, most publications were being run with old fashion mimeograph machines, many salvaged from the storage closets of schools and churches. The formulation of homemade ink was a cottage industry in many parts of the territory.

Terri had just finished sorting her assigned stack when she sensed a presence behind her. It was Chase.

"Hello, there," he smiled. "This is an amazing thing to watch," he continued, indicating the bustling courthouse with wide arms. "I've never seen anything like it."

"We're lucky to have such dedicated people who believe in the Alliance," she replied. "Heck, most of the folks you see here today are volunteers."

He continued into the small room, taking up a position where he could make eye contact as Terri returned to her work. "I want to thank you for accepting Diana's offer to be my office's liaison. While we may have gotten off on the wrong foot, I still believe we can work well together."

Terri glanced up quickly, flashing a short smile before returning her attention to the table full of papers. "Well, of course, we can. We are both professionals, aren't we?"

"Yes, yes, of course," Chase replied. "I just wasn't sure how much of a problem that night had caused you at home."

She waved off the concern. "Bishop and I are just peachy keen. We had a great week together until he got called away today. There's no problem in my house."

"Good. That's so good to hear. The last thing I want to do is cause you any difficulties."

Terri smirked, "Given what we've been through together... what with the collapse and all? It would take a whole lot more than a simple misunderstanding to come between us."

"I always wonder how my wife and I would have weathered the storm. On one hand, I think it would have pulled us closer – strengthened the relationship. Other times, I don't know if we would have survived it... how anyone does really."

"Bishop and I learned the true meaning of trust throughout the entire ordeal. It definitely made us stronger, both as individuals and as a team. If I had told my co-workers at the bank in Houston that one day I'd been representing a new government that controlled Texas, they would have laughed me out of the building."

Chase thought about the comparison for a moment before speaking. "I wouldn't have laughed. I always knew you were going to be fantastically successful one day. I thought it would be international finance, corporate investment banking, or something along those lines. I knew back at A&M that there was a greatness inside of you... some inner strength or destiny that would surface one day. It's always been there."

"Why thank you, kind sir," Terri fluttered. "I appreciate those words."

A volunteer came in just then, looking around the room, desperately searching for something. "Have you seen any staples around? We can't find any, and I'm afraid we might have just used the last batch in all of Texas."

Terri hustled around a counter and rummaged in the contents on the marble top. She lifted a box of paper, and underneath was a box of the little connectors. The nearly panicked lady exclaimed, "Thank, God!" and rushed out the door.

Chase chuckled, "Now wouldn't that suck. All this work, all these man-hours getting ready and preparing, and the entire project is halted due to a lack of staples."

Shrugging, Terri replied, "We would have found a work around or another supply. What choice do we have?"

"But where is the staple factory? What condition is it in? Is anyone left alive that knows how to operate the machinery? For both the Alliance and my government, those are the challenges we face. It's probably going to take years before the small things stop hindering the big things."

Terri nodded, "That about sums it up. I'm sure both of our governments are battling the same issues every day. But again, what choice do we have? We have to plow through and do the best we can."

"Do you ever consider what will happen when there are choices?"

Pausing, Terri looked up with a puzzled expression. "I'm not sure I understand what you mean?"

Chase hesitated and then changed his mind. "I was just thinking out loud, it wasn't important or pertinent." The deft conversationalist quickly changed the subject, leaving only the slightest of questions regarding his previous inquiry. "So, your husband is off to the north I hear, trying to settle some land dispute?"

"Yup. That's my Bishop, always galloping off to save the day."

Grunting, Chase responded, "And yet your big hero keeps his family in a camper. Doesn't seem fair."

"What's that supposed to mean?" Terri fired back.

"I'm just saying it seems like the Alliance doesn't appreciate you, that's all. From everything I've heard, Bishop and you have gone well above and beyond the call of duty. If anyone had done the same for Washington, they would have been greatly rewarded."

"Bishop and I do what we can because we believe in the Alliance and want to serve, not because we are looking for compensation or glory. We're just trying to make life better for our friends and neighbors and help build a place where our children will have a future."

The ambassador seemed to accept her response, at least enough to move on. "But the sacrifices you've made... continue to make.... Does it trouble you greatly when he's away? Surely it must worry you sick?"

Terri chose her words carefully, not liking where the conversation was going. "Of course it causes me to lose a little sleep now and then. Who wouldn't? This mission's not so bad, though. There are two families threating to fight over a parcel of land.

Bishop and his team are going to keep them separated until the Alliance gets this new plan in place. This trip doesn't sound nearly as dangerous as some he's been on. As a matter of fact, this trip sounded fascinating from a governing perspective. I would have liked to go with him."

"You wanted to go because it fascinated you? Hmmmm…. Now, that does beg the question, doesn't it? In what way was it so intriguing?"

Terri proceeded to tell Chase about the history of the dispute north of Fort Davidson, filling in the ambassador on not only the details but her take on the social aspects and how something so small as a tiny portion of land could lead to much bigger problems. "That's why I wanted to go, but I just got back home after being away for weeks, and with this new program getting ready to launch, I decided to stay here and help out."

"I heard you've faced your fair share of danger on some of these adventures. Diana was telling me about a few of them. You should write a book someday."

Terri rolled her eyes, "That would certainly be a lengthy work. Heck, maybe a whole series of books."

Bishop watched Grim's shape move through the darkness, a spool of fishing line spinning quickly as the contractor backed from the former barn to the house.

"That's the last one," Grim announced, arching his back and stretching stiff muscles. "Nobody is getting close to the place without our knowing about it."

"And the flash bombs?" Bishop asked, bending to help his man tighten the tripwire.

"All set. If anybody ventures close enough, they might get their eyebrows singed, but no one should be seriously hurt. Do you really think they'll be coming in tonight?"

"Yup. I would if I were Mrs. Baxter. She's smart enough to know that the longer she waits, the more we'll dig in, and ultimately the harder we'll be to dislodge. They'll be here. Until then, why don't you make sure the shotguns are loaded and ready? I'll take the first watch."

Grim's sleeve wiped the perspiration from his forehead as he took one last look around. Bishop knew something was bothering his teammate. "Smoke bombs, flash bang grenades, shotguns loaded with sandbags… I'm feeling a little exposed here, boss. If those guys do come in tonight, they'll have real rifles and pistols expelling high-velocity lead. We might as well be throwing spitballs back."

"We'll have our carbines close if things get out of hand. Remember, we're here to keep people from killing each other. It would be kind of pointless if we ended up planting more bodies than they could slay on their own."

Grim still didn't like it. "This reminds me of Iraq during the insurgency. We could only fire if fired upon. That was a little too late in my book. We lost some good men with that bullshit policy. Hell, even cops can draw and fire if they feel threatened."

"Nobody said this was going to be easy, partner. Such is life for those of us incapable of making a living any other way."

"Whatever. I'm going to go wash up and try to catch some shuteye. I may even talk the kid into taking the second watch."

Bishop watched Grim stroll toward the house and began making one last check of his own kit. Finally satisfied, he pulled on his pack and then followed his man inside.

On the off chance that anyone was watching them and had night vision, the Texan entered the front door as would be expected. A moment later, he was out the back, darting quickly to the protection of a strand of small oaks and scrub.

Careful not to set off his own trip wire, the Texan moved, listened, and then moved again. He didn't expect any of the local ranchers to be about, instead trying to gain a feel for the night, wildlife, and natural sounds of the area.

Finally reaching the hide they'd scouted just after nightfall, Bishop settled into a small gap between an ordinary mound and a tree that had fallen not long ago. The position gave him an excellent view of the entire homestead.

To his back were the beginnings of the black rock formation that defined the region. In high school geography, they'd taught him the name of the specific stone, including a detailed tutorial on how it had reached its current shape and state. Right now, his mental energies were otherwise engaged, and he couldn't recall a single fact.

His night vision was on a lanyard, dangling from his neck where it wouldn't be misplaced in the darkness. The pump shotgun he was holding didn't have a mount for such devices, and there hadn't been time to have Alpha's armorer work one up.

They had almost made a critical error in the selection of non-lethal weaponry. Bishop preferred an automatic scattergun over the tried and true pump variety. Stored in the bat cave were two such blasters, combat weapons designed for military use and sporting the proper rails to mount just about any furniture the shooter desired.

By chance, Bishop loaded a few of Sheriff Watt's seldom-used sandbag rounds into his favorite 12-gauge. The weapon had immediately jammed.

A second, and then a third attempt had produced the same stovepipe failures.

"Those beanbag shells don't have enough powder to work that fancy shooting iron of yours," Watts had explained. "We always used them with our pump shotguns."

"Train like you'll fight, fight like you train," Bishop whispered, recalling the old infantry wisdom. It had never let him down.

The Texan pulled the small radio off his belt and clicked the talk button once. A moment later, Butter responded from inside the home, two crisp breaks in the static announcing they have clear radio communications. Bishop hadn't expected any issue. The two devices were less than 100 meters apart.

Pulling the NVD up to his eye, the Texan began his first sweep of the surroundings. While he had little fear of the Baxter's hands being world-class stalkers, he also respected the fact that they weren't stupid and might know the lay of the land. They wouldn't come riding up in a cavalry charge, nor would they rumble up to the house like a gang of robbers preparing to storm the local bank.

Like always, he tried to put himself into his opponent's mind. How would he come in? How many men would he bring? What were the primary and secondary objectives? It didn't always work, but the exercise often exposed weaknesses in his own preparations.

He expected a dismounted approach, probably from two or three directions. They knew the squatters were heavily armed, Butter and Bishop brandishing carbines, Grim with his fake hand grenade during the rancher's initial visit. Had Bishop had more time, he would have displayed a few more of the toys he'd borrowed from the boys over at Hood. It would have been a nice touch.

So Kathy and her men would try to sneak close to the house, maybe throw a few torches onto the roof and walls, perhaps even a Molotov cocktail if they were creative. Standard irregular tactics. He'd seen it all before.

After two hours, Bishop was beginning to think he'd overestimated his foe.

Other than a swooping barn owl, there hadn't been any movement whatsoever. Butter would be relieving him soon, and the Texan had been hoping to get the first encounter out of the way so he could get some sleep.

Movement caused a start, but it was only a small group of whitetail deer meandering into the home's backyard. "How did you get in there," he whispered to the non-responsive animals. *I'm going to bust Grim's ass,* he thought. *There's a gap in his wires. They should not be in the backyard.*

It then occurred to Bishop that he'd get more mileage of harassing Grim if he knew where the hole in their defenses was located. *They will go out the way they came in*, he concluded. Still holding the NVD to his eye, Bishop found a small stone with his free hand and tossed it at the grazing herbivores.

All three deer perked instantly, scanning for a predator and then rushing directly at the cliff face behind the ranch house. Bishop watched in amazement as they disappeared into what he had thought was an impassable wall of rock, scrub, and cactus.

There is a second way out, he reasoned, his opinion of the original builders now elevated.

Slightly disappointed in having lost his leverage over Grim, the Texan made a mental note to check out the hidden game trail in the morning. If the deer could pass that way, so could people.

He returned to scanning the valley and his watch, suppressing another yawn. He wasn't sleepy for long.

The distant sound of a truck engine was the first indication of activity. "Wakey, wakey, eggs and bakey," he whispered into the radio. "I've got engine noises to the west."

A single click acknowledged the boys were awake.

Bishop grunted, visualizing Grim cussing up a storm, complaining about people being so rude as to try and burn them out in the middle of the night.

Next came the distant whinny of a horse. Finally, the night vision detected movement along the valley floor, distant, ghost-like shapes dodging among the stony mounds in the small boulder field that resided there.

"That's where I'd come in from, Kathy. Nice plan," he said in a hushed voice.

Movement from the house drew Bishop's attention. Butter and Grim were now outside, using the overgrown landscaping bushes as cover. The older contractor was heading toward a pile of concrete blocks someone had conveniently left behind. Butter was hustling for a flowerbed, its railroad-tie walls and dirt filling more than an adequate bullet stop.

"Movement," came Grim's voice. "Three, maybe four making for the barn. They should hit the first tripwire about... now."

Bishop closed his eyes, wanting to preserve his natural night vision.

A moment later, the valley was ripped by a huge explosion,

the percussion thumping against the Texan's chest. Bishop could detect the flash despite his clenched eyelids.

A second passed before another of the flash bombs ignited, this one on a fence post less than 80 meters from the house. There had been no warning. This time Bishop was caught by the brilliant white flash that resembled a lightning strike close by. The thunder was louder than even the most intense storm could produce.

The flash bombs were filled with a special mixture of magnesium, aluminum, and ammonium that produced millions of candela and over 170 decibels of sound. Anyone nearby was temporarily blind, deaf, and probably had their ear fluid scrambled to the point where balance and movement were a challenge.

With his nocturnal eyesight now completely ruined, Bishop pulled the NVD back to his eye. The green and black world illuminated through the light amplification device showed several men stumbling and rolling around from the first detonation, a similar group lying on the ground from the second.

Headlights and the sound of a rushing truck engine came next. Up the driveway careened two pickup trucks, each carrying four or five riflemen in the bed. Peppering the house with round after round, Bishop had to wonder how accurate their fire could possibly be given how badly the trucks were bouncing along the bumpy, gravel lane.

The mobile assault units stopped directly in front of the residence, no doubt an effort by the drivers to give the shooters in the back a more stable aiming platform.

Bishop was up and moving before the dust had settled.

All eyes must have been on the old homestead because none of the invaders noticed Bishop approaching. When he was twenty feet away, he tugged a flashbang from his belt, flipped off the safety and tossed it into the bed. Before the stun grenade landed, the pump shotgun was against his shoulder.

The first sandbag round struck the driver directly in the head, the man screaming in pain as he fell onto the seat grasping his temple. Working the pump, Bishop started in on the exposed men in the bed. He'd loaded the weapon with alternating rounds of rock salt and sandbags, a method often referred to as "candy striping." If one non-lethal load didn't take his opponent down, hopefully, the other would give him something to think about.

The first shot knocked a man completely out of the bed, Bishop racking and firing as fast as his arm could work the pump. After three blasts had impacted their ranks, the rest of the shooters decided they didn't want to ride anymore and began bailing out, scrambling for cover.

One man, working his bolt-action deer rifle, decided to charge Bishop, growling a respectable battle cry the entire way. He met the thick wooden stock of the Texan's shotgun, and would require extensive dental care for his trouble.

Butter was working the other truck, and soon Grim was chasing after the retreating victims of the flash bomb. They had broken the attack.

Bishop was just bending over to retrieve a dropped rifle when the pickup beside him began rolling. For a second, he thought the driver was trying to get away.

Running up beside the cab, he saw the bleeding man still lying prone across the seat.

"His foot's still on the gas!" Bishop yelled at Butter. "Get the hell out of the way!"

There wasn't anything else to be done but watch the old Ford accelerate directly toward its cousin.

The two vehicles weren't that far apart, Bishop estimating the impact at about 10 mph. But it was enough to puncture the gas tank of the jacked up 4x4 on the receiving end of the collision.

While Bishop rushed up to check on the unconscious driver, the smell of gasoline filled the air. The crash had jammed the door tight.

The Texan ran around the tailgate, hoping the passenger door was still operable. Three bullets ripped into the fender, chasing him back to cover. Butter clearly hadn't finished mopping up.

The situation was soon remedied by the blinding flash of another grenade, or at least that's what Bishop thought.

While Butter's toss had landed square in the middle of the still-resisting Baxter guns, it also ignited the gasoline with a whoosh.

"Shit!" Bishop cursed, turning his head away from the wave of hot air.

It then occurred to him that the driver was about to be roasted alive. After verifying no active guns remained aimed in his direction, Bishop hustled to the Ford's door and yanked hard on the handle. It opened.

The guy in the cab moaned when Bishop grabbed a handful of his hair and pulled hard. By the time the driver's body bounced out the door and onto the ground, the Texan figured the fellow wouldn't need a haircut for quite a while.

After the now-groaning driver had been dragged to a patch of non-burning grass, Bishop pulled a pair of nylon handcuffs from the back of his belt. In less than 10 seconds, he secured the still-drowsy man's hands and feet.

Grim appeared around the corner, four men with their hands on their heads marching in single file ahead of the contractor's barrel.

It took the three Alliance men over an hour to secure 11 prisoners, three of which were unconscious. Butter gathered weapons, assisted by the roaring fire of the two trucks while Grim searched the prisoners an applied nylon restraints.

Bishop checked each man for serious injuries but found nothing life threatening.

By the time they were done, the pre-dawn eastern sky was about to announce the sunrise. Bishop, thinking there may still be an observer up in the hills, rushed inside to retrieve a stack of old bedsheets.

One by one, he laid out the white cotton covers, each apparently covering a body lying near the house. Logs from the woodpile provided the lumps and bulges to imitate the dead beneath.

"You're evil," Grim teased, watching Bishop put the final touches on their pretend, improvised morgue. "I love it."

Bishop watched Butter standing over the prisoners. "Fetch the Sat phone and call the sheriff. He'll take these guys off our hands. Round one goes to the white hats."

Chapter 6

Cameron watched the men loading supplies into the vans, impressed with their efficiency and discipline. He had to admit, they were a rough-looking bunch, obviously cocky, and wholly capable of violence.

The oldest noticed his employer's presence and approached, "Good morning, Mr. Lewis. We're about ready to shove off."

"Do you have everything you need?"

"Yes, sir, and thank you, sir. The equipment and ammo you've been stockpiling is all first class. My team will put it to good use."

Cam handed the former Marine Corps Captain a folder. "This is everything we know, including a topographical map, the directions you will need, names of the players, and the latest intelligence I've received from our sources within the Alliance."

The sturdy veteran accepted the file and nodded but offered no additional comment.

"As I stated last night, the primary objective is to protect those ranchers down there. We will make an example out of their plight that will open the eyes of citizens all across the Alliance. Unfortunately, that will likely result in causalities, but the men pretending to be squatters already have blood on their hands. They are some of the malicious crooks who executed my people at Midland Station and seized my private property. They, like the rest of that gang of thieves running the show in Texas, have no respect for the Constitution or individual liberties."

Again, the captain merely nodded his understanding and agreement.

"And there's a bonus!" Cam continued. "I've just learned that the man in charge of the squatters holds a position of prominence in their government and is one of the leading enforcers of their socialist policies. His team and he are like the Nazi Brownshirts of pre-World War Two Germany, traveling all around and using force against any citizen who tries to stand up for his rights. This thug's demise will open additional avenues of approach for our efforts and send a strong message to the freedom loving Texans trapped by the current regime. Any questions?"

"No, sir. I think we're all set. It will be a pleasure to take these guys out of the fight and help those ranchers keep what is rightfully theirs."

"Good luck then. I'll see you all back here in a few days."

Cameron watched the captain's team load into the vans and drive away. A sense of well-being warmed his soul. Finally, after all the months of bitterness and inaction, he was taking the first step toward redemption. Justice lay just over the horizon.

The men he'd just dispatched to Texas had been gathered months ago, at a point in time where he believed the use of force and arms was the only path to revitalization. He'd almost dismissed the entire group when it had become clear that the Alliance wasn't going to be dislodged with gun barrels. Now he was glad he'd kept them on the payroll.

In addition to the information about the ranchers north of Fort Davidson, Cam had also received a copy of the new Alliance rules regarding personal property, including detailed documentation of how the system was to be implemented.

Sauntering back inside the nondescript metal building that served as his temporary headquarters, Cam headed for the main conference room where four gentlemen waited patiently for his return.

There was a stark difference between these men and the group of former soldiers and Marines he'd just dispatched to Texas. Rising from their plush chairs, Cam shook each man's hand. Rather than camo fatigues and load vests, all of the attendees wore jackets and ties. Instead of rifles, optics, and explosives, their weapons were contained in the leather briefcases scattered around the large table.

"Gentlemen, I hope everyone has had an opportunity to read and digest the information we've received from the Alliance," Cameron began.

All present nodded that indeed they had studied the massive stacks of documents.

"Good. You all know our strategy; each of you has your assignments. I want this new batch of Alliance bullshit attacked from every possible legal angle. I want it challenged in what little press exists in Texas. You are to act as representatives... legal counsel... for the common, average citizen. You are to play the role of benevolent seekers of justice and equality. But most importantly, you are to be royal pains in the local government's ass."

The four lawyers smiled and nodded, each appearing eager to begin the campaign.

"Then I'll conclude by wishing you all a safe journey and the best of luck. Hopefully, we'll meet again within a month's time and celebrate the downfall of Alpha's tyranny."

Another round of handshakes and best wishes were exchanged as the four men readied to leave. Cam soon found himself alone with his thoughts.

"I wonder which group will inflict the most damage?" he queried the empty room. "My money is on the lawyers. They're far more vicious."

"Solo rider coming in, sir. On horseback, under a white flag. It's Katherine," the anxious messenger reported.

Abercrombie Pomelos rose from the dining room table after wiping the grease of a partially consumed chicken wing from his chin. "Maybe we'll find out what all the fuss was about last night," he grumbled. "Let her come in. But make sure you keep an eye out for any of her kin trying to sneak up while she has us distracted."

"Yes, sir."

The old rancher checked his teeth for scraps via the hall mirror, rubbed the stubble of three-day growth on his chin and ran his fingers through his hair. Shrugging, he whispered, "That damn woman doesn't deserve my Sunday best anyhow."

He strode to the front porch, reassured by the two stocky ranch hands stationed at either end of the long wooden structure. After exchanging a quick nod with the sentries, Abe stepped off to wait as the lone rider approached.

The ruckus last night had kept most of his crew awake into the wee hours. While the main house was over five miles away from the disputed property, the explosions and bright flashes had been clearly visible. At first, Abe had thought there was a weird thunderstorm on the way, but that idea was quickly dispelled once he'd pulled on his trousers and managed the front yard. Rain clouds didn't create large plumes of fire and smoke like they could see in the distance.

"The Baxters are fighting with somebody," one of the foremen had speculated.

"Bullshit," another had replied. "Who would they be scrapping with? All of our men are present and accounted for."

The following morning, their scout had returned with little useful information. "There are two burned out pickups sitting in front of the old house. That's all I could see."

Katherine approached slowly, a pillowcase tied tightly to what appeared to be a broom handle waving in the air.

"You don't need that flag anymore, Kathy. I'm not going to

shoot you," Abe called from across the barnyard.

She continued riding, finally stopping 15 feet in front of Abe. "We need to talk," she insisted, getting right to the matter at hand.

"So talk."

"There are squatters on the old place, three men claiming to be from up north. We tried to push them off last night and got our asses thoroughly kicked. I lost 11 men and have another handful hurting in the bunkhouse. We've got to do something."

"What's this 'we' shit, Katherine?" Abe spat back. "Why should I give a pig's oysters that somebody kicked your outfit's ass? I should probably buy them a round of drinks."

The head of the Baxter clan shook her head, a low, mean laugh rising from her throat. "You old fool. Stop trying to be the biggest swinging dick in the valley for a minute, and think. One of your boys already put a bullet in a deputy's leg, and that has pissed off Watts and his cronies. They're not going to be doing either of us any favors for a while. Now, *we* got squatters moving in right before the new law comes down. If we don't work together, those three bastards could end up owning our water supply. Both of our herds will shrivel up and blow away in the wind. Can't you see that?"

Abe rubbed his chin, staring back hard at the woman his men called, "Old Brass Ass." Like a hundred times before, it occurred to him that the name was a perfect fit. "So what do you propose?"

"We can settle our quarrel later. Right now, we have to get those wandering scum off that property. The only thing worse than having you control that creek would be having a bunch of hostile gypsies in charge of our watering hole. You comprende?"

Abe thought it over, finally motioning for his archrival to dismount. She might be an uncompromising, old bitch, but that didn't mean she was always wrong. The fact that she had come to him, alone, carried even more weight.

"Come on in," he said, "Let's have a powwow."

She dismounted, following him inside. He offered her a drink, which she accepted. He had to dig in the cabinet for the better bottle of brandy.

"Those three squatters have the old place wired with explosives and trip wires," she informed her host after a sip of the golden colored liquid. "They claim to be ex-military, and after they chewed up my men and spit them out like watermelon seeds, I tend to believe them."

Abe started to fire off a smartass remark about the quality of Baxter fighting men but held his tongue. Deep inside, he knew

Kathy's men were as good as his. Finally, he said so. "So what's to stop these vigilantes from doing the same thing to my crew? It sounds like our little oasis has been turned into the Valley of Death to me."

"I sent in 20 of my best, and they scampered back with their tails between their legs, whimpering like whupped pups."

The two ranch owners spent the next hour and two refills exploring different options and ideas. Despite the warming effect of the alcohol, both were extremely frustrated.

Right when it seemed there was no possible solution, one of Abe's men knocked on the front door. "Sir, we've got a white van coming up the lane," the man reported, eyeing Kathrine with suspicion.

Abe reached for the gun in his belt, throwing a fiery glance at his nemesis. "If you've double-crossed me, woman, I swear I'll put a hole in your corset."

Unflustered, Katherine shook her head. "This is none of my doing, Abe. I swear it."

"We'll see," he said, using his gun barrel to wave her toward the front porch.

There were a dozen rifles covering the van as it rolled to a stop in front of the main house. Abe and Kathy watched as a single man exited and approached. He walked like a military man with squared shoulders and a measured stride. "Is this the Pomelos place?" he asked.

"Who wants to know?" came the cold response.

"I lead a SAINT team for the Alliance. I've been assigned to settle a land dispute between your ranch and the Baxter's. I'm stopping by as a courtesy to tell you to keep your people out of that valley."

Abe exchanged looks with Katherine, neither quite knowing what to make of the new arrival. Both of them had heard of the SAINT teams before.

"You're a little late, mister. Mrs. Baxter and I were just discussing a group of violent gunmen who have moved into the old homestead. They shot up a bunch of her men last night." the rancher replied.

"We're already aware of that, sir. My men and I will move them out shortly. In the meantime, I strongly suggest both of your organizations stay clear of the basin. It would be a shame if more of your men were killed in a crossfire."

Katherine stepped forward and said, "And after you move them out?"

"We'll let the Alliance settle things after that. My orders are to take possession of that valley, and that's just what I'm going to do."

"What's your name, mister?" Abe asked again.

The former Marine Corps captain's mind scrambled back to the file Cameron Lewis had provided before his team had left Oklahoma. "Folks call me Bishop, sir," he said with a sly grin.

After alternating catnaps and light meals most of the day, Bishop and his crew were hard at it after sundown. "Move the perimeter out 100 meters," he ordered Butter and Grim. "I don't think they'll be back, but just in case our new friends are feeling frisky, we need to reposition our little party favors so they maintain the delight of surprise."

The commander also changed their fighting positions.

"These aren't as good, but the combatants may have noted our locations last night," Bishop reminded his men.

After an agreement to keep the same watch order, Bishop left via the back door and stalked his way to the new hide.

The Texan settled in with his shotgun and flashbang grenades, this time using a low wall of firewood as his bullet stop.

He found it was far more difficult to stay alert, struggling to keep his focus sharp. Part of the reason was the off-hours, daytime sleep never seemed to satisfy as well as the natural nocturnal cycles.

Then there was the fact that he didn't think anyone would venture into their valley this evening.

After 90 minutes on watch, the Texan reached for the radio to check in. Maybe a few jokes with Butter or Grim would help him stay awake. His hand was about to close on the small device when the split logs around him erupted in a shower of splinters.

Instinct saved Bishop's life at that moment, his muscles forcing him to the ground before his brain ever registered that people were shooting at him.

Round after round pounded his position, the volume and accuracy driving the Texan to make his body as prone and flat as possible. A storm of dirt, wood, and bark pelted his skin and clothing, filled his mouth and nose, and stung any exposed skin.

What the fuck, he thought, trying to wiggle deeper into the soil. *When did these guys learn to shoot like this? How in the hell did they get past our trip lines?*

The relentless, withering fire continued for several seconds, Bishop barely able to breathe, let alone bring his weapon into the fray. A thousand questions raced through his mind, not the least of which was how in the hell did they know his exact position.

It then occurred to him that the incoming rounds were from weapons firing three round, automatic bursts. Only the U.S. Marines used that specific configuration. *Where in the hell did a bunch of ranch hands get select-fire weapons? How did they suddenly learn to control them so well?*

About that time, Bishop had a terrifying insight. No one wasted that much ammo unless it was suppressive fire. That translated into a focused effort to keep him down, which meant someone was advancing on his position.

Realizing his hide was about to be overrun by hostile visitors, the Texan commanded his body to rise high enough to reach one of the flashbangs hanging from his vest. He then forced his adrenaline-charged brain to focus on the angle of the incoming rounds.

He knew the assaulters wouldn't risk stepping into the line of friendly fire. They would be coming in from a different angle. That's where he needed to throw the banger.

It seemed like hours passed, but in reality, it was less than 10 seconds after the first shots before the safety was removed. Taking a deep breath and fully expecting to have his arm torn off by the incoming blizzard of lead, Bishop hurled the canister with every ounce of strength he could muster.

There was a loud "thunk" just after the grenade had left his hand, immediately followed by a voice that screamed, "Fuck!" After a few seconds of recovery, the same danger-close throat screamed, "Grenade!"

Realizing his throw had hit one of the incoming foes, and that they were far closer than he'd guessed, Bishop buried his face in the dirt and covered his ears.

The banger exploded, less than 15 feet away.

Up came the pump shotgun, Bishop working the weapon like a madman, firing blindly where his tortured brain calculated the foe would be. Was it his imagination or had the suppressive fire slowed? *Keep the shots low. They'll be on the ground now. Fire ankle high. Mow the grass.*

Cursing the non-lethal rounds in his weapon, the Texan continued to spray and pray, emptying the eight shells in less than three seconds. In a flash, his secondary, a .45 caliber pistol, was in his hands. He desperately wanted his carbine that was inside the house, leaning against the doorframe.

His pistol was barking now, four of his eight available rounds spread low and fast.

Roll right.

Two rounds at a shadow.

Roll again.

Two more shots at an outline.

Run... run like hell.

A stream of bullets chased the Texan the short distance to the house, their angry hissing seeming to swarm his head. The corner of the structure, a sanctuary from the death that was trying to shred his body, appeared to be miles away.

"Bishop! Coming in!" he screamed at the top of his lungs, hoping Grim and Butter wouldn't shoot him.

It was too far, the bullets now so close he could feel the concussion wave against his head. The enemy's aim was catching up. He wasn't going to make it.

A gun barrel appeared around the corner, emerging from the exact spot Bishop was trying to reach. The barrel began belching white fire. For just a moment, the Texan thought the attackers had somehow managed to get between the home and him. He dove headfirst, skidding painfully across the earth, his forward motion stopping just short of the house and its promise of cover.

An arm appeared, grabbed Bishop's vest and lifted the Texan like he was a rag doll. In a blink, he was pulled from the line of fire, tossed into the safety of the backyard and tumbling across the cool grass.

Bishop's hand was just closing on his knife when he recognized Butter's smiling face above him. The big kid was yelling something, but the Texan's ears had been scrambled by the flashbang's thunder.

"Are you okay?" Butter was screaming.

Bishop finally got it, nodding while trying to regain his feet. Butter handed over the Texan's favorite M4, again screaming at the top of his lungs, "Grim is pinned down on the other side. Who are these guys, sir?"

"Stay here," Bishop bellowed back. "Keep 'em busy. I'll get Grim."

Pausing for a moment to watch his man pop around the structure and snap several rounds, Bishop then hustled toward the opposite side, running across the back of the old house, still trying to figure it all out. The pop and crack of rifles increased in volume as he arrived at the far end of the yard. Grim was engaged in one hell of a fight.

The contractor had somehow managed to retreat back to the flowerbed and its bastion of thick railroad ties packed with heavy soil. Bishop counted at least three weapons spraying automatic fire into the wooden mini-fort. His stomach knotted when the outlines of two additional foe appeared, trying to flank Grim's exposed right side.

Okay, so much for saving lives. These guys asked for it, Bishop thought, the red dot of his optic centering on one of the flanker's chest. He began pulling the trigger.

His first target went down, arms flying outwards as the 5.56 bullets tore into the flesh and bone. Bishop didn't wait to see the guy fall, moving quickly to the second shooter trying to sneak up on Grim.

But the fighter had inexplicably disappeared. "What the fuck," Bishop whispered. "Are we fighting ghosts?"

The Texan found him a moment later just as a string of bullets tore into the house next to Bishop's head, large sections of the old clapboard sawed into kindling by the incoming lead.

There he is, Bishop thought as he ducked back for cover. *Damn, he reacted quickly. Who are these guys?*

"Coming in," Grim's voice sounded in the distance.

To give him covering fire, Bishop popped around the corner, found Grim's line of egress, and began snapping off rounds. He'd never seen the old contractor's legs pumping so hard.

His friend was halfway back when a familiar motion caught Bishop's attention... an arm extending in a wide arc. "Grenade!"

If Grim heard the warning, he didn't heed. While Bishop commanded his feet to step back and use the home's corner for protection, his eye caught a glimpse of the falling explosive. It landed less than five feet behind Grim's legs, spun around twice and then a blinding red flash filled the Texas night.

A body flew past Bishop's boots, Grim landing a few feet beyond his leader's legs and skidding across the ground. Bishop watched in horror as his friend tried to roll and stand, only able to fall clumsily back to the earth. The contractor's face was contorted in extreme pain.

That's it, Bishop decided. *We're out of here.*

Seeing Grim go down crystalized the tactical situation, and more importantly their mortality. *We're out. They can have this fucking valley. It ain't worth dying for.*

Bishop extended several rounds to keep the enemy back and then went to Grim. "How bad?" the Texan shouted.

"I'm still in this fight," Grim replied, his face straining with the effort to roll over.

Bishop pulled off his gloves and ran his hands up and down Grim's legs and back. The Texan grimaced when he felt several areas of warm sticky liquid already soaking through his man's clothing. *There's no big hole pumping blood like crazy. I'll fix him later.*

Bishop helped Grim move to a better position and said, "Can you keep them off my ass for a minute or two?"

Grim nodded, moved onto his side, and began firing around the corner. "Hurry," he said. "They're determined to take this backyard."

Nodding, Bishop ran for Butter's position, not surprised to find his man still engaged in a desperate battle. The Texan almost lost his footing, slipping across the growing pile of brass next to the big man's boots.

"We're out of here in two minutes. I'm going in the house to get our packs," Bishop announced.

"Yes, sir! Hurry, sir. They're working me pretty good over here. They've advanced another 35 feet since you left."

"Grim's hurt. I don't think he can walk. Get ready to use all those muscles. I'm not leaving him here."

"Yes, sir!"

Again, to buy precious, life-saving time, Bishop popped around the corner under Butter's taller frame and added a second rifle to their defense. It would give the enemy something to think about. After dumping five quick rounds, he was gone, darting for the back door.

Bishop found their gear mostly packed, the home's interior illuminated by a single flashlight somebody had left on as Grim and Butter had scrambled outside to meet the threat.

His own pack was first, quickly followed by Grim and Butter's heavy kit, one on each arm. He scanned the interior, saddened by all of the food, ammo, and gear they were leaving behind. A wooden crate of real hand grenades drew his attention. Given his arms were already maxed out, he managed to palm one of the explosive devices before grunting toward the door.

There were also two cans of gas for the ATV and motorcycle.

He hesitated for a moment, sure that whoever was pushing them out would have to clear the house. In a flash, his anger over the whole ordeal got the best of Bishop's thinking. He dropped Grim's pack, pulled his knife, and stabbed each can. It was with some gratification that he kicked the two leaking containers to opposite sides of the main room.

A second later, he was pushing through the back door, wiggling sideways through the threshold to squeeze the bulging packs out into the night air.

Saying a quick prayer that the attackers hadn't spotted the game trail at the back of the property, Bishop lifted his NVD and scanned the area rising up into the sheer cliff face. While he didn't see any sign of human activity, it wasn't going to be an easy hike. Especially with a wounded man.

The sound of Butter and Grim's weapons keeping the assaulters at bay reminded Bishop that the alternative was far worse. He doubted the men they faced were interested in taking prisoners.

Butter's end of the house was first. After dropping his man's ruck on the grass, Bishop hustled to the big shooter's side. "Put on your pack and then get Grim. Meet by the head of that backdoor game trail. We're out of here."

Nodding, Butter fired two more shots around the corner, switched to a fresh mag… and was gone.

Bishop had a pretty good idea where the attacking foe would be. His narrow escape had royally screwed up their plans, which had been to take his former position at the woodpile first and then they would have had the house completely at their mercy. Grim's fast reaction and stronger than anticipated resistance had been a second wrench in the enemy's gears.

At least that's what Bishop thought.

So now, the assault force was having to regroup, and that was buying Bishop and his team precious time. There was only one suitable place for them to stage, so the Texan focused his shots there. He had little faith the rounds were hitting anything or anybody, but it would delay their final push.

"Ready!" came Butter's distant shout.

Popping off three more shots, Bishop backed away and made for the trailhead. Butter, with a limping Grim using the big kid for support, was right where he should be.

Bishop took the rear guard while his men advanced on the trail, slowly backing into the underbrush and giving his guys a head start. He noticed one of Grim's legs was dark with dampness, but that was a problem he couldn't address with several accurate shooters hot on their heels.

Pulling the recently acquired grenade from his pocket, Bishop set up a cross-path booby-trap using a short length of paracord line. If anybody followed them, at least in the dark, they were in for a nasty surprise.

As he worked on the booby-trap, it occurred to Bishop that his foe would be preparing to storm the old house – once they'd determined that the SAINT team was no longer in the backyard, that walls of the home were the only logical place where anyone could hide. Even if the Texan and his men had been spotted disappearing into the undergrowth at the foot of the cliffs, any good commander would want the structure cleared.

Taking a chance on his muzzle blast being spotted, Bishop rose slightly and put three quick rounds into the kitchen window, calculating that the metal cabinets and appliances would provide the best chance for a hot, gasoline-igniting spark.

The Baxter home seemed to swell for a hundredth of a second, and then all hell erupted in the canyon. The remaining glass windows blew outwards, followed by roaring spews of boiling fire. Large patches of the roof shot skywards as whole sections of the rear wall began to collapse.

In the sun-like glow of illumination that bathed the valley, Bishop finally got a good look at their attackers. He could clearly see several men, a few bowled over by the shockwave from the house.

These weren't ranchers, but he'd already figured as much. What stunned Bishop was the Kevlar helmets, bulging body armor, professional looking load vests, and radio ear pieces. It was as if he was facing a U.S. Marine Corps Rifle squad. *Who the hell are you?* he whispered to the night.

The ex-Marine captain took a knee beside one of his wounded, his experienced eye taking only a moment to estimate the injuries were life-threatening. In the light of the still-burning home, he could see the medic's junk scattered around the area, used bandages, gloves glistened crimson red, paper wrappers, and the empty tubes of hypodermic needles. Litter no officer ever wanted to leave behind.

"Hang in there, Corporal. We'll get you out of here ASAP," he said softly to the barely conscious man.

While the team's pharmacist mate worked quickly on the two most seriously wounded men, the captain's expression remained stoic and unreadable. He'd watched this scene play out too many times before.

The battle to control the valley was over; the fight to save the wounded had just begun. "Get them stable enough to move," he informed the hustling sawbones. "We'll load them up in one of the vans and get them out of here as soon as you think they're ready."

"Yes, sir," the man replied, his hands a blur over a nasty looking chest wound. "I'll do my best."

Rising, the captain assessed their status. He had two dead, three wounded, including his second in command who was suffering from a badly broken nose. The injury had been a freak, the result of his man taking a thrown flashbang grenade square in the face at point-blank range.

Out of ten original men, the captain's force was now only 50% effective. They had, he reminded himself, achieved the objective. It had required twice the original estimate of ammunition, with double the number of anticipated casualties. The two bleeding men at his feet would require serious medical attention within the next few hours, which meant they would have to be transported back to Oklahoma. The trip would reduce his head-count even further. The ranch house was a complete loss.

Visually sweeping the area, he noted the light flickering off the high stone walls that bordered the valley. It was an eerie hue, red flames against the black rocks. It reminded him of a village in Afghanistan from eight years back. That had been a bad night as well.

That war is long past, he thought, bringing his mind back to Texas and the problems at hand. *You survived there; you can thrive here.*

His Marines had taken their objective, but didn't they always? The price had been high – too damned high. Like all men who lead combat units, he mentally replayed the engagement, making entries into a conceptual ledger of what had gone right... and where they had fucked up.

Tonight wasn't much different from previous battles, he decided. Fate had been against them, and there was little he could do about that. He'd also run into an enemy that had far exceeded their expectations. The men he'd dislodged from the property had been organized, disciplined, and had fought with more skill than any foe the captain had ever faced.

The former officer studied the ridge above, hazarding a guess that the men he'd just beaten were up there somewhere, staring down at the ground they'd lost.

He knew from the blood trails they'd discovered that one of the Alliance shooters was wounded. There was no way to know how seriously. Maybe his opposite was up there tending to his causalities, having the same thoughts about the price paid.

Another batch of rounds cooked off in what remained of the old farmhouse, drawing the Marine officer's attention back to the flames. Knowing that his foe had been forced to retreat without all of their ammo did little to placate his melancholy outlook.

His men, angered over the loss of their comrades, had wanted to chase the Alliance team into the hills, but he'd not allowed it. Their foe had fought harder than anticipated, obviously possessed far more skills than anyone had estimated. Given what they'd experienced so far, it wouldn't surprise him if an ambush or booby-traps awaited anyone stupid enough to go chasing after the retreating defenders in the darkness.

Who the hell are you? He whispered to the dark cliffs above.

Chapter 7

Bishop and Butter had taken turns helping Grim, the contractor's loss of blood draining his strength as they followed the game trail higher into the canyons. Thorns and cactus tugged at their skin and clothing, low branches and thick underbrush making every step difficult.

When it wasn't the high desert foliage, it was loose, sandy soil and sharp rocks. Steep ravines threatened the misplaced step, narrow ledges overlooking vertical walls that would have been difficult in the best of circumstances. In the darkness, after an exhausting firefight, with heavy packs and a wounded man, it was the most difficult trail Bishop could remember negotiating.

Every muscle in the Texan's body was burning like fire, perspiration running down his forehead to deliver stinging salt into already overtaxed eyes. Grim was getting weaker at the same time the incline grew steeper.

After just a half-mile, Bishop had to call it quits. Butter didn't protest the decision.

It was as good a spot as any, a small enclave that offered a relatively flat floor and high rock walls on three sides. They could defend it if the men from below pursued, but it would be their last stand as there was no escape route.

"This is our Alamo if they come after us," Bishop said in a matter of fact tone. "Let's hope this isn't where we die."

The Texan didn't believe they were being chased. He'd listened for the telltale "whump" of his hand grenade booby-trap, but the warning had never sounded. Unless the men in the valley were the absolute best stalkers in the world, there was no sign of anyone on their trail.

Bishop was also aware all of that could easily change come sunrise. That's what he would do, wait for good light and follow the blood.

Grim was priority one.

After cutting away one leg of the contractor's fatigues, Bishop found three shrapnel wounds. Two were no longer bleeding, deep scrapes that he doubted still contained any of the explosive metal fragments.

The third puncture in his friend's limb, however, was troubling.

Between Grim's knee and buttocks, directly in the middle of the thigh, was a nasty looking hole about the size of a dime.

While a major artery had been spared, blood continued to run out of the wound at a good clip.

Stop the bleeding, Bishop thought. That was always the first rule of battlefield medics. Keep that precious, life-giving fluid inside the body.

"I think my leg's broken," Grim croaked in a weak voice.

"Could be," Bishop responded, already having counted that possibility. "It's not a compound fracture though, at least not from what I can see."

Retrieving a small canister of antibiotic spray, Bishop did his best to keep the wounds from getting infected. His topical application would do little if Grim had a hunk of metal in his body. Next came the bandages, the largest puncture getting most of his attentions.

Grim moaned in agony when Bishop began wrapping the big wound. "Sorry friend, but I've got to get this good and tight," he told the patient.

"Do what you have to," Grim replied through gritted teeth. "I feel like there's a chunk of burning metal in there the size of a softball."

After finishing several circles around Grim's thigh with a bandage, Bishop pulled a bottle of small pills from his kit. "These will help with the pain… a little," he informed the still hurting contractor.

Grim waived them off, "I can deal with it. Give me my weapon and drag me to a good spot. I can still fight."

"No," Bishop replied. "We're fine. You need water and rest. Drink and sleep. That's an order. If they come after us, then you'll be in the shit, I promise. Until then, chill."

Grim nodded without so much as a dirty look. *The guy's got to be at his limit*, Bishop thought. *Hell, I'm toast, and I don't have three new holes in my body.*

Even the youngest of his team was exhausted; sweat pouring from his body, his breathing heavy from the exertion and sudden stress of the moment. Butter, resting nearby and drinking from a water bottle, looked like hell warmed over. "You okay?" Bishop checked.

"Yes, sir. I'm still trying to figure out what just happened. I keep replaying it over and over again in my mind. Do you know, sir?"

Butter was experiencing a common trauma, one that Bishop had felt a dozen times before. The intensity of the firefight they'd just survived combined with the lack of sleep, physical exertion, and extended adrenaline dumps was enough to rattle the human brain.

"Are your hands shaking?" Bishop inquired with the soft voice of understanding.

"Yes, sir. But I'm not scared... I just can't... they won't stop."

"You probably feel like you want to puke, too," Bishop continued with the fatherly tone. "I can't tell you why, Butter, but I can promise it will pass. You'll be okay. Go ahead and toss your cookies if you want. I usually do. No shame in it."

The admission seemed to brighten the big kid's mood. "Even you feel like this, sir?"

"All the time," Bishop responded with a warm smile. "It's normal. We just had several very well-trained, highly motivated individuals try and end our existence on this earth. Your brain probably thought you were dead a dozen times during the encounter. Now it's trying to figure out how you survived, and in the process you are reliving how close you came to death during the ordeal. Don't worry about it. It will pass."

"Thank you, sir. I've been shot at before, but *that...* back in that valley... it was... was...."

"Intense," Bishop finished for him.

"Yes, sir. I guess that's as good a word as any. I feel all hollow inside, like I left everything back there. I'm just an empty shell with a stomachache and worthless limbs."

"That, my young friend, is a no bullshit assessment if I've ever heard one. You'll be okay. I promise."

For a moment, Bishop thought about mentioning the nightmares that were sure to follow. He decided the kid had enough on his plate at the moment, and besides, the Texan didn't have any sage advice concerning the nocturnal terrors that would probably plague Butter for the rest of his life. It simply became part of a fighting man's existence until the reaper arrived and took care of the problem.

Bishop was bone tired and wanted nothing more than to lie down and close his eyes. Sucking water through his Camelbak's tube, he rose, forcing stiff, cracking knees to respond. He needed to assess their position, figure out where to post a lookout, take inventory of their remaining kit, and most importantly of all, come up with a plan of action to get Grim on a surgeon's table before infection, shock, or blood loss ended his friend's life.

"Get some rest, Butter. I'm going to run down my checklist for the next hour, and then I'll be toast. Sleep if you can... even a few minutes will help. If not, close your eyes, drink tons of water, and grab a nibble of something if you can hold it down. I'm going to need you pretty soon."

Butter nodded, reaching for his pack and opening a pouch

to produce a slab of jerked beef. After Bishop was sure the kid was okay, he moved off to get a better look at their new home. The sun would be coming up in a few hours, and if the men back in the valley still had any fight left in them, that's when they would come.

Katherine sat in her favorite rocking chair, the handmade heirloom a product of her great-grandfather's workshop. It was her harbor of tranquility, a stress reducing respite that might be occupied at any time, day or night. Hand carved of local oak, it had occupied the same position for so long that the curved runners had worn deep grooves in the porch's wooden planks. Everyone who knew the Baxter matriarch kept their distance, even the greenest ranch hand having been warned that when the boss was rocking, now wasn't the time to come knocking.

Despite the early, pre-dawn hour, there were plenty of men around to heed the warning. Awakened by the thunderous explosions, rifle reports, and flashes against the night sky, the entire Baxter contingency had grumbled outside, all wondering about the distant ruckus.

Charged with excitement and curiosity, they remained scattered around the main corral and bunkhouse even after the sounds of battle had died down.

Some clustered together in small gaggles, whispering speculations on the outcome, ferocity, and participants of the gunfight. Others rested a boot on a comfortable plank of fencing, watching the reddish glow pulse against the night sky without uttering a word.

For her part, Katherine sat rocking, her well-known temper barely held in check.

She'd agreed to let the Alliance SAINT team handle the squatters, not to sit and watch her childhood home go up in flames. It was bad enough the barn had caught fire a few nights ago, now the beautiful valley would be scarred with a second pile of ash, charred timber, and scorched memories.

She was certain the crimson hue on the horizon was her childhood home. There was nothing else in the basin that would burn with such intensity. She'd been raised in that house, brushed her first pony while it was tethered to the front porch's rail. Her bedroom was the one in the rear with the big window – a pane of glass where a daydreaming girl could watch the whitetail come down from the hills and graze in the backyard. How she had envied their beauty and grace.

Now it was gone.

From Katherine's point of view, the Alliance had been neither angel nor demon. The Baxter Ranch had suffered through the apocalypse, but not nearly as bad as most. With herds of cattle, dozens of well-armed men, and stashes of feed, hay, and food purchased in bulk, they had managed to keep everyone fed while millions had starved.

When the rumors began circulating of a new government being formed out of Alpha, most of the men and women in the surrounding county had merely shrugged with indifference. Out here, it really did not mean all that much.

Then the Alliance had shown up in Fort Davidson with a large force of armed men, eventually taking control of the county seat. The local District Attorney, D.A. Gibson, had even joined their cause.

Despite the endorsement of the county's head honcho, many residents thought the newcomers were heavy handed and willing to seize any property to advance their cause. Ownership was a gray area, with so many having died, fled the region, or gone missing.

One such example was a huge recreational vehicle retailer not 10 miles from the Baxter ranch. Men claiming to be sanctioned by the Alliance had descended on the local business and seized several Class-A motorhomes, purportedly to be used by the newly appointed heads of state.

While the representatives from Alpha had asked around about the owner of the multi-million dollar business, they hadn't invested a whole lot in research or due diligence before driving away with several of the most expensive models. The entire episode just didn't seem right to Katherine and her peers. She had invested with the owner years ago when it was a start-up. Her safety deposit box at the bank contained stock certificates that documented her 8% ownership, but the branch hadn't been open since everything had gone to hell. As of yet, no one had offered her any compensation before absconding with the dealership's vehicles.

When a drifter relayed the events of Midland Station and how the Alliance had taken control of the entire city via armed incursion, Katherine and her peers had again experienced doubts. After hearing that the owner of an oil refinery had been chased out of his own town by what amounted to a small army, many of the local ranchers became seriously concerned. Who were these people from Alpha? Where would they stop? Was any private property, claimed or unclaimed, exempt from their definition of eminent domain?

Then there was Sheriff Watts.

Out of the blue, after nearly two years of absence, men in patrol cars began roaming the countryside, claiming to have authority. Baxter ranch hands had been stopped and questioned, two of the cowpokes having been arrested in town for public intoxication.

After the run-in with Abe and his crew, Watts had threatened to arrive with hundreds of armed men to arrest both sides of the age-old feud. Katherine wanted the lawman's nose out of her business. As far as she was concerned, he was late to the party and offered no good solution. His status as a peace officer was questionable at best.

Most of the area's larger outfits had eyed the fledgling government with a healthy dose of skepticism. It wouldn't be the first time someone with a hunger for power had tried to rule the surrounding territory. There had been Mexico, various Indian tribes, the original Republic of Texas, the Confederacy, a period of occupation by Union troops, and finally the United States. Most of those "governments," hadn't worked out so well. Many had been nightmares of ruthlessness, abuse, and totalitarianism.

Of them all, the good ole' U.S.A. had been stable, long lasting, and usually fair-handed as far as the ranchers were concerned. At least in recent memory.

Stories started making the rounds, tales of the Alliance battling the U.S. Army. After that came more accounts of Texas separating from Washington and having visions of reforming the long-defunct Republic. While many cheered the move, not all of the region's citizens were convinced it was the best course. *Why?* the rancher had asked herself a dozen times. *Why separate from the only form of government that had ever worked?*

Katherine, along with most of her neighbors, had adopted a wait and see attitude. She understood that rule of law was necessary but didn't trust so much power in unproven hands.

Now, her homestead was under siege from this unknown entity called the Alliance, and the anger raged through her core over the injustice of the entire affair.

Shaking her head in disgust, she rose from her chair and strode to the southern end of the porch. "Mack?" she called to a group of men huddled nearby.

A lone outline of a large man separated from the cluster, quickly stepping toward the house. When his face was clear in the moonlight, he removed his hat and replied, "Ma'am."

"At first light, I want to go back to the valley and see for myself. I want to bring as many men as we can muster."

"Yes, ma'am. We'll be ready."

"Good night, Mack. Get some sleep if you can."

"Yes, ma'am."

Pete scanned the crowd and was pleased. Practically every stool and table was filled with a paying customer. It also pleased him greatly that his patrons were a mixture of familiar faces and folks he'd never met before. Travel was a sign of commerce, trade, and wealth. It was a good omen.

In fact, business had been so good, he was finding it difficult to keep enough help in the bar. With his other investments growing rapidly, he should be back in the office checking the books, writing letters to suppliers, and fulfilling the executive role. While he would hardly call his endeavors an empire, he now had several employees and locations to manage. Between that and his duties on the council, Pete was a very busy man.

Still, he loved tending bar. He was a social animal who took great pride in making customers feel comfortable in his establishment. His thriving business offered other, darker benefits as well. The budding capitalist had also discovered that being a good listener while pouring customers their libations was an excellent way to gather intelligence.

Both as a councilman and an entrepreneur, it was beneficial to know what was on the people's minds.

Working the counter with his ever-present bar towel, Pete noted a man he'd never seen before. The gentleman was well dressed, wearing an expensive suit, silk tie, and expensive watch. *Not your average tourist,* Pete surmised.

The well-heeled gent drew the bartender's attention for a couple of reasons. First of all, Pete was confident he had an encompassing knowledge of Meraton's ongoing business opportunities. A man, dressed so formally, most likely wasn't just passing through, but in town to buy, sell, or invest.

Secondly, he noticed that his new customer was about his own age. Not that many grey-headed folks had survived the downfall.

"Good evening, sir. Could I refill your glass?" Pete inquired with a smile.

"Why, sure. Thank you."

As the server tipped the bottle, he continued, "First time in

Meraton?"

"Yes, it is. I've heard so much about the famous market and the Manor hotel; I just wanted to see it for myself. I have business in Alpha tomorrow, so I thought I'd stop over and get a good night's rest."

"Smart move," Pete nodded. "With the government centered in Alpha, rooms there can be extremely difficult to find at times."

"That's good to know," the man replied, sipping from his glass. "If things work out, I may be spending a fair amount of time in Alpha. Perhaps I should look into acquiring a property. This is an excellent spirit. By the way, where did you come across it?"

"That's my own concoction," Pete explained proudly, extending his hand and introducing himself as the proprietor. "I own this bar, two micro-breweries, and a distillery over near Austin. That's our best grade of corn whiskey and my finest creation to date."

"Pleased to meet you," the friendly stranger replied with a warm handshake.

Pete waited for the patron to share any details about his occupation, but the man remained silent.

Again, to break the ice, Pete asked, "Coming from back east?"

"No, actually from the north."

Another customer called out just then, the new arrival calling, "Pete! Good to see you working tonight! It's about time you started earning an *honest* living. You've been spending too much time hobnobbing with all those political types over in Alpha and not paying enough attention to your real friends back here at the bar."

"A councilman's work is never done," Pete replied with a grin.

Before the conversation could continue, movement caught the bartender's eye.

The well-dressed customer was backing off his stool, a look of complete horror on his face. For a second, Pete thought the man was choking or perhaps ill.

"You okay, sir?"

There was no reply, the stranger breaking eye contact and hustling out of the bar without looking back.

Pete shrugged, glancing at the man's mostly full glass. There was a hundred dollar bill lying under the shot. "Wow," he said. "That's one hell of a tip."

As he reached for the currency, Pete noticed handwriting on the note. There was a series of numbers and an address in Oklahoma.

Dawn brought a hustle of activity to Bishop's camp. Awakened by his watch alarm, the Texan had relieved Butter after only 90 minutes of sleep. The parade of yawns just kept coming.

It was one of those mornings where every move Bishop wanted to make was hampered by the apocalypse. Desperate for coffee, he'd decided to use one of his few remaining, ultra-precious fuel pellets to heat water. The burning chemical didn't produce any smoke, and that was critical at the moment. Yet, they weren't making them anymore.

The next reminder that the world had gone to hell concerned Grim.

The contractor was running a fever, and that meant infection. With his exhausted, semi-awake mind, Bishop tried to visualize Grim's life with only one leg, a very real possibility if they didn't get him some serious medical attention quickly. The image shook the Texan to the core, partly due to his friendship, mostly because it could easily be him lying on the ground, sweaty and moaning with the first stages of gangrene.

The Sat phone's battery was dead, the charger left behind and most likely burned in the fire. Not that Bishop had a power source. Regardless, it had been a boneheaded mistake made in the rush to retreat. They couldn't call for help.

Digging in his kit, Bishop produced one of the last bottles of the antibiotic left in the region. Like his fuel pellets, they just weren't making them anymore.

He shook a pill into the palm of his hand, studying the capsule that was one hundred times more valuable than its weight in gold. "Here, Butter, make sure he gets this down. We'll give him another in two hours."

About the only good news was the fact that there wasn't any sign of pursuit from the valley. Drinking his joe, Bishop watched the trail for 20 minutes while Butter changed Grim's dressings. It looked like the men back in the valley weren't up for an early morning firefight.

Returning to camp, Bishop checked on his wounded man and then motioned Butter aside. "We've got to get him to a sawbones, or he's going to lose that leg, maybe his life."

"Yes, sir. Do we carry him out?"

Bishop knew exactly where he was, and on a paper map, a cross-country trek carrying Grim on a makeshift stretcher didn't seem like that big of a deal. Reality and the terrain, however, told a different story.

While Fort Davidson was only 11 miles away, it might as well be 111 given the canyons, lack of roads, and mid-sized mountains that dotted the area. It wasn't impossible, but by the time they crossed the rugged landscape, Grim might already be dead.

"No, I don't think we can carry him out, and using the road is a bad idea. We've got a lot of hostile people around here, and walking alongside the pavement carrying a wounded man doesn't seem like a winning strategy. We need one of the trucks we left back in the valley."

Butter nodded but didn't like the idea. "I don't think those fellas back there are just going to hand you the keys, sir. Even if you ask nicely."

The kid had a point.

Bishop turned, his gaze drifting toward the basin area. "Maybe those guys have left after pushing us off. We're assuming they're still occupying the place, but we don't know for sure. I think I need to do a little observation work before we decide on a play. Who knows, I might be able to steal one of the trucks right out from under their noses."

Again, Butter wasn't thrilled about being left behind with a dying teammate. "And if they catch you, sir?"

Bishop glanced at his watch. "If I'm not back in two hours, make a drag stretcher and head directly south. You'll eventually hit either the highway or Fort Davidson. But don't worry. I'll be back. I'm not planning on trying to retake the valley. I just want to see what's going on."

Katherine strolled across the front porch, her best riding boots and spurs clicking and jingling across the planks. She paused for a moment, scanning the gathered men under her employ.

Mack had managed to mount 14 riders, all of them armed. Given the losses of the last few days, it was an embarrassingly small number, but she was confident her foreman had done his best.

No one moved to help her climb into the saddle. Katherine Baxter wasn't some frail, city girl who needed help with a stirrup.

With the grace of a longtime rider, she was up and pulling

on the reins in a flash.

"Riders coming in," a sentry shouted from the nearby barn's rooftop. "Looks like Abe Pomelos and two of his men."

Mack acted instantly, motioning for his crew to spread out and prepare for an attack. Katherine overrode his concerns. "Wait! It's okay. He wouldn't just ride in like the welcome wagon if they were up to any shenanigans. Especially with only two guns."

The ranch's second in command didn't like it but heeded his boss's command.

Abe galloped up the lane, flanked by two of his riders and slowing their pace to a gentle trot as they entered the courtyard. The rival rancher scanned the gathering of mounted hands and shook his head. "Looks like we got here just in time," he said to Katherine. "You look like you're heading out to look for trouble."

"You had to have seen the fires last night, Abe. I want to see the valley with my own eyes," she tersely replied.

Nodding his understanding, Abe adjusted his hat and delivered the bad news. "The house is gone, Katherine. We rode along the north ridge on the way here. It's a complete loss."

"Damn it!" she spat, "I knew it in my heart, but... those sons-ah-bitches are going to pay for that. I swear it."

"That's why I'm here," Abe said. "One of my ranch hands just got back from Meraton and has heard of that Bishop fellow we met yesterday. I thought you might be interested in what he had to say."

"Go on."

"It seems this Bishop has quite the reputation as an enforcer, rabble-rouser, and hired gun. According to my man, he was involved in that massacre of U.S. Army troops last summer. He's also been given credit for shooting up no less than three towns, and he sports quite a few notches on his gun barrel. He's known far and wide as a stone cold killer."

Tilting her head, Katherine seemed pensive, contemplating the Intel. "Kind of fits now that I think about it. He drove up to your place in that van like he owned the entire county. I knew that man's swagger was a sure sign of trouble."

"It gets worse," Abe continued. "It seems Bishop's wife is a big shot with the Alliance down in Alpha. That's supposedly how he gets away with the killing... she protects him, even spins some of his deeds into positives for the government. Somehow she even managed to get his name cleared after all those National Guardsmen were murdered."

"So, he's not only ruthless but well-connected politically," Katherine observed. "Those are the worst kind. Maybe we should contact Sheriff Watts and see if he applies the law equally to all."

Abe disagreed, "Won't do no good. From what I gather, Bishop is his own law. Hell, one rumor has it that Sheriff Watts is even on the wife's payroll."

"Figures," the lady rancher barked. "I never have liked Watts. Makes sense that he's on the take."

For a moment, Katherine sat and pondered the information just received. Finally refocusing on Abe, she stated, "Our dispute over that land is a family matter. We made a mistake yesterday by not stopping that Bishop fellow right in his tracks."

"So far I follow," Abe replied.

"We need to join forces and run them off. If even half of what you heard is true, the Alliance didn't send their henchmen up here for no reason. If they control that valley, then eventually they control both of our spreads. We can't let that happen."

Now it was Abe's turn to think things through. After a bit, he countered, not quite buying into the lady's open-ended plan. "Let's say for a moment I do help you push them off. Then what?"

"Then we'll settle our differences afterward the best way we can... cross that bridge when we come to it. Right now, there's one big-ass ogre blocking the way, and we need to deal with him."

It took Abe a bit to consider all the angles, but he finally agreed. "I'll meet you at the north pass in an hour with 25 men. We'll ask them to leave, and if they don't, we'll help 'em along."

"We'll be there."

Bishop found the perfect outcropping to observe the basin oasis below. After double-checking that the sun would not reflect off the optic, he began studying the men who'd done their best to kill him just last night.

Only two of the shooters were visible from his angle, one man on sentry duty watching the backdoor game trail Bishop had used to escape just a few hours ago. The other fellow was eating breakfast, reclining in the shade of a small oak.

The house had burned to the foundation, a second patch of smeared earth not far from the old barn. All three of his team's pickups were still right where the Alliance men had parked them.

Also, a white panel van was now parked directly alongside the lane leading from the road. Bishop was sure at least nine or ten men had pushed his team out of the valley, and there was no way all of them could've arrived in that single truck. It was a puzzle, but not an important one.

Bishop began a slow, methodical search of the terrain, certain that any commander as competent as the one that had kicked their asses last night would have posted more than one sentry. Where were the rest of his men?

Less than 20 minutes later, motion on the opposite side of the canyon drew Bishop's attention. An image of dozens of horsemen soon filled his optic.

"This can't be good," he whispered, counting at least two dozen armed riders.

Then Katherine Baxter came into the Texan's view, she and an older man obviously in charge of the mounted brigade.

It wasn't only Bishop that noted the newcomers. Men were now moving in the valley, the Texan counting four individuals rushing for cover. *Four?* He thought. *Did we hurt them that badly last night?*

Evidently, Katherine had learned a hard lesson from the schooling Bishop and his team had given the rancher two nights before. Rather than come in from a single charge, her men split into several small groups and began moving off in different directions. *Smart,* Bishop thought. *Don't bunch up like before. Approach the target from multiple vectors.*

After watching her riders begin their descent, Miss Baxter and the older gent spurred their mounts and rode directly toward the valley at a measured pace. Halfway down the trail, she raised a white flag.

"They want to have a powwow with the shooters," Bishop whispered, now completely puzzled by the string of events. The only logical explanation he had come up with for the men who'd attacked his SAINT team was that they were a bunch of mercenaries under contract to the ranchers. Now, that reasoning didn't make sense. Why would Kathy need a white flag to speak with her own hired guns? Why bring so many men? Why split up like they were preparing for trouble?

Wanting answers, Bishop decided to move closer. Given the men who occupied the valley were now completely distracted by the oncoming ranchers, he thought it was worth the risk to move a bit further down the trail.

He found the grenade booby trap right where he'd left it.

"Maybe we did hurt them worse than I thought," he mumbled. "That's why they didn't pursue us this morning. They're shorthanded."

Bishop continued slowly, working his way through the thick underbrush until he was only 20 yards from the burned out shell of the old house.

One of the shooters rose from his fighting position and began his march toward Katherine and her white flag. Bishop knew instantly the now-exposed man was in charge of the team that had taken the valley last night. He held himself with the confidence of command, his step the measured gait of a military officer.

When Miss Baxter and her fellow rider were within earshot, the commander raised his palm to signal that they were close enough. The two riders heeded, reigning their mounts to a halt.

Katherine's voice carried across the quiet valley, "I'll come right to the point," the lady began. "I want you and your Alliance thugs out of here. Right now."

Bishop couldn't hear the response, but it obviously wasn't what Kathy wanted to hear.

"I don't give a shit," the woman barked in retort. "We know who you are, Bishop. We know your reputation as a murdering marauder and enforcer for those power hungry hooligans down in Alpha. Now I'm only going to ask one more time. Pack up and get out, or we'll move you out."

For a moment, the Texan thought he was hearing things. "Did she just call that man by my name? What the hell? Are there two of us walking around with the same weird handle? Poor guy."

The man sitting next to Katherine now spoke, "We don't recognize the Alliance's authority, Bishop. Nor do we need your help. We didn't know who you were yesterday when you offered to move those squatters off our property. That aside, we never expected you to burn the place to the ground. Now, why don't you and your henchmen head on back to Alpha before more people get hurt?"

The real Bishop was stunned. The man talking to the ranchers was an imposter, either by accident or intent. The Texan's head was spinning.

The conversation with the riders ended with Katherine snapping a harsh, "You've been warned." She and her mate pivoted their steeds and began riding away. When they were near the far side of the valley, Katherine dropped the white flag to the ground.

A moment later, the thunder of hooves sounded from all directions, a dozen cowboys charging the four men surrounding the burned-out home. The report of multiple rifles quickly followed.

Bishop soon realized that the riders charging up the valley were a feint... a distraction... a head fake. The majority of Katherine's men had dismounted and were now firing from the surrounding rocks. They were using cover with braced firing positions. "Smart," Bishop whispered. "Very smart, old gal."

The defenders fought like they had against Bishop's team, two riders falling, and another shooter in the rocks screaming out in agony as he was hit. Still, there was no question in the outcome, the numerical superiority of ranch hands was overwhelming.

The hailstorm of accurate bullets quickly began taking a toll on the four men trying to hold the valley. Bishop saw one fall in the first volley, another go down less than a minute later.

The riders circled after their initial pass and then charged again. This time, with the defenders reeling, their speed and numbers came directly into the fray.

Bishop watched a group of riders pass right in front of his position, one of the men shot out of the saddle as a bullet tore through his chest.

It was over in less than two minutes, the rancher's forces now circling, checking the dead and wounded.

The Texan saw an opportunity to retrieve one of the trucks his team had left behind. The valley was a swirling mess of horseflesh, downed men, and general confusion in the aftermath of the battle. In a few seconds, he was out of his load vest and hat.

Waiting until no one was in the immediate vicinity, he darted out of the brush and to the man lying nearby. Bishop scooped up the cowboy's hat and lever-action rifle and then walked with purpose toward the dead fellow's nearby horse.

The animal was a bit suspicious of the stranger, but Bishop managed to grab a handful of reign, and then began leading the mare toward the pickups. He said a prayer that no one had snatched the keys from the sun visors.

Keeping the horse between himself and the majority of the surviving ranchers, Bishop continued with his stolen hat low, eyes darting here and there, ready to mount up and ride like hell if discovered. At worse, he could use the horse to help transport Grim.

No one seemed to be paying attention as Bishop passed close to a large cluster of the victorious cowpokes. That's when he noticed they'd taken one of the defenders alive.

The man who Bishop knew was in charge of the mystery team was on his knees, several of Kathy's men pointing their weapons at the captive. The Texan could see blood pouring from the prisoner's scalp.

"I tried to warn you," Katherine taunted. "I tried to end this without more bloodshed. Now we have to dig more graves. I should probably kill you right here and now... get it over with."

The older man who'd accompanied the lady rancher stepped forward, placing a calming hand on her shoulder. "He might have value," Bishop heard. "Don't forget his wife is some big shot down in Alpha. He might be a good card to have up our sleeve."

The Texan kept walking but slowed his pace. *They are talking about Terri and me*, he realized. *What the hell is going on?*

The captive said, "My name isn't Bishop. I told you that to scare you. My real name is...."

One of the surrounding ranch hands stepped in and barrel-whipped the prisoner before he could finish, growling a harsh, "Shut up, you lying sack of shit!"

Evidently, the blow was delivered with more force than intended, the captive falling over onto the grass and no longer moving. Katherine didn't seem to care.

"Tie him up and take him back to our bunkhouse," she ordered. "Abe is right. He might be a good bargaining chip."

A flurry of activity followed as two of the ranch hands rushed to execute her orders while others gathered weapons and bodies, and tended to the wounded.

Bishop reached the nearest pickup, opening the door as if someone might be hiding inside. The keys were still there.

After making sure no one was in the immediate vicinity, he smacked the horse on the ass and then pointed toward the cliffs, screaming, "Hey! Hey! I just saw one of them running that way!"

The Texan didn't wait to see how many heads turned in the direction of where he was pointing. In a flash, he was behind the wheel, hitting the ignition and flooring the gas.

Gravel, dirt, and dust flew from the back tires as he raced down the lane, leaving a group of bewildered, startled ranch hands in his wake. Bishop kept low, his eyes barely able to see over the dash, but not a single shot was fired in his direction.

He turned south onto the county road that fronted the valley, speeding in Butter's direction. A few miles later, he spied an excellent spot to hide the truck.

Taking the keys with him, Bishop began hiking toward his teammates, wadding up the western hat and shoving it in his pack. Butter might shoot him if he approached the nervous kid while wearing the disguise.

Bishop felt like Santa Claus on Christmas morning, so happy was Butter to see his leader alive. "I heard the shooting, sir, and I thought for sure they'd caught you spying on them," the big kid gushed, embracing the Texan in a rib-crushing hug. "I can't tell you how glad I am to be wrong, sir."

After realigning his spine, Bishop relayed the events that had just occurred in the valley, including the part about the mysterious imposter.

A pained expression crossed Butter's face, "I know some people don't agree with our SAINT team's missions," he confessed. "When I worked at Pete's bar, I'd tell people I was training to work with you guys, and some folks would get a little mouthy. I guess rumors, gossip, and exaggerations can spoil the best intentions or results."

The Texan thought about his man's comments, for a moment wondering who on earth would have enough gumption to get mouthy with the huge kid. Shaking off that unproductive line of thought, he continued, "There are still citizens of the Alliance who believe I killed all of those National Guardsmen not far from this very spot. It's like we used to say about the Internet – haters are going to hate. The apocalypse wasn't enough of an event to modify human nature."

Grim's weak moan snapped both of them back to reality.

Butter, believing his boss had fallen to gunfire in the valley, had already constructed a makeshift drag-stretcher. Bishop admired the craftsmanship, citing that it would be perfect to haul the contractor back to the waiting pickup.

Constructed of two wrist-thick saplings and a webbing of paracord between, Bishop was proud of his man for having enough foresight to make the gurney large enough to not only handle Grim, but his pack as well.

An hour later, the two upright SAINT members were carrying their wounded comrade out of the rocks. It was a hot, difficult trail back to the road, but nothing compared to what they would have had to endure walking all the way back to Fort Davidson cross-country.

As they scrambled, climbed, slid, skidded, and hauled Grim toward the truck, Bishop had time to reflect on what he'd seen in the valley that morning.

The ranchers were obviously pissed about the house being burned to the ground. The Texan didn't blame them but figured there was more at play than just the loss of a home that neither clan used for its primary residence.

Watts had been very clear – the conflict was over the water that flowed through the surrounding property. That's what they had been fighting over for decades. So why have such a harsh

119

reaction to the fire, real Bishop or pretender?

And who was this imposter? *Now, it is true that Terri does have a great pair of legs... but that aside... who the hell would want to change lives with me?* Bishop mused.

The Texan's initial thoughts gravitated towards a group of opportunists, roaming the countryside looking for a place to settle, or leverage for financial gain, or just ramble around scavenging for survival. They could have heard about the SAINT teams. His name was unusual and thus easy to remember.

That reasoning, however, didn't fit with the skill, equipment, and organization the strangers had shown as they had pushed Bishop's team out. The Texan hadn't seen anybody fight like that since Deke and his group of Darkwater contractors had tried to take the ranch so long ago.

The Alliance was full of rugged, capable men and women. Merely surviving the collapse often required some level of skill with a firearm and the willpower to use it. Often, it was the bold, aggressive sorts who prevailed. The meek had not inherited the earth – or at least not the part labeled Texas.

The team that attacked Bishop had been different. They were professional fighters, disciplined and experienced. Everything from their controlled usage of ammunition to their coordination of movement led the Texan to believe they were most likely a unit that had either trained or served together in a combat zone.

Why *that* specific ranch at *that* specific time?

They found the pickup right where Bishop had left it. Grim was quickly slid into the bed, Butter riding in the back to make sure his friend was comfortable.

As Bishop drove toward Fort Davidson, he continued trying to solve the mystery.

Even if a team of former military men had banded together, it was still a troubling coincidence. They had bypassed Grim's web of trip lines as if the booby traps had been anticipated, maybe even expected. Obviously, Bishop and his team had been scouted before the assault had begun. It was almost as if the imposter and his men knew the SAINT members were there. But how could that be? Bishop shook his head to clear the cobwebs, afraid that the heat of the desert was causing erratic thinking. *Not the time to get on some paranoid tangent,* he told himself. But where was the logic in all of this?

Now, all of the attackers were dead but one, and he was in Katherine's custody. Why hadn't she killed the man outright? What was all this talk about using the prisoner in negotiations? The list of unknowns kept piling up, and Bishop didn't have any answers.

A bump in the road diverted Bishop's attention to his comrades in the pickup's bed. A quick thumbs up from Butter assured the driver that his passengers were handling the trip as best as they could. But there was no doubt; if his friend were to survive, he needed the attentions best delivered on an operating table. Bishop knew that his primary concern right now had to be getting medical attention for Grim, providing a safe trip to Davidson.

But at the same time, the puzzle before him begged to be solved.

One thing was for certain, if the man detained by the Baxter ranch hands died, there most likely would never be any resolution to the Texan's multitude of questions.

His inner voice kept nagging him about the element of his identity. An undeniable benefit of a post-collapse environment absent electronic banking, email, on-line ordering, and credit cards was the elimination of identity theft from a man's list of daily concerns. Or so he thought.

What really troubled the Texan was the fact that a man claiming his name was being prosecuted for Bishop's past sins... or perceived wrongdoings. As the pickup approached the outskirts of Fort Davidson, that dawning, little epiphany troubled Bishop greatly.

While he produced his credentials at the Fort Davidson guard's outpost, he combed the corners of his mind for the captive's exact words. He envisioned the prisoner's quivering voice saying, "My name isn't Bishop. I told you that to scare you." *What the heck did he mean by that?* the Texan wondered. While he appreciated a little respect as much as the next man, why should his name strike fear in any honest heart?

From what he had overheard, Katherine and Abe had a bone to pick with the Alliance and more specifically with the man they thought was Bishop. Words like henchmen, murdering marauder, thugs, and other derogatory terms had come spewing out of the ranchers' mouths. *Why?* Even for West Texas, those were some pretty strong accusations.

Yes, he'd been involved in a gunfight or two. Sure, the SAINT team had run into the occasional trouble here and there. But, for the most part, Bishop thought he'd acted honorably the vast majority of the time. *Haters are going to hate*, he repeated.

He made up his mind. There was only one way he was going to get to the bottom of this.

As Bishop watched Grim being loaded into the county's only functional ambulance, Grim started grumbling at the two EMT's for their rough handling of his sensitive carcass. The Texan nodded with a knowing smile - his friend would be okay. He'd be in

Alpha soon, undergoing surgery in a matter of hours.

"I want you to go with him," Bishop informed Butter. "I'm going to poke around that valley some more before I head back home."

"But... but sir... by yourself?"

"I'll be very careful. Some man is walking around using my name, and I want to find out what he's up to. I have a very bad feeling about all this. Besides, Nick, Sheriff Watts, and Terri need a full briefing on what's going on. Tell them to give me two days, and if I'm not in touch by then, send in the cavalry. Got it?"

"Yes, sir. Be safe, Mister Bishop. You're the best man I've ever known."

Chapter 8

Hunter, for some unknown reason, had slept in. Mom thought it was a miracle or at minimum a sign that it was going to be the grandest of days.

With the Alliance's new policy now being distributed all across the territory and a few extra hours of sleep, Terri was in the best of moods as she pushed her son's buggy toward the Alpha courthouse.

She needed to go to the ranch for additional clothing and to check on the homestead. Neither she nor Bishop had been home for quite some time.

Nick, sporting his typical overprotective reaction, had insisted that Terri take at least one security man along. "I wouldn't feel right about a young lady and her child traveling by herself *before* everything went to hell, let alone after," he'd said. "Stop by the courthouse, and I'll assign a man to drive you out."

In the end, Terri had agreed, secretly thankful for the escort and protection. Hunter could be a handful at times, and a distraction was the last thing she needed while venturing into the desert. While she was sure everything was fine, a girl just never knew.

At Main Street, she decided that intruding on the inner workings of government could wait, choosing instead to depart on a quest to find something yummy and sweet. While donuts were still uncommon, cakes and other treats were often available. She'd let somebody else make her a cup of tea for a change.

"We're going to spoil ourselves today," she informed a smiling Hunter. "You dad is out playing with his friends and their guns, so we're going to get our share of the good life. I promise you'll like chocolate icing. It's a gift from God."

Mother and son meandered casually down the sidewalk, stopping a few times to window shop or greet a passerby. The weather was cooling off, the sky a royal blue, and there wasn't a single thing on her calendar with a deadline. Paradise.

A handbill mounted on a nearby utility pole advertised a bake sale to raise money for the Alpha Elementary School. "Perfect!" Terri said to Hunter. "We can shop for goodies and meet some of your future teachers and friends."

For his part, Hunter seemed in agreement with the plan, flashing a toothless grin and cooing as Terri knelt and examined his diaper.

Pivoting the buggy and reversing course, Terri made

straightaway for the chocolate treats. As she paced the short distance, the first dark cloud of the day drifted into the mother's mind. Bishop had fought inside the very school building that was now hosting the fundraiser. That was the day the president had been killed, setting off a sequence of events that, even to this day, made her shudder.

She pushed away the memories, determined not to let the past foul what was turning out to be the best weather of the year so far. Bishop and she had survived, and that was all that mattered.

It wasn't easy to clear her head of the negatives.

Seeing her husband arrested, on his knees, handcuffed, and accused of heinous crimes was an image no loving wife ever wanted to catalog. Waiting for traffic to clear at an intersection, she longed for the days when a girl's wedding album and family portraits were the most vivid memories.

The worst of it all hadn't been the threats to Bishop's freedom. Nor was it the lonely nights when he was off on some dangerous trek. How many times had she stared out the camper's tiny window, absolutely convinced her man would never come home?

No, by far the mental pictures that were burned the deepest… the ones that would haunt her forever… were the bodies.

Hunter somehow managed to eject his favorite blanket overboard at that moment, the act followed by a hearty chuckle from the stroller's cockpit. It obviously was a major accomplishment, the boy giddy with his success.

Terri stopped to retrieve the worn security-cloth, exchanging the now-soiled unit for a spare she kept in the diaper bag. Kneeling to face the boisterous young man, she gently reprimanded the lad, "We're not going to play this game, Hunter. This is the last clean one I've got until I can do a load of wash."

She passed the blanket to her son's eager, outreached hands. In a flash, with a squeal, it was sailing over the edge.

Terri managed to catch the flying cloth before it hit the ground, her quick movement adding to the boy's delight. "A<i>ugggh!</i> You are as hardheaded as your father," she scolded. "No."

Hunter seemed hurt by the rebuke, his frown deepening when mom held the blanket close to her chest as if she wasn't going to return the projectile.

After a bit of fussing, she again handed it over. Hunter hugged and snuggled the article, and then tossed it with glee.

"You little turd," Terri said, trying hard to keep a straight face while pretending as if she wasn't going to return the blanket.

"Having trouble with the men in your life?" a voice behind Terri questioned. It was Chase.

Rolling her eyes, she responded, "Of course. What woman doesn't?"

The ambassador smiled, spreading his arms wide, "What a glorious morning for a walk."

"Hunter and I were just on our way to the school bake sale. I promised him a treat with chocolate icing."

Chase peered up and down the street, a puzzled expression crossing his face. "Bake sale? Seriously?"

"Sure, why not? It is a great way for them to raise money. They're trying to start a centralized textbook exchange."

It was clear from his expression that the diplomat didn't get it.

Terri handed her son back the blanket while issuing a stern warning to Hunter. She really didn't want to be bothered at the moment, but then considered that it was now her job to act as a liaison. Besides, she could use the opportunity to show him a small part of what the Alliance was about. "Come on, you can walk with us and see for yourself," she offered.

As they ambled toward the school, Terri explained. "Books are a valuable commodity these days. They're not making any more and probably won't be for a while. As the recovery continues, reading about how to grow a crop, fix an electrical appliance, or repair a car's brakes is often the only option people have for problem solving."

Chase shrugged, "Makes sense. I suppose if there aren't any surviving repairmen in your town, and no phone service to call someone, it would be do-it-yourself or do without. But I still don't see what that has to do with the school?"

"Our schools have been forced to change their curriculum from the old days. Yes, we still have reading, writing, and math, but we also have to teach practical skills. Our 4th graders learn how to grow vegetables. In the 6th grade, there is a class on small engine repair. The problem is finding enough books. Someone came up with the idea of starting a centralized book repository where school systems from all around the Alliance could trade, swap, buy, and sell with each other and the general public at large."

Chase didn't seem impressed. Nodding toward Hunter's stroller, he chided, "I'm not so sure I'd want my child's traditional education altered so drastically. What we teach to the young ones has been basically unchanged for decades."

Terri shrugged, "Really, there's no choice. A lot of parents didn't come out of the downfall in such great shape. Many still barely have enough to eat, and often larger families depend on the children to work. In some cases, the kids might be the only household members who can do manual labor. Remember, there's no Social Security anymore. No Medicare, or unemployment insurance as a safety net."

"So how have the handicapped, sick, and invalid citizens survived? Who fed and cared for them? Who is caring for them now?"

Stopping mid-stride, Terri turned and faced him. "They didn't survive, Chase. At least not very many. And those that did manage to live are getting by with the help of friends, family, volunteers, churches and other private organizations. Like I said, we have to teach as many people to be self-sufficient as possible, as quickly as possible. Those that can help themselves will hopefully have the bandwidth to help others."

"Can't the Alliance as a government help?" he asked, still mulling her responses around in his head.

"Yes, the council tries to make sure everyone has enough food at a minimum. But beyond that, there are simply not enough resources or manpower to recreate all of the services that existed before the collapse."

Chase rubbed his chin, "Some might argue that such a government's priorities are all wrong then."

A sly grin crossed Terri's face, "Others might say that the 'nanny state' was a big part of why it all fell apart before."

"Touché," Chase responded. "Still, wasn't it Pearl S. Buck who said, 'The test of a civilization is the way that it cares for its helpless members?'"

Grunting, Terri replied, "Yes, but she'd never experienced an apocalypse before. We have."

After giving Chase a moment to digest her words, Terri continued pushing the buggy. Chase remained silent but kept up.

After a few more strides, he said, "I'm sorry I sidetracked the conversation. I'm having a glorious morning, and should have known better than to start a conversation about politics. Check these out."

Terri stopped pushing and accepted a handful of photographs the ambassador had extracted from his jacket.

She saw a beautiful home sitting on a hilltop, the landscaping, although overgrown, had at one time been spectacular.

The next photo was of the backyard, a huge swimming pool and summer kitchen dominating the picture. The remaining images of the mansion were just as impressive.

"This is a beautiful home," Terri said, thumbing through the photos a second time. "Where is it?"

"One of the men Diana assigned to help with my relocation knew of it. I guess it's secluded, just a few miles outside Alpha. From what I understand, the owner didn't survive the downfall, and now the place is unoccupied. The people running the Alliance's housing assignments were saving it for someone with the resources to fix it up... bring it back to its original glory. I think I'm going to take the project on, and maybe even try to convince Washington that it would make an excellent embassy. Want to see it with me?"

Terri stood staring at the pictures of the dream home, a pang of jealousy rising in her chest. Ignoring Chase's direct question, she responded, "I bet it would take a small fortune to get everything back shipshape."

He waved her off, "I've been very lucky as far as money is concerned. I married well and have had some success in business. Fortunately, most of my assets survived the downfall, so I'm in pretty good shape, financially speaking. I wouldn't want to cause any marital rifts, but since Bishop is out of town, you should see it with me. After all, you are my liaison, right? Plus, I've always valued your opinion and taste. You could help me decide."

The rolling hum of an electric golf cart interrupted the conversation, Terri's heart sinking into her stomach when she turned and saw Nick, along with a filthy, grime-covered Butter racing down the street. Both approaching men had "that" look on their face.

Bishop! Something's happened to Bishop!

How many times had she dreaded the news? How many dreams had played out a crushed, dejected Nick informing the new widow of her husband's demise? How many nights had she sat, staring out the camper's window, waiting for her man to come home? Terri's hands started shaking, her legs suddenly as cold as ice.

The cart stopped at the curb despite Terri's deepest desire that it continue down the street and pass them by. Her first instinct was to pull Hunter from the stroller, but she couldn't move, couldn't force her legs to work.

Nick sensed her trauma immediately. "Bishop's okay, Terri. That's not why we're here."

A flood of relief poured over the wife and mother, her apprehension staggered by a tidal wave of respite. She started to take a step toward Nick but stumbled on unsure legs.

Nick and Chase caught her, strong hands helping to steady the still-reeling girl.

Then the polarity inside Terri's head reversed, a backlash of emotion welling up. Growling, and then striking Nick's chest with a clenched fist, her body was racked with sobs. "Don't you scare me like that!" she gushed between breaths.

The big operator pulled her close, mumbling, "Sorry we rushed up on you. Bishop's okay, Terri. Really... he's fine."

Then Butter was there, trying to be helpful. "I just left him a bit ago, Miss Terri, honest. He's not hurt or nothing," the kid offered, still a little confused about what had just happened.

Terri finally composed herself, sniffing and drying her eyes, now more embarrassed than anything. "It's okay, guys. I don't know what came over me."

The three men stood for a while, giving her a minute. Butter occupied the time playing with Hunter, who seemed enthralled by the equipment on his playmate's load vest. The image brought Terri back to the moment. "So if Bishop's okay, why are you here?"

"There's a problem, and it involves you in a way. Grim's been hurt and is in surgery, but he should be fine. Diana wanted to bring you in on the situation, and more specifically, what to do about it."

"We were in one heck of a fight, Miss Terri," Butter offered. "The men who attacked us... well... Bishop said to tell you they were almost as good as Deke's team. Real professionals. We barely got out of there with our asses... err... sorry... our lives."

Nick continued, "And the leader of this group of strangers claims to be Bishop. *Your* Bishop."

"What? Who would... why.... I don't get it?" Terri stammered, still trying to grasp it all.

Nick grinned, "And now you know why we came rushing up so rudely. Again, I'm sorry about that. I should know better."

Terri waved him off, and then put her arms around the huge operator's neck, pulling him down for a forgiving peck on the cheek. "It's okay. I shouldn't be little Miss Paranoid. We're good."

It was the only time Butter had ever seen his boss flush red.

Terri pointed toward Hunter and explained, "We were just on our way to the elementary school bake sale. I probably didn't need the calories anyway. I'll meet you back at the courthouse."

"Bake sale?" Butter said, his attention perked. "Like in cakes and pies and stuff?"

Terri nodded with a sly grin, "Uh-huh."

"If it will help you, Miss Terri, I'll volunteer to take Hunter to the sale. He and I can check it out," Butter rushed.

Nick tried to restrain his chuckle, "Umm... Butter... shouldn't you be thinking about a shower before you go shopping?"

The young man sniffed his armpit and grimaced, then his head turned toward the school and its promise of treats. "You know, I'll just take the little tyke with me and clean up a bit... before we head over to the bake sale. I can bring him over to the courthouse after we're done."

Mom nodded, "Okay, Butter, but not too much for the little guy. I don't want to take care of a fussy fella with a stomachache tonight. Hear?"

"Yes, ma'am."

In a flash, Butter was behind the stroller, hustling toward what Terri knew would be the quickest shower in the history of bathing. As her son and the ranch hand rushed off, she could hear Butter preparing his little buddy for the experience, "We'll try some apple pie first, Hunter. Then we'll move on to sugar cookies, if there are any. Not to worry, though, blackberries are in season, and there is nothing finer than...."

Nick shook his head, "I remember when I could eat like that. The citizens of Alpha will be lucky if there's enough left to feed a church mouse after that kid's done."

By the time Bishop returned to retrieve his gear, the basin was unoccupied.

He'd heard Katherine Baxter instruct her foreman to take their captive back to the bunkhouse and assumed her victorious cowpokes had retired to that location.

Retreating back into the rocks and out of sight, the Texan inventoried his kit, made a quick meal, and pondered the next move.

Only a few miles away was a man being held prisoner... and most likely either about to face his maker or find himself a pawn in hostage negotiations with the Alliance. A big part of the imposter's predicament was due to the fact that his captors thought he was Bishop.

The real Bishop was troubled by that detail.

Like most men, he didn't embrace the thought of leaving enemies in his path's wake. Sure, the men who are forced to live by the gun aren't going to navigate their days without impacting others. Bishop, however, carried a clean conscious that his acts had been justified, either for his personal protection or for the greater good of society.

Taking human life isn't a natural act, and virtually every aspect of the Texan's existence was affected by his past. He'd left more than his share of widows and orphans... had been forced to pull the trigger far too many times for any one man.

Yet, in every single case he'd eventually resolved his damaged, nagging soul. It had been his life or theirs. His choice had been to let innocents die... or put down the man in his sights. Terri, Pete, Diana, Nick, or people he didn't even know would have died... or been subjected to some variation of hell on earth.

The Texan's mind drifted back to the bugout from Houston and the bridge over the Brazos River. He'd killed some of the men holding that bridge, and he had no regrets. They were the few preying on the many, evil souls who had lost their humanity. Wolves, really, nothing but guiltless predators harvesting the game animals around them. Should he feel remorse over eliminating such beasts?

He remembered Sarah Beth, the college girl he stumbled across in Alpha, living off of dove eggs and whatever she could scavenge. The Goulish had tried to gang rape her. After satisfying their needs, she was to be sold as a sex slave to convicts who ran the town. The Texan had ended their lives and felt no remorse over the bloodletting.

Bishop shook his head, squelching the parade of memories. He'd already watched each episode a dozen times, already replayed the events where blood had stained his hands. It wouldn't do any good to repeat the process again.

Still, the revelation that his fellow citizens hated his name and reputation bothered the Texan. Why did they think he was some sort of monster? What was driving their anger to the point of violence? As far as he knew, his path hadn't crossed any of those involved.

For a moment, the Texan thought he knew the answer. Fear. It was the only piece that made the puzzle whole. The ranchers were frightened of the man they knew as Bishop.

That, however, didn't make a lot of sense.

The Texan knew the type of people he was dealing with, well aware that it really wasn't one man or one gun that terrified people like Katherine or Abe. They were hearty souls who had survived the collapse and all of the hardship that comes with earning a living in West Texas. These weren't meek individuals who shivered or ran when faced with adversity, whether it came from the barrel of a weapon, disease ravaging their herds, or an aggressive neighbor trying to dominate a limited water supply.

No, it had to be the Alliance that generated the rancher's reaction. Somehow, these people believed the new government in Alpha was out to do them wrong, and that was more troubling to the Texan than any personal accusations or notoriety surrounding his name.

For a moment, Bishop considered just walking away.

He'd accepted the job to help the sheriff while his SAINT team was on the mend and unable to fulfill its regular duties. Now, he was down another man until Grim recovered. Their primary objective, to keep the two ranches from starting a countywide range war, was no longer a viable concern. There had been a loss of life, but that hadn't been Bishop's doing.

"I should just go hop in the pickup and head for Alpha and Terri," Bishop whispered to the surrounding rock. "My part in this is over. I should let Diana and the Alliance brain-trust handle this situation from here on out."

The captive at the Baxter ranch had tried to assassinate Bishop and his team. There'd been no warning, parlay, white flag, or discussion. They'd introduced themselves with a sneak attack, offering only a high-velocity greeting, and had made it clear that killing the basin's occupants was their goal. The Texan thought Katherine's prisoner deserved what he got while in the fuming landowner's custody.

Yet, some instinct in Bishop's core wouldn't allow him to bail and return home.

There was little doubt in the Texan's mind that Kathy's prisoner was a professional soldier... or at least had been at one point in time. Their assault had been impressive from a purely objective point of view. It was extremely unlikely the U.S. government had sent in active duty military to take one small valley in the heart of Alliance territory. That left Bishop with only one logical conclusion – hired guns.

Who would do such a thing and why? The seemingly endless, rolling parade of questions bombarded him, frustrating Bishop's already overworked brain.

One thing was certain – he wasn't going to get any answers by packing up his toys and going home. He needed to "interview" Katherine Baxter's captive. That man was at the center of the dilemma, and any help from Alpha might arrive too late to save his life.

Even if Nick and 100 men showed up at the Baxter spread this afternoon, the irate ranchers might execute the prisoner rather than turn him over. More people would surely die if the slightest little thing went awry during the confrontation. The body count could be significant, and that would likely result in even more upheaval and violence throughout the region.

No, Bishop needed act and do so quickly - before the entire affair spiraled out of control.

The light of dusk was fading as Bishop approached the sentry's position. The Texan had spent three late afternoon hours probing and scouting the spread's security perimeter, keeping stealthy and taking his time.

The configuration of guards surrounding the Baxter property wasn't the best Bishop had ever seen but was far from the worst. In fact, he'd had trouble detecting a couple of the cowpoke's well-hidden spots. The outposts were, however, intended to detect large groups of riders or dismounted assailants, not a single man with thermal imaging and patience.

His plan was simple – infiltrate the big spread, locate the hostage, and interrogate the man vigorously. While Bishop had a hundred questions tumbling around inside his head, he doubted there would be the time to completely debrief the fellow. If he was still alive. If the ranch hands hadn't beaten the captive silly.

After boiling it all down, Bishop had one critical piece of the mystery he needed to solve. Who had hired the professional riflemen to take the valley? That answer, if he could extract it from the prisoner, would unravel the entire affair.

Squeezing between a slab of lava rock and a small mound, Bishop wiggled his way to the best vantage point not already occupied by Baxter sentries. There was just enough light left to study the main house and the buildings surrounding the farmhouse headquarters.

Below, he could see what would be considered a typical setup for a working West Texas spread. In addition to the oversized barn and primary residence, the tin-roof outline of stables, storage sheds, bunkhouse, and a variety of other outbuildings came into the circle of Bishop's optic.

While the spread's layout offered no surprises, the activity below caused the Texan's eyebrows to seek his hairline.

Bishop had anticipated everything from a gallows being constructed to a sleepy, tranquil scene while the Baxter gang recovered from the battle and licked their wounds. Even a rope hanging from a tree with the hangman's noose swaying in the breeze was within the realm of possibilities.

Instead, the scene below reminded the Texan of an evacuation. Men were hustling to load a line of pickup trucks while others rushed here and there packing supplies. There was an urgency to the activity as if some pending natural disaster was about to strike the ranch.

"What the hell?" he whispered, studying the anthill of motion and resolve below.

Despite adding another layer to the deepening mystery, there was some good news. Bishop would be able to penetrate the chaos with little chance of being detected.

Quickly replacing his bush hat with the stolen cowboy model, Bishop took a moment to remove his vest and pack. He had to look like one of the hands... had to fit in.

With a grimace, he stashed his kit as well as his carbine. While the lever-action rifle scavenged from the valley's firefight was a quality piece, it couldn't produce the same rate of fire as his favorite blaster. It was a chance he'd just have to take, and if all went well, there wouldn't be any shooting anyway.

The Texan snaked his way through the rock formations and patches of scrub oak, descending onto the flats where decades ago some ancestor of the Baxter clan had broken ground for a home site.

As he approached the bustling main area, Bishop studied the men in the low light. If he stayed in the shadows and kept his brim low, it would be difficult for anyone to spot a stranger in their midst. He neared a group loading cardboard boxes into the back of a pickup, and soon was toting a load himself.

After depositing his cargo, Bishop moved off, circumventing the barn and main stables, working toward the bunkhouse.

"You there!" someone shouted, Bishop knowing instinctively that the challenge was aimed in his direction.

He didn't stop, forcing his head to remain forward, a purpose in his step just like those around him. *I belong here*, he kept telling himself. *Act as if you're just one of the hands*.

It didn't work.

"Hey! You... with the rifle... hold on a second!" came the commanding voice.

Bishop had no choice. He hesitated, looked around until he made eye contact with a barrel-chested man vectoring in his direction and then touched his chest with a gesture intended to mean, "Who? Me?"

"Yeah you," the ever-approaching man growled.

Bishop tensed, his eyes scanning for the nearest cover and eventual escape route. His grip on the old Winchester tightened.

Then a sickening bolt of fear shot through Bishop's stomach. He hadn't checked to see how many rounds were in the old rifle. He wasn't even sure if it was even loaded. *Hellfire and damnation,* he thought. *Here lies Bishop, stupid enough to start a fight with an empty gun.*

The big fellow strolled right up, now close enough to make

out facial features. *Knock his front teeth out with a butt stroke and run like hell*, Bishop schemed as the local eyed him up and down.

"I don't know you," the challenger said in a low tone. "You must be one of Abe's boys."

"Yes, sir," Bishop responded, thankful for the out.

"I thought Abe had agreed all of you would stay over by the corral. What are you doing here?"

"I was looking for the outhouse," Bishop lied. "I've had a touch of Montezuma's revenge in my gut lately," he continued, the second part absolutely accurate, as least at the moment.

The local eyed Bishop again, almost as if he was trying to match a face with a name. From across the courtyard, a voice interrupted the big guy's focus, "Mack? Mack? Anybody seen Mack?"

Turning his head to shout over a shoulder, Mack replied, "Be right there!"

He then returned to Bishop and barked, "I want all you Pomelos people to stay together. We don't need any old grudges causing a fight right now. You hear me?"

"Yes, sir."

"If you got a case of the shits, go dig a hole in the woods… hear?" Mack added, pointing a finger at Bishop's stomach.

"Yes, sir."

"Now get," came the last order before Mack pivoted and made for the distant summons.

Bishop exhaled deeply, taking a moment to let the tingling leave his limbs. That had been a close one.

Not wanting to risk Mack's wrath, Bishop ordered his legs to move, walking towards the corral as ordered. Fortunately, the bunkhouse was in the same general direction.

The sound of truck motors echoed through the ranch, one engine after another being started. Soon after, shouted voices and hustling shadows were everywhere.

"Everybody up to the main house," called out a voice of authority. "Come on now, get moving. Up to the main house."

Not wanting to stand out and curious as hell, Bishop began following the general flow of ranch hands making for the Baxter residence.

The Texan lingered back on the fringe of the gathering throng of men. He quickly estimated there were at least 60 cowboys present, all in a semi-circle and facing the front porch. Headlights from two pickups illuminated Katherine and two other men standing beside her.

The Baxter matriarch raised her hand to quiet the milling

crowd and then began speaking in a strong voice. "As most of you know, our men have been traveling the entire county today, spreading the word of a town meeting tonight in Fort Davidson. It is my intent to tell our neighbors and friends the truth about the Alliance and their land-grabbing scheme to seize private property."

She paused for a moment, scanning the sea of western hats and admiring faces. Low voices and murmurs wafted through the crowd, Bishop detecting a few, "You go, Miss Baxter," and "Damn right we need to spread the word," comments here and there.

"Your job," she continued, "isn't to bully, debate, or cause one iota of trouble. You all were witnesses to the corruption and evil that occurred in our valley over the last two days, and the people of this county need to hear the truth from your own lips. Is that clear?"

"Yes, ma'am," the choir of voices agreed.

"There is also a chance that the Alliance will attempt to take their enforcer back, perhaps even by force. We can't let that happen. This man is the key to making our case with the good people of this county. Let's load 'em up and head 'em out," she ordered.

Keeping his head low and moving toward the corral just in case Mack was watching, Bishop noticed a commotion at the front of the bunkhouse.

Four burly cowboys appeared, carrying a man in chains. Bishop knew instantly it was the leader of the force that had assaulted him in the basin – the imposter.

The Texan watched as they hauled the barely-conscious prisoner to a nearby hay wagon where he was secured using heavy rope. The man was still bleeding from the scalp, nose, and mouth, his clothing ripped and filthy. It was clear the fake-Bishop hadn't enjoyed the hospitality of the Baxter ranch.

"Shit," Bishop hissed, knowing his infiltration and risk had been for naught. There was no way he could get to the captive.

Again, a round of shouted orders and moving bodies rang over the area, "Load up! Come on now! We've got to get moving!"

Bishop spied a narrow gap between the toolshed and a pen. After glancing around to make sure no one was nearby, he rolled quickly under the fence and then crawled to the outbuilding.

After waiting for several seconds to make sure no one had noticed his movement, Bishop moved to the back of the small storage building and then sprinted toward the hills and the spot where he'd hidden his gear.

"I'm going to a town meeting," he announced to the rock as he began gathering his equipment. "And this time I'm going to make sure I've got a loaded weapon."

Chapter 9

It was easy to find Kathy Baxter's meeting. To begin with, Fort Davidson wasn't that big of a place. This, combined with the huge bonfire roaring into the night sky, made it easy for Bishop to locate the gathering.

For such a small berg, a surprising number of people were in attendance. Evidently, Katherine had been true to her word, as the lack of parking was a sure indication that many of the attendees had driven into town. Bishop had to abandon his pickup almost a quarter of a mile away.

There was a quiet anticipation among the people Bishop encountered as he walked toward the center of town, hushed voices and nervous laughter drifting through the calm Texas evening.

"Even the Fourth of July parade doesn't draw this many visitors," the Texan mumbled as he followed the crowd. "I should have gotten here early and opened a beer stand. Pete and I could have made a mint."

Next to the bonfire was the hay wagon, complete with the still-shackled prisoner. Bishop could see several people hovering around the captive, a few of the onlookers pointing and gawking like they were at a zoo.

Just as he reached the edge of the throng, Bishop saw someone helping Katherine into the bed of a pickup. Facing the crowd, she held both hands wide to quiet the low background of voices and announce that the festivities were about to begin.

"I'll get right to the point," she shouted over the onlookers. "As most of you already know, the Alliance out of Alpha... our supposedly elected government... is about to embark on a program that straightens out the mess of private property ownership in the wake of the collapse."

Kathy scanned the crowd, noting many of the heads were nodding north and south.

"We've all heard rumors and speculation about the rules and processes involved. I, as one of the county's largest landowners, had initially adopted a wait and see attitude. After the events of the last few days, that is no longer the case."

A rumbling shot through the crowd, Kathy's statement surprising several of the attendees. Obviously used to speaking to large groups, the lady rancher waited until her words had sunk in before continuing.

"Three days ago, we found squatters in the valley that separates the Baxter and Pomelos ranches. We were in the process of moving them out when a heavily armed Alliance SAINT team, led by a man who identified himself as Bishop, informed both Abe and me that they would take care of the problem for us. We agreed."

Scanning the crowd, Katherine paused for a breath, the fire in her eyes enthralling the listeners.

"The very next night, the old ranch home was burned to the ground by those men. They couldn't produce the squatters. They refused to leave the property, warning Abe and me to stay away or there would be violence."

The reverberations grew from the listeners, several people able to predict where Kathy was going.

"When we came back in force to claim what is rightfully ours, those Alliance thugs began shooting at us, killing several of our men. Their intent was clear; occupy that valuable land and its precious water. They intended to seize it for that so-called government."

The reaction from the crowd was growing sharper, more defined. Kathy's words were striking a sour cord with her neighbors.

"We've all heard what's coming out of Alpha," she said, raising her voice to a new level while sweeping an arm through the air. "Everyone knows that possession is going to be a huge part of the new law. But what good is any claim to ownership given what we've seen in the last three days? Any right is meaningless if the Alliance can send in heavily armed enforcers to take whatever they want."

Now she had them going, Bishop noting a couple of men on the fringe shaking angry fists in the air.

"I say we tell those heavy-handed, power hungry hooligans down in Alpha to stay out of Davidson County. I believe we should stand up for our rights as freeborn Americans! Let's band together to fight this evil, and keep our liberty and individual rights!"

The woman's energy was spreading through the throng, her words striking at the heart and minds that surrounded the bonfire.

Katherine's voice then returned to a less-rousing pitch, now projecting as a friend and neighbor. "But... don't take my word for it. Abe and I have brought along several eyewitnesses. Talk to our men one on one, look them in the eye, and make up your own minds."

With that and a helping hand from Mack, she hopped down from the wagon and began circulating among those closest to the makeshift podium.

Bishop was pivoting to leave, certain there wasn't anything he could do. His frustration was due to several different factors, not the least of which was the fact that the Alliance was getting a bad rap.

As he began strolling toward his truck, he noticed two men standing and watching the gathering. He recognized one of the men as a deputy.

Marching up to the pair, Bishop asked, "Do you know who I am?"

After studying the Texan for a second, the man nodded, "You're Bishop.... But then... who's that man the Baxter woman has tied up?"

"An imposter," Bishop replied. "How many men does Sheriff Watts have here?"

"Just us right now," replied the lawman. "We've asked for backup, but there're not that many men in this area."

Bishop rubbed his chin, an idea forming in his mind. "Do you know where the 11 men we captured at the old Baxter place are being held?"

""Yes, sir. We're holding them at the ranger station up by the interstate."

"Can you bring them here?" Bishop asked, his mind now rolling at high speed.

"Ummm... I guess. There are two deputies guarding them, and they both have trucks. I suppose we can get them here... but...."

Bishop cut the man off. "Go. Please. Bring them back here as soon as you can. I'm going to stop a lynching and maybe turn the tide of public opinion to the Alliance's favor."

The two deputies looked at each other and shrugged. "If you say so, sir. We'll be back in an hour or so."

"Hurry," Bishop pleaded. "The sooner, the better."

After watching the two lawmen rush for their car, Bishop jogged quickly to his own ride. Twenty minutes later, he'd substituted his cowboy garb with his full SAINT loadout, including carbine, armor, vest, and balaclava mask.

Bishop waited, watching the distant crowd as Kathy and her men circulated. When he thought it wasn't prudent to delay any longer, he began moving toward the hay wagon, mounting a steady, confident stride directly through the middle of the throng.

The first people that saw the Texan approaching simply stopped their conversations mid-sentence. A few managed to mumble, "Who the hell is that?" or similar inquiries.

Bishop was almost to the wagon when the first serious challenge occurred. It was Mack and one other man, "Who are you?"

the muscular foreman asked, stepping directly into the Texan's path.

"A concerned citizen," Bishop said calmly, sidestepping the roadblock of flesh. "Just a man who wants to exercise his right to free speech."

As Mack moved to intercept Bishop's maneuver, the Texan flicked the safety off his carbine, the metallic "click" unmistakable. It froze Kathy's man just long enough.

The Texan climbed up on the wagon and instantly the crowd drew silent. He held up a single piece of paper, and said in a strong voice, "This is a wanted poster printed by the Army a while back. We all saw them. They were everywhere, offering a reward for a man named Bishop. This prisoner up here beside me doesn't look anything like the picture of the man the military was looking for."

Bishop walked up and down the hay wagon's edge, holding out the old paper for everyone up front to view. After he'd passed the entire length, he gave a nearby onlooker the poster and said, "Pass it around. See for yourself."

As the real Bishop's picture began circulating, the Texan continued, "I was here the day the Alliance came into Fort Davidson and met with D.A. Gibson. I was also here when the trucks full of food arrived, delivered by those '*thugs*' from Alpha. Doesn't anyone else remember those '*power-hungry monsters*' delivering a doctor and first aid?"

Bishop scanned the crowd, noting that his words were having the desired effect. "And what about the electricity those '*hooligans*' from Alpha delivered for everyone – free of charge? What about the relocation for the homeless? Am I the only one who remembers all of those charitable acts?"

Just as several in the crowd were beginning to agree with Bishop's words, the throng parted, Katherine and four of her men making for the stage. "Who the hell are you?" she challenged, hellfire and brimstone behind her eyes.

"It doesn't matter who I am," Bishop retorted calmly. "I'm just another freeborn American, exercising my right to free speech. You're not against that. Are you, Katherine?"

"Why are you hiding behind a mask and a gun? Doesn't seem like the actions of an honest man."

Bishop ignored her questions, instead pointing toward the prisoner. "I know Bishop. That's not him. You're the one not being honest with these people."

The look on the lady rancher's face was as if Bishop had walked over and slapped her across the cheek. "How dare you call me a liar!" she shouted, pointing a shaking finger at the captive. "That man identified himself as such, a well-known enforcer and killer who works for the Alliance."

Bishop pulled off his hat, and then his mask. "Ma'am, I know he's not Bishop... because my name is Bishop. I don't know who you captured, Katherine, but it wasn't me."

Most people would've been at a loss for words, or knocked completely off their game. Not Katherine Baxter. After glancing back and forth between the real Bishop and the imposter, she immediately turned to the crowd and said, "This man is one of the squatters. He is a liar, and murderer. He is responsible for killing 11 of my men! We should hang both of them from the old oak at the courthouse."

Bishop just shook his head, "You're credibility isn't running so high tonight, Miss Baxter. I've never murdered anyone. I would have thought by now you'd know better than to make unfounded accusations."

"You killed 11 of my boys!" she shouted at the top of her lungs. Then pointing at Mack, she screamed, "Take this man!"

"Hold on there!" a voice from the edge of the mob demanded. "Are you talking about these 11 men?"

All eyes turned to see a large group of cowpokes being led by two deputies. Mack unintentionally answered his boss's question by rushing over and looking at new arrivals. "George? Red? You guys are alive? Praise be!"

The big foreman was soon joined by several of his crew, all of them shaking hands with their friends and coworkers now back from the dead.

Katherine was stunned, glaring back and forth between Bishop and her men. "If you're Bishop, then who is that?" she spat, pointing at the mystery prisoner.

"Now that's one hell of a good question," Bishop answered, walking over to the prone and bound man.

Pulling his knife, Bishop sawed through the thick rope bounding the captive's wrists and legs. The Texan knew the man at his feet was in trouble when his battered body didn't move or acknowledge its new freedom.

Kathy didn't like it, "What are you doing?"

"This man is almost dead," Bishop responded. "He's not going anywhere, except to see a doctor."

The Texan then looked at the two deputies, and said, "Carry him to my truck. I'm taking him to Alpha to see a doc."

It was all too much for the crowd, many of those attending completely confused by what they had just witnessed. Bishop detected it and quickly moved to the front of the wagon stage. "Please! Everyone! Please, listen to me. None of us know what the new Alliance process is going to entail. Doesn't it make sense to wait and see... to read the rules with your own eyes and *then* pronounce judgment? I'm sure it won't be perfect. I am positive it won't be some panacea or miracle cure. But... I am also just as sure that the intent behind it is for the good of the citizens of Texas and the recovery. Can we really ask for more from *any* leader during these difficult times?"

The vast majority of the crowd were nodding their heads north and south, Bishop's logic seeming to resonate with all but a few outliers.

Without another word, the Texan jumped off the wagon and hustled to catch up with the deputies and their gravely wounded cargo. "Put him in the bed. I'll get a blanket."

Returning a moment later with a poncho, blanket, and bottle of water, Bishop and the two lawmen did their best to make the captive comfortable.

Putting the water to the captive's lips, he managed a single swallow and then his eyes seemed to focus on the Texan. "Who are you?" Bishop asked.

"It doesn't matter," the guy croaked. "I'm not going to make it out of this one."

"Maybe. Maybe not. Do you have any family? Is there anyone we should get in touch with?"

"No," the sad voice replied.

"Why did you attack my team in the valley?"

There was a brief moment of confusion in the wounded man's eyes before Bishop's question finally registered. "That was you?"

"Yes, that was two of my teammates and me. Why? Who hired you? Why did you claim to be me... Bishop?"

The response was a coughing fit, a pink and red frothy foam draining down the captive's chin. When the convulsions finally stopped, the man's voice seemed weaker. "I was only following orders. My employer doesn't seem to like your Alliance much."

"Who hired you?" Bishop repeated.

There was no answer as the light faded from the injured man's eyes. One of the deputies tried to find a pulse, finally announcing, "He's gone."

Bishop grimaced, a wave of sadness overcoming all other emotion. The dead man lying in his truck might have been a mercenary, and there was little doubt he would have killed the SAINT team without mercy. Yet, the man had also been a wounded prisoner, helpless, without any recourse or ability to impact his status.

Capture was every soldier's worst nightmare. More than being wounded or killed, anyone who carried a weapon into a fight dreaded such an outcome. Bishop had experienced similar feelings dozens of times.

"Shit!" Bishop spat, turning to look back where Katherine and her men were loading into their trucks. "Damn it! That woman is the one who should be arrested for murder. Now we're back to square one."

After a quick shower, fresh clothes, and an embrace of his wife and child, Bishop's first priority was to check on Grim's condition.

Nick and Diana met Terri and him at the Alpha medical clinic.

The doctors had removed two hunks of shrapnel from Grim's leg and expected a full recovery. Infection, as was usual in the post-apocalyptic world, was still a serious concern. The patient was sleeping, his wife and daughter keeping watch and apparently handling the situation as best as could be expected.

Everybody scribbled a little message on a makeshift get-well card and left it by the recovering man's bedside. All of them promised to stop by later.

"They knew we were there," Bishop explained to Nick as the two couples walked back toward the courthouse. "I don't know how, but I'm convinced that whoever hired those shooters was well aware of the situation and my team's role."

Terri wasn't convinced. "How do you know that guy didn't tell the ranchers his name was Bishop just to cause panic? No offense, my husband, but you do have a wee bit of a reputation."

"I considered that, but these men were professionals, hired and equipped to do a job. They weren't the sort to namedrop or bluff. They didn't have to. If it had been some gang of vagabonds or drifters trying to snatch a prime piece of real estate, I could believe they would resort to such posturing. But not these guys."

Nick scratched his head, trying to figure it all out. "Sheriff Watts and some of his men knew what you were doing. The guys over at Fort Hood didn't know the location or mission profile, so they're clear. A few of my guys and I were up to speed, but I can't believe any of those folks would betray you or the Alliance."

"Should we delay the rollout of the new property law?" Diana asked, her voice far away in thought.

"I wouldn't," Terri responded. "This is just one isolated example, and if Bishop's is right, there was an outside influence stirring up trouble. Those rules are as fair and equitable as anyone could expect given the situation."

Nick grunted, "Even if we wanted to, I'm not so sure we could stop that juggernaut now. There must be 2,000 people spreading out across Texas to communicate the new rules. We've got radio broadcasts, town hall meetings, a whole string of presentations, and even the military and police spreading the word."

"Let's hope the general public reacts a little more favorably than our friends in Fort Davidson," Diana replied. "We can't handle widespread public unrest. The whole ball of wax will come apart at the seams."

The foursome continued their stroll, enjoying the cooler weather and clear night... all of them apparently deep in thought.

After a bit, Bishop paused and waited until his friends and wife gathered close. In a low voice, he said, "What bothers me the most is how believable Katherine Baxter's spin job came across. She basically rewrote recent history with negative accusations of the Alliance's role, and if I hadn't pulled off my little stunt, it would have worked."

"Why?" Diana replied. "To whose advantage is it to make us look like the bad guys?"

Terri nodded, "You know, I feel like sometimes I get the same reaction from Chase. It seems like our new ambassador looks at everything we're trying to accomplish as some sort of threat. It's almost like he expects the council to be these evil, power grabbing bunch of megalomaniacs."

Bishop waved his hand through the air at the mention of the diplomat, "That doesn't surprise me one bit. That inbreed is not to be trusted."

"Maybe you are right," Terri replied, ignoring the politically incorrect assessment about Chase's lineage, "but we can't discount that line of thinking. The more the recovery progresses, the less effort people have to spend on basic food, shelter, and security. The average Joe Nobody is going to have more time to dissect every move we make. I think Chase already expects us to be corrupt, probably because that is what he found in the world of professional politics before the apocalypse. Other folks might expect us to abuse our authority as well."

"Private property has always been the touchiest of subjects," Nick added. "Machiavelli wrote about it over 500 years ago. His book, *The Prince*, basically stated that a ruler could get away with murder, war for profit, consignment, outrageous taxation, and sleeping with every female in the village, as long as he didn't seize private property."

Sighing, Terri continued, "I dunno. I think it's more than just that. It's almost as if Chase is waiting for the power and authority to go to our heads. He keeps looking for proof that the Alliance is becoming authoritarian or some sort of brutal dictatorship."

"Power corrupts," Bishop added. "Always has and always will. The difference with the Alliance is that its authority is tenuous as best. I worked with Diana day and night the last few weeks, and her role is about as far away from a dictator as you can get. You poor woman," Bishop continued, smiling as his friend, "Anybody who thinks your office is the pinnacle of political desire should walk a mile in your shoes. I'm sure they would be rambling lunatics in a matter of days."

Diana smiled warmly, a twinkle of appreciation in her eyes.

The conversation was interrupted, the sound of a racing car engine drawing everyone's attention. Around the corner squealed a police car, its red lights flashing their urgent warning.

The two couples watched as the deputy raced down Main Street, the responding officer pulling a hard right turn at the next intersection. Before anyone could react, another squad car followed.

"Wonder what's going on?" Nick said, glancing at his mates. "Anybody want to walk over and be nosey civilians for a change?"

"Sure," Bishop replied. "I'm always up for a little excitement. My life is so routine and mundane, ya know?"

The foursome found the two flashing police cars parked outside a small office building that Nick recognized immediately as his doctor's office. "What the hell... I was just here yesterday."

The two officers then appeared, both of them holstering their weapons after clearing the interior. "No one is inside now, Doc. It looks like he left via one of the back windows," one of the lawmen stated. "Did you get a good look at the guy?"

"No, not really," replied the frightened physician. "I returned to get some forgotten paperwork off my desk. I heard a noise in the back and saw the burglar walking down the hall. It was dark, and he had his back to me. I ran over to the courthouse and asked one of the security men to radio for help."

"Come on inside with me, and we'll see what is missing," the deputy replied. "They were probably after prescription meds. We're seeing a lot of that lately."

"But I don't keep any medications here. Those are all down at the pharmacy in the safe."

"Yes, sir," nodded the deputy, "But criminals are stupid. They probably don't know that. Let's go check to see if they took anything. My bet is that you scared them off before they could dig around for anything valuable."

Terri subconsciously moved closer to Bishop, her hand checking the pistol at her belt. "Should we help the officers try and find the culprit?"

Bishop shook his head, "Naw. I've not had a lot of luck lately helping out law enforcement. We need to let the cops do their jobs. Besides, somebody might get shot if a bunch of us start poking around. They'll find him."

"I hope so," Diana shuddered. "Nothing worse than some creepy guy stalking around at night."

Nick remained silent, staring at the doc's office with a faraway look. His thoughts were being carried back to his last visit and the issues associated with his condition. It was a reminder the big man didn't need or want.

"You okay?" Diana asked, sensing his unease.

"Yeah... yeah, I'm good," he lied.

She started to challenge his statement but then reconsidered. Hooking arms, she said, "Let's head home. It's been one hell of a day, and tomorrow is going to be worse."

Nick's coffee seemed extra strong for some reason, the ex-operator frowning as he swallowed the first sip. It wasn't a good omen.

He was about to water down the steaming brew when a rap on his doorframe sounded. Looking up, he was a little surprised to see Chase McGuire standing at his office's threshold.

"Sorry to drop by without an appointment," the ambassador greeted, "but this visit is of an unofficial nature anyway."

"Oh?"

Chase entered Nick's small enclave, closing the door behind him without seeking approval. Nick decided, for the advancement of diplomatic relations, to let it go.

"I heard about the break-in at the doctor's office last night, and... well... I was out walking about the same time and spotted something quite troubling," Chase began.

"You should inform Sheriff Watt's department immediately," Nick replied, despite having his curiosity piqued.

"Normally I would, but given what I witnessed, I thought it best to come to you first."

"Go on."

"The big guy who works with Terri's husband... the same man I saw the night of our confrontation... I'm pretty sure I saw him running away from that office building last night, right before I heard the police cars responding."

Nick grunted at the absurdity of Chase's statement. "Butter? Seriously? You think that kid broke into the doctor's office?"

"I can't be 100% sure given it was dark and I only got a quick glimpse, but there aren't that many men walking around Alpha, Texas who are that big and that fast. I'm pretty confident it was him."

Nick rubbed his chin, trying desperately to control the belly laugh fighting to escape his throat. *No need to cause an international incident*, he thought.

"I'm sorry, Mr. Ambassador, but I'm having a little trouble believing that. Any of my SAINT team members could walk up to the doctor's house, day or night. Butter, or any of those men, would have no reason for breaking and entering."

Chase shrugged, "I'm just trying to be helpful. I'm afraid I'm in no position to speculate as to the reason why that man would do such a thing. What you choose to do with this information, however, is up to you."

"There is no reason why Butter would even consider such an act," Nick replied instantly. "That's why I'm having a little trouble taking this seriously. I'm sure it was someone else."

"The man's loyalty to Bishop is amazing," Chase continued. "That was clear the night we tangled. I was quite surprised he and the older guy... Grim was his name as I recall... didn't back down when you issued what sounded like a direct order."

Waving off the incident, Nick replied, "We had a little talk about that. SAINT team members face some of the most challenging conditions of all those who serve the Alliance. They tend to become an extremely tight-knit brotherhood. In the heat of the situation that night, I don't blame Grim and Butter for supporting their leader. Still, we had a clearing of the air regarding the chain of command."

Chase began to rise, a look of disappointment on his face. "I'll leave you to your calendar then," he said with a hint of exasperation. "Clearly I'm adding two plus two and coming up with five. You know your people, and I should just butt out."

Tilting his head, Nick said, "Mr. McGuire, I'm not much of a diplomat. I've been a fighting man most of my career and am not well versed in the subtleties of your profession or language. In my world, if a man has something to say, it's best to come straight out with it."

The ambassador seemed to ponder Nick's declaration for a

moment before retaking his seat. "Okay, I'll be blunt. I like you and think you are doing an excellent job with your responsibilities. I can say the same of Miss Brown. As an outsider, I see things a little differently than others, and I've become aware of certain troubling events."

"Go on."

"For example, my security men now work with your forces. My guys report to me that while you were in the hospital at Fort Bliss, Bishop was spending an inordinate amount of time in the company of Miss Brown. Now, what I've heard is purely secondhand, but you are familiar with security professionals and must realize that such men don't normally partake in gossip and wild rumor. I'm being told that Bishop's activities were completely inappropriate and had several members of Diana's protection detail concerned."

"That's ridiculous!" Nick snapped. "Bishop is my closest friend on this earth. I have put not only my life but also my only son's well-being in his hands numerous times. I'm well aware of his activities while I was away, and appreciate his helping Diana through a very rough time."

Chase held up both hands in mock surrender, "I meant no offense, nor have I heard a single word about Miss Brown accommodating his advances. I'm just the messenger, sir."

Nick half rose from his chair, the big man's anger showing in his intense gaze and red cheeks. "You'd better be careful of what messages you go around delivering, *sir*. If Bishop got word that you were spreading bullshit like that around town, I think you would have another confrontation on your hands... and I'm pretty sure you wouldn't survive it."

The ambassador didn't seem to be intimidated by Nick's ire. In fact, the big man's reaction appeared to have a calming effect. "I don't think my facts are bullshit, nor am I worried about your hot-headed friend. The Alliance is on the verge of obtaining incredible power, wealth, and control. We both know such prizes can corrupt the best of men. I'm merely pointing out a series of undisputed facts that, in my opinion, indicate the distinct possibility of treachery within your inner circles."

Nick wanted to throw Chase out of his office, to bounce the ambassador's ass right down the courthouse steps and onto Main Street. It took all of his discipline to remain seated and calm. "What sequence of facts? What treachery?"

"Please, think about this for a minute, Nick. I strongly advise you to open your mind and hear me out. Bishop's last two operations were, by all accounts, dismal failures. He specifically requested that you and Miss Brown stay away from Fort Davidson during the confrontation with the ranchers. Why? All of the supposed witnesses to the crux of his story are now dead, and the situation is far from resolved. Even if his actions during your hospitalization were honorable, the appearance of such inappropriate conduct could be very damaging. A true friend would have considered public opinion before spending the night... several nights... in Diana's private quarters."

Grunting, Nick decided to let the lunatic continue. *How far will this crazy bastard go with this shit?*

"Your friend's former boss, a man he worked for long before he met you, is now the President of the United States," Chase continued. "It was on Bishop's counsel to Miss Brown that I was given this very assignment. Has it ever occurred to you that your friend might not want Texas to succeed as an independent nation? Have you ever looked at his actions in that light? A man like that could be having second thoughts about his loyalties."

"And I suppose you think Terri is part of this subterfuge?"

Chase nodded, "Yes, in my conversations with her, I detect a very distinct edge to her words. I know Terri better than anyone, and I can say with certainty that she isn't confident in the path the Alliance is taking. Didn't she resign from an official position within the government just a short time ago?"

"Yes," Nick admitted. "She wanted to spend time with her family. I can certainly understand that."

"I see," the ambassador said, rising from his chair, aware that his concerns weren't being taken seriously. Chase turned to leave but then paused at the door, deciding to take one last shot at making his point.

"Nick, I know you think I'm insane or have some hidden agenda. In a way, I don't suppose I blame you. But please, look at this from my perspective. First, I hear official reports of Bishop's failures and unexplainable acts during his recent missions. Secondly, I know his men are absolutely loyal to him. Then there's the fact that I saw you leaving the doctor's office just a few days ago, and you were clearly troubled at the time. And now, last night, I saw this man Butter running away from the scene of a crime at that same office... where private information about your health is filed... information you clearly don't want to be made public. Am I really being absurd?"

Nick rose, somewhat stunned by how a man assigned as an ambassador could connect the dots in such a bizarre manner. Still, he had to humor the man. "No, you're not absurd, Mr. McGuire. I'll look into a few of the facts that's you've shared with me... ask a few questions. I appreciate your coming by."

After shaking hands and watching his unscheduled visitor

leave, Nick returned to his perch and thought about the oddity of it all.

"Bishop was right," he whispered, staring at the door. "That guy isn't to be trusted."

Still, Nick was troubled by the break-in. No matter how outlandish, the concept that someone could have been reading his private medical records was troubling. There were some things that were better left to patient-doctor privilege.

After checking his calendar, Nick marched into his assistant's office and said, "Can you reschedule my first two meetings? Something's come up. Oh, and which guesthouse is Butter staying in? I need to speak with him."

It had taken some convincing before Mack had allowed Sheriff Watts to inspect one of the dead strangers' vans.

The vehicle, like so many in the post-apocalyptic world, didn't possess license plates, an inspection sticker, or any sort of registration papers. Nor did the Alliance lawman have access to the vast network of state and federal computers database that had been so commonly used before the collapse.

That, however, didn't mean that Watts was completely helpless.

With the practiced eye, he circled the late-model panel van, taking note of various details. The first major clue to catch the sheriff's eye was the sticky outline where the old registration sticker had once resided on the windshield. It was a unique, unmistakable, shape. Watts was reasonably sure the van had at one time been registered in Oklahoma.

He also found it interesting that all three of the vehicles were the same make, model, and year. Each van was identically equipped, and obviously a base model with few bells and whistles. These were fleet units, probably purchased by a corporation or other business entity, and most likely were from the Sooner State.

The vehicles' remarkable lack of fingerprints, food wrappers, cigarette butts, or any other sort of human-generated debris was also troubling.

In a way, Watts felt like he was a sheriff from the old days, depending on only what clues his eyes, ears and sometimes sense of smell could collect.

Years ago, when computers had first started working their

way into the daily routine of rural law enforcement, Watts had been slow to embrace the technology. He was old school, beginning his career in an era when a man's judgment and common sense played more of a role than DNA samples or mobile phone tracking.

That, however, quickly changed. As a dedicated peace officer, Watts found his ability to protect the county's citizens was far more effective if he utilized technology. It was his sworn duty, and if any tool increased his efficiency, he was all for it.

Now, post-downfall, it was back to square one, the primary instrument in his arsenal today being experience, closely followed by common sense.

In reality, the vehicles Nick had asked him to investigate could have come from anywhere. Watts didn't think so. Gasoline, up until a short time ago, had been in such short supply not many people would've had the resource to move one, let alone three vans around the middle of the country. No, he would report back that it was his learned opinion the three vehicles had arrived in Texas most likely from some corporation in Oklahoma.

Cam lowered the report to his desktop, only a slight grimace showing at the corners of his mouth. His team of Recon Marines had been wiped out by a man, Bishop managing to yet again escape the reaper's hand.

"It doesn't matter," he whispered, "we are sowing seeds of discourse, and not all of them can be expected to grow."

His plan was moving forward, mostly on schedule. The opportunity to discredit, or perhaps kill, one of the Alliance's leading figures had been a long shot, not a prerequisite to success.

Flipping to the next report, his attitude improved.

The pieces were in place for the grand opening of the new property law. Interviews were lined up with the few operating radio stations, carefully scripted editorials ready to be delivered to a multitude of start-up newspapers.

Diana Brown would be in Amarillo, hosting one of the larger announcement sessions she had quaintly named, "Town Hall Meetings." His men were already in place.

Cameron rose and poured himself a glass of water, sipping the cool liquid as his gaze redirected to the window. "I'm going to be coming home soon, Texas. And when I do, I'm going to show you what true leadership is all about."

Chapter 10

As part of the roll-out plan for the Alliance's new property laws, Bishop and Terri were tasked with setting an example. When Diana had discovered that the couple had been pre-collapse homeowners, she insisted that they return to Houston and claim their property.

"A lot of our citizens have heard of you two," the Alliance leader had stated with beaming confidence. "We need to walk the walk and talk the talk. It will help smooth the roll-out."

Bishop, from the beginning, thought it was a bad idea.

While the couple had traveled extensively throughout the territory since the downfall, those journeys had been performed as part of an entourage or in an official capacity. This would be the first time they ventured back along that original, harrowing bug-out route that had nearly cost them their lives. It would be a voyage through a minefield of harrowing memories.

If retracing those steps wasn't emotionally daunting enough, seeing their old home was sure to produce a strong reaction.

"Haven't we done enough already?" Bishop had questioned after his wife had relayed Diana's request.

"Diana has been a Nervous Nelly over this new law. Folks don't like change, and with Katherine Baxter stirring the pot, emotions are running high for sure. Plus, Diana wants to make sure it is logistically feasible for folks to be able to travel into the Alliance and make a claim within the timeframe the new law proposes." The stateswoman paused to give her husband time to mull over her words before continuing. "It's a small thing to ask of us, and besides, it will be interesting to see how the recovery is progressing. It's really not a big deal, is it? I mean, together, we can handle anything, my love."

The Texan, as usual, was thoroughly trounced in the debate that followed.

As he loaded the spare gas cans into the pickup, Bishop experienced a mixture of emotions. On one hand, he was proud of his mate and her fearlessness. She seemed more than willing to face what had been the most dangerous and trying episode of their lives. With her usual vigor and energy, Terri had set about planning and packing, almost as if they were preparing to head out on a family vacation.

Still, Bishop had his doubts.

From the time the trip had been scheduled, he had wondered if the foreboding cloud that consumed his thoughts was out of concern for his wife's... or his own well-being. There were some memories better left quarantined in the past.

While he'd faced danger numerous times during his career in security, the 10 days it had taken them to travel across the post-apocalyptic landscape of Texas had been the first time Terri's life had been on the line. Bishop had almost lost her on several occasions, and it made him shudder to think about it. How would she react when they retraced their steps? Would the flood of memories consume her?

Of even greater concern was how the two would respond when they saw their first home after abandoning it.

The Texan knew their former residence had hosted at least one uninvited guest since they had fled the subdivision. The Colonel, along with his grandchildren and Mrs. Porter, had used their house as a hideout during their escape from Houston. That had been over two years ago, it was likely that their structure was worse for the wear.

According to his way of thinking, they were volunteering for more trauma, and he couldn't embrace that. It just wasn't logical. Terri, on the other hand, didn't seem to be concerned.

With Hunter secured in the backseat, two suitcases of clothes, the normal array of firearms and survival gear, Bishop decided to take one last shot at talking his wife out of the adventure.

The outskirts of Alpha had just disappeared in the rearview mirror when Bishop informed Terri that the truck had been running a little rough as of late. "I hope we don't have any troubles on the way to Houston," the Texan remarked in a nonchalant tone. "Even with the recovery, I'm not sure how easy it would be to find a mechanic."

"Should we go back and ask Nick for a loaner?"

Foiled yet again, Bishop's reply was deflated, "No, it will probably be fine."

The miles passed quickly, the couple glancing longingly at the Manor Hotel and Pete's Place without stopping. Once outside Meraton and rolling east, Bishop began to reconsider his melancholy outlook. Terri had found a decent compact disc of classic rock 'n roll, her slightly off-key voice happily belting out a favorite tune. Hunter, egged on by his mother, did his best to provide backup vocals.

All of that changed as they approached Sanderson. Terri abruptly stopped her serenade, silently staring at the abandoned structures where Bishop had almost died of a gunshot wound.

"It looks even smaller and... and... so lonely now," she

mumbled. "I thought I'd lost you that first night. Then I thought we were both going to die of dehydration."

Bishop smiled, "You came through. You saw the devil and rather than fold up and quit, you faced the challenge and prevailed. I always knew you were a strong person, but that little episode showed an inner strength even I couldn't have guessed."

Terri blushed slightly, reaching across to touch Bishop's arm. "I just wanted you to hang around a little longer."

They continued driving across West Texas, occasionally encountering other travelers in automobiles, horse drawn wagons, tractors, and even a few semi-trucks carrying cargo.

"It's good to see people out and about," Bishop noted. "Sure is one hell of a lot different than the last time we traveled this road."

Even navigating through the small towns was a completely different experience. The couple didn't encounter a single roadblock, barricade, or guard post. One of the bergs even offered gasoline, another contributing a fresh produce stand attracting several shoppers. Terri wanted to stop.

The locals were friendly, chatting up the traveling family while posing mildly curious inquiries and making over Hunter.

"Where are you folks headed?" asked an older man with a handful of potatoes.

"Houston," Bishop answered.

"Oh? Do you think that's safe? We've heard so many stories from people, most of them trying to get away from that town."

"We hear the recovery is going well there," Bishop informed the gent. "We're going back to claim our home."

"We are supposed to have a township meeting about property ownership in two nights," came the response. "A lot of people are leery of how things are going to go with this new law. The Alliance has done right be me so far, so I'm going to hear what they have to say and make up my mind, I guess."

"I've read the rules," Bishop countered. "It's not a perfect solution, but I think it will treat most property owners fairly."

Terri appeared, along with a small bag of grapes and a smiling Hunter. "He loves them," she grinned, feeding the boy another of the small fruits. "I don't think I've ever seen him enjoy food like this."

After popping a couple of the purple orbs into his mouth, Bishop had to admit they were delicious. "I wonder if we can plant an arbor at the ranch? Maybe I'd have more luck growing these than I did with my other attempts at gardening. We could even open a winery."

"Umm, sure," Terri replied with a healthy dose of skepticism. "Just don't quit your day job, okay?"

Back on the road again, a sign reminded Bishop of another significant landmark – the Brazos River.

The crossing had been a terrifying ordeal, rogue National Guard troops taking control of the only bridge in the area and demanding a high toll before allowing anyone to cross. Bishop had coordinated with a group of the stranded travelers, sniping the villains while several men charged the structure.

While the bridge was eventually liberated, Bishop had fought a running gun battle with two of the defenders, barely escaping with his life. His nightmares frequently revisited the event for him in the dark of night.

Terri seemed to sense the foreboding in her mate. "Remember how kind Ben and Maggie were to us," she reminded the Texan. "They took us in and helped free all those people. Just concentrate on how good it will be to see them again."

She's right, Bishop had to admit. *Focus on the positive.*

They found the farmhouse after only two wrong turns along the unmarked, narrow country lanes. Bishop sensed instantly that something was wrong.

Cooter, the old hound, wasn't at his usual post on the front porch. The growth of weeds around the barn and homestead gave the place a sense of emptiness. Terri, after scanning the property, announced, "I don't like this Bishop. I hope...."

Pulling a carbine from the back seat, Bishop hopped out of the cab and headed for the house. "Hello!" he greeted, not wanting to spook their old friends. "Anybody home?"

There was no response.

A solid pounding on the front door produced no answer. The curtains were drawn.

The Texan then moved to the back of the structure, checking the windows as he went. Finally, spotting a gap in the draperies, he found the interior was much the same as he remembered.

A nearby coffee table was coated in dust, a pair of Ben's work boots resting near the door. There was no sign of foul play, but Bishop's gut told him that the place hadn't been occupied for several months.

Returning to the truck, Bishop informed an anxious Terri of his findings.

"You have to go inside and check it out. They might have left a note or something... or they might be in there."

Shaking his head, Bishop replied, "You know I hate that. Going in somebody's house sucks. But... I suppose you're right. You stay here with Hunter."

The Texan returned to the back door, sucking in a breath

155

and poking a small pane of glass with his rifle barrel. He then reached inside and unlocked the door.

"Hello! Hello! Anybody home?" he shouted.

Again, there was no response.

Bishop cleared the house, every new room bringing a dark curtain of dread that he was about to stumble onto the decaying corpses of their friends. It was simply a vision the Texan didn't need.

After checking every room and finding no sign of foul play, he went back through a second time looking for any hint, sign, or clue that Maggie and Ben had packed up and intentionally left their home. It was a difficult, if not impossible riddle to solve.

The master bedroom's closet was a picture of tidiness, the lady of the house clearly dominating that space. Ben's smaller section was filled with hanging overalls and other work clothes, as well as two suits that the Texan assumed were for Sunday services and funerals. There were empty hangers, but it was hard to tell if someone had intentionally packed up and left – or not.

"We just didn't have the chance to get to know you very well," Bishop whispered to the empty dwelling. "I don't even know where you kept your suitcases, or how many you had."

Discovering neither a note nor indication of foul play, Bishop returned to the truck to inform his anxious bride of his findings.

Terri wanted to look for herself, returning ten minutes later with the same conclusion. "Where would they have gone?" she asked, not really expecting Bishop to have an answer.

"Family? Friends? Little Ben's parents? There no way to know," Bishop replied. "Why don't you fix us a quick meal while I walk around the farm? Just to double-check."

A short time later, Bishop returned, none the wiser than when he'd left. "I didn't find any graves or other signs of issues. Ben's truck is gone, so I guess we have to assume they left of their own accord."

"Should we inform the local sheriff's department?" Terri asked, frowning at the empty home.

"And say what? I don't even remember Ben and Maggie's last name. What would we tell the deputy? There's no sign of any problem or foul play."

Swallowing a mouthful of her ham sandwich, Terri vented, "It is so frustrating. We have no way of knowing, and we may never find out what happened to them. It's one of the most troubling aspects of the collapse... the lack of communication."

"I hear ya," Bishop replied. "It's terrible to think about all of the family members that can't find each other. I think every town we have driven through has had one of those bulletin boards plastered with pictures of missing loved ones. Even with the recovery, it's still a major problem."

"I'm just going to assume they're okay," Terri finally announced with an uplifting tone. "I'm not going to let this spoil our trip."

"That's my girl," came the Texan's reply.

The couple finished the remainder of the meal in an uncomfortable silence, both of them seeming to be occupied with their own thoughts.

"That was good, darling, thank you," Bishop said, announcing he was done eating. "I'll either change Hunter or clean up the dinner mess... your choice."

"You'll do both," Terri teased, putting her hands on her hips. "I was going to use the old water pump out back to wash some of this road dust off my person."

"No problem," Bishop answered with a grin, secretly worried that his wife was taking Ben and Maggie's disappearance more seriously than she was letting on. "I got this."

As Terri disappeared around the corner of the house carrying a change of clothes and a small bag, she glanced back over her shoulder and said, "No peeking!"

"No promises," came the reply along with the underlying chuckle.

"Come on Hunter, let's get a dry diaper on your little bottom," Bishop said, lifting his son.

Terri returned a bit later, drying wet hair and looking refreshed. "Damn that water was cold, but it felt good in a way. You should give it a try," she said with a wink. "One never knows what benefits a clean man who does the dishes might realize."

With an eyebrow waggle, Bishop started digging for a change of wardrobe. As he was pulling a shirt from his bag, he asked, "Do you want to stay inside the house tonight, or should I set up the tent?"

Shaking her head, Terri said, "No. I wouldn't feel right sleeping in there. I'll help you pitch the tent."

Judging it was going to be a cool evening, Bishop had to agree, "Yeah. It would be weird crashing inside their house. I'm good with another night on the ground. We'll make a family camping trip out of it."

After his pump-bath, Bishop gathered wood and staked out the tent. When he realized he'd subconsciously picked a spot behind the barn and hidden from the road, he had to laugh at himself. "Old habits die hard," he whispered to the fading light. "When will you stop being so paranoid?"

With a small fire crackling and Hunter now asleep in the tent, the couple sat mesmerized by the flames. Finally, Terri broke the silence. "Today, we found our friends missing without a clue. I ate a cold meal, took a cold bath, and now I'm getting ready to sleep on the ground. So much for the recovery, huh?"

Grunting, Bishop flashed her a smile, "I set up the tent back here behind the barn so it wasn't visible from the road. I didn't even think about it. That, of course, was after I'd walked the area, looking for shallow graves. It's amazing what you can get used to, isn't it?"

"I'm not unhappy... or worried... or sad," Terri replied with an uplifting voice. "As a matter of fact, I'm quite content sitting here with you and enjoying the fire. Still, sometimes, I wonder if our world will ever get back to normal... or the way it was before society tumbled off the edge."

Bishop shrugged, moving close to his wife and wrapping an arm around her shoulder. "What is it you always say? As long as we're together?"

Kissing her husband on the cheek, Terri snuggled into his embrace, resting her head on his chest. "Come inside my tent, cowboy. I've got plans for you."

The drive into their old neighborhood was spooky to say the least. It seemed like every block brought back some memory or recollection, most centered on those early days following the collapse.

The bank branch where Terri had worked was the worst, most of the glass windows broken or cracked, waist-high weeds growing in the parking lot. Every business nearby was in practically the same condition.

Some structures had suffered worse fates. Bishop stopped counting the burned-out skeletal remains of grocery stores, gas stations, and restaurants after a few miles.

While the Army had been working on clearing the millions of stalled, abandoned vehicles that clogged every major traffic artery, suburban areas had been low on the priority list. Twice Bishop had to change his route, the roadway impassable due to hulks of rusting trucks, vans, or cars.

There were, however, some signs of life.

The couple saw children playing in a yard, another home sporting clotheslines heavily laden with laundry. Bishop even encountered the occasional car or truck on the roadways.

Small columns of cooking-fire smoke darkened the horizon here and there. At one point, the aroma of a BBQ came drifting through the cab.

Three blocks from their home, Bishop yet again had to backtrack. A large pine tree had fallen, blocking the paved lanes.

"Looks like that's been there for a while," he informed Terri. "Notice all the smaller branches have been removed? Probably for firewood."

Then the truck turned onto their street.

The first thing Bishop noted was the overgrowth of grass, weeds, and shrubbery in what had once been a well-manicured subdivision. "These people should take better care of their yards," he quipped to Terri. "Real estate values are going to plummet."

"Wait until I speak with our neighborhood association," she answered, never taking her eyes off the passing houses.

All of the homes had another thing in common.

On the side of each, in bright orange spray paint, was a symbol. It reminded the Texan of New Orleans after Hurricane Katrina.

A simple checkmark seemingly indicated the home didn't contain any residents, dead or alive. A number probably noted how many people were living in the structure. A number with a circle was evidently a body count. There were a lot of circles and check marks.

Bishop's old yard wasn't any different, his once-sculptured bushes now covering significant portions of the windows, his "grass" almost waist high in places.

"Did you forget to pay the yard crew?" Bishop asked, pulling into the driveway.

"I thought you were paying them," Terri replied, but her heart clearly wasn't in the banter.

Bishop glanced over, hoping to reassure his wife. Terri didn't notice, her gaze absolutely fixated on their former home. "It's bigger than I remember," she whispered.

Jumping down from the cab, Bishop retrieved his carbine from the backseat. "Give me a few minutes to make sure we don't have any uninvited guests."

It suddenly dawned on Bishop that he didn't have a key... had no idea where the original would be. Finding the back door partially open solved the issue.

The first thing he noticed was the clutter. Leaves and other debris covered the floor at the entrance, a thick layer of dust adding to the sense of a place that hadn't seen human occupation in a long time. The Texan checked for any signs of footprints in the thin film that covered the floor. He found none.

A musky odor overwhelmed him as he stepped in, a combination of mold and dampness waffling just inside the entrance.

The kitchen had obviously been ransacked, every drawer and cabinet open, the contents strewn across the floor. The refrigerator door was ajar, the shelves absolutely bare. Glass crunched under his boots as the Texan bent to retrieve a sizable hunk of his favorite coffee cup.

A rustling sound from the den had Bishop's carbine snapping to his shoulder, but it was only a squirrel shocked by the sudden appearance of a higher predator in its adopted abode. Exhaling as he watched the critter's fuzzy tail disappear through the broken glass of a window, he returned to clearing the rest of the house.

Other than the kitchen, most of the homestead looked untouched by looters. A few things were out of place, but it was obvious that food had been the primary interest of the intruders.

Two windows were shattered; one by a downed tree limb provided the primary squirrel entrance ramp, the other broken by some unknown force. The carpeting around the missing glass was dark with mold and soil.

Dust was on every horizontal surface, thick and undisturbed. Cobwebs were also in abundance.

After clearing the home, Bishop returned to the driveway and informed Terri it was safe to venture inside.

"How bad is it?" she asked with a worried expression.

"Not as bad as I thought, but it is a mess… especially the kitchen."

"Looters?"

"Only in the kitchen. A couple of windows are out, so the bugs, squirrels, and moisture have ruined the carpet."

Terri looked at her home, doubt flashing behind her eyes. "Is it safe to take Hunter inside?"

"I'm not sure. It smells pretty bad, probably mold… but other than that and the broken glass, there are no overt dangers."

Terri again scanned the structure, indecision governing her expression. At one time, the home had been the primary focus of their lives. Scrimping, saving, and doing without had been the couple's motto for months as they struggled to realize the American dream. The fact that a horrible recession was roaring through the economy at the time had made the effort even more intimidating.

Terri could still remember the day when the bank had finally approved the mortgage. Bishop had been out of the country, gallivanting off to some distant land to guard an oil well, or something similar. She had somehow managed to hold off celebrating, waiting patiently by the phone until he called so that she could share the good news. They had whooped and hollered for a full five minutes via the static-laced, long distance connection.

After signing more documents than either had anticipated, the couple had poured their hearts and souls into creating a home out of a building. They had only been able to afford a fixer-upper. The place had good bones but needed a ton of work.

Then, in what seemed like the blink of an eye, the world had gone to hell, and they had been forced to leave most of their worldly possessions behind.

Peering up at Bishop with fear, Terri said, "I don't know if I want to go in. I'm thinking you were right... this might be a bad idea."

"Up to you," Bishop answered as warmly as he could. "We can turn around right now and head back to Alpha if you want."

Her eyes darted between the structure and her husband, a tennis match of contemplation governing her thoughts. "You know I wanted to raise our children on this street," she said in a far-away, hushed tone. "I always thought we would grow old together in this house."

"If the recovery continues to roll along, we still might," Bishop replied. "Isn't that why we're here?"

"I don't... I don't know, Bishop," she stumbled. "I thought so, but now that I'm here, I'm having second thoughts."

Terri exited the truck after handing Bishop his wiggly son. Hunter, as always, was fascinated with his father's rifle sling. While mom scanned the home and continued to weigh the decision, Bishop took in the neighborhood, looking for any other residents.

Two of the homes further down the street appeared to be occupied, pathways of flattened grass leading to the pavement. "I wouldn't want to be a lawnmower salesman," Bishop informed his son. "No one is going to waste gas money on trimming the lawn for a very, very long time."

Terri called out, "Bishop, I'm going in. Will you come with me?"

"Of course, my lady," he replied, smiling at his wife's stubborn determination.

She inhaled sharply when the kitchen came into view, but it wasn't the mess of broken plates and scattered utensils. No, what had fixated Terri's gaze was a collection of old family photographs still hanging on the wall.

Her mind wandered back to that day when they had made

the decision to get out of Houston. There simply hadn't been room in the truck to pack everything. Water, food, and ammunition had been the top priorities.

Terri took a step closer, her hand gently brushing the dust from one of the frames. "Hi, Mom, I've missed you," she whispered.

"We've got more room in the truck now… if you want to take some of our belongings back west," Bishop offered.

Like she hadn't heard him, Terri's gaze continued around the room and then she moved toward the center of the house.

With Hunter bouncing on his hip, Bishop followed his wife, wanting to be close at hand, but trying not to press.

"It seems so big," she mumbled at one point, then reversing that observation later. "It feels smaller than I remember."

Bishop could understand the flood of emotions. His reloading equipment, still on the garage workbench, had elicited a similar reaction. The master closet had been the worst.

Terri again became fixated, holding a piece of china that had rested proudly on a living room shelf. "This was my grandmother's," she told Bishop as if he was a stranger in her home. "It's the only heirloom I have of hers."

"Bring it back with you," he offered.

With a flash of anger, she pivoted and held the precious object at arm's length, her hand shaking with rage. "I can't bring the whole house full of memories with me. I can't pack up a life that no longer exists. Stop saying that."

The Texan retreated, deciding she needed some space. He wasn't angry, just worried. Hunter, hearing the tone of his mother's voice, was frowning as well.

The two males skulked outside, Bishop wading through the high weeds to check the outside of the home and give mom some time to adjust.

Terri appeared a short time later, her expression making it clear she regretted the earlier outburst. "I'm sorry," she said. "I don't know what came over me. You were being sweet."

"No problem. I'm just worried about you; that's all."

They couple exchanged a hug, and then Terri took her son and snuggled him close.

"What now?" she eventually asked.

"I need to patch up the two broken windows and get rid of the moldy carpeting. We are supposed to make our claim in the morning, so we'll have to figure out someplace to sleep tonight."

Turning to face the house, Terri said, "I don't want to sleep in there. It smells musty and stale, and I don't think it's good for Hunter to be inside for extended periods of time. Let's pitch the tent in the backyard. We can camp out just like my cousins and I used to do when we were little girls."

"Sure," Bishop answered, looking around with a frown. "It's not like we're going to hurt the grass or anything."

"It will be like coming home, but not. This whole trip is just weird anyway. Why not top it off with more strangeness?"

Nodding, Bishop stroe for the truck. "I'll get Hunter's playpen, and you can set it up on the back porch. I'll get started on my domestic duties after he's all set."

Chapter 11

There was a line at the county annex building where Bishop and Terri were to claim ownership of their property.

Already troubled by the exposure to their former lives and exhausted from sleeping on the ground for a second straight night, Terri peered at Bishop and suggested, "Is it too late to forget about the whole thing and head back to Alpha?"

"Let's go," Bishop responded immediately. "Ready, willing, and able."

For a moment, she actually considered it. Then her commitment to Diana returned to her thoughts. Sighing, she shook her head. "In for a penny, in for a pound."

Taking turns carrying Hunter, the couple slowly followed the line as it snaked its way into what had once been where citizens of H-town stood to renew their driver's licenses and other automobile related issues.

As they idled in the cue, Bishop grinned at Terri. "Do you remember when the pre-collapse legislators used to have all those arguments about new spending bills and budgets? They were always debating about where the money would come from to pay for some new law or program. You'd hear them going on about Senator So-and-so's new bill was a great idea, but some other program would have to be cut to fund the latest, greatest need."

"Yeah, I remember those sound bites. In the end, our esteemed elected officials would always end up raising taxes to pay for whatever seemed so important at the time. They always called it a balanced budget, but in reality, it should have been called an expanding budget," Terri vented.

"This line reminds me of an idea I once had," Bishop continued. "How about you use your influence and political capital to convince the council that we need a 'balanced time,' amendment to the Republic's Constitution?"

Terri frowned, sure that the heat had taken its toll, having absolutely no idea of his meaning.

"It would limit the government's intrusion on a citizen's time to only three days per year. Whatever new law is passed, whatever bureaucracy is created, an individual's time is protected as an inalienable right. One of my biggest fears is that we'll end up right back where we were pre-downfall. I remember spending hours in line to register the car while you spent days trying to figure out our federal tax returns. If you wanted to protest property taxes, you lost a day of work after wasting several evenings figuring out the confusing letter they sent in the mail. Then there were the safety inspections, state taxes, and God help you if you wanted to build a new room onto your house. It required weeks obtaining all of the permits and inspections. All that's not even counting Social Security, health insurance, and jury duty. Voting was another lost day because of the long queues. It just never ended."

Terri rubbed her chin, pretending to take him seriously. "I see what you're saying, but how would you measure and enforce something like that?"

Bishop was ready with an answer, "Time is money, right? So this new amendment would hit them square in the pocketbook. Just like business expenses are deducted from your tax bill, you get to charge the government back for the time you spend executing all of their bullshit. Whenever someone wants to pass a new law, the politicians will have to take into account not only how much the new program will cost, but how much tax revenue they will lose from people standing in line. After a while, they'll be forced to cut older programs because no one will have any 'gov-time' to fill out their stupid forms and wait their turns to be helped."

Terri shook her head in amazement. "I wonder about you sometimes. It's almost like you want the recovery to fail."

"Nope," he responded, glancing at the slow-moving cue. "I just don't want to repeat the same mistakes, and by the look of things here today, we're well on the road to doing just that."

A row of several booths was servicing the anxious queue, Bishop noting that despite the early hour, many of the Alliance workers already appeared tired and frustrated.

"There's supposed to be a reporter here to snap pictures of us going through the process," Terri whispered. "You're going to be famous."

"I'm sure they'll edit me out of the frame," Bishop teased back. "It's your gorgeous face everyone wants to see."

"You think?" she grinned. "But I forgot my low cut top and mini-skirt," Terri continued, striking a model's pose.

Bishop smiled at his wife, still delightful and charming after the endless waiting. "You, my darlin', are always a beauty."

Bishop watched several residents as they approached the booths. Some folks seemed to breeze right through while others appeared to be frustrated with the process. One man was arguing with a raised voice, clearly unhappy with the new rules.

There was also a substantial law enforcement presence in

their general vicinity, two of the officers idling in the corner while keeping a keen eye on the massed citizenry. Bishop was reassured by their presence. During their time in line, he had spotted at least a dozen people with pistols and assumed practically everyone was armed. For sure, Terri and he both were toting iron.

A well-dressed woman appeared next to them, her badge indicating she was a supervisor. "Are you two the famous Bishop and Terri?"

"Yes, that's us," Bishop replied. "My name is Terri, and this is my wife, Bishop."

The woman didn't get the joke, her brow knotting in confusion.

After throwing her husband a dirty look, Terri straightened out the introductions. "He's nervous around all these people," she explained in a hushed voice. Then cupping her hand as if to share a secret, she added, "He's a bit of an introvert."

"Ahhh," smiled the public servant, casting a worried look at the Texan. "That's understandable.... I suppose. Anyway, you two don't have to wait in line. I've been instructed to expedite your claim in my office. There's a reporter here from one of the resurrected Houston newspapers who wants to take a few pictures and ask you both a couple of questions."

"Thank you for the offer, but we really don't want any special treatment," Bishop interjected. "We'll stand and wait like everyone else."

"Oh," the surprised woman responded. "Are you sure? It might be a while before it's your turn."

Scanning the multitudes, Bishop lowered his voice to share his own secret, "We really don't want any special favors. It wouldn't be fair to everyone else. We'll be fine."

Shrugging her shoulders, the supervisor responded, "Up to you," and then disappeared through a door marked, "Employees Only."

An hour later, it was finally their turn.

Bishop had a copy of the bank mortgage, several old utility bills, and, of course, his new Alliance-issued driver's license. Terri had her original "State of Texas," version as well.

The woman serving them was polite and seemed relieved that the couple had presented reasonable documentation. The entire registration took less than 10 minutes.

After signing three different forms, the lady behind the counter produced two official-looking pieces of paper. She penned in their address, stamped them with a loud "thud," and then informed Bishop that he should keep one on his person and display the other in a window visible from the street at the referenced address.

Miss Supervisor magically appeared again, this time waving for them to follow her into the hallowed halls of Alliance bureaucracy.

"We're important," Bishop whispered as the couple followed. "I feel like a VIP."

"Just imagine if I'd worn that low-cut top."

"How do you think I have been entertaining myself the last two hours?" he responded with an eyebrow waggle.

They arrived at a small, government-issued office where a man waited next to an empty plate of what had been cookies. Bishop noted nothing but crumbs remained and instantly regretted not cutting the line when it had been offered. The municipal coffee pot was empty as well. "Damn those budget cuts," he whispered to Terri.

The newshound asked the anticipated questions, covering what the couple thought about the claims process, recovery, and local progress. Bishop kept his mouth shut, allowing the more diplomatic Terri to handle the inquisition.

Then the fellow produced a cell phone. "There's no signal or working towers just yet," he explained, "but it still has a great camera." The photo shoot was over quickly, the couple posing with their certificates. Hunter fussed, wanting desperately to hold the reporter's flashing gadget.

After shaking hands and thanking all involved, the family exited the inner sanctum only to run into Chase McQuire.

The ambassador was talking to a huddled group of residents, all smiles and chuckles. Another man was with him, typing furiously on a laptop computer as the U.S. representative asked questions.

Looking up and spotting the couple, Chase said, "There you are! I'd been told you would be here today. I'm glad I caught you."

Bishop bristled. Terri was confused.

As they approached the ambassador, Bishop bent and whispered another secret in Terri's ear. "I thought I'd never utter these words, but now I'm glad you didn't wear that top."

"I'm here conducting a survey of the people who are making claims," Chase bubbled after receiving a cool hug from Terri and a reluctant nod from Bishop. "We're collecting some very interesting data about how people are reacting to the new law."

"Oh, really," Terri responded, obviously puzzled by not only the man's presence but his quest.

"Remember," Chase smiled, sensing her confusion, "the

United States is probably going to implement a similar process in the future, and I want to document how this first attempt could be improved."

To be polite, Terri pretended to be interested. "And what are your findings so far?"

Indicating the man with the laptop, Chase said, "It's early yet, but we have collected enough data for some preliminary results. You should take a few minutes and go over it with me. I'll be presenting my findings to the president in a few days."

Bishop interrupted, glancing at his watch. "We really should be going, hun. Remember, we've got to make it to Diana's presentation in Amarillo this afternoon, and that's a long drive."

The ambassador, however, was insistent. "I promise… it will only take a few minutes. I was really looking forward to your participation, as I don't want to give my boss any inaccurate information."

Terri's eyes darted between the two men and the laptop, torn between her civic duty, and a strong desire to be done with the entire affair. *Diana asked me to take this job and keep Chase out of her hair*, she considered. Responsibility won the internal debate.

Peering up at Bishop, she said, "It won't take long."

The Texan didn't like it, nodding in frustration as he took Hunter from his mother's hip. "Hurry. Remember, Diana is expecting us at the town meeting, and we still have to go back to the house and spend *gov-time* posting this official certificate."

Grinning with satisfaction, Chase motioned for the family to follow. He led them to the building's lobby where several vacant chairs and two empty vending machines resided.

Bishop managed to tolerate the discussion about five minutes, Hunter having expressed his boredom before that. "I'm going to take our son for a walk," the father announced, interrupting a mind numbing conversation that including such highlights as participation rates, satisfaction indicators, and the mean age of those registering a property.

Both father and son were relieved to get outside and into the fresh air. Bishop had spotted a park nearby, complete with overgrown playground equipment. Perhaps Hunter and he could salvage the slide, or trample down the weeds enough to use a swing.

It was over an hour before Terri finally appeared. Her mood, already in a low place, hadn't improved.

"He just droned on and on and on," she declared. "Even after all that, he was still pissed when I got up to leave. I thought he was going to order one of his men to hogtie me to the chair so he could bore me to death. Get me out of here before I pull my gun and kill that man," she insisted.

"Yes, ma'am."

They rushed back to their home, Bishop displaying the required document in a street-visible window while Terri hustled to pack the personal items she wanted to take back to West Texas.

The Texan headed for the garage, his reloading equipment in high demand in their new hometown. *This will fetch enough at the Meraton market to keep me in bacon for years,* he mused. Next came the boxes of books his wife and he had accumulated. They would make a nice contribution to the repository.

When Terri reappeared a short time later, Bishop could tell her efforts had further deepened an already impressive funk. "I made room in the truck's bed for your treasures. How much are we taking back?" he said in a cheery tone.

"Just this," she responded, holding out two photographs, one of her mother, the other taken on the house's front stoop the day they had moved in.

"That's it? No clothes? Shoes? Nothing else?"

"None of my clothes fit anymore, and insects have damaged a lot of our stuff. I took my best shoes with me the first time, besides, I don't have much need for heels anymore. There's just not much here that we really need."

Rubbing his chin, Bishop didn't know if his wife's statement was positive or negative. Throwing another glance at his watch, he decided they didn't have time to discuss the issue anyway.

"Okay, you're the boss. Let's head west."

While Bishop and Terri drove headed for Diana's meeting, a pair of well-dressed men approached the property claims counter in Midland Station.

Seeming unaffected by enduring the long wait, the older of the two hefted a briefcase onto the counter and popped the twin locks. He then began withdrawing several large stacks of documents. "I'm here as the representing attorney for Mr. Cameron James Lewis. These are our property claims," he stated, shoving across the massive amounts of paperwork to the clerk.

"We claim all buildings noted, including the hospital and elementary school that bear Mr. Lewis's family name. In addition, we demand compensation for the use of these assets, most specifically the petroleum refinery and distribution facilities listed within, as well as the fair reimbursement for the oil and other products processed through that location."

The bewildered clerk began thumbing through the mountains of paperwork, unsure of how to handle such a massive task. No sooner had the first briefcase been emptied, than the second man plopped his leather attaché onto the counter and began producing a similar-sized pile of documents.

"In addition to the real estate listed, we are seeking compensation amounting to 9.7 trillion dollars," he said with a serious expression.

"I beg your pardon?" the clerk stated, sure she hadn't heard the figure correctly.

"Mr. Lewis has the right under the new law to make such a claim, as his personal property was used by the Alliance for several months. By the well-established legal precedents regarding ill-gotten gains, the value of any automobile, truck, or other machine that performed while consuming our property is rightfully ours. Also, numerous critical employees were killed in the illegal seizure of our client's resources, and we have the right to demand compensation for the loss of those human assets as well."

Stunned, the woman behind the booth called over a supervisor. The lawyer repeated his speech.

"That's ridiculous," the supervisor responded, scanning the piles of documents. "It's almost as if you're trying to bankrupt the entire Alliance."

"I assure you, madam, that we have dissected the new law thoroughly. Our claims are legitimate and well founded. We'll accept payment in gold or other hard form of currency," the attorney replied with a straight face. "If the Alliance can't pay, then I'm afraid we're going to have to let everyone in Texas know that their government is insolvent."

"This will have to go before the special review board," the supervisor replied. "We're not set up to handle anything like this here."

"We're well prepared for that contingency," the lawyer stated with confidence. "Very well prepared."

Bishop hadn't been so worried about his wife since she'd been kidnapped. The drive back from Houston was passing with very little conversation, a wall of ice dividing the two front seats. Even Terri's interaction with Hunter seemed inhibited.

The Texan had been married long enough to know when his mate needed to be alone with her thoughts and emotions. Any conversation he offered was short, pleasant, and to the point.

In reality, he couldn't blame her. Bishop was dealing his own melancholy mood.

Memories of their previous life were one thing. Walking through the physical ruins of a former existence was quite another. The struggle to survive had served as a mental barrier, allowing so much of their former lives to be shoved back and minimalized. Seeing their old place removed much of that protective insulation, exposing the couple to a tsunami of "what if" emotions.

Bishop had always understood that having their own home meant more to Terri than to him. He had often chalked it up to one of the many differences between a man and a woman.

While no one had worked harder or enjoyed home ownership more, Bishop was well aware that more of Terri's heart was contained in the structure of plaster and wood than his own.

But, that didn't mean he could walk through a museum of their former life and not be affected.

Forcing the discomfort aside, he spent the last several hours trying to focus on the best method of helping Terri through the experience. He knew that she would, in turn, help him get past it all.

A quick glance at the truck's GPS informed Bishop that they had reached the point where it was time to head north to Amarillo and Diana's presentation.

"Where are you going?" Terri asked, noticing the change in direction.

"To Amarillo and the big town meeting. Remember? We promised Nick and Diana we would attend on our way back."

Terri's frown deepened, "Shit. I forgot."

That's not like her at all, Bishop thought. *She's always the one who remembers the social commitments. Now, I am worried.*

His anxieties increased exponentially with Terri's next statement. "I don't want to go. Let's just head back to Alpha," she announced.

"Are you sure?" Bishop replied gently. "We did promise them we'd be there. It's only a few hours out of the way."

Terri, however, was firm. "I know, but I don't feel like going. Please, just take me back to Alpha. Besides, like you said before we left, 'Haven't we already done enough?'"

Shrugging, Bishop pulled a U-turn, sending them motoring along their original route. Again, the cab was filled with nothing but the big V8's purring and the whine of the rubber against the road.

Diana's security team was on edge, heads pivoting sharply right and left as they escorted the Alliance's leader into the gymnasium.

"No long guns... and no hovering directly behind me," she had informed the team of bodyguards. "This is a public meeting of citizens, who, I might add, elected me. I'm not a queen or dictator. Keep it low key, gentlemen, and that's an order."

The high school facility was packed to the gills. After managing a parking lot full of buses, horse-drawn wagons, cars, trucks, and motorcycles, Diana straightened herself and prepared to enter the main auditorium.

The reaction from the crowd was positive as she appeared via a side door. Several people clapped, others shouting encouragement as she made for the stage. She found herself smiling and waving at a sea of people fanning themselves with whatever was handy. The air conditioning had failed just an hour before the gathering.

After shaking hands with several location leaders, Diana took a seat and watched as the lights were dimmed and a huge projection machine illuminated the entire back wall of the facility.

After a shrill from the microphone had caused many to wince, the mayor of Amarillo, Texas began addressing the gathering.

"Ladies and gentlemen, as I'm sure most of you know, we are gathered here this evening to present the Alliance of Texas's new program concerning the ownership of private property and other private assets."

Pausing to scan the crowd, the mayor then turned and indicated the dignitaries seated behind him on the stage. "It is also my pleasure to introduce several of our new nation's servants who have honored us by attending this evening's town hall meeting."

One by one, the mayor introduced various council members, trustees, and other local leaders. He saved best for last.

Again, a broad round of applause greeted Diana as she was introduced. Standing, smiling broadly, and waving to the folks. With a measured step, she approached the podium.

"My fellow survivors of the collapse," she began with a strong voice. "Thank you for your support and patience. Due to your hard work and seemingly boundless spirit, the recovery continues. Starvation no longer annihilates our ranks. The availability and quality of medical care are improving every single day. Roving bands of marauders and thieves no longer threaten the vast majority of our lives. We now live in a society governed by the rule of law."

The sound of cheers and clapping filled the gym, several people standing to show their support.

"But our work is not nearly complete. We are far from finished," Diana continued. "To progress down the path to a higher standard of living, we must have manufacturing, communications, transportation, automation, and a long list of other capabilities and services. Our factories must again ship products. Our hospitals, schools, shops and churches must reopen and produce."

More applause and shouts of encouragement followed.

After waiting for the reaction to die down, Diana's gaze swept the crowd as her voice took a serious tone. "Without banking, taxation, and a larger government presence, none of these advancements will occur. We, as a society, need a financial system. We require a fair judicial process. We must protect the private ownership of the property at all costs."

The volume of support was less but still strong. *At least no one is booing me*, she thought. *Or shooting at me.*

"So often I hear my fellow Texans talking about life getting back to where it was before the collapse. It's only natural for all of us to yearn for the 'good ole days.' Tonight, you will hear what the other council members and I believe is the next step to achieving not only that goal but what may establish a foundation for an even higher standard of living for our citizens. Together, we can build a Texas that is better than before, with a quality of life that exceeds any in the history of mankind. We can do this if we work as a team. It can be done!"

The cheering was louder than ever, Diana scanning a throng of smiling faces and supporting eyes. After casting a friendly gesture to each section of the arena while mouthing, "Thank you," she then leaned back into the mic and continued, "and now it is my pleasure to introduce Councilman Williams who will provide the details of this afternoon's presentation."

A middle-aged man in a suit made his way to the front of the stage, the local official tasked with delivering the nuts and bolts of the new law. The rules were simple, projected boldly on the wall for all attending to see.

Williams was well spoken and accustomed to addressing large crowds. His portion continued for several minutes, highlighting the important parameters and even managing to crack a few jokes.

As Diana had anticipated, the initial phase of the presentation drew a positive reaction from the gathering. Now it was time for the controversial sections of the new law.

Someone had estimated that over 85% of the private property in Texas had been pledged as collateral of one sort or another to various banks and credit unions. Prior to the collapse, the vast majority of financial institutions had survived by collecting interest on mortgages, lines of credit, and other loans secured by real estate or physical assets. None of those streams of income existed anymore.

For years, no one had been making monthly payments. With half of the state's population now deceased, many of the council's experts were doubtful that banking could be revived in any form. Others argued that, like the first failure of the economy in the 1930s, blame was to be placed at the feet of the banks. Many learned people blamed the Second Great Depression on insolvent financial institutions, claiming that the economy was pushed over the edge by their mismanagement and unworkable policies. Why should the same mistake be repeated?

The Alliance had already imitated a few of the cures implemented to reverse the contracting economy so many decades ago. Roosevelt's Works Progress Administration had its modern day equal in the Agriculture Relocation Program, or ARP. Tens of thousands of unemployed, starving citizens had been relocated to temporary camps where they tilled the fields, raised livestock, and received food, shelter, medical care, and security in exchange.

But there were differences between the collapse of Diana's time and that of her great-grandfather. Some banks had remained open during the 1930s. The council in Alpha hadn't inherited a single functioning teller's window. Unemployment had reached a crippling 25% in 1933. Diana's apocalypse had seen 99.9% of the population without work.

Entire cities, courthouses, and government office complexes had burned or been looted during society's latest fall – a problem the Roosevelt White House hadn't been forced to overcome. That, combined with the fact that most counties kept their records on computers, left massive gaps in the government's ability to reconcile who owned what land, factory, homes, or apartment buildings.

No, Diana thought as Councilman Williams prepared to continue his presentation. *We need banking.*

The gym grew quiet as the next projection flashed on the wall. Its title was two large font, bolded words: **Eminent Domain.**

The concept wasn't anything new. Since the beginning of government, tribal leaders, kings, dictators and eventually democracies had exercised a process that forced citizens to sell land or other assets if the action was deemed to benefit society as a whole.

There were, however, rules. The most important criteria in the United States had been ensuring that the citizen received fair value for the property being acquired. This was not always as simple as it might sound.

One of the most complex examples occurred when the federal government began constructing a system of interstate highways. While the narrow strip of land needed for the paved lanes wasn't significant to many individual property owners or tenants, the planners in Washington soon found that acquiring the properties was going to be far more difficult and expensive than anyone had anticipated.

To many farmers, it was as if the Great Wall of China were being built directly through the center of their fields.

Tractors, combines, and other implements couldn't just cross the multilane freeway to plant or harvest the crops or care for livestock. In fact, such slow-moving machinery wasn't even allowed to utilize the freeway. Access points, such as overpasses and crossroads, were often several miles away. How was the rancher to cross the road?

As the federal government quickly discovered, the "fair" value of a thin strip of land was minor compared to the financial impact realized by an individual citizen. Over time, the court's and public opinion agreed, and the cost of construction soared.

Williams continued his explanation and justification of the new rules and regulation. After nodding at the projectionist, he then pointed to the large display and said, "In the future, the Alliance will again exercise a similar process and take possession of unclaimed property."

A murmur swept through the crowd, Diana noting the sharp tone of a few individual voices. The unrest didn't go unnoticed by the man behind the podium.

"If there are office buildings... or vacant land... maybe a factory or other real estate that are not claimed by legitimate owners, then the Alliance will take possession of the property. This is no different than how every county in the United States did business before the collapse. If a citizen didn't pay property taxes to the local jurisdiction, the land was taken and then auctioned off for the good of the community. The proposal before you today is no different."

The explanation seemed to placate the crowd, or at least

most of the naysayers.

For another 10 minutes, the councilman repeated the rules, covering the specifics of how individual citizens were to go about claiming their property. After wrapping up his portion of the presentation, Councilman Williams returned to his seat followed by a smattering of applause.

The next item on the agenda was the question and answer session.

The first man stepping to the floor-mounted microphone was a gentleman who appeared to be in his early 60s and was dressed in apparel that led most onlookers to believe he was a rancher. "My brother didn't make it through the collapse," he stated with a sad voice. "I have a copy of his Last Will and Testament, which clearly states his home and land were to be mine if he passed first. Is this strong enough documentation for me to make a valid claim given this new process?"

The next two citizens of Amarillo to approach the podium all voiced similar concerns and questions. The fourth man to reach the mic was dressed in an expensive looking suit and spoke with a powerful tone as if he were a man comfortable with addressing large gatherings.

"My question is for Chairperson Brown," he began, staring at Diana with a hostile gaze. "I wish to ask Ms. Brown how the government intends to compensate citizens who have already had their property seized or destroyed by the Alliance?"

Diana acknowledged the challenge by approaching the podium. "Thank you for attending this evening, sir. Your question is very broad based, would it be possible to provide a few more details so that I can give you an accurate answer?"

Despite Diana's attempt to be accommodating and polite, the questioner seemed to take offense. "You arrived at this evening's gathering in a very expensive class-A motorhome," he began with a sneer. "I assume from what I know of your background such a vehicle was not in your possession before the collapse. Is that accurate?"

"Yes, that is accurate. As the Alliance began to spread across Texas, we acquired several motorhomes from an abandoned dealership on the outskirts of El Paso and have used them for long-distance transportation."

Mr. Suit-and-Tie grinned as if he'd caught the rat in a trap. "And did you compensate the owner of that business?"

"No, not that I'm aware of. We were informed that the owner was deceased. The RVs were just sitting there, rusting away."

Pointing an accusing finger at Diana, he barked, "My client is the rightful owner of that RV dealership. He is the son of the owner and was away on vacation when the collapse occurred, only recently able to return to the area. Will he be compensated via these new laws?"

"No," Diana replied honestly. "But, he can file a claim on the dealership, and the Alliance will find an alternative source for any future vehicles we may require."

Instead of continuing his conversation, Mr. Suit turned and faced the crowd. Spreading his arms wide in appeal, he began addressing the gathering in a bellowing voice. "My fellow Texans, this is not justice. The actions by Miss Brown and her cohorts were illegal, immoral, and go against the grain of the values we all hold true. The rightful owner of this business has suffered millions of dollars of losses, and is unlikely to ever recover."

He stopped for a moment, scanning the audience, and then half turned and pointed at the stage. "These thieves... who call themselves our government... they are nothing more than greedy, power hungry thugs who readily admit they have, and will continue to plunder whatever they want. While the rest of us struggle to put food on the table and clothe our children, they are seizing luxury motorhomes and other upscale amenities for personal use."

A shockwave traveled through the crowd, many of the attendees surprised that someone would attack Diana so blatantly, others voicing their agreement with the harsh accusations.

Waiting until the background noise subsided, Diana finally voiced a rebuttal, "Your words are slanderous, sir. I, as well as all of the council members, acted to save lives, restore order, and improve the lot of our neighbors. For over a year, none of us were paid for our service, nor did we receive any special personal benefits. Many of the Alliance's founders were killed or wounded in the line of duty. All of us put our lives on the line to help our communities. I have no regrets and carry no guilt in my soul."

Mr. Suit shook his head in disgust, his voice booming through the arena to drown the crowd's murmur. "No personal benefits? No special treatment? Let me ask this; where did you get the gasoline and diesel to power your opulent motorhome, Miss Brown? While the rest of Texas was succumbing to malnutrition, sickness, and shivering in the cold, dark corners of the rubble, where did the fuel come from?"

Diana didn't get a chance to answer.

A man two rows back stood, his chest heaving in anger, his fist shaking at Mr. Suit he yelled, "Why you lowlife piece of shit, I'll kick your ass!"

Someone else shouted, "Wait! Wait! I want to hear her answer!"

"That bitch was driving around with her ass wrapped in leather seats while my kids were starving?" another voice cried.

Everyone started talking at once, the volume increasing exponentially as all wanted their voices heard. Hundreds of people were now standing, some shouting insults at Mr. Suit, others taking out their frustrations on the leadership sitting on the stage.

The head of Diana's security team sensed that things were escalating quickly, the din of the crowd now so loud that his men were having trouble hearing his commands through their earpieces.

Years of frustration, stress, and fear were all percolating just below the surface of the attending masses. Not only had their world been shattered by the apocalypse, but change was also now rolling into their lives at an ever-increasing pace.

Several islands of dispute developed throughout the seating areas, individuals of varying opinions now bickering with each other. Diana's team, sensing the rage that was simmering inside the gym, began to collapse their perimeter.

One man shoved another, sending his flaying arms and legs into the midst of a separate argument. Someone else threw a punch. A woman screamed while another man shouted a warning. A chair flew through the air. A gun was drawn. A shot thundered through the enclosed facility.

In seconds, absolute bedlam erupted.

Screaming, alarmed people were rushing for the exits, the swirling horde of humanity moving in all directions like a school of fish trying to escape the shark. While long guns weren't allowed at the meeting, a vast majority of the attending survivors carried pistols. More and more shots rang out as the panic and desperation intensified.

In a flash, Diana was surrounded by her bodyguards. With their weapons drawn, the four stout men literally lifted her off the ground with the press of their well-conditioned frames. "Get her out! Get her out!" the team leader shouted over the chaos.

The plan had always been to egress through the same side door that Diana had used to enter, the sanctuary of her motorcade being close by. As the security team pushed and muscled their way through the pandemonium, they soon found the route blocked by dozens and dozens of people all trying to exit via the same door... and all at the same time. The few deputies assigned by Sheriff Watts had mostly been stationed outside. Their eagerness to enter at the same moment when everyone else was trying to leave added to the gridlock. The surging, struggling mass of flesh was wedged tight in the threshold, horrific sounds coming from the throats of those being crushed by the throng.

The body of a trampled woman tripped one of Diana's protectors, another knocked to the floor by a fast-moving fistfight.

Realizing there was no hope of pushing his charge through the exit door, the team leader spied an empty corner that, for the moment, was unoccupied. "Over there! Get her over there!" he commanded.

In a flash and blur of movement, Diana found herself shoved roughly against the concrete block wall. "Get down!" one of her men commanded.

The Alliance's top official found herself kneeling in the corner, peering out at the riot through the legs of her protectors. Aside from the indignity of being manhandled, corralled, and forced here and there, Diana was infuriated by the violence.

Just then, she noticed two men who seemed out of place. They were walking across the gym floor, apparently impervious as they strolled with purpose through the whirling upheaval. Something in their steely gaze made her shiver as they made a beeline for her position.

Before she could shout a warning, both men reached inside their long coats and produced what she recognized as submachine guns.

The security men saw the movement at the same time, someone shouting, "Guns! Guns!"

The buzz of automatic weapons, combined with the bark of her team's pistols filled Diana's ears. One of her men fell, as bullets thwacked into the wall around her.

Pushed down by the weight of her fallen guardian, Diana longed for her own weapon. She regretted her decision not to carry a piece, now feeling a sense of helplessness as another of her protectors went down. She could feel the hot flow of blood flowing across her face.

Fear now enveloped her core, her thoughts confused and darting. Defenselessness and vulnerable, she was hopeless. She wanted to help her men fight. She should be giving aid to the wounded. A vision of Nick filled her mind.

It was a one-sided gunfight, the blizzard of spraying lead overwhelming Diana's men in less than two seconds. One of the attackers went down as her security chief corkscrewed to the floor, a series of slugs tearing through his torso.

Pinned under the fallen bodies of her team, Diana watched with horror as the surviving attacker slammed a new magazine into his weapon and then began walking toward her with murder in his eye. The man wasn't angry, frightened, or rushed. His face was that of a calm, cool, professional.

Some instinct forced Diana to push, struggle, and crawl

away. She knew the wall was behind her, the weight of her own men making every muscle ache and strain. Still, her brain screamed for her to retreat… run… get away from the advancing predator.

The floor was sloppy and wet from the blood and gore, making traction impossible. She saw the machine gun rising to the shooter's shoulder. Her struggles doubled as a whimper escaped from her throat.

Her hand came in contact with something hard, the familiar shape of a pistol's grip in her palm. She could see the assassin's knuckle tightening against the trigger as her fingers closed around the slick weapon. She wasn't going to make it.

Shards of concrete exploded from the wall next to her head, slicing, stinging debris pelting her skin as the incoming rounds worked toward her face. Diana never noticed.

Her wrist felt a tug of recoil as she fired, her finger working the trigger over and over and over, pulling as fast as she could command. She couldn't see anything; no sound reached her ears. There was only silence.

The world went black.

Chapter 12

By the time the outskirts of Alpha appeared on the horizon, Bishop's frustration and foreboding had peaked. Other than being as kind and gentle with his mate as possible, he was stumped for a way to help his wife heal.

In addition to the obvious source of Terri's foul mood, Bishop couldn't help but ponder Chase's part in the entire affair. Well past the anger he had experienced that first night, the Texan had spent significant mental resources trying to figure out the ambassador's angle.

The man's surprising appearance at the registrar's office had not only been ill-timed, but also unjustified. What possible knowledge could Chase have expected to gain from such an odd endeavor?

For the last few miles into town, Bishop tried to push aside his personal dislike of the U.S. diplomat and approach the mystery from a cool-headed, logical perspective.

Again, he had failed, unable to arrive at any reasonable explanation.

"Do you ever think about what our life would have been like if everything hadn't gone to hell?" Terri's voice questioned out of the blue.

"Yes, on occasion... I don't spend a lot of time dwelling on it. The collapse was something neither of us could control."

"Of course, you're right," she said in a hushed monotone. "Still, I can't help but wonder what it would have been like to cook dinner in a real kitchen and put Hunter to sleep in his own room."

Bishop knew his wife was in a very delicate place. He had to choose his words carefully. "Do you think you would have been that much happier?"

It was Terri's turn to vet a response. Only a small fraction of her discomfort bleeding through with her next words. "I don't think 'happier' is the word I would use. I love Hunter and you. And both of you make me a very happy girl. What I keep going over is far more complex than feeling happy or sad. Seeing the old neighborhood got me to longing for more of a permanent existence... of having a station in life."

"I understand," Bishop began. "Shelter is not the same as a home. A roof over our head is the same as establishing a place to raise children or call our own."

"I'm glad you get it," Terri said, a small smile showing at the corners of her lips. "I don't blame you, nor am I angry with the world. No one could ask for a better mate than you, darlin'. But… going back to Houston has opened a jumbo-sized barrel of mon-key-questions. I've been sitting here asking myself how long it will be before Hunter has a real home, not just four walls and a roof. What has to happen before we stop sailing dangerous seas and drop anchor in a safe, stable port? I'm feeling the need for establishment… to lay a foundation for our family."

"Let me ask you this," Bishop replied. "I'm sure we both agree that the residence we just left isn't a neighborhood where either of us would want to put down roots any more. I'd be pissed at the realtor for even showing it to us. Do you agree?"

"Yes, I agree. But… I'm not speaking of any specific town or address, I'm talking about a community where we could live what I used to consider a normal life."

Terri was resurrecting want had always been a minor point of friction in their relationship. When it had been utilized as a hunting lodge and weekend getaway, the ranch's isolation was actually a positive attribute. She had often accompanied him to the remote locale just to escape the hustle and bustle of subur-bia.

He had always known it was not even close to her idea of a preferred retreat. As the newness of their marriage had faded, she occasionally would stay home, sending him on the journey to West Texas alone.

Bishop had always written it off as discomfort with the primi-tive facilities and barren landscape surrounding the old camper. Now, after having been forced to live full-time at the isolated location, he realized that there was more to it than any lack of a flushing toilet or microwave oven.

In no way did her lack of enthusiasm come across as a negative. The fact that his wife didn't share his love of the se-cluded environment actually made her the healthier example of humanity.

Bishop's work and the trauma associated with carrying a weapon for gainful employment prompted the Texan to crave being a hermit of sorts. He not only tolerated being alone better than most, he actually enjoyed it. Bishop could remember several times, after returning from a particularly difficult assignment, when the ranch had been his salvation.

Terri, on the other hand, was like most healthy human be-ings. She needed social interaction, conversation, and a sense of belonging.

In some ways, the ranch's isolation had helped both of them through traumatic times following their bug-out from Houston and the events that followed. The quiet surroundings had allowed both of them to recover after the worst of the post-collapse episodes.

Before the recovery had taken hold, Bishop had even held out hope that the secluded stretch of land would one day be their permanent home. Much of the fantasy had been fueled by a lack of any other reasonable alternative. They had even contacted an architect at one point, discussing the possibility of the man drawing a special design to marry well with the box canyon.

Now, the ranch would have to be low on any reasonable person's priority list when it came to choosing an address. It was going to take years to build a herd, and Bishop's gardening skills hadn't exactly been top-shelf. Even the wild game in the area was in decline.

"We *will* find a place to call home," Bishop said firmly. "I can't promise when or where, but I won't rest until we have someplace to begin over again."

Terri reached across the truck cab, gently resting her hand on his arm. "I appreciate that. It means a lot to me. But, the truth is that neither of us has control over our destiny at the moment. That's probably the most frustrating thing about life after the downfall. Before, we had more control... more of an influence in the direction our lives would take. Now, it seems like we're not steering our ship at all. Like the ocean's currents are taking us wherever they wish and we have to go along."

Bishop had seen examples of Terri's current perspective before. Lately, it was a common topic of discussion amongst Diana and the Alliance's leadership and a growing trend in the communities they served. When there was no hope, when empty stomachs and midnight raiders occupied the mind, thoughts of a future and a better quality of life were easily dismissed. While hope had always been an ingredient in the recipe of survival, drastic circumstances led most people to limit the importance of optimism.

Obviously, Terri was yearning for more than just the basic hierarchy of needs. Bishop had to admit, he had felt flashes of the same desires.

After visiting their old home, he'd experienced his own flashbacks to their pre-collapse existence. The spare bedroom that held his gym equipment reminded the Texan of a convenience no longer available in their lives. As Terri had stared longingly at the stove, oven, and dishwasher, Bishop's attention had been drawn to his garage workshop, reloading bench, and gunsmithing tools. While their motivators may have been different, the resulting sense of emptiness was the same.

It was just as he had feared before they had left Alpha. An easy prediction of the problems associated with visiting the past. Yet, Bishop felt no desire to say, "I told you so."

What Terri and he were experiencing was bound to occur sooner or later. What frustrated the Texan most was the fact that he could provide no solution to his wife's discomfort. He hated seeing Terri troubled by anything.

Arriving at the temporary bungalow assigned to the couple by the Alliance didn't help the melancholy atmosphere that still dominated the mood in the pickup.

Sure, it's a shelter, Bishop considered, looking at the structure in an entirely new light. *There is a roof, some walls, and a relatively safe place to fall asleep. Why does it look so hollow to me now?*

It was temporary. Like a hotel room on an extended journey.

For a moment, Bishop felt the stirring of embarrassment over his thoughts. Not so many months ago, they would have given much to have such a comfortable residence. The claustrophobic environment of the camper and its aluminum walls was not yet a distant memory. They had electricity… running, drinkable, water… and police cars cruising the streets keeping the bad guys at bay.

For a second, Bishop felt like a spoiled brat, whining and unhappy with the plethora of toys just received on Christmas morning because the gifts hadn't satisfied every little need. "I'm not content where we are," he finally said, "but, I don't think we should lose sight of how far we've come."

Terri didn't immediately respond, her head tilting slightly with consideration. "I know, I know. I'm coming across like a rotten little princess. You probably think nothing will ever make me happy."

"Not true!" Bishop replied honestly. "The minute we lose the desire to better ourselves is when we stop being truly alive. All that I am saying is that it's been a rough couple of days, and we shouldn't forget that we're gaining ground."

Nodding her understanding, Terri moved closer to her husband, pouting her lips for a kiss. She paused, looking at him with admiration in her eyes. "Promise me you won't let that happen," she whispered.

Bishop's answer and kiss were interrupted by the thunderous thunder of several helicopters roaring overhead. The Texan stood puzzled, watching as the birds rushed north, quickly disappearing over the horizon.

"Something's going on," he said, catching a last glimpse of

the military machines. "I've got a bad feeling about this."

The parking lot surrounding the school was a sea of red and blue flashing lights, an army of ant-like figures rushing here and there.

Nick sat on the edge of the helicopter's bay, his eyes taking it all in as rage boiled in his soul. He should have been there… should have overridden Diana's protests about his healing and been at her side.

Two deputies were working hard to keep the football field clear as the three Blackhawks roared over the massive rescue effort. The warbird's wheels were still four feet off the turf when the big man jumped and rolled, regaining his feet quickly and moving toward the campus without pause.

As the flight landed, two squads of fully loaded assault troops poured out onto the grass, their NCO's shouting orders as boots were hitting the ground.

Hustling to catch up, the officer in charge listened as Nick began barking his own series of commands, "Find her. That is the top priority. Find Diana and get her back to Fort Bliss. Do it. Right fucking now!"

"Yes, sir!"

Please, Diana, hang in there. Just a few minutes more. I'm coming. I'm so sorry… so very sorry, Nick thought as he quickly crossed into the main parking lot.

He noted the troops spreading out, a local deputy pointing a sergeant in the direction where the wounded were being triaged.

Nick came into a mass of confusion – firemen, EMTs, law enforcement, and medical personnel rushing everywhere. There were rows of bodies lying along one wall of the gymnasium, each covered with a white bedsheet. Many were soaked through with red and purple splotches of blood. The fact that some of his men were among the casualties fueled his fury even more.

After passing the rows of dead, Nick spied a large group of people sitting on the ground. Nearby were several uniformed deputies, apparently interviewing the survivors. Someone had set up a series of folding tables, the surfaces covered with stacks of handguns.

Then a sergeant was beside him, "Sir! We've located Miss Brown. This way, sir."

The two men jogged off, approaching what was obviously

the triage area for the wounded. Nick was stunned at the number of people lying scattered here and there. *This is like the aftermath of a major battle*, he thought. *What the hell happened here?*

Spotting Diana was easy, her prone form now surrounded by several riflemen. The squad's two medics were unfolding a stretcher.

"She looks worse than her true condition, sir," the sergeant warned. "According to the docs, she's in no danger."

Despite the warning, Nick's heart stopped when his fiancé came into view.

She was literally covered in blood, a thick, soaked bandage wrapped around her head. He was beside her in an instant.

"I'm here," he said in a hush as her eyes focused. "You're going to be okay."

It was a tremendous relief when a slight smile crossed her lips. "Some men will use any excuse to get out of the house," she said in a hoarse whisper. "I love you."

"I love you, too. We're going to take you back to Fort Bliss. There is a trauma team on standby," Nick announced, squeezing her hand.

"I'm okay... really, it's just a scratch," she replied, trying to rise.

"Relax and stay down. That's an order," he grinned. "Besides, I don't care how minor the wound is, I want you taken care of by the best."

"No," she protested, finally managing to sit. "There are a lot of people here hurt far worse than I am. Take them if you can. They need the help a lot more than I do."

A ruckus with one of the infantrymen interrupted the conversation, the soldier following orders and blocking a man who was trying to approach Diana.

"I'm a doctor," the fellow protested. "Please, let me through."

Nick looked the man up and down and then nodded to the sentry. "It's okay. Let him pass."

"I understand you've got helicopters waiting to medevac the wounded?" began the physician.

"I came here to take Diana back to Fort Bliss," Nick responded with a frown. "We can take another as well."

Shaking his head, the physician glanced at Miss Brown, "She's fine. Really, it's just a flesh wound and potential concussion. I've got several patients who are going to die unless we can get them better care than I can provide here."

Nick started to dismiss the request, but Diana's hand on his arm stopped the rejection. "Nick... let the critical people use the copters. Please. I'm okay... really, I am."

The big man pondered her words. As always, his decision came quickly. "Okay. I'm outnumbered. Doctor, pick three of your most critical, and the sergeant will help you get them loaded."

After a quick exchange, the doc and NCO were off to load the patients. Nick remained, his mind now working on the next set of problems.

Taking a knee, he asked Diana, "What happened here? A deputy in Alpha received a radio transmission that there had been a riot and that gunfire had erupted. According to the report, there had been an assassination attempt on your life."

"I filed that report," a voice stated.

Nick looked up to see a senior deputy approaching. After the two men had shaken hands, the lawman said, "Please come with me, sir. I think you'll be interested in seeing this."

On the way inside the gym, the officer reported on the events leading up to the riot. Inside, they came upon a scene of utter chaos. Shoes, pools of blood, scraps of clothing, and debris were scattered everywhere. A dozen policemen were roaming the area, looking for evidence and clues.

Nick's escort pointed to the corner where three of Diana's security team were lying in the twisted positions of death. One deputy was taking pictures while another outlined the virtual carpet of shell casings.

Recognizing his dead men, Nick's anger returned, the ex-Special Forces Operator barely controlling his emotions. "Explain it to me," he grumbled.

The deputy replied, "Given the number of dead and wounded, we might have missed this, but one of Miss Brown's protection detail survived long enough to warn the responding officers of the crime. After receiving medical attention, she confirmed his story and filled in a few more details."

"Where is that man?"

"He didn't make it, sir."

"Fuck!"

The lawman then walked a few steps and pointed at a pair of dead men lying nearby. "These two were the assassins. They carried no identification and were armed with fully automatic MP5 weapons which had all identifying serial numbers filed down. I'm no expert, but I would say they were professionals."

Nick walked over to gain a better view of the two hitmen and then shook his head. "I've never seen either one of them before."

"There's more, sir," the officer continued. "Several people described a man in a suit and tie who verbally attacked Miss

Brown during the meeting. Yet, we can't find that individual. It's as if he vanished into thin air. I have one witness who claims she saw him getting into a white van with three other men. According to this very shaken woman, the van had Oklahoma plates."

With a frown, Nick digested the deputy's report. Finally nodding, he said, "Thank you, officer. You've done an excellent job. I'll put in a good word with Sheriff Watts."

"Thank you, sir. But there's one more thing you should know."

"Go on."

The lawman hesitated for a brief pause and then the words spilled out. "The second shooter... the closer one... Miss Brown killed him, sir. We found her with the empty gun in her hand. I don't think she remembers it just yet, but I thought you should be aware of that."

Nick actually chuckled, the thought of Diana killing the son of a bitch elevating his mood. The cop's expression indicated he didn't get it.

"It's okay, deputy," Nick explained. "She's been in more than her share of firefights. That gunman didn't have a chance."

Without another word, Nick pivoted, exiting the gym with a motivated pace. A few moments later, he was again at Diana's side. "Did you know the guy in the suit or either of the shooters?"

"No," she said, her eyes beginning to water.

"Are you okay?" he asked, worried over her reaction to his question.

Her body was racked by sobs as she buried her head into his chest. Still puzzled, Nick held her tight until the worst of it had passed. Finally regaining some control, she looked up and said, "I thought it was over. I thought I was dead. I was so... so scared."

The weeping returned, Diana's body shaking as Nick held her close. "You're braver than anyone else I know," he whispered. "You'll be okay, I promise."

While he continued to support her, Nick realized he hadn't seen Bishop or Terri anywhere. He'd been so worried about Diana and his men.

Embarrassed by the oversight, he looked down at her and said, "Where are Bishop and Terri?"

"They never made it to the meeting," she replied. "I hope they're okay. You don't think someone was going after all of the Alliance leadership, do you?"

Nick had already thought of that, dispatching protection to all of the other councilmen and women. "No, I think that you were the only target. Still, something must have gone wrong…. Bishop promised me he'd be here."

The county road was bumpy as hell, the blacktop having gone without maintenance since the collapse. None of the occupants in the van seemed to mind.

Taking the less traveled route had been a necessary precaution as it was less likely that any law enforcement would be traveling the seldom-used roadway.

"Diana Brown survived," commented the passenger in the backseat, pulling a radio headset from his ear. "The police are looking for a van with Oklahoma plates and three men inside. Someone must have gotten a look at us."

"The boss isn't going to be pleased," added the driver, casting a nervous glance at the man in the passenger seat.

Loosening his tie, the well-spoken gentlemen who'd initiated the entire episode didn't seem to be concerned. "The boss will be just fine," he stated. "We accomplished our primary goal. Killing that bitch would have been a bonus, but everyone knew it was a longshot from the start. We did our job, and did it well."

They continued on, the mood inside improving when an old road sign stated, "Oklahoma State Line – 2 miles."

"Did you see the look on that guy's face when I threw that chair at him?" asked the man in the backseat.

"Yes," replied the driver. "He was almost as shocked as the guy I shot."

"I missed all the fun," responded Mr. Suit-and-Tie. "On the next job, one of you two clowns has to play the respectable role and let me enjoy a little *incitement*."

Sheriff Watts eagerly scanned the initial reports coming out of Amarillo, relieved that Miss Brown wasn't listed as one of the victims.

He almost missed the section containing the eyewitness report, the word "Oklahoma" registering immediately as his brain sorted the facts as known.

Turning quickly to a stack of folders lying on his desk, the lawman flipped through several open cases until Bishop's report on the incident in Davidson County was in his hand. There it was again, the van's inspection sticker. A white van. Most likely from Oklahoma.

Then there was a conversation he'd had with Pete just that morning.

The councilman and former law enforcement officer was often interested in the criminal activity occurring throughout the territories. Being Bishop's friend, Pete was especially keen to hear about the Texan's adventures outside Fort Davidson.

Upon hearing about the van's registration sticker, Pete recalled the strange encounter he'd had the previous day at the bar. Producing the $100 bill, he described the man who'd left the super-sized tip and his odd behavior. Oklahoma, yet again.

Watts scratched his head, his mind screaming that he was missing something very important. Finally, it dawned.

The man who may have incited the riot in Amarillo had been wearing a suit and tie, described by many as "well dressed." Pete had used the exact same description of his customer.

Watts wondered if it might possibly be the same man.

Grabbing a pen and notepad, the sheriff scribbled an order to be broadcasted immediately. He wanted a sketch artist to work with key witnesses to create an image of the supposed troublemaker. He could show the drawing to Pete, and if it was the same man, he would start passing the image around Alpha to see if he got a hit.

After handing his written command to an assistant, Watts then flipped open his notepad and found Nick's emergency Satphone number.

The head of Alliance security needed to know his initial findings, as well as his suspicions regarding Pete's customer.

Opening a drawer, the sheriff retrieved the high-tech device and dialed Nick's phone.

The big man answered, and then listened as Watts relayed his findings.

"Now isn't that all quite interesting, Sheriff. You've given me a lot to consider. Has anyone seen Bishop, by the way?"

"No, I thought he was with you."

"He never showed up."

"Do I need to put out a bulletin?" Watts asked, his concerns now going wider.

"Not yet. Let's see where he turns up."

It took a while, unpacking the truck, verifying Terri and Hunter were shipshape and grabbing a bite to eat. After cleaning his weapons, the Texan decided to walk down to the courthouse and see if anyone knew what all the helicopter fuss was about.

A few blocks away, he ran into Butter taking an after-dinner stroll and enjoying the cool air.

"Hey, boss," the always cheerful kid greeted.

"What's up, Butter? You doing okay?"

"Yes, sir. I just found a place serving great hamburgers. They were so yummy, I had four."

Grunting at the mental image of a bewildered waitress and harried cook, Bishop asked the question that had been weighing on his mind all evening. "Hey, any word on what those three Blackhawks were doing in Alpha?"

With his eyes growing large, Butter spouted, "You haven't heard? Miss Brown was shot up in Amarillo. I hear she's going to be okay, but a lot of people were hurt or killed. Some sort of riot."

Bishop grew pale at the news, his mind moving in a thousand different directions at once. "You sure? She's not hurt bad?"

"Yes, sir, that's what I heard over the radio. I was hanging out with the security guys at the courthouse when the news came through that she was going to be fine. It was a tense afternoon, that's for sure."

"And the copters?"

"Mr. Nick went tearing ass up there with two rifle squads and a whole load of pissed law enforcement. Sheriff Watts is on his way as well. I hope they catch whoever is responsible. I want to watch Mr. Nick skin the asshole alive."

Butter continued with his report, relaying to his boss the few details he'd heard over the airwaves.

The two men then continued their stroll, Bishop wanting to go by the security office and see if there was any additional news. Terri would want to know the latest.

They were just walking up the courthouse steps when two police cars rounded the corner, followed by Diana's RV and bookending, black SUVs.

"Speak of the devil," Bishop said, and then as an afterthought, he added, "Butter, do me a favor and go tell Terri what's going on. I'm sure she'll want to be here."

"Yes, sir," sounded the instant response, and then Butter was hurrying toward the bungalow at a fair clip.

Nick obviously wasn't taking any chances, a massive security presence appearing around the courthouse in just moments. Bishop didn't blame him.

In addition to the police, the Texan spotted a least a dozen of Nick's best men positioning all around the area. There were even two counter-snipers stationed on a nearby rooftop.

Next came the doctor.

Evidently pre-warned of the convoy's arrival, the sawbones was rushed to the idling RV and where he quickly disappeared inside. Not wanting to get in the way, Bishop hung back, letting the professionals do their jobs.

Motion drew Bishop's eye, Terri and Butter hustling up the street, a look of concern coloring his wife's distraught face. A gleeful Hunter was bouncing on the bigger kid's shoulders.

"What are you doing out here?" Terri snapped. "How is she? What's going on?"

"I don't know," Bishop replied. "The doc just went in the RV, and I've been trying to stay out of the way."

Casting a frown at her husband, Terri snipped, "They're our best friends in the whole world. How can you not check on her?"

And with that, Terri made for the RV.

Just as his wife arrived at the door, Nick appeared on the steps. Nodding curtly to Terri, the ex-Green Beret stepped out of the way and let her past. Bishop had never seen his friend look so bad; concern over Nick's health now added to his list of worries.

Bishop decided Terri was right, and with Butter and his son in tow, the Texan approached his friend.

"Hey, how is she?"

"She'll be alright," came the brisk response.

He seems really sideways about this, Bishop thought. *I guess I would be, too.* "Anything I can do to help out?"

Nick threw Bishop a look that nearly froze the Texan's soul. "A little late for that, isn't it?" the big man snarled.

"What? What are you talking about?"

Stepping forward and poking a finger in Bishop's chest, Nick barked, "You were supposed to have been there, my *friend*. You and your wife told me not to worry... that I could stay here and mend... that you two would be there. You'd better have a class-fucking-A excuse, *Judas*."

The confrontation was so out of character, so unexpected, Bishop seemed to have trouble forming words. Nick didn't give him time to recoup, pressing in a fast and furious tirade. "Diana told me you didn't like this new property ownership law. You made it quite clear that it was a bad idea. So just because you disagree, you let her down? What the fuck is the matter with you? Don't you have any honor?"

The insult hit Bishop hard, the fact that the words were

coming from the man he considered his best friend multiplying the effect. "Nick... I know you don't mean that. Chill out, man."

"Chill out? Where the fuck were you? Diana came *this* close to getting her head blown off!"

"Terri wasn't feeling well.... We were running late...."

Nick stepped in closer, his face blistering with rage, "Terri! Now you're going to blame this shit on your wife? I can't believe I ever called you or that backstabbing, two-faced bitch of yours, my friends. Why on earth did I bother saving your sorry asses? How many times have I bailed you out? What a fool I've been. If you or your wife want Diana's job, why don't you just step up and say so? Fucking cowards... both of you."

Bishop could take any man's words, his time in the military helping to develop an extra-thick skin. The insults to Terri were a different story.

Now it was the Texan's turn to step into the larger man, his voice going low and mean, "Back that shit down, trooper... right fucking now. Say anything you want about me, but leave Terri out of this."

"Or what?" Nick bellowed back. "Go ahead, little man... bring your best... I'll stomp your sorry ass right here, right now."

Neither man seemed to notice the small crowd of onlookers their raised voices had attracted. Butter, sensing things were about to get completely out of control, handed Hunter to a woman he recognized and then stepped between the two quarreling men.

Wrapping his massive arms around Bishop before his boss could react, Butter began backing the Texan away, calmly saying, "Come on, boss.... Let's finish our walk... get some air... cool down."

Nick kept it up, "That's about what I figured out of a pussy like you! Your man had to come and rescue your yellow ass."

Bishop stopped struggling against the stronger Butter, spreading his arms wide in surrender and saying, "Thanks. I'm cool. It's all under control."

Taking his mentor at his word, Butter loosened his grip.

In a flash, Bishop sidestepped the kid and charged.

Butter may have been fooled, but Nick was ready. Stepping into the rushing Texan, the operator's right fist shot out with all his weight behind it. The target of his wrath, however, was no longer there.

At the last millisecond, Bishop shifted into a baseball slide, his boot slamming into Nick's lower leg with tremendous force. Still off-balance from his punch, the big man fell, hitting the ground hard.

Nick was bigger and far more experienced in unarmed combat. Normally, Bishop would have had little chance against the highly skilled warrior, but Nick had just spent weeks in the hospital and was still healing from his wounds.

Both men rolled, regaining their feet quickly. Nick, wanting to take advantage of his size, dove for Bishop in hopes of shortening the contest via a grappling match. The vision of ripping his foe's arms from his torso filled his mind.

Bishop wanted none of it.

Sidestepping the flying giant, Bishop struck hard with the heel of his hand as Nick flew by. The blow, however, damaged little but the retired operator's ego.

With a roar, Nick landed in a perfect roll. As Bishop stepped in to deliver another strike, the big man's boot lashed out, landing a painful kick just above the Texan's knee and spinning him away.

Both of them paused for just a moment, breathing hard as they readied to re-engage.

The thunderclap of a pistol shot stopped the battle cold.

All eyes turned to see Diana and Terri standing nearby, the Alliance leader's pistol still pointing in the air as smoke rolled out of the barrel. "Stop it! Both of you… right now. Have you both gone insane?"

"I'm giving this cowardly fuck what he deserves," Nick shouted. "Stay the hell out of this."

"Now whose girl is saving his ass?" Bishop taunted, his eyes never leaving the opponent.

Butter reappeared, along with a half-dozen confused security men, all of them moving to stand between the two combatants.

"You little fuck," Nick roared, "I'm going to ram my fist down that smartass throat of yours and tear out your heart."

"You're too old and slow to kick my ass," Bishop snapped. "C 'mere, fat boy!"

With a deep-chested growl, Nick dove for Bishop, Butter and two husky security types struggling to restrain the infuriated behemoth.

Seeing an opportunity with his foe being restrained by three strong men, Bishop went for Nick's throat, his hands straining to crush a windpipe. Two, and then three, and then four deputies finally tackled the thrashing Texan to the ground in a dogpile of uniforms and straining men.

Next, the girls were between them, both shouting for their mates to stop.

Terri got through first, getting in Bishop's face as he tried to shake the cops off his arms and legs. "Quit it! I'm serious… stop this nonsense right now. What the hell do you think you're doing?"

Running out of gas, Bishop managed, "Defending your honor," between gasps of air. "You wouldn't believe what that ass bag just said about you."

With the Texan no longer struggling, the two deputies started to relax their grip. Terri warned them, "Don't fall for it. He's still pissed... I can see it."

Foiled, Bishop threw a dirty look at his wife. "Okay... okay... I promise. I'll quit."

"Let him up," Terri commanded the lawman, "But don't let go just yet. He's sneaky as hell."

Ten feet away, Diana was having a similar exchange with Nick. With over a dozen bodyguards now between them, the two men were gradually herded away from each other.

Terri, finally convinced that Bishop had regained his senses, motioned for the now hovering Butter to retrieve Hunter from the ad hoc babysitter. After verifying her son was okay, she then hooked arms with her husband. "Come on, we're going home. You've got a lot explaining to do."

Bishop, still looking over his shoulder as if he expected Nick to come charging, didn't have much to say at the moment.

The walk back to the bungalow helped clear the adrenaline from Bishop's system and refocus his mind. With Butter standing by just in case, Terri put Hunter down for the night while her husband washed up.

"Okay," she announced, joining the two men on the front porch. "Explain this to me."

"We can let Butter go home," Bishop responded. "I'm fine."

"No, I want him to stay," Terri stated. "I just saw my husband act like he'd completely lost his mind, and quite frankly, I'm not sure I trust his lucidity just yet. Butter stays."

"Fine. The long and the short of it is that Nick was taking out his frustrations on me, blaming me for Diana getting shot. I was cool with that, but then he started accusing you of a bunch of nasty shit, and I lost my temper."

Terri tilted her head and then switched her laser-like gaze on Butter. "Is that how you saw it?" she asked.

"Yes, ma'am, that's exactly what happened," the suddenly-shy fellow responded.

Now back to Bishop, she barked, "And what exactly did Nick accuse me of that caused you to start a fight with your closest friend?"

"Basically that you were after Diana's job. He said, and I quote, that you were a 'power-hungry, back-stabbing bitch.'"

Not believing Nick would have made such an accusation, Terri's gaze shifted to Butter. She didn't have to voice the question. Looking down, the kid mumbled, "Yes, ma'am. Mr. Nick said those words."

Terri couldn't believe it. With her hands on her hips, she took a few steps to the edge of the porch and stared off into the distance for nearly a minute.

"Something's not right," she finally whispered. "I don't know what's going on, but somehow this is all spiraling out of control. We'll let this settle overnight, and in the morning we'll find out what in the hell is happening. Hopefully, cooler heads will prevail."

"You're right," Bishop added, his voice now sad. "I've never seen Nick like that before. I'm sure we can talk tomorrow and work it all out."

Terri stepped toward the somewhat cowering Butter and took his hand. "Thank you for all your help tonight. You should head on home and get some sleep. We'll be just fine now."

"Okay, Miss Terri. Good night... and same to you, boss."

After Butter had disappeared down the sidewalk, Bishop rose and went to his mate. "I'm sorry," he said sincerely. "I just couldn't handle someone speaking about you that way. We've both put our lives on the line for the Alliance so many times I've lost count. To hear Nick talk like that just made me crazy."

She stretched long, kissing him on the cheek. "We'll straighten this all out in the morning. Come to bed. Tomorrow looks like it's going to be a long day."

Chapter 13

Diana's head was throbbing, the aspirin doing little to counter the discomfort. Instead of rest, as prescribed, she had rushed from the RV, fired a weapon, and been stressed even further by Nick and Bishop's fight.

Once everything had settled down, she'd ordered the doctor's return – this time for her future husband.

Physically, he was in decline, having pulled three staples from one of his wounds suffered in New Mexico. Mentally, the man seemed to be a wreck.

"I order bed rest for at least two days," the physician had stated strongly. "Seriously, keep him off his feet, or he's going to do a lot more damage. Between his activities in Amarillo and the fisticuffs in front of the courthouse, he's lucky not to be bleeding internally and in even more trouble."

"And his mental state?"

"I'm a medical doctor, so by no means an expert. He was very stoic during my examination, but that's nothing new."

"I need to talk with him…. I'm sure you understand why."

The sawbones rubbed his chin, finally conceding. "Not for long. I mean it… he needs rest."

She entered the RV's master suite, finding Nick lying comfortably on the large bed. His face remained emotionless, despite her best attempt at a warm smile.

"How's things?" she said softly, sitting beside him.

"I'm okay. How are you doing?" he asked, pointing at the bandage still wrapped around her head.

"To be blunt, I've felt better. What happened, Nick?"

"Bishop and I had a disagreement; that's all. It's over now," the monotone voice answered.

"Bullshit. I'm not buying that for one second. Come clean. Trust me."

Nick's gaze drifted toward some undefined point in time and space. With a distant voice he said, "To be honest, I'm not sure what happened. During the entire drive back from Amarillo, I kept thinking about why Bishop hadn't shown up at the town meeting. The events of the past few months kept replaying in my head, over and over again. I was so furious by the time we pulled into Alpha, I guess I lost control."

Taking his hand, Diana tried to reassure him with a warm touch. "What events? What set this off? I know you aren't the type to cause trouble without a good reason, especially with someone like Bishop. What is this all about? What's eating you?"

The question seemed to trouble him. There was a frown, then a grimace, and finally a look of helplessness. "I know this is going to sound pretty farfetched. I'm reluctant to say it aloud."

It was Diana's turn to express hurt. "Nick, I love you with all my heart. You're going to be my husband soon. If you can't trust me.... If you can't tell me everything...."

"No, no," he came back quickly. "I do trust you in all things. It's your trust in me that I'm protecting."

She leaned over, kissing him softly on the forehead. "I have to know. Surely, you understand that. All sorts of people saw Bishop and you fighting right in front of the courthouse. Rumors are no doubt spreading across the Alliance, even as we speak. But more importantly, we are going to have to face Bishop and Terri sooner or later, and I want to have all the facts straight before that occurs."

He nodded, "You're right, as usual." Then came a pause as he gathered his thoughts.

"The short of it is, I'm convinced that Bishop is trying to undermine the direction you are taking the Alliance, and I think Terri is onboard with his position."

The shocked expression drained the color from Diana's face. "What? How on earth did you come up with that?"

"Hear me out," Nick snapped back, rising from the pillow. "We know there was a confrontation between Bishop and the cops in Meraton a while back. Terri has relayed his frustration with a lot of the new rules and regulations. You said yourself that he didn't want to execute the plan in New Mexico. He failed up in Palo Dura. Then this latest fiasco in Fort Davidson, where he wanted me to wait before arriving with the cavalry? That was just plain weird. You told me he was against the new property law and tried several times to talk you out of it. He didn't even want to go to Houston and claim his own home. He started a fight with our new ambassador. I could go on and on."

Diana shook her head, not believing what she was hearing. "All of those points have a perfectly logical explanation. While you were in the hospital, Bishop was the best friend I could have asked for. Sure, he disagrees with some of the stuff the council is doing, but doesn't every citizen?"

Nick wasn't budging. "Why didn't he show up in Amarillo? That's not the Bishop and Terri we know and love. Why did Grim and Butter not follow my orders the night he attacked Chase? Why did Bishop have Butter break into the doctor's office and steal my medical records?"

"He did what?" Diana snapped, stunned by the new revelation.

"Chase told me he saw Butter running away from the area the night Doc's office was burglarized. We both know that kid wouldn't do something like that on his own."

Rising from her bedside perch, Diana began pacing. With her mind moving a thousand miles a minute, she tried to analyze Nick's accusations one by one. A single question kept burning in her mind.

"Why?" she asked, returning back to Nick. "What possible motive could Bishop and Terri have to undermine my administration?"

Breaking eye contract, Nick's gaze again drifted someplace else. "I can't answer that, at least not just yet. Believe me, I've been pondering that same question for several days now. It could be Terri wants to run the Alliance, and Bishop is supporting her. They might have someone else in mind... or could be having second thoughts about Texas being independent. Who knows how or what conspirators think?"

Again, Diana wasn't buying it. "It was Terri's idea for Texas to be independent. No one has done more for the Alliance and to support my position than those two. I just can't accept that there is some hidden agenda with our best friends."

Nick's face softened, his eyes growing warm. "Your loyalty to friends and supporters is part of the reason why I love you so much. It shows the quality of person that you truly are. But not everyone is like you. Over my lifetime, I've seen traitors, schemers, and common men develop an unquenchable thirst for power and money. You can never, never let your guard down. Never."

"I bet you've also seen leaders grow paranoid, afraid of their own shadows, and see boogie men under the bed," she countered.

Sighing, Nick said, "Yes, I've seen that as well. If you truly think I've left the reservation, let me ask you one last question before we both turn in. Don't you find it about the biggest coincidence in the history of mankind that our new ambassador is actually an acquaintance of Terri's? Don't you find it the least bit strange that Chase was assigned by Bishop's former boss... a man he obviously respects and has risked his life to protect?"

"Yes, it's odd, but not impossible. I've wondered about that before."

"Combine all of what I've said, Diana. Connect the dots any way you wish. I might be wrong about all this, but for sure I've not completely lost my mind."

She again kissed his cheek, her mind still reeling from his words. "We both need to rest now. I've got a lot to digest. I'll see you in the morning."

Terri rose early, giving up any hope of sleep. She had tossed and turned all night, Bishop's fight, and more specifically Nick's words, keeping her from achieving any beneficial rest.

So troubled was the young mother, she decided that seeking a babysitter for her son was the morning's top priority. Bishop, fully aware that his mate hadn't slept well, offered to take care of Hunter for the day.

"We should see if I can get someone else," Terri protested, still sipping her morning cup of tea. "We need to visit Nick and Diana together."

"I don't think that's wise. I know I'm still stinging from Nick's words, and can only assume he's still thinking like a crazy man. How about us boys hang out here while you sensible female-types solve the world's problems?"

"Fine."

After a quick shower, Terri threw on a pair of jeans and a T-shirt. Today, comfort was a higher priority than image.

After kissing Hunter and Bishop goodbye, she was off to the courthouse, still unsure how she was going to approach the subject with Diana.

Halfway there, a familiar voice called from behind her.

"Oh shit, not now, Chase," she whispered, trying to pretend as if she hadn't heard his greeting.

"Hey, Terri! Wait up!" he repeated after rushing to catch up.

"Good morning, Mr. Ambassador."

"I heard about the festivities last night," he continued, short of breath. "It seems like your husband has been experiencing confrontation issues of late. Are you okay?"

Terri stopped, spinning to face him with anger in her eyes, "That, sir, is none of your business. Furthermore, I don't appreciate your gloating tone of voice."

The diplomat became stern as well, "But it is my business, madam. I am charged with interaction at the highest levels of the Alliance government. The fact that the head of security services was in a fistfight with the husband of my liaison is well within my scope of operational responsibility. Throw in the fact that the same man assaulted me less than a week ago warrants my attentions."

"Keep out of this, Chase. It doesn't concern you. The two incidents are unrelated, and last night's affair has nothing to do with the United States or its interests."

Chase relaxed, just a little, his tone becoming reasonable. "Really, to be honest, I just wanted to check on you and make sure you were okay. What the hell is going on, Terri?"

"It's no biggie," she replied. "A misunderstanding is all."

Pretending to accept her answer, he replied, "Good. I was afraid it all had something to do with Butter's arrest. I'm glad you cleared it up and that everything's okay."

"Butter's arrest?"

"Well, as of just a few minutes ago, his attempted arrest. I think they're calling in a SWAT team or something."

"Shit!" she barked, pivoting to push past the messenger.

Darting the few blocks to the house, she burst in the front door and told Bishop what she'd just heard.

Mumbling, "I told you he was thinking like a crazy man," Bishop grabbed his carbine from the closet after handing Hunter to his mother.

"What are you doing?"

"I'm going to figure out what the fuck is going on," he snapped. "It's one thing for Nick to pick a fight with you or me. Taking out his frustrations on my loyal teammates is another."

Terri blocked his way to the door, her expression making it clear she wasn't going to be moved easily. "Leave the rifle here."

"No."

"Bishop... please... don't take the rifle. Nothing good can come of it."

For a moment, she thought her plea was hopeless. Bishop had that look in his eye, the one that was normally followed by a lot of shooting and carnage.

"Please."

He changed, much to Terri's relief. One of her recurring nightmares last night had been of Nick and her husband's brouhaha escalating into a full-blown gun battle.

He returned the long gun to its resting place, and then sighed, "There. Are you happy now?"

"Yes, thank you. I'll get Hunter dressed, and we'll be over in a bit. Please, be the cool head, whatever is going on."

"You got it," he said, bending to kiss her forehead before hustling out the door.

It was six blocks to the former hotel where Butter had a room. Bishop ran the entire distance; the only noise reaching the Texan's ears was the pounding of his heart and boots.

He rounded the corner to see several police cars and Alpha's only functional ambulance parked in front of what he knew was Butter's residence. There were dozens of people standing around.

He spotted Sheriff Watts, Nick, and a deputy standing in front of the crowd, the huddled men talking out of earshot of the gathering onlookers.

As he drew closer, he also saw two EMTs and the doctor bent over a prone deputy. Another was already on the stretcher. "Fuck," Bishop muttered. "What have you gone and done, Butter?"

The window fronting Butter's unit was shattered, shards of glass sparkling all over the sidewalk. Bishop could see small pockets of blood intermixed with the remnants.

The door to the former hotel room was partially open, at least four deputies pointing pistols at the threshold. There was no sign of Butter.

Ignoring Nick, Bishop stepped directly to the sheriff. "What's going on?"

Watts turned and said, "Your man in there just put two of my officers in the hospital," he spat. "He threw one out the window and broke the other's jaw."

"Butter wouldn't do that without damn good reason, Sheriff. What happened?"

"Nick radioed me early this morning and said he had information that Butter had been involved in a burglary. I sent two deputies over to search his quarters and things obviously went wrong."

Finally acknowledging Nick, Bishop stared at the big man and said, "Burglary? Seriously? Butter?"

"There was an eyewitness," came the cold reply. "Someone saw a person resembling Butter leaving the doctor's office the other night."

"Butter? Now why on earth would he break into the doctor's office?" Bishop replied, trying to keep his cool.

"After we had arrested Butter, I was going to ask you that very same question," Nick replied with an edgy tone. "After all, that kid would only do something like that if he was ordered to."

The accusation was clear, Bishop's temper rising quickly. Seeming to struggle to control the building rage, the Texan hissed, "You and I can settle our shit later. There's no need to involve innocents."

Watts sensed he was about to be caught in a clash of titans and moved to defuse the situation. "I can't stop you two boys from having your schoolyard brawl, but please, not right now. I've got men down and a very skilled, heavily armed shooter inside that room. If a firefight breaks out, a lot of civilians might get hurt."

Shaking his head in frustration, Bishop shot Nick a nasty look and then pivoted toward Butter's room. Watts said, "I wouldn't do that... he's pretty desperate."

Ignoring the warning, Bishop strolled directly toward the threshold and then stopped about 20 feet away. "Butter!" he said loud and clear, "It's Bishop. I'm coming in. If you shoot me, Miss Terri is going to be pissed."

"I wouldn't shoot you, boss," came the distant reply.

Bishop entered the dark room, finding Butter behind the bed with his weapon trained toward the parking lot. A pile of magazines was beside the clearly frightened kid.

"Good morning," Bishop greeted as if nothing was wrong.

The response came in a rush. "Sir, those deputies said I broke into the doctor's office... but I didn't. They pointed toward the file sitting over there and said I'd stole it. I'm not a thief, sir. I've never taken anything that doesn't belong to me."

Frowning, Bishop reached for the office folder Butter had indicated. Sure enough, it was full of medical records – Nick's records. "What the fuck? Where did you get this, Butter?"

"I've never seen that before, sir. The two deputies found it behind the dresser while they were searching my room. I swear I didn't know it was there."

"Do you ever leave your door unlocked?" Bishop said, turning to examine the opening.

"No, but a few nights ago, my key didn't work the first two times I tried. I just thought it was getting stiff or something and sprayed some gun oil on it."

Bishop bent and looked at the keyhole, finding several fresh-looking scratch marks. There was no way to tell if the lock had been picked, or not.

Returning to Butter, Bishop sat on the bed next to the nervous kid. "Look, you're going to have to surrender. I'll make sure Watts knows the truth and treats you fairly, but this standoff is going to end badly, and you know it."

"But... but, sir, I didn't do anything wrong."

"I know that, Butter," Bishop replied with the softest voice he could manage. "I believe you, 100 percent. On the other hand, Watts has to do his job, and the deputies will keep coming and coming. End this, my friend, before it all spirals out of control."

The look of helplessness on the kid's face nearly tore Bishop's heart out of his chest.

"Why is this happening to me?" Butter asked, tears rolling

down his cheeks. "I didn't do anything wrong, sir."

"I promise you I won't rest until your name is cleared. I swear it. Now secure that blaster, and let's go talk to the sheriff."

Nodding, Butter did as Bishop asked.

Bishop grabbed the folder while Butter put away his weapon and stood to straighten himself out.

"Stand tall, Butter," Bishop said kindly. "Square those shoulders and walk out of here like the innocent man you are."

"Yes, sir."

Bishop went to the doorway and shouted out, "We're coming out! Hold your fire! We are unarmed!"

Turning and nodding to his teammate, Bishop said, "Keep your hands out wide and don't make any sudden movements. You hurt two of them. Think about how we would feel if someone kicked the shit out of our teammates."

"Yes, sir."

Bishop went first, his hands wide. Butter followed as instructed.

After they were a few steps outside, two deputies rushed up, one reaching for the handcuffs on his belt.

"No," Bishop commanded, "that won't be necessary."

The two lawman threw a questioning look at the approaching sheriff, not sure what to do. "It's okay," Watts said calmly. "At least for now."

Bishop held the folder out for Watts to see. "Is this what you're looking for?"

As the sheriff reached for the evidence, Nick stepped in and rudely snatched the documents away. "That's private information," he hissed.

Deciding to ignore his ex-friend's reaction, Bishop motioned toward the hotel room door. "Sheriff, Butter claims that he never saw that file before, and I believe him. He also stated that a few nights ago his key wouldn't work as usual. If you look at the lock, it has some odd scratches around the keyhole."

"A likely story," Nick spouted. "Do you really expect anyone to believe that shit?"

Before Bishop could reply, a commotion at the edge of the crowd drew everyone's attention. Terri, Diana, and Ambassador McQuire, along with their significant security entourages, had arrived.

Nick apparently forgot all about Butter, Diana's appearance now the big man's highest priority. Walking toward her, he said, "I thought you were going to sleep late this morning? Really, you shouldn't be out of bed. There's no need for you to be involved in this."

Diana didn't even hesitate, her mind set on getting in the middle of the fray, "What the hell is going on?"

"There's no need for you to be here," Nick repeated. "This doesn't involve you."

"I think it does involve me," Diana stated, clearly prepared to hold her ground. "Terri came to me a few minutes ago, afraid you two were going to try and kill each other again. Somebody explain to me why half of the police force and two of our most highly regarded SAINT team members are in a standoff."

Watts took less than a minute to brief the Alliance leader.

Diana took it all in, never saying a word until the sheriff had finished. She then motioned Nick to follow her out of earshot.

"I want to support my man," Diana began. "Truly I want to back you up more than anything. But until you start talking to me, that is becoming more and more difficult with each passing moment."

"I told you last night, I'm convinced that Bishop and Terri are up to something. Chase told me the day after the break-in at the doctor's office that he'd seen Butter running away as the police arrived. After what happened yesterday, I decided to see if there was any proof."

Nick then held out the doctor's folder and said, "And guess what? The cops found this in Butter's room this morning. Do you still think I'm crazy?"

Diana started to reach for the file in Nick's hand, but the big man pulled it back. "It's my medical records is all," he said, clenching the documents tightly.

"Why, Nick? Why would someone break into the doctor's office and steal your records? What possible value could they have?"

His answer came quickly – too quickly. "If my health were poor, that weakness could be used against us both. I think Bishop and Terri were fishing for leverage."

Not in a million years would Diana have accepted the explanation were it not for the fact that the folder was in Butter's room, and someone had broken into the doctor's office. Diana's headache came rushing back.

"Okay, I need time to think this through. What's next?"

"We take Butter into custody and try to get him to confess that Bishop ordered him to do the dirty deed. Then we'll arrest Bishop and his wife."

"Are you serious? How can you even think like that? After everything we've been through together?"

Nick didn't answer, his attention diverted by the sound of Terri's voice as she was speaking with Sheriff Watts. A scowl crossed the big man's face.

Holding up a finger, Nick said, "Hold that thought," before rushing back to the main gathering. He arrived in time to hear Terri saying, "Release him into my custody, Sheriff. I promise you he won't be going anywhere."

"No!" Nick snapped, "I want to interview Butter and get to the bottom of this quickly."

Bishop stepped directly into Nick's path, "I have one over-riding question for you. Who is the eyewitness that saw Butter leaving the doctor's office?"

"That's not important," came the curt response.

"It most certainly is," sounded Terri, her words fast and sharp. "Anyone charged with a crime has the right to face their accusers. That's been a basic right for hundreds of years... or has the paranoia around here gotten to the point where we're suspending the Bill or Rights? Who is the witness?"

Nick, taken aback by Terri's assault, briefly flashed his eyes in Chase's direction.

Bishop saw it.

"You!" Bishop barked, pointing a finger at the ambassador. "You son of a bitch," he continued, stepping toward the indignant man. "None of this shit started happening until you arrived. I should have killed you that first night."

Chase didn't answer, instead reaching for his pistol and drawing the weapon.

Despite the gun pointing at Bishop's head, the Texan kept coming. "You low-life bag of shit.... You're in the middle of all this, stirring up trouble for God knows what reason."

Watts came between the two men, shouting for the ambassador to put the weapon away. Terri was tugging on Bishop. Several deputies rushed in. Chase's security team, as well as Diana's, all seemed to appear out of nowhere.

For a moment, it looked like a full-out brawl was about to erupt in the hotel's parking lot, tempers, fear, duty, and egos flaring in all corners.

Diana, feeling the need to take charge, raised her voice, "People! People! Stop this right...."

The Alliance's leader's eyes rolled into the back of her head as her legs gave way, and she crumpled toward the lot. Only Nick's cat-like reflexes saved her from another head injury.

Chapter 14

Pete glanced at the pile of newsprint, the stack of papers drawing yet another frown.

By pre-collapse standards, they weren't much, individually or as a whole. Thin paper, cheap, smearing ink, and a few pages per edition, they were hardly worthy of a birdcage's gutter.

Yet the councilman, bar owner, and brewer knew they were a sign of progress and recovery. Newspapers were communication and an important part of governmental checks and balances. They represented free speech.

All of that was fine and dandy until the press lost its neutrality. Pete recalled a quote by the famous French General, Napoleon Bonaparte; "Four hostile newspapers are more to be feared than a thousand bayonets."

It wasn't so much that the reporters had turned hostile, or suddenly developed a dislike for the leadership in Alpha. In reality, they were merely relaying the events of the last few days to their readers.

A series of events that Pete was still having trouble comprehending.

Rumors and the retelling of the attempt on Diana's life had spread like wildfire all across the Alliance's territory. Even when stated accurately, the news was worrisome to many. When truthful recounts of the "Incident in Amarillo" were lacking, slight exaggerations and misinformation filled the gaps.

It was only to be expected. People were always hungry for information, inaccurate gossip or not. Many of the embellishments sent waves of outright fear rolling through the population at large. The citizens were a nervous mess. Having survived one apocalypse lessened the average person's tolerance of instability, the unknown, and rapid change. Optimism was declining at an alarming rate.

When news of that incident was followed by headlines of other town hall meetings gone awry, tremors of unrest began to rattle through the Alliance.

Pete picked up a copy of the Dallas paper, the headline reading, "Property Claims Suspended by Unrest in Plano." Someone had started firing a weapon while standing in line. A woman and her child were badly hurt by the throng's stampede to escape the gunfire.

Midland Station's rag was even more troubling. In large,

bold font, the words, "Massive Claim Filed by Lewis Oil – Could Bankrupt the Alliance," stared back at Pete. The story contained few details but was troubling nonetheless. Someone was making a claim for the local oil refinery and all of the product it had produced since the Alliance had liberated the town. That claim was for trillions of dollars.

Every single one of the small, struggling news outlets contained similar stories. Austin's town meeting had broken down into a swirling pool of arguments and was quickly shut down by the authorities before another riot took place. San Antonio's mayor had canceled her presentation after several attendees refused to surrender their firearms at the door. It was a pure, unadulterated, hot mess.

The negative impact of those stories was nothing compared to the near panic that was generated by reports of fighting amongst the leadership in Alpha.

While printed details were sketchy, the quarrel between Bishop and Nick had been publicized as rift based on a difference in politics that had gotten out of control. The article had served little purpose other than to divide readers, some siding with Bishop, others relating with the incumbent's camp.

Now, this morning's paper had delivered the worst. Diana had fainted, rekindling conspiracy theories that her injuries were far more serious than originally reported. The Houston Post was calling for the chairperson to step aside, questioning her ability to run the government. The Texarkana Times was calling for Texas to cease its "…failed effort to become an independent nation, and reintegrate with the United States as soon as possible."

There was more than just the headlines.

Well-worded editorials were carried by many of the fish wrappers, all questioning the Alliance's government, elected officials, and the direction the fledgling country was taking in general.

The few radio stations in operation were hosting guests that spouted every possible angle of conspiracy imaginable.

Pete had rushed to Alpha upon hearing of Diana's collapse. Despite being one of the original councilmen and a close friend, Nick had denied all access.

Instead, the head of Alliance security had grilled Pete on his relationship with Bishop and Terri. The questions, really more of an interrogation, had been troubling to say the least.

When Pete had tried to locate his friends and find out what the hell was going on, Bishop and his family were nowhere to be found. Even Sheriff Watt's lips seemed to be sealed. Not even the old "one cop to another," posturing had been effective. He could only assume they had retreated to the ranch.

Returning to Meraton, Pete found himself fighting off a growing sense of helplessness. It seemed like everything they'd worked for was crumbling beneath his feet. The council, despite surviving numerous threats in the past, had become dysfunctional. Untrusting. Frightened.

Close friends and trusted allies were now viewed with suspicion. The government's boldest move yet, the new property law, was causing chaos and unrest throughout the land.

Pete found himself desperately wanting to speak with Terri. He recalled how many times her cool head and perceptive logic had saved the young movement. She always had a unique view, and her creative solutions were one of the reasons they'd made it this far.

Shoving the newspapers aside, Pete rose from his desk determined to find his friends. He knew the location of the ranch. It wasn't that far. He could drive there in less than an hour.

A knock on the door interrupted his train of thought. "Yes?"

The bartender's head appeared, "Pete, some kid just left a message for you. He said it was urgent."

"What? That's odd. Let's see it."

Pete was handed a sealed envelope, his first thought being, "What now?"

The handwritten note inside was signed, "Love, Terri." He began reading it in a rush: As you are no doubt aware, things have gotten a little strange in Alpha. Bishop and I need someplace to hole up, out of sight, but not the ranch. Would you have time to meet us at Betty's old bed and breakfast with some ideas? We'll be here the rest of the night."

Pete set the paper down, mumbling, "Have things degraded so far that Bishop and Terri have to sneak into Meraton and pass secret notes?"

He could remember the day Bishop was given the honorary title of Texas Ranger and the ensuing ceremony. How many times had the couple saved the Alliance and thousands, upon thousands of lives?

Rising from his desk, Pete stepped to the front of the bar and informed the barkeep that he was going out for a bit.

As he drove out of Meraton, he cursed his own paranoia after glancing in the rearview mirror to make sure he wasn't being followed. "I guess it has gone that far."

The old bed and breakfast hadn't been occupied since Betty had taken over the Manor. As he pulled in front of the overgrown driveway, Pete thought about the woman he'd one day hoped to marry. Her untimely death during the hurricane in Galveston had been one of the saddest days of his life.

For a moment, he thought he'd messed up and gone to the wrong house. There was no sign of Bishop's truck or the couple. Pushing down the knee-high weeds as he rolled closer to the porch, Pete saw the Texan standing in the dark, rifle slung across his chest.

Terri and Hunter appeared a moment later, all smiles and hugs. "I'm so glad you came," she gushed. "It's difficult to know who is still a friend."

Meraton's councilman soon found that Bishop had hidden his pickup in the backyard. The couple had already set up a tent – just in case Pete hadn't answered the note. Given the gear Bishop was wearing, it seemed as if the Texan was ready for a less than friendly response as well.

After helping the couple load their belongings into his car, their impromptu host chaperoned them to the back of the Manor. "I keep a suite available for visiting businessmen and other guests. I'll tell the front desk that you two have just arrived after a long journey and shouldn't be disturbed."

"Thanks, Pete," Bishop replied. "We appreciate your hospitality. We considered hiding out at Betty's, but there were no supplies there. We should only be in your hair a few days."

"I owe my life to both of you," replied the older man. "The entire town probably wouldn't be here if it wasn't for your heroics. Now, once you're unpacked and comfortable, I want to know what in the hell is going on in Alpha."

"You're not the only one," Terri replied. "We probably have the same questions as you."

Two hours later, sitting in an isolated corner of the Manor's famous gardens, Pete sighed and shook his head in disbelief. "How did this happen? What the hell is Nick thinking?"

"We're as stumped as you are," Bishop responded, his voice colored with sadness. "We're hoping to lay low for a few days and see if things cool down."

"I was planning to go to Alpha tomorrow. I'll try to see Diana again," Pete said. "Maybe she can shed some light and make sense of it all."

Everyone was tired and decided to call it a night.

As he walked back to the bar, Pete paused and looked back at the Manor. "I wonder where they'll go if this doesn't get resolved? I wonder if they'll take me along?"

210

The next day was like most at the Manor, relaxing and quiet.

Terri decided to take a chance on being recognized. Wearing her hair in a schoolmarm's bun and accessorized with oversized, dark sunglasses, she went for a swim with Hunter. Bishop, after numerous "patrols" around the grounds, eventually joined them. His wife thought it was hilarious when he splashed into the pool wearing a disguise that included a frizzy mop head as a wig. Hunter didn't agree.

Frightened of his father's creation, the kid wouldn't go near his dad, eyeing the strange-looking character with suspicion, screaming loudly whenever Bishop tried to approach with extended arms.

Noting that there wasn't anyone around anyway, the father soon discarded the camouflage so he could play with his son.

By late afternoon, the Texan was restless, pacing around the grounds. By early evening, he had finally settled in one of the hotel's numerous rocking chairs, working back and forth at a steady pace.

When Hunter went down for a nap, Terri joined him on the porch.

"It's Chase," Bishop stated out of the blue. "I've finally figured it out. Chase is behind all this."

"What? How did you come to that conclusion?"

"It all makes sense. He's had his nose in every single thing that has gone wrong lately. He was in Houston and caused us to get a late start and not go to Amarillo. He was the one accusing Butter of stealing those medical records. I'm telling you, he's behind all this."

"Did he cause Nick to verbally attack us?"

"Not directly."

"Did he incite the riot or shoot Diana?"

"No… not that I know of."

"I think you're just jealous. It's cute and very flattering, but your timing is poor."

Bishop's face got red. "I'm getting a little tired of people thinking I'm that shallow and insecure. I especially expected a little better from my wife of all people."

For a second, Terri thought he was teasing, or exercising that infamous, ill-timed humor. It quickly became clear, however, that her husband was serious. "Oh come on, Bishop," she pushed back. "You know I was making a joke. You understand the value of laughter when times are stressful."

"I know you were joking," he stated in a low monotone.

"That's not what's pissing me off. It's the fact that my analysis is dismissed so easily. You're not the only one who can read people, my dear."

She didn't like his tone or statement. "Seriously, Bishop? You want to dissect recent events with an eye toward Chase McQuire? Fine. Let's roll down that path and see where it leads us."

"Fine."

"First of all, he's not been in the right place at the right time to be involved in half of the incidents. Where would you like to begin?"

Bishop rubbed his chin, almost as if he was regretting the conversation already. "The first fiasco after his arrival was that bullshit up by Fort Davidson… that weird, still-unexplained team that arrived out of nowhere and shot up my men."

"And Chase was involved in what way?"

"You told him where I was, didn't you?"

Now it was Terri's cheeks flushing red. "Yes, I probably mentioned it. It wasn't a secret or anything. Hell, your guys and you were loading up trucks full of supplies in broad daylight. Remember?"

"So he knew. Maybe he called in some old friends. You said he was in the military, right? Those guys that hit us in that valley were ex-military…. I'm sure of that."

It all came welling up inside of Terri, an eruption of painful memories and strong sensations. The trip back to Houston, seeing their old home, and Chase's reappearance in her life. It all combined with Nick and Diana's strange behavior to make her feel as if her world was collapsing – as if her head was about to explode.

"Bishop! Is there some virus going around that is converting testosterone into stupidity and paranoia? First, it infected Nick, and now you? Do you really think Chase wants in my pants so badly that he would hire a team of professional hitmen to take you out of the picture?"

Bishop stood abruptly, his face cold with anger. "There you go again, and quite frankly, it's getting a little old. You're a stunning young lady, but not *that* hot, sweetheart. Of course, Chase wouldn't go through all that just for a piece of your ass. It was the new property law that he was trying to sabotage."

With her lower lip trembling in rage, Terri stood and glared at her husband. "In all our years… with all the threats and tragedy and death we've endured, you've never spoken to me like that, *sweetheart*."

Bishop knew he should apologize, but he didn't. Instead, he

turned his back to her. "I need space," he informed his shell-shocked wife. "I need some time and open spaces to think. I'm going to go hunting."

"You're what? You're going to leave Hunter and me here by ourselves with the second apocalypse looming on the horizon?"

"You guys are as safe here as anywhere."

"Maybe I'd feel safer in the new house that Chase is fixing up," she hissed. "He invited me to come see it. I'm sure it's a little nicer than the camper."

"See... see what I mean," he growled back. "That little lard worm is just trying to drive a wedge between us. I should have gutted that shit shark when I had the chance."

Terri knew she'd struck a nerve, the veins on the side of Bishop's neck pulsating, the corded muscles on his arms tight like a guitar string. Deep down inside she knew it was wrong, but her fury eroded all restraint. "I don't think he's trying to come between us at all. I think he's merely trying to open my eyes," she spouted, instantly regretting the words.

In all their time together, she'd never once thought Bishop would, or could, strike her. Her husband's reaction, there on the front porch of their favorite place on earth, challenged that belief. His fists balled as his weight shifted forward - a lion preparing to pounce. For the first time in her life, Terri was frightened of the man she'd married.

Fortunately, it passed in a heartbeat, the Texan's stance returning to a non-threatening keel, almost relaxed. "Suit yourself. I'm going hunting."

Terri was over the top pissed. "I can't believe this! Right when we need each other the most, you're running out on me. What the hell has happened to you, Bishop? Maybe Nick was right. Maybe you have lost your honor."

"Nothing has happened to *me*," he replied coldly. "I just need to go hunting. I'll be back in a couple of days."

Without another word, Bishop went inside their room and gathered his equipment. He emerged a few minutes later after giving his sleeping son a soft kiss and whispering, "I love you."

Terri stood speechless by the door, arms crossed and mind burning from their fight. Bishop paused in front of her, bending to deliver a forehead peck. She moved away, purposefully avoiding the kiss.

Sighing, he walked out into the Texas night without another word.

Terri held it until she was sure he was too far away to hear and then began to sob. "Oh, God. What is happening to us?"

Bishop drove out of Meraton, a hunting trip to the mountains the last thing on his mind.

He hated deceiving Terri and would no doubt pay a price for that later. In his mind, however, he was completely justified. After all, she wouldn't even consider that her former lover was a wolf in sheep's clothing.

What he needed now was proof. Unquestionable, clear as day evidence.

He continued driving west toward Fort Bliss, his mind digesting the facts as fast as the truck was eating up the miles.

Twenty minutes outside the Alliance's largest military installation, he pulled to the side of the road and began to formalize his plan. It was all so risky, an all or nothing gamble, but he had to do it.

He'd snuck in and out of Bliss before, delivering a message to the visiting president, and then having to escape with the chief executive after an attempt on his life by the Independents. He knew the layout well.

Checking his watch, he knew there were only four hours until dawn. He needed the night to accomplish his mission. That's when the base's personnel would be the least active.

He thought about driving to the neighborhood he'd once used as a springboard to penetrate the base's perimeter. He could leave the truck and go in on foot. It was a 10-mile hump from there to the building that housed the base's primary communications center. If he hustled and traveled light, he might just make it in and out.

Then what?

He'd be exhausted, that's what.

No, he decided. There was a better way. He was getting too long in the tooth to go rushing off into the desert with a pack and a rifle.

Pulling out onto the road again, Bishop made for the front gate.

The sentry approached cautiously, traffic at the wee hour unusual, even for a facility as large as Bliss. "I have a priority one message from Chairperson Diana Brown," Bishop informed the sleepy soldier.

"Identification, please," the specialist stated, following procedure.

Bishop handed the man his new driver's license. "Check the

list," he told the soldier. "You'll find I'm cleared for entry."

The trooper did just that, waving Bishop through a few minutes later. "Finally some respect," Bishop whispered as he pulled through the gate.

He drove directly to the communications building, pulling the exact same stunt on the LT sitting behind the desk. "Give me the message, and I'll see to it," the officer offered.

"No," Bishop answered curtly. "This is POTUS eyes only."

"Fine."

Bishop was shown into the room where Diana and he had recently spoken with the Colonel. A few minutes later, the young sergeant on duty said, "The White House is on the line, sir. Press here to talk; release to listen. It takes the computers a bit to decode each transmission, so you can expect a slight delay."

"White House operations," came a metallic sounding voice. "State your message."

"Message is for POTUS and reads as follows; Code Red. Call Bishop at 1714419292 ASAP. End Message."

The voice in Washington repeated the words back to Bishop, and then the transmission was over. The Texan exited the building and the base as quickly as possible.

The "Code Red" was an old phrase from the days when Bishop had worked for the Colonel. The Texan hoped his old boss would remember. The number was the satellite phone he'd been issued while searching Palo Dura for the pot growers.

Two hours later, he pulled the truck into a secluded spot and waited for the President of the United States to call.

Three times Bishop checked the phone's battery level, nervous that he'd foul up his best opportunity by making a mistake with technology he wasn't used to operating.

After another 40 minutes, the phone rang, causing Bishop to jump.

"Hello, sir. Thank you for calling."

"What's wrong, Bishop? This is highly unusual."

"Sir, I need to speak with you about the ambassador you assigned to the Alliance. How well do you know this man?"

There was a pause on the other end before the familiar voice said, "I don't know him, son. I've never met the man. He was recommended to me by a private individual who's been doing good work with our recovery. I checked his resume and offered the post."

Bishop briefly explained a few of the events that had occurred since the ambassador's visit and then asked for a huge favor. "Does he have a satellite phone like the one I'm using, sir?"

"Yes. He is supposed to use it for emergencies or other critical communications that can't wait for the normal courier."

Bishop hesitated for a brief time and then popped the big question. "Sir, could you check his call records for me?"

"What? Did I just hear you ask that I check up on my own ambassador's activity like he was a teenager who was going over on his cell phone minutes?" sounded the indignant voice.

"Yes, sir, you most certainly did hear me correctly."

"And exactly what do you expect me to find, son?"

"I think you'll find your representative have been making numerous calls that have nothing to do with his assignment here in Texas. If that winds up being the case, I would very much like to know where those calls are going."

"That man is a diplomat of the United States of America, Bishop. His communications are considered confidential and property of this country. He also has immunity. What exactly are you accusing him of?"

"It's very complex, sir, and I can't prove anything just yet. I do believe, however, that the future of the Alliance, as well as the U.S. recovery, may depend on this information. We both know that if Texas goes over the edge again, there's a good chance you'll be dragged into the abyss with us. No one wants that to happen."

The president knew Bishop well. The Texan had saved his life and was one of the most competent operators the Colonel had ever employed. He wasn't a man to go flying off the handle, nor had the chief executive ever known his former subordinate to subscribe to wild theories.

Bishop had risked his life to save the Colonel's predecessor and to stop a second civil war. But most importantly, he'd never made any sort of request like this before.

"Give me an hour," POTUS finally responded. "I'll call you back at this number."

"Thank you, sir."

Relieved that his request hadn't been rejected outright, Bishop again found himself idling while he waited. It was maddening.

"I can't just sit and wait any longer. I'm gonna head back for the ranch," he finally announced to the empty cab. "I have a feeling I'm going to need some extra gear."

216

Sleep again eluded Terri, her mind replaying the previous day's events over and over again. The worst was the fight with Bishop.

A whirlwind of emotions circled in her mind – anger, regret, curiosity, and most importantly, love. As she bathed Hunter in the bathroom sink, she wished for the hundredth time she could take back her words of last night.

A knock on the door gave her a rush. Thinking it was Bishop coming back to make amends, she wrapped Hunter in a towel and rushed to the threshold. She was greatly disappointed to see Pete's face when she cracked open the door.

"Good morning," the councilman greeted.

Pete then got a good look at her and knew instantly something was very wrong.

"Bishop and I got into an argument last night," she explained, her eyes watering with the telling. "It was terrible, Pete. He left in a huff, and I've not heard from him since."

Pete's expression changed at the news, his face turning pale. "Oh, no," he mumbled, moving to sit on the bed as if his legs had suddenly weakened. "That's not good... not good at all."

"Why, Pete? What's wrong?"

"Ambassador McQuire is missing," Pete answered. "Nick is turning Alpha upside down trying to find the man. Everyone already thinks Bishop may have done him in."

Terri soon joined her friend, needing to sit just as badly. "Bishop wouldn't do that," she began. "At least not the Bishop I used to know."

"You're right," Pete tried to reassure her. "He's not a murderer."

Unable to hold it any longer, Terri began crying, feeling like her entire world was disintegrating. Pete moved to embrace the distraught woman, holding her gently against his shoulder.

After a bit, Terri got it under control, and with a sniffle, she said, "I have to keep the faith in my husband, no matter how crazy everything has been. I have to do that, don't I?"

"We both do," Pete replied. "Bishop has never let us down. I'm sure he's not involved... it's just a coincidence."

"Tell that to Nick," Terri said in a hush.

Bishop pulled into the ranch, wanting desperately to catch a few hours of shuteye, pack his gear, and get on the road again.

Despite the stress, lack of sleep, and troubles with his mate, he was in a good mood. The president had delivered some very interesting information.

Chase's phone records revealed some telling facts that could only lead to one conclusion. The man had been spying, providing critical information to someone in Oklahoma. The satellite phone on the receiving end of his calls registered the longitude and latitude, a location Bishop wanted desperately to visit.

Before the mystery team arrived and shot up the valley outside Fort Davidson, a call had been made. The same number had been used when Diana's schedule in Amarillo had been finalized. The list of satellite calls corresponded exactly to times when bad things were happening all across the Alliance.

As he turned into the box canyon, it was only a mild surprise to see Sheriff Watts, a handful of deputies, and of course, Nick scattered around the camper.

The Texan parked his truck and exited, noting that the lawmen immediately moved for a tactical advantage. Had it not been for the frightened look in their eyes and the fact that all of them were carrying rifles, it would have been amusing.

"What's up, Sheriff?" Bishop greeted, trying to keep his voice friendly.

"There's been a new development," Watts began. "I'd like to know where you were last night."

"I was out driving around, clearing my head," Bishop answered honestly.

"All night?"

Bishop shrugged. "Yes, sir. Times have been difficult lately to say the least. Driving clears my head."

Watts tilted his head, the lawman's mirrored glasses reflecting the morning sun.

Looking at Nick, Bishop added, "Besides, it's been a little stuffy around town lately."

The senior lawman didn't acknowledge Bishop's remark. Instead, the questions just kept coming. "Where is your wife?"

Now the Texan grew serious. "Okay, Sheriff, I've played nice up to now. What's going on? I know you didn't bring all these men out here just to talk about my relaxation habits or Terri's recent travels."

Watts looked at Nick, the big man giving his approval via a quick nod. "Ambassador McGuire is missing," the officer stated. "His staff has no idea where he is, and we've searched much of Alpha. Given the history between you two, I wanted to come out and see if you could shed any light about his whereabouts."

Bishop stiffened, his attention now on Nick. "So you not only think I'm a traitor but a murderer as well. Nice."

When Nick didn't reply, Bishop turned back to Watts. "I was driving around all night, Sheriff. I didn't see or speak with the ambassador."

"And Terri?"

"We had what I believe you would call a non-violent domestic disturbance. I don't know exactly where she is at this moment. Perhaps she and the ambassador ran off together."

Watts stiffened at Bishop's jest, the cop not having considered the possibility. In a way, Bishop was glad.

It was obvious that the sheriff wasn't happy with Bishop's responses, yet there was little else he could do. Now fishing, Watts fired the next question completely off the cuff. "Any chance your wanderings last night took you up to Oklahoma?"

The inquiry caught Bishop completely off guard. Now it was the Texan who got aggressive, "Oklahoma? Now just why would you bring up our neighbor to the north, Sheriff?"

Something in Bishop's body language alerted Watts that he'd hit a nerve. "You didn't answer my question, sir. Did you drive up that way last night?"

Now recovering from the shock, Bishop's answered honestly. "No, sir, I didn't travel north at all. I left Terri at about 10 PM. There's no way I could drive up there and back in 9 hours. Now, I've answered your question, how about you return the common courtesy and tell me what Oklahoma has to do with any of this?"

Again, Watts received permission to share the information from Nick. "One of the vans used by the men who attacked you up by Fort Davidson had at one time been registered in Oklahoma. There is a witness who saw persons of interest getting into a similar van after the incident in Amarillo."

Bishop found himself smiling for the first time in days. It all fit, the final pieces of the puzzle coming together in a flash of realization.

Watts and Nick noted the instant change in the suspect's demeanor and found Bishop's reaction interesting. The big man finally spoke, "Well now, don't you just look like the cat who swallowed the canary? Care to share what has lightened your mood all of a sudden?"

"Nothing important," Bishop responded with a cocky grin. "Now if you gentlemen will excuse me, I'm going hunting and need to get some of my gear together. If there are no other questions, Sheriff, then I will ask you kindly, get the fuck off my land."

Watts exchanged the third glance with Nick and then nodded. "I'm sure I'll be back," he said to Bishop, the intentional threat left hanging in the desert air.

Motioning his men, the sheriff watched as the small platoon of deputies made for their cars. He then turned to Nick and said, "Are you coming?"

"No," Nick stated coldly, his eyes never leaving Bishop. "I think I'll hang around for a bit longer. I'll see you back in Alpha a little later."

Watts started to protest, knowing damn good and well the two former friends had been at odds. A curt look from Nick halted the sheriff's objections.

While the lawmen exited the ranch, Bishop retrieved his rifle from the truck, checking the chamber.

A few minutes later, he found himself standing and staring at the big ex-operator.

Nick's face was stoic as he stepped close, the two men well within striking distance of each other. Then, without warning, he smiled broadly and wrapped his arms around Bishop in a bear-like hug.

Both men were emotional as they exchanged the embrace, each patting the other on the back as if they were long-lost relatives reunited.

"I think we pulled it off," Bishop gushed, glad the charade was finally over. "Although I have to admit until you used the code word 'Judas,' you had me going. Scared the crap out of me to be blunt."

"We both deserve Academy Awards," Nick responded, finally letting loose of his smaller friend.

"I don't think they give those out anymore," Bishop chuckled. "Besides, the girls are going to kill us when they find out," Bishop noted. "That shit with Diana scared the hell out of me, yesterday. Is she okay?"

"Yeah… she's fine. Damn it, I told her to stay put and rest, but she didn't listen. I thought the whole thing had blown up in our faces when she fainted. That's what you get for falling for a hard-headed woman."

Bishop nodded toward the ranch's lane and the dust trail still lingering after law enforcement's exit. "Watts and about a dozen other important people are going to be super-duper pissed at us when they find out we've been playacting all along."

"They'll forgive us after we explain. Given we couldn't be for sure how deep the problem went, the extra caution and cover story were necessary. After all, we can't be sure Chase is our only spy. And everyone knows that loose lips sink ships."

Grinning with a nod, Bishop added, "Hell, you even had me going a couple of times. I was a little scared that you were really going to kick my ass."

Nick shared in the memory with a hearty chuckle before becoming stoic. "Will Terri ever forgive me? I didn't sleep at all that night after I said that shit about her. I bet she'll hate me forever."

"Naw," Bishop responded. "I helped you out and diverted her rage last night. Now I'm the one in the doghouse. She's forgotten all about your transgressions."

"Thanks, buddy. I always knew you'd take a bullet for me."

"You don't know how close that little joke came to being a reality last night." Bishop punctuated the intensity of his encounter with Terri by a loud whistle. "My gosh. I have never seen that woman so pissed," Bishop chuckled. "Anyway, I've got work to do," he continued, walking toward the bat cave and the equipment stored there.

Nick followed, "So the president confirmed our man Chase has been making some unauthorized communications?"

"Yes, and guess where most of his Sat-phone calls have been going?"

"I don't have to guess. The look on your face when Watts mentioned Oklahoma let the cat out of the bag. You should really work on your poker face a bit. It was written all over you."

"No wonder Terri could always guess what I got her for Christmas. Anyway, I looked up the coordinates and you were right – it's your old buddy, Cameron James Lewis. You should be a little more particular about who you pal around with."

"I knew the day that jerk got away from us that he'd be back. He's just not the sort that gives up. We need to put him down."

Nick's statement brought Bishop back to the job ahead. "Is Butter out of jail, or am I going to have to break him out with horses and ropes around the window bars? It's not a problem either way, I just need to know what extra equipment I might need to stow in the pickup," he mocked, arranging rifles and gear.

"I had Watts let him go with a promise not to leave town," Nick replied. "While you're packing up, I'll get my kit ready. Are we taking your truck or mine?"

Bishop stopped his arranging and stood straight. "What's this 'we' shit? You just got out of the hospital, brother. The last thing I need is your big ass bleeding out on me up in Indian country."

"You're not going by yourself," Nick pushed back. "Besides, I'm in a lot better shape than I've been letting on. It's all been part of the act."

The Texan didn't buy it, not the last part anyway. "Come on, man. I'm already in so much fucking hot water, I'm not sure if I'm the lobster or the potato. Let me get Butter or one of the other guys. We can handle it."

"No," came the firm reply. "I'm going, and that's that. These assholes have killed a bunch of our people and set the recovery back months, if not years. I'm going."

Bishop stepped closer and put his hand on Nick's shoulder, "I understand the need for payback, but you're a government official and have no permission to operate outside Alliance territory. If things go badly up there, I'm just a private citizen committing a crime. Your large-ass presence, on the other hand, could be twisted into an international incident… something just short of an invasion."

"Then we have to make sure nothing goes wrong, my friend," the retired operator countered.

Bishop studied his comrade for a moment, weighing the positives and negatives. Finally, he shrugged, capitulating, "Okay. You're the boss."

As the two men loaded up their gear into the truck, Nick mused, "You know, we haven't been in the field together for a long time."

"I'm actually glad you're tagging along," Bishop teased. "I wouldn't trust anyone else to keep your old, crotchety self out of harm's way."

"Hell," Nick poked back, "You've probably forgotten everything I taught you. This will be a good refresher for you…. get your skills up to a minimal standard. Maybe with some hard work and my expert guidance we can eliminate a few of your bad habits." Before Bishop could counter, Nick added, "I am touched, though. It's good to know you still care about me," and then he blew the Texan a kiss.

Grunting, Bishop couldn't let it go. "I hate to bust up your man-crush, but honestly I don't give a shit about you. If I let something happen to you, Diana would cut off my baby-maker, and *that* scares the shit out of me."

The banter continued as the two men loaded equipment into the bed of Nick's truck. Boxes of ammo, medical kits, jugs of water, body armor, and several weapons.

Nick assisted Bishop as he arranged the trip's necessities. "This ain't no after church on Sunday picnic, ya know. You packed my favorite .308, didn't you?" Nick asked, taking a moment to wipe the perspiration from his brow.

"Sure did."

"Good. I love that rifle. It seems kind of ironic that the last time I used it was against the same ass-clown we're going after now. Maybe I'll get a chance to finish the job this time."

"I was going to speak to you about that," Bishop smirked. "Speaking of skills, how is it you let that guy go the first time around? I can't keep cleaning up your messes forever, ya know."

"My bad. Won't happen again, boss. I swear it."

Bishop became serious for a moment, "We're going up there for a snatch and grab, right? I mean, I'd love to shoot Chase and this Cameron Lewis dude, but that's not in the cards, is it?"

"No. I want to bring them back here, have a formal, very public trial. I want everyone in the Alliance to know what these two tried to pull off. Then, I'll shoot them. They tried to kill my future wife, and Texas has dozens of new graves now because of their treachery. We'll make them pay, but do it the right way."

"And if they resist?"

"Kill them like the dogs that they are. No regrets. No hesitation. Think about all those people killed in the riot. Think about the ranch hands Kathy Baxter lost. Remember how close they came to killing Grim and your team. If they want to play hardball, then put them down... hard."

"No problem."

Chapter 15

The drive across Texas passed mostly in silence, the two men spending the miles alone with their thoughts.

Bishop, for his part, fell into the typical routine of questioning his abilities and desperately hoping he didn't let anybody down. Nick, as a former Green Beret, was a card-carrying member of an elite tier of fighting men – one of the most highly skilled purveyors of violence in the world. His large boots were difficult to walk beside.

Nick was experiencing a different set of insecurities. Had his body mended to the point of performing in combat? Was he too old to be effective? Would he get Bishop killed, leaving a widow and orphan behind?

Both men shared one specific worry; what would happen to the Alliance if they failed? Nick had left Diana a letter in his safe that he hoped would send her down the right path if they didn't return. He had also expressed his unending, unconditional love for the woman of his dreams.

Another thought they shared was absolute confidence in each other.

Nick's capabilities were proven and obvious to Bishop, the Texan having no reservations about Nick's health or wherewithal to accomplish their goals. If the big man said he was good to go, then he was, and that was that.

For Nick's part, Bishop was an established entity as well. Sure, the Texan hadn't been through the world's finest combat schools, nor had he ever served on a Special Forces team. The retired sergeant was worldly enough to know none of that really mattered after a point.

He knew Bishop's rare combination of heart, motivation, physical prowess, and intelligence was unbeatable. The military courses Nick had both attended and taught were designed to instill the skills and attitude that his friend had achieved from experience and natural gifts.

The appearance of the old state line didn't draw a comment from either man. It was a line on a map and the boundary of authority, neither of which meant diddly at the moment.

An hour later, their attitude had migrated from loose and cool to professional and cold.

The location where they expected to find one Cameron James Lewis and Chase Matthew McQuire wasn't near any city or town.

Originally a regional supply depot and low-level administration site, the cluster of metal structures, house trailers, and dominating three-story office building was hardly worthy of note before the collapse. While the two travelers had no way of knowing, Cam had never visited the unimportant facility while CEO of Lewis Oil.

The location's centralized placement in the massive gas fields of western Oklahoma did offer some advantages as a bug-out destination.

First, and most obvious, it was isolated. The nearest town was almost 20 miles away. The nearest city four times that distance.

Because of the remoteness, Lewis Oil had been forced to provide their site with some unusual assets. It even offered a reasonably well equipped emergency room, designed to accept injured roughnecks and other personnel requiring medical attention.

There was also quite the warehouse, the larger than normal structure stockpiled with food, fuel, and other critical supplies. Freight costs, supply-chain logistics, and availability had been the primary justifications for its existence – no one had even considered a post-apocalypse stash.

There were other accidental advantages.

The helipad, including a large underground fuel tank, facilitated mobility. The on-site security, complete with its own pistol range, ammunition storage, security fence, and even a barracks for the guards were all of benefit when the world had gone to hell.

Still, it wasn't a locale that emitted a positive first impression, no matter how desperate the visitor. On that fateful day when the barbarians had stormed his gate, Cam Lewis had looked down from his corporate helicopter with the same mindset as a prisoner condemned to Alcatraz. His was an exile onto an island of desolation.

Now, years later, he understood how fate had actually smiled upon him. Compared to the vast majority, he had survived the anarchy and suffering in relative luxury.

Bishop and Nick discovered yet another advantage to the facility as they drove north – the terrain sucked for anyone trying to accomplish a clandestine approach.

When they were within 20 miles, Nick switched places with Bishop, the big man wanting to study a map as they drew closer. It was an old habit that had paid dividends more than once.

Three miles away, Bishop pulled the truck behind an abandoned shed that had at one time been used to store farm equipment. The Texan wasn't liking the local scenery one bit.

Their surroundings, like most of the panhandle, were tabletop flat. There was little ground cover and only a smattering of trees. "This is going to suck," Bishop grumbled as the duo began pulling on packs, vests, armor, and weapons. "I know that no terrain is ever as level as it looks. There are always low spots and hidden recesses, but that looks like the carpenter's daughter – flat as a board."

"This reminds me of Iraq," Nick replied, grunting at his comrade's description. "The first thing we said when faced with miles of flat, featureless sand was, 'How in the hell does anybody hide here?' But they did."

Other than the outbuilding concealing their truck, the two men didn't see a single feature, ridge, undulation, or bush to use as cover. Nick, however, didn't seem to be concerned.

"So?" Bishop inquired, strapping on his armor. "How do you intend to infiltrate? Morph into a ghost?"

"Nope, c'mere."

Nick spread his map out on the tailgate, an oversized finger tracing a line. "This railroad track comes within half a kilometer of that facility. Engineers, whether they're building a road, rail, or outhouse always worry about drainage. If somebody built something to last for the long haul, you can bet it is elevated or has some method of taking care of precipitation. We'll just follow the tracks and stay low."

The thought of crawling for miles along a rail bed didn't tickle the Texan's fancy, yet there didn't appear to be much choice. Reaching in his duffle, he extracted both kneepads and an extra pair of gloves.

Before departing, each man double-checked the other. Loose straps, rattling buckles, and dropped equipment could alert a sentry. Plus it would suck to stalk across a long, rugged trail only to arrive and find out a critical piece of kit had fallen off a vest.

Then they were ready.

Daylight was fading quickly as the duo began hiking toward the objective. "Do you remember when we started that war between the two gangs?" Nick asked, a smile of reminiscence crossing his lips.

"How could I forget?" Bishop replied with a similar expression.

"That was when my dad got killed," Nick continued. "At least that old Marine went out fighting."

"That was also the night Terri had to shoot to kill for the first time. I think she handled it better than I did. How on earth did we survive that shit? I look back on that now and wonder what the hell I was thinking."

The two continued to exchange bits and pieces of shared memories. It was a way to burn off the stress of pending danger, a method to build confidence and prepare for a fight.

It was completely dark by the time they approached the tracks. Bishop was in the lead, using his infrared to scout their intended route. They had no idea how serious Cam Lewis would take his security, and running into a random patrol could ruin the evening. Nick was using light amplification, an NVD (night vision device) monocle hanging around his neck via a length of paracord.

"Do you think they have any sort of night vision?" Bishop inquired, taking a minute to study the rails.

"Let's assume they do," Nick responded.

"I was afraid you'd say that," Bishop complained. "Bending to stay low means my back is going to be sore for a month."

"What are you complaining about?" Nick chuckled. "I'm five inches taller than you are. Quit whining like a little girl and go scout those tracks."

Bishop had good news when he returned, "The grade is much higher than it looks. We're not even going to have to crawl."

Keeping the railroad between themselves and the facility, the two Alliance men continued their approach. Cam's hideout wasn't difficult to find, the bright lights of several pole-mounted security lights illuminating the entire complex.

When they were as close as was prudent, Nick found a comfortable spot and began scouting their objective with the 24x magnification scope mounted on his rifle. Less than 500 meters from the barbed wire perimeter, he could discern an amazing level of detail.

Bishop watched their flanks and rear, his carbine's optic not nearly as powerful.

"A lot of activity over there," Nick announced after a few moments. "Looks like they're loading up a rifle platoon into a school bus. Looks like a U.S. Army unit. Why the hell would soldiers be involved with these assholes?"

"Those guys that hit my team by Fort Davidson were definitely ex-military. Maybe our friend, Mr. Lewis has a connection with a local base?"

"They're loading a semi-truck with boxes of supplies. Looks like they're preparing to invade or some shit."

"Any sign of my buddy Chase?" Bishop asked, hoping to find the ambassador onsite and red handed.

"Negative. I don't recognize any of these clowns."

After a time, Nick offered to change places and let Bishop study the layout. "While we can't go barging in there with all that activity going on, you still need to know the layout," the big man stated.

After Bishop was behind the powerful scope, he could see why Nick was puzzled. From a man acting as the observing officer to the gents playing the role of the sergeants, the men preparing to board the old school bus looked and acted like a military unit. Their uniforms, down to the patches, appeared authentic.

Patches?

"Hey... wait a minute... that's not a U.S. Army unit.... That's one of ours."

"What?"

"I just got a clear view of their stitches, and it's a Lone Star, not Old Glory. Now I know they're imposters. None of our guys would be involved with these creeps, and if General Owens had that many guys AWOL, he'd be screaming to high heaven."

"Seriously?" Nick said, now wanting the scope back to see for himself.

After five minutes, Nick sighed. "You're right. One of them just wandered under a light, and I got a clear view. They're wearing Texas uniforms."

A moment later, Nick added, "There's your buddy, Chase.... He's walking with another fellow... Mr. Cameron James Lewis in the flesh."

"What are they doing?" Bishop hissed, the confirmation that their target was indeed present and accounted for making the Texan eager to get on with it.

"It appears that the honchos are inspecting the troops," Nick replied. "Here, take a look."

Ambassador McQuire's image came into view, Bishop's heartrate increasing as he watched the man responsible for so much damage and death promenading along the line of fake soldiers. They were all smiles and nods, conducting themselves as if they were feeling a high level of confidence.

"They're excited about something," Bishop noted, studying body language and gestures.

The Texan moved the scope back to Chase, the crosshairs now resting directly on the bridge of the man's nose. For a fleeting moment, he considered doing the son of a bitch right here and now. It was an easy shot, well within the range of the blaster pushing against his shoulder. He could probably dispatch Mr. Lewis as well.

"I don't even want to hear that safety click off," Nick whispered, obviously reading Bishop's mind.

"Now do you really think I'd do that?" an innocent voice replied.

"Yes, I do. That's because I was thinking about it myself just a minute ago. Don't. We need to parade the ambassador all over Alpha, Texas. We need him chirping like a morning bird, telling the world of his past evil deeds and misconduct. Then you can shoot him... after I hang him... after Diana cuts off his balls."

Bishop didn't reply for several minutes. When he finally backed his eye away from the optic, he said, "Well I hope we don't regret that decision. They're loading up. Looks like to me that the party is moving elsewhere."

"Fuck!" Nick replied, exchanging rifles and again focusing on the compound.

A few minutes later, things went from bad to worse. "Oh shit, Chase is going with them. He's riding in the lead escort vehicle. What the hell is going on?"

Bishop knew the question was rhetorical and didn't bother to speculate.

"What now, boss?"

"We follow them. I don't know where they're going, but I want to be there."

The rumbling engines now reached them across the prairie, the small convoy pulling out of the Lewis Oil facility in single file. Nick's sense of urgency spiked.

"Let's hump it back to the truck," Nick quickly decided. "If they head south or east, we'll follow them."

"If Chase is leading that parade, I'll follow them to hell," Bishop quipped.

The Alliance duo moved with far greater speed on the way back, no longer worried about sentries or patrols. They found the truck undisturbed and were soon hustling to strip off most of the bulky equipment and get on the road. "They've got almost an hour's head start, but I'm thinking that old school bus isn't a speed demon on the road. We'll be able to catch up... I hope."

After a quick exchange, it was decided Bishop would drive and Nick would navigate. "There are not that many roads in this neck of the woods, and they seem hell bent on creating trouble for us, so I'm guessing south. Turn back the way we came."

"They must be heading toward an objective that's pretty far away," Bishop commented as he turned onto the blacktop. "Why else leave at this time of night?"

"Let's see.... If I wanted to arrive at my target at dawn... and give myself an extra hour in case something went wrong, that gives me roughly six hours of driving time. Say the old bus can do 50 miles per hour... that gives them a 300-mile range. Hell, that's a big hunk of Texas, including Alpha."

It then dawned on Nick what Chase's objective might be. Diana.

Throwing a worried look at his partner, Nick's voice was full of dread. "You don't think they're taking another try at Diana, do you?"

"I don't know. Maybe. Chase knows our security procedures and already has people in place. On the other hand, if I were going to try and take her out, I'd bring a hell of a lot more men than what boarded that bus."

Nick's foreboding grew. "They don't have to kill her. Even the appearance of a military coup would push the Alliance over the edge."

Bishop pulled out his NVD and switched off the truck's headlights. He could actually see further down the road with the light amplification technology than with the illumination generated by the high beams. When they did catch up with the convoy, without any headlights behind them, there would be little chance that Chase's men would detect the tail.

The driving technique reminded the Texan of the bug-out from Houston so long ago. Like now, Terri and he had navigated the post-crash landscape at night, using the technology to guide them. There was a difference, though. His wife and he had been the prey on that journey. Tonight, he was the predator.

They spotted the semi's high-mounted trailer lights just over 90 minutes later, aided by the flat terrain and Nick's running stream of "Turn right here," and "Head south here," guidance.

Bishop kept the pickup well back, cautious of giving the men in front of them any hint that they were being followed. It was stressful work, each small town and intersection slowing the head of the inch-worm and causing the Texan to react and avoid the ass slamming into the head.

An hour later, the convoy made an unanticipated turn. "What the hell?" Nick grumbled, looking at the map with his red-lensed flashlight. "They should have taken a right back there if they were heading to Alpha. This road runs south and east. Where the hell are they going?"

Tagging along, the duo was now completely stumped. It was 4 AM when the convoy's brake lights signaled they were stopping. Bishop did the same.

"Now what?" Nick asked, not really expecting his driver to answer.

"Piss break?"

"Lord knows I could use one," Nick agreed, reaching for the door handle.

"Wait," Bishop snapped. "If you open that door, the dome light will come on."

Nick glanced from his friend to the plastic lenses mounted on the roof. Clenching a fist, he punched the offending light once, twice, and then crushed the bulb with the third strike.

"There. You happy?"

"Yeah… I happy I'm not your insurance agent."

"When a man's gotta go, a man's got to go," Nick replied, opening the door and stepping out into the night.

After a 30-minute stop, the Lewis forces were again on the road, most likely with empty bladders.

The cat and mouse game continued across northern Texas, Bishop and Nick eagerly watching every turn and marker, trying to predict the imposters' final destination.

"Should we use my Sat-phone and call Sheriff Watts?" Bishop offered at one point.

"And say what?" Nick replied. "That we're following a group of men in Army uniforms riding in an old church bus, and we're positive they're up to no good? Even if the good sheriff could muster a few deputies, what are they going to do? Execute a traffic stop and then get ambushed and killed?"

Bishop had to admit, the big guy had a valid point.

"We'll call for the cavalry once we've figured out what they're up to. Until then, given the time of night, putting the entire territory on alert just doesn't seem prudent."

A few more miles had passed before Nick reconsidered. "Give me that phone. There is one precaution we can take."

After Bishop had fished the high-tech device out of his pack, Nick dialed a number from memory. A sleepy sounded voice answered, "Hood, Duty Officer, state the nature of your call."

Nick said his name, a special code word, and then stated, "I want four rifle squads on ready-5 status. Unknown, armed force of approximately 60 men in Texas Army uniforms traveling south from Oklahoma."

Bishop listened as Nick continued his report, giving the location and additional details of the caravan they were following. The head of Alliance Homeland Security ended the conversation with a forceful, "Now listen carefully, Captain. When I call the next time, even if there's been a shift change, I want rifles in the air within five minutes. Got it?"

Evidently, the response was what Nick wanted to hear, the call ending shortly after that.

"Smart move," Bishop commented, keeping his eyes on the

distant taillights in front of them. Just then, a roadside sign drew his attention. "It looks like were heading toward Fort Worth. That sign back there said we were only 20 miles outside of town," he added. "Now what in the hell would they be after in..."

"Oh shit," Nick barked, his face blanching pale. "The gold."

"The what?"

"The gold we've been gathering to back the new Texas currency. The repository is just outside Fort Worth in an old bank building."

Bishop knew the gold he'd captured from the bank robbers had been moved from the bat cave to some unknown location. He'd also heard that the council had been sending men to various bank vaults to gather as much of the precious metal as possible. The fact that the stash was in Fort Worth was a surprise.

"Why there?" the Texan asked.

"It was the only vault large enough that had one of the old fashioned locks. We found an old, retired guy who was a locksmith who remembered how it worked. The newer, electronic mechanisms weren't stable enough, and there's no source of spare parts, so we choose this location."

"How well is it guarded?"

"There are normally about 20 soldiers surrounding the place. We tried to keep their presence low profile so no one would start asking a lot of questions. No armor or machine gun nests, but more than enough to hold off the typical robbery."

"Well, hiding in plain sight didn't work out so well. I think Chase knows your secret, and the party he's getting ready to throw is a bit more potent than the typical heist. You'd better be calling the cavalry," Bishop recommended.

"Let's make sure. I don't want all those birds buzzing half of Texas in the middle of the night if we're wrong. Even with the men they have on that bus, it would take them a while to overcome the security and blow the safe."

"Unless he has the combination," Bishop countered.

Sure enough, the lead convoy pulled off the road less than a mile from the old bank. Bishop followed suit, quickly finding a good place to hide the truck.

Again, the duo was pulling on packs and weapons. A few moments later, they were trotting off into the night.

Evidently, Chase and his men were confident that their little scheme remained a secret.

Bishop and Nick managed to get very close without encountering any sort of sentry or picket line. The old grocery store parking lot, selected as a jump-off point for the bank robbers, was bustling with activity.

After watching the proceedings for less than a minute, Nick said, "Let's get in front of them. We can spring a little ambush and warn the bank's security force. We'll call in the Blackhawks from Hood as soon as I'm positive of their objective."

"You're the boss," the Texan replied, double-checking his extra magazines.

Four hundred meters from the repository, Nick spied the perfect place to set up an ambush.

Two stout-looking buildings sat at the intersection, neither appearing to be occupied by much more than cobwebs. Nick quickly pointed to the distant bank and said, "That's our rally point after we spring the ambush. Cut them up as best we can and then hightail in that direction. I'll call Hood as soon as the shooting starts."

Then, much to Bishop's surprise, Nick said, "Wait. Hold on a second. We can't do this… at least not this way."

"What? What are you talking about?"

"We can't just cut down a bunch of men walking along the street, fake uniforms or not. What if they're on their way to rescue a long, lost relative? What if they're reenactors, or making a movie or something?"

Bishop was stunned, not believing his friend's restraint. "Really? Seriously? Do you want to just walk up and ask Chase if he's trick or treating for Halloween?"

"No, that's a good way to get killed. On the other hand, we need to be absolutely, positively, 100% sure these guys are trying to steal the Alliance's gold."

Glancing nervously at the spot where over 60 armed men were about to appear, Bishop said, "Okay, boss, what's the plan?"

Nick didn't have to think long, "You go and warn the guards… get them up and at their posts just in case."

Bishop shook his head, "They don't know me from Adam. You're the Alliance's honcho. You go warn them. I'll inquire as politely as I can what my buddy Chase and his friends are doing under the cover of darkness."

"Politely?" Nick asked, the skepticism dripping from the word.

"I promise," and then as an afterthought, Bishop continued. "Why are we dicking around with this? Call in those birds and barrels from Hood. We can sort this out after Chase and his boys are disarmed, on their knees... with their hands on their heads."

Nick pondered his friend's request, but then decided against it. "There's more than enough security at the bank to hold them off until help arrives. If we end up killing the ambassador and his motley crew of U.S. citizens before we have undeniable proof, the headlines in Washington will drone on and on about the massacre in Fort Worth. We have to handle this in the right way."

"Fuck them," sounded Bishop's hasty reply, but then he immediately softened. "Okay, Mister Diplomat, I'm not walking in your boots. Go warn the white hats. I'll delay these clowns for as long as possible. By the way, I want to be buried on the ranch, and I want my tombstone to say, 'Damn it, Nick! I tried to tell you...'"

Nick didn't wait for his friend to finish, vanishing in an instant, a shadow trotting toward the bank. Bishop was left alone in the street, looking for a position where he could both issue a challenge and withstand what was sure to be a withering hailstorm of gunfire.

A few minutes later, he spied them, glowing bright red in his thermal imager. They were spread like a rifle company, single file on each side of the street. Some of the men were carrying what appeared to be RPGs or Rocket Propelled Grenades. All were armed, with at least three belt-fed weapons visible in the lead elements. "Shit," Bishop whispered. "Me and my big mouth."

He waited until they were a half block away and called out from his hide. "Good day, Ambassador McQuire. Out taking in the air kind of early this morning, aren't we?"

Bishop wasn't overly impressed with the approaching riflemen's reactions. They hesitated just a moment before moving for cover. *Too slow*, he thought. *Definitely not pros.*

"Who is that?" called back a voice from the night. "This is Captain Steven Reedy, Texas 7th Cav, first of the third. Who goes there?"

Bishop had to grin at the man's bluff. "Don't bother with the bullshit, Captain, or whoever you are. We know you just left the Lewis Oil facility in Oklahoma. The real Texas 7th Cavalry is on the way here. A lot of them. And they're pissed that you posers are wearing their colors."

"Bishop?" a voice called from the right. "Is that you?"

Stall, Bishop thought. *Give Nick time. Nobody is shooting... just yet.* "Yes, Chase, it's me. You have to stop stalking me like this, Terri is going to get suspicious of your sexual preferences."

There was a hushed conversation on the other side, Bishop unable to make out the words. One thing was almost certain;

they weren't planning on asking him for Halloween candy.

Finally, Chase called out again, "Come on out, Bishop. Let's talk this over."

Yeah, right, Bishop thought. *I'm sure you won't shoot me on sight.* "I'm quite comfortable right here," Bishop responded. "Why don't you turn around and head back to Sooner Country... and stay there."

Now there was movement on the other side, the scrape of boots and rush of cloth signaling the Texan that the opposing force was zeroing in on his voice, trying to flank his solo ass.

Bishop moved, scrambling half bent and retreating another 25 yards down the street. "Flank *this,* assholes," he whispered.

"I'm afraid I can't do that, Bishop," Chase finally shouted. "Why don't you show yourself, and perhaps we can strike a deal."

Before responding, Bishop scouted his next move. In an urban environment, sound bounced off walls and streets, increasing the difficulty of identifying the source. Still, he would have to move quickly after answering. "Chase, we both know why you're here. I've got men with me, and the guards are alerted. I wasn't bullshitting when I said the real 7th is on its way. Leave... now... before a lot of people die."

While Bishop's plan to talk and then move, speak and then retreat, was noble, it didn't work. The Texan saw a yellow-red glow appear just down the block and then a shower of sparks. RPG!

The Texan dove for cover as the hiss of the rocket's exhaust grew louder, and then a blast of hot air and thunder disturbed the night.

Chunks of concrete block, mortar, and lead shrapnel sizzled through the air as Bishop rolled hard to escape the primary kill zone of the grenade. Then he was on a knee, firing a spread of five shots where he thought the foe would be.

At least 10 guns responded, geysers of dirt, rock, and pavement adding to the smoke and airborne debris created by the RPG. Bishop, however, had already moved.

Twice more he executed a shoot and scoot, spraying haphazard bursts and then moving before the counter fire could zero in on his position. It wasn't a tactic for victory, merely designed to delay.

The enemy, however, was catching on, dozens of zipping rounds coming closer and closer as the Texan scurried for cover. He decided not to make a third attempt and ran like hell for the old bank.

Saying a quick prayer that Nick's nervous sentries wouldn't pepper his carcass with friendly fire, Bishop zigzagged down the street, altering his direction and changing speeds.

Just when a sturdy looking building came into view, a voice called from the darkness. It was Nick. "Bishop! Bishop! Over here!"

He didn't need to be summoned twice.

Running toward the sound of his friend's voice, Bishop was chased across the pavement by incoming fire. The imposters knew the element of surprise was no longer with them, and they were coming hard.

Nick's next statement made it all worse, "They had a man on the inside. Most of the guards are dead, shot while they slept."

Before Bishop could react, all hell erupted around the sleepy outskirts of Fort Worth, automatic weapons, grenades, and the roar of exploding rockets signaling that the two forces were fully engaged. The Texan knew in less than a minute his side was going to lose.

The security around the repository had been designed to discourage bank robbers with small arms, perhaps even a few sticks of TNT. It didn't have a prayer against a full bore, heavily armed assault by a military-grade unit.

What remained of the bank's security force automatically went to their stations, lightly fortified corners of the building's roof, along with a few key positions around the perimeter of the structure. Chase's men had thoroughly scouted the site and knew exactly where the defenders would be. Hell rained down.

One by one, the small clusters of defenders were subdued, mostly by .50 caliber machine gunfire and blazing rockets. "This is going to be over in less than five minutes!" Bishop shouted as he poured rounds into an advancing group of attackers. "How long before the white hats arrive?"

"Flight time from Hood is 50 minutes," Nick yelled back, his carbine snapping lead at a shadow racing along the sidewalk.

"We're fucked!" Bishop screamed back as a hail of heavy lead descended on their position, driving both Nick's and his face into the dirt.

In the profession of gun fighting, there were two basic ways to achieve victory – maneuver, and direct application of ordnance. With the bank's location fixed, the first method was eliminated, leaving the defenders with the option of throwing more lead at the foe than what could be returned.

Bishop and Nick were good. Damned good. The duo fell into an effective rhythm, one always shooting while the other reloaded. Their aim was accurate, target selection never wasted by duplication. But it wasn't enough.

"We can't get over the top," Bishop shouted, slamming another box of pills into his weapon.

Nick knew exactly what his friend meant. Facing belt-fed weapons and far outnumbered, the two Alliance shooters couldn't produce enough suppressive fire to get "on top," of the exchanges. They were being driven down behind cover more than they were shooting back, and the ratio was degrading with every volley.

"Fall back," Nick screamed at anyone who could hear. "Fall back!"

Bishop didn't need to be told twice.

Leapfrogging each other with covering fire, Bishop thought his body would be shredded at any moment. The intensity of the incoming ordnance made it nearly impossible to concentrate, aim, or do much more than run like a pack of demons was trying to bite his ass.

Finally, after scrambling several blocks, the pursuing blizzard of lead subsided. The two men, gassed and stunned at the ferocity of the firefight, paused to catch their breath.

"Holy shit that was nasty," Nick panted.

"What now," Bishop managed between drawing lungs of air. "He has the repository."

"No way they can load up that much gold and get out before the boys from Hood show up. There's nearly 20 tons of the stuff in that vault. He may hold the building, but soon enough it will turn into a tar baby."

"I don't know," Bishop gasped. "So far they've been one step ahead of us."

Just then, a huge explosion vibrated through the earth, the rumbling, shaking ground leaving little doubt that someone had just blown the vault.

A moment later, the sound of several engines disturbed the night.

Nick looked ill. "He's using heavy equipment to load the gold."

"It would only take a couple of forklifts to make short work of the treasure," Bishop nodded. "They could load it onto that semi and be gone before help arrives."

Nick shook his head, "But where would they go? Half of the Texas Army would be flying around in Blackhawks, hunting them down from the sky. They're smarter than that."

The sound of footsteps halted the conversation, Bishop and Nick both raising their weapons as a man stumbled around the corner, holding his shoulder and walking with a slight limp. It was one of the guards.

Nick identified himself and moved to help the wounded survivor. The ex-operator quickly surmised the man's injuries were not fatal.

"I heard two of them talking," reported the new arrival as Nick applied a bandage. "I think they're going for the airport. I heard one teasing another about being afraid to fly."

"Makes sense," Bishop pondered out loud. "If I were stealing all that loot, I'd want to fly out of Texas, not drive. A good size transport plane could handle that much weight."

"The old municipal airport is about two miles from here," the guard chimed in. "It's not been used since the downfall."

Nick glanced back at the bank and then at his watch. "We've got to slow those guys down until help arrives."

"Best place is going to be that airport," Bishop speculated. "Since we don't know their route, and they have us completely outgunned, an ambush isn't likely to work. Given the lack of prep time, I say we try and take out the plane before they can get off the ground."

Nick looked at his friend, his eyes still holding hope, "You up for one more fight tonight?" he whispered.

"Can I have some of the gold to buy Terri a new house?" Bishop teased.

"How do we get to the airport?" Nick asked the wounded man.

Both of them listened intently as the man gave directions, and then they were off, jogging for the truck. Their speed over ground was painfully slow.

It seemed like Lewis men were everywhere, patrols, lookouts, and sentries between the duo and their escape vehicle.

"We're not going to make it," Bishop said, watching a group of five men patrolling the street ahead. There are too many of them."

As Nick started to reply, a small pop sounded in the distance, immediately followed by a flare rising above the old bank. Both Alliance fighters watched the streaking rocket soar into the sky and then ignite in a glowing ball of green light.

The unit to their front then did something very strange.

"There's the signal, boys," someone shouted, "Let's get this done."

Without any hesitation, they all started getting undressed, shirts, trousers, and boots flying everywhere.

Bishop frowned at Nick, clearly perplexed by the odd behavior. "An orgy?" he mumbled.

Grunting, the big man shook his head. "They're ditching the uniforms. Probably going to try and melt into the population and then sneak away."

"Smart," Bishop admitted. "They've been working on this little scheme for a long time."

"We need to get moving," Nick stated, looking right and left for a way around.

"How long before the boys from Hood arrive?"

Glancing at his watch, Nick's scowl deepened. "Twenty minutes, give or take. If you say, 'Daddy, are we there yet,' one more time, I'm going to put your scrawny ass on the deck."

"They're not going to make it in time," Bishop mumbled, pushing off to follow Nick's lead.

The two men finally arrived at the pickup, jumping in and then racing toward the airport. "What are we going to do once we get there?"

"Hell if I know. Shoot out the tires of the plane or something. We'll just have to play it by ear. The good news is that most of their forces are fading into the night and won't be around the plane."

The key word there is 'most,' Bishop thought, but he didn't state the obvious.

The short distance passed quickly, Nick having to slow as they got close. Sure enough, they could see the huge tail section of a massive plane sitting on the runway.

Nick rolled the truck to a stop behind an old hangar, the two men hustling to the building's corner to spy on the activities taking place on the field.

There they found a massive C-17 Globemaster on the runway, its cavernous interior being fed by two forklifts scooting up and down the lowered ramp. Bishop spotted Chase standing at the rear of the cargo bay, directing traffic and shouting orders to the small group of men scurrying to get the aircraft loaded.

"Not many sentries," Nick observed.

"Enough," Bishop countered. "We'd be cut in half before we even got close."

"I'm going to try and use this big blaster of yours to damage the plane. They'll come after me like the devil's hounds once I start firing. I want you at the far end of this hangar where you can get an angle on their counterattack. Receiving fire from two directions will confuse them for a bit. Keep them off me as long as you can."

"You can't hurt that plane with that pea shooter," Bishop protested. "It's just not got enough ass for the job. Even if you did pop a tire or damage an engine, that thing can still take off and fly. Get on that Sat-phone and scramble some jets. Shoot that fucker out of the sky."

"They will be out of Texas airspace in minutes. Besides, we

don't keep interceptors on the runway. There's never been a need, at least not up till now. It's up to us or we lose the gold, and we both know what that means. We've got to try."

Nodding, Bishop asked, "Okay. And after they push you back, where are you going to pick me up? Or do I have to walk home?"

"Go to the south end of the field," Nick pointed. "Down by that warehouse. I'll come around with the truck and meet you there… if I'm still able."

Bishop didn't like the plan, not one bit. As he started to debate his friend, the C-17's enormous jet engines began spinning up. "They're almost done loading," Nick snapped. "Now move your ass, trooper."

As ordered, the Texan hustled off, keeping the hangar between the bad guys and him. He reached the far end a few moments later and found an old engine block sitting in a pile of plane-trash. It would have to suffice for cover.

The .308's report sounded like a kid's firecracker against the background of the big jets. So much so, Chase and his cronies didn't realize someone was shooting until the second round impacted.

Just that quickly, a dozen rifles began firing back as Nick continued to snipe at the plane.

Bishop waited, not wanting to give away his position until someone actually moved toward his friend. If Chase and his cohorts were content having a long-range gun battle, that was just fine with the Texan. Nick's superior marksmanship and blaster's longer range would win the contest, at least until help arrived.

Somebody on the other side must have come to the same conclusion at the same time. Suddenly, Chase's arms were waving as orders were shouted over the drone of the jets. It was clear he was trying to get his men to form up and charge the sniper.

Two of the Lewis men motioned for one of the large, gas-powered forklifts to come closer. In a flash, they jumped on the back of the yellow machine and commanded the driver to advance on Nick's position.

Bishop raised his weapon, centering his red dot on the driver's chest.

Evidently, Nick saw the countermove at the same moment, his aim moving from the plane to the makeshift armored vehicle now speeding in his direction. As Bishop flicked his carbine's safety to the fire position, the sparks of incoming rounds began flashing off the forklift's metal surface.

The Texan pulled the trigger, the loading machine's operator jerking hard as he was struck. The forklift, still rolling hard, zigged and swerved so violently that Bishop's follow-on shot missed one of the passengers.

"Oh shit," Bishop hissed as the fast-moving machine steadied its course. The damn thing was pointed right at him and barreling across the tarmac at a good clip.

The two shooters hanging off of each side must have realized their chariot was doomed and abandoned ship, hitting the concrete hard and rolling like rag dolls.

Bishop poured several more shots into their now-prone frames, but it was probably a waste of ammo as neither man moved after jumping from their fast moving ride. He then turned and ran as the forklift slammed into the corner of the hangar just a few feet from his hide.

Crumpling metal and splintering wood overrode the background noise of the jet, the hardy forklift destroying the corner of the hangar and then coming to rest on the scrap heap. The driver's body was nearly thrown half out of his seat.

Bishop returned to cover his friend, but Nick was no longer fighting. As the Texan peered around the still-running forklift, he spotted several of Chase's men closing in on the location where the big man had been just a few moments before.

The Texan had no idea if his friend was dead, retreating or setting a trap for the pursuing forces. What he could see clearly was there was no one remaining at the rear of the C-17.

Yellow lights started flashing on both sides of the aircraft's ramp, warning all that the huge aluminum door was about to close. "Chase doesn't want to share the gold with his friends," Bishop whispered. "He's taking off without them."

The Texan's thoughts were confirmed when the plane's engines began to power up to a deafening roar.

Glancing at the forklift, he made up his mind quickly. After taking the dead driver's hat, Bishop tossed the body aside and climbed into the seat. It took him a moment to figure out the controls, and then the loader was backing off the trash heap. Bishop said a short prayer that Nick wouldn't shoot him in a case of fratricide, and then the Texan was racing across the tarmac toward the slowly closing cargo ramp.

Fully expecting someone to start pelting him with lead any second, Bishop crossed the entire distance without a single incoming round. Slamming on the brake, he leapt from the machine's seat and surged for the ever-narrowing opening above the ramp. He jumped, catching the edge, and then looked down as his carbine clattered on the pavement below. Cursing the loss of his weapon, he did a chin up and then throwing a leg over, pulled himself inside the ever-darkening cargo hold.

Off balance and scrambling to get away from the still-moving door, Bishop stumbled, rolled, and then crawled to hide behind a huge crate of what he assumed was Alliance gold. The interior of the aircraft went black as the door sealed shut.

The plane began rolling.

Thinking he would visit the cockpit with his pistol and convince the pilots that today wasn't a good day to log hours, Bishop started up the aisle.

He was halfway to the front of the aircraft when a searing bolt of white-hot pain shot through his arm – the flash of a metal pipe shattering the Texan's limb and sending his .45 flying across the bay.

Knocked to the deck and completely confused, Bishop tried to gather himself. Stunned and nearly blinded by pain, he barely saw the boot flying toward his ribcage.

The kick landed squarely, but most of the kinetic force was dissipated by the Texan's body armor and load vest. Still, it hurt like hell, rolling Bishop over onto his broken arm and sending blistering waves of agony through his skull.

When his vision cleared, Bishop looked up to see Chase's sneering face hovering above him, murder in the larger man's eyes.

"I'm sorry, sir, but your ticket isn't valid for this flight," the ambassador quipped. "On this airline, we execute stowaways."

Bishop saw that boot again, this time its aim was to stomp his face. He rolled hard, barely avoiding the strike.

With one bad arm and confined by the narrow space between two crates, the Texan couldn't reach his knife. Chase seemed to have already grasped his enemy's helpless state and moved in for the kill.

Blows rained on Bishop's retreating body, hammer-like impacts that rattled every bone in the Texan's core. Chase was insane with fury, swinging his pipe and kicking relentlessly as the Texan retreated, stumbled, and absorbed the painful wrath.

Finally, the energy bled from Chase's muscles, the commotion subsiding as the two men stood panting. "I'm going to kill you and then take your wife and child," the ambassador growled. "I'll enjoy Terri's body in my bed. And I will raise your son as my own. He'll never know you existed."

Half blinded by the blood flowing down his cut and battered face, Bishop's brain screamed for him to attack, but there was no strength left in his limbs. He could barely stand, his lungs struggling to draw breath.

Chase recovered first, hefting his pipe and moving in for the kill. The plane achieved wheels up at that moment, the deck tilting steeply under the two combatant's feet. Bishop felt the crate he was leaning against shift, the nylon strap securing the container pulling taut with the strain of gravity and angle.

In desperation, Bishop pulled his fighting knife, slashing viciously at the retaining strap. His first attempt failing to slice through the thick material, the blade flashed again and again.

Knocked off balance by the aircraft's ascent, it took Chase a moment to regain his equilibrium and charge. As he lifted the tube for a tomahawk-like strike, the frayed nylon restraint gave way, and the heavy box of precious metal began to slide.

Chase's strike missed Bishop, the tubular weapon's arch fouled as the wooden container gained momentum.

Bishop watched as the crate increased its speed, Chase's limbs trembling with the strain as he tried in vain to slow its progress. Commanding his own legs to move, the Texan took four big steps and crashed his shoulder into the opposite side of the container, shoving with all his might.

The plane banked, the additional angle facilitating Bishop's cause. A moment later, with a resounding thud and Chase's agonizing scream, the gold came to rest against the side of the aircraft.

Bishop moved to continue his attack, but the action was unnecessary. Pinned from the chest down from the bone shattering impact, he found Chase was no longer in the fight. One of the man's legs was twisted at a horrible angle, bloody bone protruding from the sandwiched ambassador's pants.

Bishop stood and watched as Chase struggled to breathe, the man's eyes rolling around in his skull as he fought the pain while his ribs heaved to take in oxygen.

"He's going into shock," the Texan muttered his diagnosis. "Maybe the fucker will bleed out before we land. I wish I could stay here and watch it happen."

Wiping the blood from his face, Bishop found his pistol lying nearby. Checking the weapon's status, he began limping toward the cockpit.

The pilots, expecting to see Chase, were stunned by the bloody, haggard man that appeared behind them. "Do you gentlemen know the way to Alpha, Texas?" Bishop grumbled, his .45 caliber sidearm unwavering.

"Ye... ye, yes, sir," answered the nervous flyboy.

"Good. This is now my aircraft. Take me there. Oh, and please radio ahead to tell them we're coming in."

Chapter 16

A sea of flashing emergency lights awaited the plane's arrival, Sheriff Watts and the Alpha security forces arriving to greet both the gold and the two passengers aboard.

Terri was there as well, holding Hunter and pointing as the huge aircraft circled Alpha twice before lining up for their final approach. "I've got to hand it to your Dad, Sweetie, when he goes hunting, he *really* goes hunting."

Once stationary on the tarmac, the C-17 was swarmed by law enforcement and medical personnel. Bishop was escorted down the ramp by two very unhappy EMTs, the Texan refusing to be placed on a stretcher. "I'm walking off under my own power," he declared. "And that's more than I can say for the other guy."

After handing off her son to the hovering babysitter, Terri rushed to greet him, not sure whether her husband was going to receive an ass kicking or a hug. When she finally laid eyes on the badly beaten Texan, she went with the embrace. Clearly, someone had already kicked his ass.

She didn't say a word as he debriefed Watts and Diana, along with a huddled mass of several other Alliance bigwigs. The story would have been unbelievable were it not for the oversized aircraft sitting nearby, as well as the tons of Alliance gold within. Chase McQuire was icing on the cake.

All the while, paramedics were cleaning his wounds, applying bandages, and checking his arm. "You're going to need to get that x-rayed," one of the EMTs announced, pointing at the battered limb. "Looks broken to me."

As Bishop continued his sordid tale, Diana and Pete occasionally asked for clarification, as did the sheriff. Terri, however, remained silent. Throughout it all, she didn't speak a single word.

The thumping of a distant helicopter interrupted Bishop's recounting, the military bird landing at the far end of the field. Nick hopped off and was rushed to his friend's side via an electric golf cart.

Stepping toward Bishop, the big man's smile was genuine. "I saw you sneak on the plane," he said. "Glad you pulled it off."

"Sorry to leave you back there, but somebody had to clean up your mess," Bishop mumbled through swollen lips.

The two men then continued with their tale, Nick now helping Bishop explain the finer details to the eager listeners.

Finally, after the question and the answer period was clearly over, Bishop had a moment alone with his wife. "I know you're pissed," he said with a lowered head.

"No, I'm not mad. I'm hurt... but we can talk about that later after the doc is through patching you up, and you've had a chance to rest."

"I want to talk about it now," Bishop countered, looking at her through the one eye that wasn't swollen shut... yet. "You don't know how badly I've felt during this entire charade. I love you. You're the most important thing in the world to me."

Terri merely nodded, and then Bishop noticed her eyes were moist with emotion. "You didn't trust me," she snapped. "Nick and you didn't think I was worthy of being let in on the secret, and that hurts more than anything I've ever felt. Why? What have I ever done to deserve that?"

"He didn't have a choice," came Nick's voice, stepping up from behind. "He was under strict orders not to let you or anyone else in on our suspicions. If you want to blame someone, put it on me."

"I didn't know either," comforted Diana, "and I almost had a stroke over the entire affair."

With Nick's admission came Terri's temper. Standing abruptly, she poked the big man in the chest with an accusing finger, "All right, Mr. Bigshot, I'll ask you the same question... 'What on earth have I ever said or done that caused you to lose your faith and trust in me?'"

"Nothing," Nick replied softly, gently taking her shoulders in his hands. "But you have to understand, we're now dealing with extremely serious people who are ruthless, clever and willing to sacrifice anything... *or anyone*... to bring us down. The Alliance is being taken seriously, and that means the stakes are increasing every day. One misspoken word... one badly timed glance by any of us and the whole house of cards could have collapsed down around our heads. My decision not to bring you two into this wasn't based on any mistrust or lack of faith – it was because you didn't have a need to know. It's my job to keep you both safe, Terri. I had to do it this way."

"Bullshit," she spat, a mixture of anger and hurt coloring her face. "You can call it your job all you want – that still doesn't make it right."

Nick remained calm, "I know you're angry. I know you feel betrayed by our deception. But please believe me... there is solid justification why 'need to know' has been a method utilized for decades. It has been implemented by security services and counterintelligence agencies all over the world and for damn good reason. Bishop asked me a half dozen times to let you in on the secret. I refused, partly because I thought Diana and you had enough on your plates as it were, partly because the more people involved, the more chances someone would inadvertently clue in our mole."

She still wasn't buying into Nick's logic, spinning out of his grasp and turning away, hot tears streaming down her cheeks. "It's okay," she lied. "I'll get over it."

Bishop stood to comfort his wife, but she refused his embrace as well. Even Diana's approach was shunned.

Nick took another shot, moving to face her. "If I had told you, do you realize how much stress that would have put on your shoulders? Chase McQuire knew you well. Every conversation... every exchange with that man would have been a pressure cooker. You would have laid awake at night, wondering if you had said something wrong or phrased a sentence badly. Then, in the loneliness of darkness, you would start worrying if your mistake was about to get your husband killed. Why would I allow that heavy load of bullshit to be dumped into your lap? You're my friend, Terri. I respect you as much as anyone on the planet. I don't do things like that to my friends unless it's absolutely necessary. In those circumstances, more than any other time, I hate my job."

Something in Nick's words seemed to resonate with the hurting woman, her eyes softening as she studied his face. "I suppose I should thank you, but I'm just not feeling it. Right this moment, I feel like an outlier... someone who was kicked out of the cool kid's club. I guess I'm just being silly."

Diana moved closer, handing her dearest friend a handkerchief. "We both were barred from the clubhouse, sweetie. I say, 'Who needs boys anyway?' I think we should get some chocolate and wine, and forget these two Neanderthals exist for a while."

Terri nodded with a sniffle, a slight smile crossing her lips for the first time since Bishop had returned. Turning to face her husband, she said, "Are you sure you're going to be okay? Medically speaking, that is?"

Her question made him attempt a smile, which his busted lip quickly turned into a grimace. "Yeah, I'm fine," he managed.

"Good," she said, placing her hands on her hips. "*I'm* going hunting."

She pivoted with purpose, hooking arms with Diana. "Men!" Bishop heard her exclaim as the duo stomped away. Then Terri stopped, and ran back to Bishop with a sly grin on her face. "I love you," she whispered, kissing him gently on a bruised cheek.

"Love you, too," he called out as she rushed back to the waiting Diana.

The two men watched the ladies as they headed to one of the waiting, black SUVs. "I wonder how much trouble they're going to get into tonight?" Nick pondered.

"I don't know," Bishop replied, "but I sure hope it's a lot."

It was the third day of the trial, one of the biggest events in the Alliance's short history.

Every radio station and newspaper of any size sent reporters, filling every available room for rent as far away as Midland Station. The smallish Alpha courthouse was bursting at her seams, holding a standing room only crowd.

So intense was the public's demand, a group of military audio/visual experts from Fort Bliss set up large projection systems on the courthouse lawn, as well as other facilities all across the Republic. Rumor had it that the Pentagon had offered satellite bandwidth, and that even the White House was watching the proceedings.

D.A. Gibson was representing the State, Chase choosing to represent himself.

When the judge had read the two full pages of charges, Chase had shocked the entire courtroom by pleading guilty to all counts.

As was prescribed by Alliance law, the accused was required to admit his acts in open court, as well as answer any questions posed by the judge or the state.

It was Chase's third day on the stand, his stunning testimony sending ripples of shock and awe throughout the territory.

It wasn't so much D.A. Gibson's hard-nosed questions or the physical evidence gathered by the state that had the entire republic talking. Chase was being absolutely forthright and honest in his responses, holding nothing back.

Bishop, with his arm in a sling, sat on the front row, Terri next to her husband. The couple had decided that Hunter would be happier in the nursery. Nick and Diana were right beside them.

"So it was one of your staff that broke into the doctor's office and removed Nick's medical records?" the prosecutor asked the former ambassador.

Sitting in his wheelchair with a crushed hip and leg, Chase responded with a loud and clear, "Yes, that's true."

"Why did you order that act?"

"I had talked with Nick just a short time before, and he was clearly upset after visiting the physician. If there was something seriously wrong with a man in his official position, I thought I could use that information to leverage additional strife amongst the Alliance leadership."

"And was there any such information?"

"No, not really. Despite finding nothing useful, I decided to make the best of the burglary and planted a seed accusing Butter of the crime. This was done to cover my man, as well as causing additional friction between Bishop and Nick."

On and on, continued the testimony, Chase admitting to calling Cameron Lewis several times a day. During those conversations, he openly recalled relaying various facts learned from the highest levels of the Alliance government.

"I informed him of Bishop's travels to Fort Davidson and of the location when the Alliance team was supposed to operate. I also divulged Diana's schedule, as well as intentionally delaying Bishop and Terri in Houston."

"So you were an accessory to the attempted assassination on Diana's life, correct?"

"I suppose," Chase shrugged, seeming not to be taking any of it seriously.

The general public learned that Cameron Lewis had executed extreme measures to topple the Alliance government. The man had hired scores of hired guns, spent untold sums of money, and had even gone so far as to bribe two Oklahoma Air National Guard pilots into stealing the big cargo jet that now claimed the tarmac at Alpha's small airport. Sheriff Watts had been forced to post deputies all around the airliner, it now being the most popular tourist attraction in all of West Texas.

So flippant and casual was Chase's testimony, D.A. Gibson became concerned that someone would start a new conspiracy theory claiming the mass-murderer and multi-count felon had struck some sort of deal in exchange for his cooperation and admissions.

To squash those rumor bugs before they left the nest, she decided on a direct approach. She asked.

"You seem very relaxed, Mr. McQuire, especially given the gravity of the charges against you. You openly admit your guilt and participation in several heinous acts. Why? Why aren't you taking this proceeding and the ramifications it has on your future seriously?"

"I'm neither ashamed of my actions, nor concerned about my future. I am an officially appointed Ambassador of the United States of America, and thus I have full immunity from prosecution."

A bolt of anger shot through the gathered onlookers, murmurs of disbelief and whispered curses rising in volume to the point where the judge's gavel and strong commands were required to restore order.

Bishop exchanged knowing looks with Nick, both men having already agreed that Chase wasn't walking away from justice, diplomatic status or not. It just wasn't happening. The big man had already picked a lamppost in front of the courthouse, a new length of rope in the bed of his pickup truck. *Nothing but the best for the fellow who sent so many of our people to early graves,* Nick thought.

At another point in the proceedings, D.A. Gibson's questioning centered on the defendant's motive. "Were you in any way acting under the orders of the President of the United States, or the U.S. Department of State while executing these acts of sedition?"

"No. Neither of those two authorities was aware of my actions. My sole co-conspirator was Cameron Lewis," Chase testified.

"Why did you join his cause?"

"Because I am a patriot and consider myself a citizen of the greatest nation on earth. Texas shouldn't be allowed its independence, nor should she be enabled to seize private property and hoard resources. American needs her people united and pulling together, or our great nation will not survive. I accidently discovered Mr. Lewis and got to know the man as a victim of your council's ruthless practices to gain and hold power. He introduced me to powerful men in Washington, and soon I was posted as the ambassador. You know the rest."

"And where might Mr. Cameron Lewis be at this time?"

The question seemed to catch Chase off guard. For the first time during his testimony, he faltered. "I'm not sure. I've been in custody and out of contact."

On and on he confessed, details emerging about how the new personal property law had been the springboard for Cameron Lewis to initiate his campaign of treachery and deceit. Chase, all along, had been feeding the Oklahoma-based mastermind with a constant stream of intelligence. The ambassador had even freelanced on several occasions when the situation allowed.

At just after 4:15PM, Gibson announced, "No further questions, Your Honor."

The judge's gavel descended, his honor straightening a tall stack of notes. After clearing his throat, he began, "Chase McQuire, you have waived all rights afforded by this court and admitted your guilt openly and publicly to an extensive list of charges, not limited to treason, conspiracy, numerous counts of accessory to murder in the first degree, and grand theft. For these reasons, this court has no alternative but to sentence you to death by hanging. Your execution will take place at 8AM tomorrow morning. God have mercy on your soul. Court dismissed."

A loud cheering rose from the gathered attendees, everyone smiling and happy with the outcome.

Bishop and Nick watched as Sheriff Watts, along with an entire squad of his men, escorted Chase through the basement of the courthouse, several threats having been made against the prisoner's life.

"See you in the morning," Nick said. "I'm glad this is finally going to be over."

"It will be good to get this behind us," Terri added. "He deserves what he's getting."

Bishop, however, wasn't overjoyed. "He'll file an appeal, or try some legal shenanigans," the Texan predicted.

The following morning, Bishop and Terri sat eating their breakfast while Hunter enjoyed oatmeal and orange slices. A knock on the door signaled the babysitter's arrival.

Both of them felt the weightiness of the event they were about to attend, neither offering much in the way of conversation.

They arrived early at the courthouse, finding Nick and his men standing around with disgusted looks on their faces. "You were right," the big man stated as Bishop strolled up. "Chase filed an appeal last night."

"How can he do that when he plead guilty?" Terri asked. "I thought that eliminated any additional legal steps?"

"According to D.A. Gibson, he can appeal the sentencing. I'm sorry folks, but there isn't going to be any justice served today."

"Where's Diana?" Terri asked.

"Oh, that's the worst part. We received word this morning that the president is flying in from Washington. Air Force One landed at Bliss two hours ago. She left early to offer an official greeting."

"Shit," Bishop grunted. "Here we go with the diplomatic immunity routine. I knew that smug bastard wasn't through being a pain in the ass."

The couple milled about, helping Nick's men explain the situation to the masses who expected to see justice delivered to a man who had taken so many Alliance lives. Most were extremely disappointed by his legal maneuver.

A short time later, Diana's motorcade rolled down the street. Consisting of the usual mix of escort SUVs, augmented with the President's limo and entourage, the long parade pulled into the restricted area at the rear of the courthouse.

"You might as well come on in and see your old boss," Nick offered. "Maybe you can talk him out of trying to pull his man out of this mess."

"Do you really think that's why he's here?" Terri asked. "That doesn't fit the character of the man I know."

"He didn't fly in just to say hello," Bishop replied, a worried frown on his brow. "This isn't going to be good, I can just feel it."

After warm greetings, handshakes, and hugs, the president was shown into Diana's office along with Bishop and Terri. Nick and one of the Secret Service types rounded out the attendees.

"I watched part of Ambassador McQuire's testimony," the president began. "I must say, I'm shocked and personally embarrassed that a representative of my government would be involved in such deplorable acts."

"We're convinced neither you nor your administration carry any blame whatsoever for his actions," Diana offered. "There are no hard feelings, at least not in Alpha. As a matter of fact, I want to officially request that you assign a new ambassador as soon as possible. We all believed the concept was the right move and don't want this isolated incident to ruin the potential benefits."

Nodding, the Colonel said, "Thank you, Miss Brown. I sincerely appreciate the Alliance taking that stance. However, there is still an issue to be resolved between us."

"Go ahead," Diana said, dreading what she knew was coming.

The chief executive looked at Nick and spoke like a friend delivering bad news. "I can't let you execute our diplomat, son. I know he deserves it, but I can't let that happen. It would set a precedent that could negatively impact my government for decades. The entire world, including all of the rogue players, would be emboldened by such an act."

Nick's expression flashed hot, but one glance from Diana squelched his retort. She wanted to respond. "I'm sorry to hear you say that, Mr. President. I also know that you understand our citizens are demanding justice. I hope this situation doesn't escalate and open a rift between our two governments. How do you recommend we resolve this?"

"Before we get into that, I would like to speak with my diplomat. Privately, if you please."

Nick tensed, not liking the chief executive's request one bit. "I'm not so sure that's wise," the big guy said, glancing at the Secret Service bodyguard as if to say, "Help me out here."

The Colonel, however, wasn't going to budge. "Wise or not, I would like to speak with Mr. McQuire. After we're finished, I'll be happy to discuss possible resolutions to our dilemma."

It was clear that Nick was on the verge of losing what little diplomacy existed inside his super-sized frame.

Bishop had been studying his former boss from the far corner. The Texan detected a slight nuance in the Colonel's language. "There's nothing wrong with letting a conversation take place, is there Nick?"

For a moment, it looked like Bishop was going to receive the big man's wrath, but then Nick softened after exchanging glances with his friend.

"I suppose not," Nick begrudgingly acknowledged.

Word was sent for Chase to be wheeled to the courthouse while a conference room was prepared for the meeting. A few minutes later, the condemned man was waiting for his Commander in Chief.

The Colonel entered the small room and then stopped his Secret Service agent at the door. "I need to have a *private* conversation. This won't take long. Besides, he's in a wheelchair, and I'm not some toothless old hound. I can take care of myself."

Closing the door behind him, the president left several puzzled faces in the hall. Everyone from Diana to Terri stood around, trying not to drift too far away, yet not wanting to appear as eavesdroppers hovering around the threshold.

While the sound of Chase's voice occasionally drifted into the corridor, the old courthouse's thick walls didn't allow anyone to make out specific words.

Nick was in a state. Stepping close to Bishop, he said, "We can't let him take that bastard out of here, immunity or not. It's just not going to happen."

Before Bishop could respond, a single shot rang out from the conference room.

In went the Secret Service man with weapon drawn. Nick was right behind him, security from both heads of state rushing into the hall.

They found the president sitting calmly at the table, a smoking .45 pistol in his hand. Chase was slumped over in his wheelchair, a small, red hole visible in the center of his chest.

Once the Secret Service agent was assured his protectorate was unharmed and in no danger, the president calmly explained, "He tried to escape."

No one believed it, not for a second. Yet there wasn't a single challenge to the president's claim. Bishop merely glanced at Nick, a sly smile on his face.

As the president rose to leave the room, he stopped and leaned close to Diana. In a whisper, he said, "I'm sorry, Miss Brown, but I couldn't allow you to execute that pitiful excuse for a human being. I, on the other hand, sure as hell could. Have a good day, madam."

Epilogue

The twilight of dawn hid the dust trails as four M1 battle tanks rolled across the Oklahoma prairie.

Accompanied by Stryker fighting vehicles, the armored units approached the Lewis Oil facility from four different vectors.

The Strykers lowered their rear ramps, the sound of heavy, thumping boots disturbing the otherwise quiet morning.

Scores of U.S. infantry poured from the transports, racing for the perimeter fence in a well-rehearsed choreography of assault. The deadly cannons and machine guns atop the tanks swept left and right, their gunners ready for any form of resistance.

Moments later, green-uniformed troopers were inside the compound, spreading out to search every nook and cranny.

It wasn't long before the bad news began to spread.

"There's not a soul here," reported a sergeant on the command radio. "This place is completely abandoned. Looks like they packed up and left some time ago."

"Damn it," replied the officer leading the operation. "The old man's not going to be happy about this. Leave behind enough men to hold the facility and then get everyone else mounted back up. I'll radio HQ and let them know our status."

THE END